Reckless
Intentions

MELINDA LOUISE
BOHANNON

Copyright ©2014 Melinda Louise Bohannon
2014 Ellechor Publishing House Edition

Reckless Intentions/ Bohannon, Melinda Louise

Paperback ISBN-13: 9781937844035
eBook ISBN-13: 9781937844165
Library of Congress Control Number: 2013951938

www.ellechorpublishinghouse.com

More By This Author

THE INNER SOCIETY SERIES

The Inner Society, Book 1
Reckless Intentions, Book 2
The Induction, Book 3

For my mother, who has been my best friend and supporter throughout my life.

This series contains subject matter intended for ages fourteen years and up.

Disclaimer: Although several of the events in these stories have been taken from the lives real teenagers, the characters are fictitious and there is no relationship intended between the Norfolk High in the story and any high school in the actual city of Norfolk. There is also no connection between the story and the true police department of Norfolk, VA.

Table of Contents

And what are humans but temporary transients
upon an ancient land –

a vapor briefly seen and then no longer
remembered.

For we do not know how many have gone before
us,

only the impact of what remnants they left behind.

And so it is that the impact of man's deeds will
outlast

the fragile memory of his existence…

PROLOGUE

Maggie quickly popped the hood open. She soon realized she couldn't see into the pitch blackness of the trunk. She felt around for the tire iron but found a flashlight instead, and flicked it on.

The light bounced off of a small object. When she leaned closer to see what it was, the blood in her veins turned to ice.

It was a gold earring, covered in blood. There were more stains in the gray lining of the trunk. She stared unbelievingly at them and then back at the earring. Something in the back of her racing mind told her that it looked familiar. Then she remembered…it was the D.A.'s!

"He killed Ms. Riley!"

C H A P T E R
one

It was a cold, misty afternoon in mid-October. Maggie sat silently beside the gravestone of her friend. The weather patterns had been odd that year, changing from warm to cold and back to warm. On this particular day, though, a white blanket of frost had covered the dreary landscape. The skeletonized trees that branched out over the grounds punctuated the sadness of the solitary graveyard.

Maggie's eyes were unwillingly drawn to the letters chiseled into the gravestone: JESSICA CARTER. She was only too aware that the ghosts of her past hovered over this lonely graveyard. Not far away lay the fresh graves of the youth who had lost their lives in the violent battle for power that had taken Norfolk hostage such a short time ago, a battle that was still raging.

But there was another ghost that lingered. The ghost of the girl she had once been.

She was no longer the tragic victim of her circumstances, living in rebellion against her own helplessness. She was now the product of a human being who had been saved by grace. She had a sense of self-worth, and hope had been born within her long-dormant heart. But now a new journey stretched before her, a journey of self-discovery in which she would have to learn how to battle her old instincts and walk in the newness of her faith. But this was easier said than done, and her dreams still haunted her.

The rage was always close to the surface; calm water that ran deep, it sometimes threatened to suck her down and drown her. Maggie knew only too well how easily she could become consumed by the injustice of her friend's death. Jessica was dead, and the court system had failed to punish those responsible. It was true that two of the killers were dead now, but there were others who had gotten away with murder. Old Man Keller's murder had only been the beginning, and there was no telling what new horrors lurked on the horizon. Still too new in her faith to bear this cold reality, Maggie's fear and anger often became a force that sometimes eclipsed the precious peace she'd found in Christ.

She knew her ordeal was far from over. The final phase of the trial loomed over her – the State trial of those who had concealed the murder of her friend and then unconscionably harvested her body to save one of their own. Maggie could not bring herself to regret the fact that their actions had saved the life of a beautiful child and others as well, but the manner in which they had done so was nothing less than sinister. This kind of power and blatant disregard for humanity was terrifying. Maggie shivered inwardly as she anticipated just how far these powerful people would go to get what they wanted. Indeed, she had nearly paid with her life when she had dared to bring charges against them.

Courage, her faithful companion, lay quietly beside her, staring intently into her eyes as if he was trying to discern her thoughts. As always, the German Shepherd sensed it when her spirit was troubled. Maggie's eyes met his, and a worried whine escaped his throat. She lovingly ran her fingers over his furry head, her heart swelling with the love she felt for him. This dog had given her a reason to live when she had given up on living.

A boy's form materialized out of the fog as he approached her. Maggie looked up at her fiancé, marveling anew at the magnificence of his features. He had been genetically designed to look like a Greek god; but she knew that his true beauty was really within. It was a natural strength, honor, and faith that had never existed in so many of the others like him. She still could not fathom why he was so determined to be with someone like her.

Coming to stand beside her, Peter reached out a hand to her. She took it and he pulled her to her feet. He looked into her eyes, and her gaze dropped before his scrutiny. She knew he was only concerned about her, but it unnerved her how easily he could read her.

Peter cupped her cheek and forced her head up. His lips molded around hers, a warm and gentle persuasion designed to distract her from her darker ponderings. He wrapped his arms around her to pull her close, and was satisfied when he felt her relax.

"Have I told you that I love you today?" he breathed, the deep resonance of his voice making her pulse race.

"I believe you texted me with the message twice this morning." She smiled ruefully, her love for him shining in her eyes.

They were silent for a while as she rested her head against the solid wall of his chest. His sweater was soft against her face, and she closed her eyes, breathing in the fresh scent of his cologne. Her heart ached with the love it contained for this fair-headed boy who had turned her world upside down, but there was still a part of her that feared the vulnerability that love represented.

"Marry me now, Maggie." His voice had a husky urgency that was becoming all too familiar. There was pain in his eyes as his fingers brushed over the diamond engagement ring on her finger.

"Peter, we've been over this. We're too young to take such a huge step so soon. I told you I would marry you if you would only give me a little more time."

"I don't think waiting is a good idea—" His words abruptly cut off as though he was reluctant to say more.

"What is it that you're not telling me, Peter?"

"There are a lot of things I haven't told you," he answered carefully.

"So I'm supposed to start a life with you built on secrets?"

"My world is not the same as yours. I am Inner Society, whether you like it or not, and I follow a different set of rules, a different reality than yours. There are things that you're just not ready to deal with yet. You knew it would be this way between us, honey. I never lied to you about it."

There was a silence between them as Maggie tried to sort out what he was saying and the frustration it was causing her.

"Please don't be angry, Maggie. You know I would never do anything to hurt you."

"I think you don't want me to live with my dad

because you think I'm still in danger."

"We both *know* you're in danger. We have no reason to doubt there will be another attempt on your life, and I'm seriously ticked off at you for the trouble you keep giving Tennyson. The D.A. wouldn't have picked him to protect you if she didn't trust him."

She made no reply. She wouldn't win in an argument with Peter, but neither did she intend to let the agent hover over her every move. Marrying Peter and moving in with him was also not an option right now. The truth was that she was afraid to leave her father alone so soon after he'd been released from rehab. He'd been drinking for so long that he couldn't remember doing anything else. It didn't help he was also dealing with guilt over not protecting her from the horrors he had recently learned that she'd faced at the hands of Bret Chambers and his friends.

Maggie eased herself out of Peter's arms. "I can take care of myself."

Peter gave her a look that spoke volumes, and when she dared to look up at him, she knew immediately what he was thinking.

"Please don't say it, Peter. I don't need any reminders. You might also keep in mind that Tennyson is parked across the street from my house nearly 24/7."

"You're not stable yet, honey. You still shouldn't be alone."

"You don't trust me," she breathed in conclusion.

His silence was answer enough. After a long pause, he finally said, "You can't trust yourself, sweetheart."

"I'm stronger than you think I am, and I'm not alone."

"No, you're with an old man who is just as unstable as you are. Whether or not your father stays sober is not your responsibility. You're not going to make this decision for him, Maggie."

"What happened to trusting in God, Peter? Don't you believe God will protect me?"

"What happened to trusting in God, Maggie? Don't you believe God will protect your father?" She gave him a look of annoyance, but he cut her off before she could voice her irritation. "Don't bother to give me that look. I had to live through hell thinking you were going to be murdered while I was unjustly locked up and unable to do anything about it."

"And God intervened and saved my life, didn't he?"

"You know I believe God's in control, Maggie. But God also allows us the free choice to make bad decisions, and I honestly believe waiting is a *bad decision*."

"It doesn't take away my right to make this decision," she carefully inserted. "The Bible also says that we are to be strong for the weak. I am being strong for my father right now."

He eyed her, obviously frustrated. "You know I'm very irritated with you."

"I'm irritated with you, too."

"I still love you, though." He pulled her into his arms once more and brushed his lips against the side of her face.

"I love you, too."

Maggie went home that Tuesday afternoon and found her father sitting quietly in an armchair, his face resting against his palm. The TV was off, and she knew he was brooding.

Courage went up to him and nudged his arm, and Mr. Kraus absently stroked his soft head.

Maggie sat in a chair opposite him, her hands resting on her knees as she leaned forward. "Hey, Dad. What are you doing?"

"Oh nothing, honey."

"It looks to me like you're thinking dark thoughts again." Even as she said it, she was unpleasantly reminded of her recent nightmares, and she knew her own thoughts had been following a similar path. Peter had warned her more than once about taking control of her thoughts.

"I'm trying, Mags. That's all I can do."

"That's all either of us can do, Dad. Didn't the counselors at New Hope warn us that it would be like this for a while? We just have to hang on and let God help us. We have to do it for each other, if not for Mom. She would have wanted us to go on."

She turned away for a moment as she fought the tears that threatened. She had her own emotional battle to fight every day. Maggie loved her father more than words could say—understood his pain—but she still could not understand why he had reached out to a bottle for solace for so long rather than reaching out to her.

When Mr. Kraus looked into her eyes, Maggie could sense the love and pain that clutched his heart, and knew his pain was derived from his own weakness. This weakness had led him to abandon her to face the horrible journey through the aftermath of the accident alone. She also knew that he was finally beginning to understand how much danger she was really in, and he could not even contemplate the thought of losing her, too.

Maggie got up and put on a praise-and-worship CD. It played softly in the background, ministering peace into the little home with such a long history of heartache. She sat on the armrest and took her father's hand. "I love you, Dad. You can do this," she whispered.

He blinked back tears and squeezed her hand. "I don't deserve your faith in me, but I'm so grateful for it, sweetheart, and I'm going to try hard not to mess up this time."

They sat in companionable silence for a long while, taking comfort in one another's presence and the understanding that they were no longer facing the struggle alone. They were facing this road together now.

Later, Maggie went to her room to write another letter to Chris Fischer. When she had first written to him in prison, he had been so overwhelmed by life and the constant barrage of hate mail over the terrible things he'd done that he'd been unable to feel remorse. He was a damaged human being who society wanted exterminated, and it was not hard to understand why.

But Maggie knew what it felt like to be completely broken, and she knew that everyone needed love—even those who didn't deserve it. So she had tried to reach out to Chris. He had written back to her in fuming contempt over her new faith and the fact that she'd stopped him from killing Jason Shelton during his rampage at the high school. But she had expected as much, and she wasn't deterred from writing to him again several times, encouraging him to believe that God still cared for him.

The next letter she received from him was at least less hostile, and Maggie knew that Chris was beginning to feel the pain over what he'd done, even if he was fighting it. But if there was hope for her and her father, then there had to be hope for someone like Chris, too.

C H A P T E R
two

Wednesday after school, the Sunrise Baptist Church youth group prepared to take a missionary trip into Richmond. Depending on traffic, Richmond was about an hour and a half away from Norfolk.

"Hey, are you guys ready?" Jacob asked when Peter answered his cell.

"Yeah. Are you going to pick up Marci?"

"In about five minutes. It won't matter if we're seen together where we're going."

"Just keep the girls within sight. I'm not too keen on them going with us, but Eric insisted on letting them come."

"What did Maggie's bodyguard have to say about this?"

"They had a fight over it. Maggie didn't want him coming because she thought he might put off some of the people we're trying to reach. I mean, he does have cop or something written all over him. He finally agreed to follow at a distance, but he's seriously ticked at her, and I'm sure he'll complain to the D.A."

Despite it being late afternoon, it was cold by the time the teenagers parked the church van along the curb beside the rundown apartments in Richmond's inner city. Peter was the official leader of the youth group, but Eric Bryant was the church overseer for all Sunday school classes and youth activities, and the 25-year-old was coming along to ensure everything went safely. As agreed upon, Tennyson would also be following in his black Mercedes a couple blocks away so that he could be on call, if needed.

Dressed in jeans and sweaters, the teens got out and retrieved their flyers. Maggie noticed Marci standing quietly in a spot by herself. She looked uneasy and Maggie wondered if this venture was a little daunting for her.

"Do you *want* to do this, Marci," she asked, "or are you doing it because you feel obligated?"

"I want to do this, Maggie. I'm just a little nervous. Those guys on the corner looked a little alarming. Then again, so does your bodyguard."

Maggie cast a look of annoyance behind them to the end of the block where the Mercedes was parked. "You need to get some backbone and learn how to stand up for yourself, Marci. There won't always be someone around to fight your battles for you, and you're going to have to stand on the power of your own faith sometimes. If you believe God wanted you to come tonight, then you have to believe he'll protect you."

"I know you're right, and I'll be fine. It's not like we haven't done this before. I've just never had the guts that you have."

"Fear has a purpose, Marci. It's to keep you wise, not to utterly paralyze you. Keep your mind focused on what you want for your life, or others will run your life for you. I know what I'm talking about."

Jacob came up behind Marci then, putting his arms around her and resting his head on top of hers. Marci closed her eyes, relaxing in his arms. "I love you, Marci," he whispered, his heart aching with the feelings he was constantly forced to repress.

"I love you, too."

Maggie smiled at them. These moments between them were precious because they were rare. As a biracial couple, Jacob and Marci had to be careful. Despite all their education and advancements, The Inner Society was deeply prejudiced in a lot of areas, and Marci and Jacob didn't want any trouble.

The team went from apartment complexes to homes, passing out certificates for free food and witnessing to the residents about the love of God. They were confronted by everything imaginable that evening. Drug dealers came by in low-riders and stared them down. Dogs came after them, and people slammed doors in their faces. Like Marci had said, the youth had done this before, though, and they knew what to expect.

"I don't know, guys, we don't seem to be getting anywhere tonight," Kevin said, tossing his head back to get his thick brown locks out of his face. He zipped up his black leather jacket and stuffed his hands into the pockets.

"They're accepting our tracks and the food certificates," Kristy pointed out. "We're here to try to help these people, but that doesn't mean we'll see the results tonight."

Kevin's brown eyes softened in affection when he looked down at Kristy. He smiled at her optimism and sighed. "I guess you're right."

It was getting dark by then, and Peter realized the group had become dispersed. Maggie had gone on ahead, and was about to turn a corner. Marci was trailing behind her by some twenty feet.

"Jacob!" Peter called, sensing impending trouble.

Eric snapped to attention and shouted at the girls, but they were way ahead by then and didn't hear him. Peter and Jacob ran after them.

"Oh no," Jacob choked as a dark form suddenly came running across the street, heading directly for Marci. Jacob shouted her name, but she didn't hear him, either.

Maggie turned the corner before she heard Marci cry out.

Marci had not even seen him coming. The boy came up on her so fast she had no time to react. He knocked her down, snatched her purse, and ran.

He rounded the corner just as Maggie turned back to see what was happening. In the same moment, the Mercedes came speeding down the street.

Maggie only had a few seconds of warning, but that was enough to spot Marci's purse in the boy's clutches. As he passed, Maggie kicked his legs right out from under him and sent him sprawling on the pavement, the purse flying out of his hands.

The Mercedes came to a skidding halt beside them.

"Epic fail!" Maggie mocked sarcastically.

The Asian boy looked up at her with wide, startled eyes. He would have gotten up and fled, but there wasn't any time. Tennyson leaped from his car and tackled him before he got the chance. In an instant, he had the kid in an unbreakable hold.

"Where the heck did you come from?" the kid asked stupidly.

Tennyson looked back up at Maggie. "This is the kind of thing I was talking about!" he snapped at her. "Don't you *ever* get in the way of a criminal. Don't you have any brains at all? I swear you can't go anywhere without brooking trouble."

Maggie was saved from the smart reply that was dancing in her head when the kid began to yell, "Get off me, man! I'm sorry, all right?"

"Not as sorry as you're going to be," Peter said with a calmness that only served to punctuate his frightening intensity as he came to stand beside Tennyson.

Maggie realized the boy couldn't be more than sixteen. She noted his ripped, faded jeans and open blue flannel shirt that he wore over a white T-shirt. No doubt Tennyson was hurting him as he held his arm twisted behind him and placed his knee in his back to keep him on the ground. Peter had put her in that same unfortunate position when he had intercepted her at the cemetery after she'd run away from home.

"Why did you take her purse?" Maggie asked perceptively. "Were you looking for drug money?"

"No! I was just hungry. I swear! I'm sorry. I didn't mean to knock that girl down. Please don't call the cops."

The others had caught up with them by then, surrounding them. Marci was in shock, and Jacob tried to comfort her. He and Peter were deliberating on how to handle the situation.

"Let me get up, man. I won't run. I swear."

"Oh, that's reassuring coming from a *criminal*," Peter said.

"Let him up," Maggie said quietly. "We came here to help people like this kid."

"That's just great," Tennyson said under his breath.

"She's right," Eric spoke up. "Let him up, please."

Tennyson rolled his eyes, giving a sigh of irritation. "You try to run, kid, and you'll be kissing the pavement again before you even finish the thought!" he threatened as he got up, jerking the kid up with him and keeping a steel-like hold on his jacket.

The boy was obviously sore. "Doesn't feel so good to be knocked down, does it?" Jacob commented dryly.

"Look, man. No harm done, right? You don't have to turn me in."

"If we don't, you'll go after another victim," Eric reasoned.

"No. I swear I won't."

"Of course you won't," Kevin laughed. "You're going to turn over a new leaf in the next few seconds and morph into a model citizen!" He folded his arms over his chest and rolled his eyes.

"Where do you live?" Maggie asked. "Do your parents know where you are?"

He looked with amazement at the girl who had just sent him sprawling. His face was scraped up from hitting the pavement, and he wiped the blood from his mouth. At that point he had a whole new respect for girls. "I…I don't have a place to live right now."

"It's fifty-seven degrees!" Maggie said.

"Tell me about it."

"The county jail has some nice cots available," Tennyson pointed out.

"Well then, you have two options," Eric inserted, assuming leadership. "You can go to jail, or you could come with us. We'll get you something to eat and set you up at the shelter, but the condition is that you will attend a church and help them with yard work for three weeks."

"You've got to be kidding? *Me in church?*" By then the boy was regaining enough of his composure to put on a tough front. He glanced at Maggie in annoyance. It obviously stung his pride that he'd been knocked down by a girl.

"You know we're not kidding. You just attacked and robbed an innocent girl…*my girlfriend*," Jacob retorted.

The kid thought it over. His gaze shifted from Jacob to Peter, who were both looking intimidating as they glared at him. He was obviously resentful of being forced into an unfavorable decision, but he eventually consented to go with them.

Walking back to the van, Kevin caught up with Maggie. He bumped her to get her attention, and she looked up at him in question. He was smiling a mischievous smile, his brown eyes twinkling, and she couldn't help but smile back. "What?" she asked.

"You rock, girl! That was totally awesome! I would have given anything to see that kid hit the ground."

"Yeah? Well, it was pretty funny, but Tennyson failed to see the humor. I don't think the kid knew what hit him until he was eating pavement and realized the ground had jumped up and slapped him in the face! I guess I'm lucky he didn't turn on me and stab me or something," she said as she rubbed her bruised ankle.

"You probably still could've taken him," Kevin teased, his ornery character showing through. Maggie grinned, but she knew Peter was going to be upset with her.

Jacob intercepted Peter when he saw him heading toward Maggie. "Go easy on her, man. I could remind you that it's the very fire in her which attracts you that you're trying to put out."

"I know," he groaned.

Maggie braced herself when she saw Peter coming, but he merely put his arms around her, holding her with her back against his chest, his head bent, resting against hers.

"What am I going to do with you?" he asked with exasperation.

She smiled. "What do you want to do with me?"

"That was a loaded question. You better stop teasing me. Do you not understand how dangerous the people in this area are?"

Maggie twisted around so that she could look up at Peter, her eyebrows raising as she gave him a meaningful look. "Are you kidding me? This is my turf, sweetheart!"

Peter looked at her with dawning understanding, and then closed his eyes. "That's right. How could I have forgotten that? No wonder you're such a brazen little hussy!"

"Excuse me?" she snapped in mock offense, and then kicked his shin.

"Ow!"

"Well, that's what you get. You know you shouldn't be messing with people from around here. They could be *dangerous*," she added sarcastically.

It was nearing seven o'clock by the time they reached a Denny's. The kids got out of the van while Tennyson waited outside in his car. The parking lot was lit by streetlamps, and Tai Lee saw Maggie in the light for the first time.

"You!" he exclaimed. "I saw your picture in the newspaper." He had the accent of a kid who had been raised in a Hmong home, but it was obvious that he'd probably attended schools in America from day one.

"And her notoriety follows her," Peter commented dryly.

The youth group watched as the boy wolfed down a super huge cheeseburger, two cokes, and a large plate of fries. All the while he chatted on, bragging about this and bragging about that. He had obviously gotten over the fear of being turned in to the police.

When everyone was finished, Maggie turned to Tai and asked, "Are you seriously going to have us take you to a shelter, or are you going to tell us where you really live?"

He looked at her in surprise. "I told you—"

"Don't give me that crap! You told us a lie so that your family wouldn't know about your delinquent behavior. The minute we drop you off at a shelter, you're going to split back home. You could save us all the trouble and just tell us where you live."

The others looked at her in question and then back at Tai, but Peter trusted Maggie's instincts. She had street smarts.

"How did you know?" Tai asked incredulously. He was becoming more impressed with Maggie by the minute.

"Never mind. You attacked one of us, and we returned the favor by taking you to dinner. We didn't have to do that. Are you going to come clean or not?"

The boy looked away somewhat sheepishly. Then he finally confessed. "All right, so I'm not homeless."

"Where do you live?" Eric asked.

"In the old brick apartments on the south end of the city," he said making an effort to conceal his guilty conscience. The others remembered passing by the large dilapidated building. It looked like it was about to fall over and obviously was not up to any codes.

When Tai was finished eating, they drove him home. Tennyson parked behind the van, coming to stand behind Maggie as he scanned the area.

"I'm not telling you which apartment," Tai muttered. "You're not gonna to tell my mother nothin'!"

Again Maggie looked at him steadily, discerning his spirit. "No dice. We need to know where you live so we can find you, in case you skip out on our church deal or try to hurt someone else."

He gave her a mutinous look, but he couldn't hold it for long. "I'll let *you* walk me in," he conceded to her at last. "You're a babe!"

Tennyson immediately grabbed hold of Maggie's arm. "Like heck," he said darkly.

"She's not going alone with you *anywhere*," Peter asserted.

Tai thought that over for a minute. "What are you going to do about it if I just refuse to tell you where I live?" he said with renewed rebellion. He had taken on a cocky stance, his arms folded in mutiny.

"How about we drive you to the police station?" Peter replied, mimicking his tone. "Don't push it, kid. We wouldn't have any trouble dragging you in. I think you know that."

They could tell Tai was thinking that over, and it was pretty obvious he wasn't ready for another physical confrontation.

"Well, are you going to say something to my mother if I show you where I live?"

"The police will definitely say something to her if you opt for the other route."

"We won't say anything to her *this time*," Maggie offered. "But if we come across you again and catch you doing something you shouldn't be doing, we'll report both incidents."

The boy finally consented, however reluctantly.

"I'm going with you," Tennyson said in a tone that didn't brook any argument. "I'll check out the apartment, and then I'll wait outside the door, if it makes you feel any better."

"Fine," Maggie agreed. She, Peter, Jacob, and Tennyson followed Tai up a flight of stairs to the door of his apartment.

Kristy and Kevin waited in the van. Maggie hoped they'd make their relationship official soon, as well. It was obvious to everyone, except perhaps Kristy, that Kevin was crazy about her. Their mothers had been best friends for years, and the two had practically been brought up together. Kevin had brought his acoustic guitar, and he quietly strummed while the two of them talked about everything that had happened that night. Eric decided to knock on a few more doors in the meantime, giving the two a chance to be alone.

Meanwhile, Tai was giving the others pointers on the Hmong culture. "Okay, so, I better tell you that Hmong women don't shake hands, and if you look a woman in the eyes, it's considered rude in our culture. Oh yes, and my mother understands quite a bit of English, but she speaks very little."

"Thanks for the tip," Maggie said.

Since Tai didn't have a key, he had to knock. After

a few seconds, they heard slow footsteps, the sound of a deadbolt being unlocked, and a chain being removed. Security was obviously an issue.

The Asian woman who stood in the doorway was undoubtedly surprised to find several people at the doorstep with her son. She rattled off something in Hmong to him, and he rattled something back that they couldn't understand. Tai looked at his escorts with slight embarrassment, but then he remembered he had brought a celebrity home. His countenance brightened, and he spoke a little more with his mom in an excited tone. She looked from him to Maggie, her eyes widening with surprise. She motioned to them and said a few more words to her son. "Koj tuaj los," she said to them.

"Uh…my mom says that you are welcome to come in. I…uh…will understand if you don't want to. Our apartment is not in very good shape. But if you choose to come in, you will have to sit down, or my mother will think there is something wrong with our furniture."

"Tell your mother that we'd be honored," Maggie said.

The woman, who had unquestionably been beautiful in her younger years, nonetheless had shadows under her eyes. It was plain to see that life had taken a toll on her, and the visitors had suspicions that she might be sick. It was no wonder that the boy didn't want her to know about his bad behavior.

Tennyson went in first and made sure the apartment was safe. Then he went out and the others entered.

The woman didn't have much to offer them, and it was clear that this embarrassed her, but she had tea and so she offered them that. They graciously accepted, realizing that turning her down could be considered offensive. Remembering Tai's warning, they all sat down on the crates that the family was using for chairs and quietly sipped their tea.

The apartment was, unsurprisingly, dirty. The Lees had a small kitchen table, but other than that they were using milk crates with cushions for chairs. Cockroaches climbed the walls, and there was an unpleasant odor that was slightly nauseating. Thus it shocked the socks off them when Tai proudly dragged Maggie into his bedroom to show her his computer equipment.

The guys followed them in, doing a double-take when they saw all the expensive merchandise. They also took in the bookshelves that were lined with every imaginable book sold on computer technology, programming, and hacking.

Jacob picked up one of the latter books, flipping through the pages. "I'm surprised it's legal to even publish these books," he commented dryly.

"You're not going to tell us that all this stuff wasn't stolen, are you?" Maggie chastised.

His face turned a little red with guilt. "Well, maybe."

"What are you doing with all this stuff?" she asked.

Tai's eyes lit up with pride once more. "I am smart with computers. I can do anything. I can make web pages, do computer graphics—"

"Hack into others' computers to steel their ID," Jacob finished for him.

"Well, maybe," Tai said sheepishly, "but I haven't

stolen too much, and I only steal when I have to."

"Well, that's a relief to your neighbors, I'm sure," Peter said with dripping sarcasm.

Tai ignored him, though. "I'm going to become a computer programmer, and I'm going to make a lot of money someday so I can take care of my mother. I won't have to steal nothin' then. I'll make my own money—more money than *you*." That last part was tacked on with an attitude.

Peter was about to make another derogatory comment, but Maggie cut him off. "I don't doubt that you will, Tai. You can do it if you set your mind to it. You might find it a little difficult to manage from a prison cell, though."

He flashed her another guilty smile.

"You've got all this stuff and yet you went after Marci's purse?" Peter asked incredulously.

Tai's eyes dropped to his shoes. "I told you why I got this stuff. But stuff is stuff and we needed the money…."

Peter fell silent. Being a more than successful entrepreneur himself and born into the wealthy Inner Society, he knew he had no call judging someone in such a difficult position as this kid. He couldn't really know what he'd do if their roles were reversed.

Before they all left, they gave Tai a business card from a local church and told him they would be checking in with the pastor there to see if he showed up or not. They planned to speak with the pastor ahead of time and give him a heads-up so that he could have some groceries ready to send home with Tai. Gift giving was a tremendously important part of the Hmong culture, and the groceries were obviously needed.

CHAPTER
three

It was nearing nine when the youth finally returned to Sunrise Baptist Church where they had met earlier in order to carpool to Richmond. They were way past their estimated return time by then, and everyone was tired. Peter kissed Maggie goodbye, and she got into her new white Audi that he'd bought her as an extravagant engagement gift. She pulled out of the driveway with Tennyson behind her.

The streets were mostly deserted by that time of night, and Maggie was more than exhausted. She pulled onto Tidewater Street and looked into her rearview mirror. She could see headlights in the darkness a hundred yards behind her. The vehicle shadowed her every move. It made her ill at ease to have someone following her—even Tennyson, even despite the fact that he wasn't right on her tail.

A creepy sense of déjà vu seeped into her senses as she was unwillingly reminded of the nightmares she'd been having of late. Maggie tried to shake her rising sense of impending doom, but its dark presence only settled more deeply into her consciousness.

Just then the vehicle tailing her briefly passed

beneath the light of a streetlamp, and Maggie was alarmed when she realized it was not the black Mercedes. Where was Tennyson, and when had she gotten separated from him?

Maggie chastised herself for her tension, telling herself that just because the wrong car was behind her didn't mean it was following her. Annoyed by her own weakness, she determined to prove to herself that she was only imagining things. Swallowing her fears, Maggie made a quick turn onto another road.

She watched in her rearview mirror as the other vehicle did the same. She circled back around to Tidewater again, but the other vehicle still trailed behind her.

Now Maggie's senses were racing, and she could no longer ignore the inner trembling within her body. As they passed under another street lamp, Maggie glanced into her rearview mirror again and was able to get a brief glimpse of the other vehicle, noting a silver or gray sedan with local plates.

She reached for her purse and fumbled for her cell phone nervously. Her fingers sought and found the cool metal and retrieved it, but she hit a bump at the crucial moment, and the phone slipped from her fingers onto the floorboard on the passenger's side. "Great!" she mumbled, realizing she would never be able to reach it without first pulling over and stopping the car.

There was no help for it. Maggie upshifted and put more pressure on the gas pedal. The Audi smoothly launched forward, momentarily increasing the distance between her and whoever was following her. However, the other car picked up its pace as well and moved up directly behind her. It was becoming clear that the driver wanted her to know she was being followed.

Maggie could feel her tension rising as she pushed the Audi faster still.

In a few more minutes, she had made it to Granby Street and was rapidly approaching Bayview Boulevard. There was a car in her lane ahead of her, already stopped at the light. Another car was in the lane to her left approaching the light. In seconds she would have to stop, and she could only wonder if whoever was following her would be willing to do any harm in front of witnesses.

She didn't want to take any chances.

Her senses were on full alert as she scanned the intersection for cars and saw none. In a split-second decision, she sped up and swerved her car in front of the vehicle in the lane beside her and ran the red light, swerving left on Bayview. As she did so, the car that had been approaching the light came to a stop. With a car now in front of it in each lane, there was no way the gray sedan could follow.

Just then the light turned green. Maggie knew the driver of the sedan had seen her make the turn. Panicked, Maggie cranked the wheel and the Audi skidded left around another corner and into a residential neighborhood.

"Lord God, help me lose this guy!" she prayed as she spotted the nose of the sedan coming around the corner after her.

In that same second she approached a house that just happened to have its garage door open. She immediately took advantage of the fact and pulled the Audi into the garage, killing the lights just as the sedan passed by. The driver had apparently not seen her.

Maggie closed her eyes and breathed a sigh of relief.

She took a moment to get control of her senses and ponder the implications of what had just happened.

Somebody was still after her. This meant she wasn't going to be safe anywhere.

When Peter found out about this, he would come unglued. He would insist that she move in with him again, and that would leave her father alone. Her resistance would easily lead into a fight. She let out a groan of frustration, just as she suddenly became aware of a girl who was standing in front of her car, looking at her in wide-eyed confusion.

"Oh shoot, busted!" Maggie said under her breath. She quickly started the car again and shoved it into reverse. "Sorry, wrong house!" she called to the bewildered little girl. The absurdity was too much, and she couldn't help but laugh. Maggie realized there probably wouldn't be more than a few seconds before the little girl told her parents that some screwball stranger was parked in their garage. She quickly backed out of the driveway and headed down Culfor Crescent Drive.

Maggie briefly peered into her rearview mirror yet again…but when she looked back at the road before her, a form suddenly materialized out of the darkness.

She slammed on the breaks too late, and shock cut through her system as she heard the horrifying thump of her car hitting a human being.

Skidding to an immediate stop, Maggie forgot about any sense of danger as she leapt out of her car and went running to the older man who lay on the ground.

"Oh my god!" she cried. "Mister, are you all right?"

The man, who was somewhere in his sixties, was

already stirring. He sat up, rubbing his fingers through his short-cropped salt and pepper hair and winced upon touching a sensitive spot on his head. He looked up at her accusingly through angry, pale blue eyes and pointed a shaky finger at her.

"You deranged teenagers are all alike! You get in a car and focus more on texting than driving!"

"I am so sorry, sir. It was dark and I didn't see you. Are you okay?" She put an arm around him and helped him up, despite his unwillingness to receive her assistance. He was around 5'11" and seemed pretty robust for a man his age. She was extremely grateful he had not been some frail, brittle old man.

"Let go of me. I'm a career vet, for crying out loud! I can take more than this."

"Maybe I should get you to a hospital."

"Like heck. I don't need a stupid doctor fussing over me!"

Maggie looked the man over, noting the blood on the back of his head. He returned her regard with a contemptuous glare. *If looks could kill….*

"You're hurt. You need to see a doctor," Maggie persisted.

"I don't need a punk kid telling me what I need to do!" he raged as he angrily brushed off his camouflage pants.

"Well, then maybe you need a 'punk kid' to help you get home," she said, not being dissuaded in the least by the man's temper. Before he could protest, she cut him off. "Where do you live?"

"Just across the street. I'm not in diapers. I can make it by myself!" But even as he spoke, he staggered slightly, and Maggie knew he had hit his head a little harder than he thought.

Maggie took hold of the man, despite his attempts to throw her off, and carefully walked him to his house. He was leaning on her for support—whether he said he needed it or not. She threw the door open and helped him to the couch, which was about five feet from the door.

"Nice house," she commented.

"You're trespassing!"

"And you're acting like a deranged juvenile yourself," Maggie retorted. "Now where do you keep your medical supplies?"

He rolled his eyes as he realized there was nothing he could say to get rid of this teen until she was ready to go. "Down the hallway, in the bathroom," he finally relented. His head was throbbing by then.

Maggie quickly retrieved the supplies. She cleaned up the bloody bump on his head, and he growled when it stung. "How are your ribs?" she asked.

"How do you think they are? They feel like they were hit by a car!"

Maggie looked at him doubtfully. She knew he'd taken a hit in the ribs, but she thought the worse injury was to his head, considering he had not once grabbed his midsection.

"I'm not going to thank you," the man persisted. "You stupid kid, I wouldn't have my head banged up in the first place if you could keep your freaking eyes on the road!"

"Maybe so, but I wouldn't have hit you in the first place if you had kept your own eyes on the road and decided not to step in front of my car."

"Well, you impudent little—"

"You can insult me all night long. It won't bother me in the least," she called back as she went into the kitchen and searched the cabinets until she found some aspirin and a glass, which she filled with water. Returning, she handed them to him. "Here, take this. It might take the edge off your headache, if not your crotchety attitude."

He took them. "A glass of whiskey would help more."

"I doubt that. Alcohol isn't exactly the best cure for a headache." She retrieved a throw blanket from a nearby chair and draped it over him.

"If you're so danged determined to clear your guilt, you might as well grab me the remote while you're at it," he griped. "I can't sleep. I thought a walk might help. Of course, you nearly helped me to sleep *permanently*."

She spotted the remote on the coffee table and passed it to him. "I have a friend whose dad is a doctor. I'm going to ask him to check in on you in the morning."

"I have a doctor, you little snippet."

"Are you going to go see him?"

"No!" he roared, and then winced as pain shot through his head again.

"Which is why I'm going to ask my friend's dad to

come and see you."

She left him her phone number in case he needed anything further. "Just in case you want to sue me," she said with a hint of sarcasm.

"I'm thinking about it!" the old man called after her as she headed for the door.

It was nearly ten o'clock by the time Maggie hit her beeper and unlocked her car. She looked around her, cautiously surveying her surroundings. The street was deserted, but the thought did occur to her that her car could blow up the minute she got into it. It wouldn't be the first time something like that happened in Norfolk.

Maggie said a prayer under her breath as she slid into the leather seat. Her heart was beating hard, and she realized belatedly that she was feeling the tingling sensation that comes from breathing in shallow gasps. Closing her eyes, Maggie held her breath, forcing herself to get a grip on her fears. For the first time, she wished Tennyson was with her.

Maggie took her car key and slowly slid it into the ignition, hesitating once more. She didn't know much about car bombs, and she wondered if there would be anything that could give rise to any warning – a blinking light or ticking sound perhaps? She gave a violent start when she indeed heard a loud buzzing sound. She barely caught herself as a cuss word nearly slipped from her lips, but she soon realized the sound she'd heard was coming from her cell phone. She searched for it, following the sound until she found it under the passenger's seat where it had fallen.

Five missed calls, all, unsurprisingly, from Peter. She checked the text message: **WHERE THE HECK ARE YOU? WHY AREN'T YOU ANSWERING YOUR PHONE?**

No doubt he was alarmed when she failed to answer. She dropped the phone back into her purse. She needed more time to think about how she was going to respond, and right then, all she wanted was to go home.

Maggie decided that blinking lights and beeping noises on bombs were probably only something that happened on TV. If someone had planted a bomb in her car, they could not have done so from the inside of the cab anyway—not since it had been locked. They could not have opened her hood, either. The hood could only be opened by remote or from the inside; therefore, if someone had tampered with her car, that person would have had to obtain access from underneath, and he wouldn't have had a whole lot of time.

Maggie glanced around, straining to see into the shadows once more as she contemplated with dread who had been following her and what his intentions had been. Seeing no movement in any direction, she decided the danger had passed—at least for now—and she was probably suffering from paranoia, however well-founded. She finally turned the key in the ignition, and the car roared to life. She relaxed for a moment.

Then the image of her totaled Corolla came to mind, and she realized that a person would only require mere seconds to cut her brake line. Maggie hesitated, and the unnerving thought occurred to her that she could be living with this kind of uncertainty for a long time.

She retrieved a flashlight from the glove compartment and got out of the car. For the hundredth time, her eyes searched her surroundings, finding no sign of anything out of place. She circled the car, looking for evidence of any kind of disturbance on the frosty ground that may not have been caused by the old man or herself. Nothing. She then squatted low and looked under the car to see if there was any liquid dripping from underneath. Again nothing, not that she would even be able to detect anything under such poor lighting.

Maggie let out the breath she'd been holding, the warmth of her breath leaving white puffs in the cold air. She wondered if this night would ever be over as she returned to her car and locked the doors. She put the car into drive and turned on the heater, but the engine was not warm yet, and the air that came out was brutally cold. She shut it off and finally made her way home without further incident.

She pulled into her driveway just as Tennyson's car pulled to the curb across the street.

She got out and went to his car. "Where were you?" she asked.

"Where was *I*? You were supposed to take the agreed upon route home, young lady! You don't want me on your tail, but then you pull this crap and lose me."

"I looked back and you were gone. I was being followed by a gray sedan. I took an alternate route to lose the guy."

"I know what was happening. I was behind him. You lost us, so I followed him for a short while trying to get a take on his plates, but they weren't lit and I couldn't see them. It was more important that I double back to find you, so I had to abandon pursuit. I just now located you when you were heading back home."

"So you were absent for at least twenty minutes, right?"

He blinked. "Did I miss something?"

"Oh, never mind."

"I might point out the obvious that none of this would have happened if you had been riding with me."

"I am not going to have you on top of me for the next several months. I'm not trying to be difficult, but this whole thing is driving me crazy! Everyone is following me around trying to either tell me what to do or hurt me. Do you know what that's like? I just can't stand feeling…trapped."

"How about feeling shot? Would that work better for you?"

Maggie rolled her eyes and breathed a sigh of exasperation as she turned and stomped back to her house. She really wasn't trying to be unreasonable, but rebellion had been part of her nature for a long time, and she was constantly battling the urge to tell Tennyson where he could get off. Walking away was her best bet at the moment.

Maggie walked in the door and was surprised to see her father sitting up waiting for her. "Dad," she asked, "are you still up?"

"You didn't think I was going to go to bed before you came home, did you, Maggie? I've been worried sick! Peter called and said that you left the church an hour ago."

"Oh, I see. I'm sorry, Dad. I…uh…." What the heck was she going to tell him? That someone had been following her? That she had hit an old man with her car? For crying out loud, he would come unhinged for sure!

"Where have you been, honey?" There was a suppressed urgency in his tone that told her he'd been terrified by her absence.

"I had some car trouble," she finally answered. That was pretty much true. Her car had caused her trouble when it had hit an old man!

"Car trouble?" he asked incredulously. "But it's a *new car*."

"Yeah, well, don't worry. Everything is fine now and I'm home. Okay, Dad? Go back to bed now. It's late."

They both heard a car pull into the driveway.

"Yeah, well, I don't think it's going to be that easy, sweetheart. Your boyfriend just showed up."

Maggie rolled her eyes in frustration. She wasn't ready for a confrontation; she'd had no time to come up with what she was going to say to Peter. She watched her dad head for his room just as she heard the abrupt knock at the door. She was clearly not going to get any backup from that quarter.

As Maggie opened the door, Peter entered immediately. He was standing inches from her, and she knew that he was either furious, terrified, or both. He knew something was off, and he took her by the arms so she couldn't turn away. A soaring moment of silence passed between them as he struggled for composure.

"You scared the living daylights out of me, Maggie! Why the heck didn't you answer when I called?" His gaze was penetrating through her, and she sensed that he was watching for any indication that she was about to lie to him. He was only too aware that she had not been a Christian for very long, and old habits die hard.

She knew the "car trouble" excuse wasn't going to fly with him any more than it had with her father. She looked away for a moment as she tried to form the right words, but when she looked back up at him, there were tears in his eyes.

"You can't go to pieces, Peter, every time I am unable to answer my phone right away," Maggie sighed.

"Really? Is that the best you can do? For crying out loud, Maggie, you've had people trying to kill you! What do you expect me to think when it takes you an hour to make a ten minute trip home? I'm surprised your dad isn't reaming you right now!"

"No, he figured he could leave that to you."

"Please don't get smart with me. You know I have a right to be upset with you."

"I'm sorry, Peter. I didn't mean to scare you. I just… didn't have time to get back to you right then. I barely just got home when you got here."

"Tell me what happened, and don't lie to me. If you lie to me, I'll never be able to trust you. Please, Maggie."

She couldn't hurt him that way. She sighed.

"Okay, Peter. I was followed tonight."

His eyes flashed. "Where was Tennyson?"

"Apparently following the guy who was following me. I managed to lose the jerk, but I also lost Tennyson in the process. I was scared, and I wasn't paying attention to where I was going and…."

"You wrecked the Audi?" he asked in trepidation.

"No. Nothing like that."

He seemed to visibly relax until she unloaded the next bombshell on him.

"I hit an old man."

"*What?*"

"He came out of nowhere and stepped right in front of my car!"

"Is he okay?"

"I think so. I helped him home. He wouldn't let me take him to a hospital. He was extremely angry and totally noncompliant. I planned on calling Jacob's dad and asking if he would see him first thing in the morning before he went to work."

Peter closed his eyes in denial, raking a hand nervously through his hair. "You're going to be lucky if he doesn't sue you. Although, if it was like you said and he stepped in front of you, it's a possibility that it could be decided it wasn't your fault. I swear, Maggie, I've never met anyone who drew so much danger!"

"I seriously don't need to hear that again right now."

"You're right. I'm sorry." He pulled her over to an overstuffed armchair and sat down, pulling her into his lap. She lay against him, so exhausted she wanted to cry. "Come home with me, baby. I can't sleep without knowing you're safe. It's driving me crazy. There isn't a night that I don't wake up wondering if something's gone wrong in my absence. If you're not ready to marry me, it will be enough to have you in the next room. You must know this isn't about anything...*physical*. It will be respectable."

"You know I can't, and you know why," she answered sleepily.

"Are we going to have this conversation again? You

can't protect your father if you're dead."

Courage whined at that point, clearly puzzled by whatever it was that was upsetting the two humans.

"God will protect us. Courage will help," she said as she yawned and cuddled into Peter.

"If it comes down to life and death, they're going to take the dog out of the equation first," he answered grimly.

She mumbled an incoherent reply, but he realized she was already half asleep.

Peter rested his head against the back of the chair. He swallowed, feeling his heart ache at the prospect of someone harming her—at the thought of what it would be like to live without her. He could only imagine how badly this night could have turned out. One thing he knew for sure–this was not close to being over. His hopes that she would be out of danger after the first trial ended were obviously in vain.

CHAPTER
four

It was early in the morning and dark outside when Maggie awoke to find herself curled up on the couch with a blanket. She blinked and looked across the gloomy living room to see Peter still asleep on the chair. She stretched, acutely aware of her exhaustion, and wondered what had woken her.

An odd sound from outside drew her attention then, and Maggie could feel a tingling at the back of her neck. *Something was not right.* She sat up and listened but did not hear anything further. She continued to listen.

Still nothing, but somehow her anxiety was not relieved. The silence itself seemed to be deafening.

Her eyes slowly adjusted to the darkness. She stood, still trying to shake the overwhelming feeling of uneasiness that had come over her. She padded across the cold hardwood floor on bare feet to where Peter sat sleeping.

"Peter," she whispered tentatively. No response. "Peter," she said again, this time gently shaking him. There was still no response, and she wondered if he was sleeping off his own exhaustion from the night before.

Maggie made her way to the window. She pushed back the curtains and peered out into the darkness. Nothing seemed amiss. She nervously glanced back at Peter, unsure of whether or not she should try to wake him again. No doubt he needed his sleep.

She made her way to the kitchen to get a drink of water. The pitcher was cold against her fingers when she lifted it, and she noticed a slight gritty substance beneath her fingers. "What on earth is that?" she asked herself, her uneasiness growing by the minute.

She wiped a finger across the glass, and it came away with slight traces of a white powder. She brought it to her nose, noting an odd smell. Anxiety suddenly washed over her. Something was terribly wrong. She could feel her chest tighten and an odd taste coated her tongue—the taste of *fear*.

Hurrying back into the living room, Maggie flicked on the light. "Peter, wake up," she said. Still no response. Her eyes darted to the coffee table, and she saw the empty water glass.

It only took a second for her to connect the glass to the powder she'd found on the pitcher. Someone had poisoned him.

"Oh my god, Peter!" she shouted then, shaking him hard. She brought her ear to his chest and listened for his heartbeat. She was almost weak with relief when she detected the steady beating. She listened for his breathing. His breaths were even, but shallow.

Maggie rushed toward her father's room and fell over something that was in the way. "Oh, Courage, I'm *so* sorry!"

She tried to get him to move, but he was limp. "Courage? Come on boy!" She tried unsuccessfully to get a response out of him. Heartsick, she let his head fall back to the floor. Had they gotten to *everyone?*

Leaping to her feet, Maggie flung open the door and ran into her father's room. "Dad? Dad!" she cried, but he was out cold, too. Her eyes took in the empty glass by his bed, and utter trepidation washed over her.

"I'm alone. Dear God, what do I do?" Her voice sounded strange and unfamiliar to her own ears.

Maggie snatched up the phone on his nightstand, and her heart skipped a beat when she realized the line was dead. Her next instinct was to go for her cell phone. Running into the kitchen, she grabbed her purse from a chair, frantically rummaging through the contents before spilling them on the small kitchen table, but she soon found that her cell was nowhere to be found.

She stood frozen in terror, too scared to move. She could feel an eerie sense of dizziness wash over her. For a frightening second, she thought she had also been poisoned or drugged or whatever. But she had not drunk from the pitcher, and she dismissed the possibility. So now what was she going to? She listened again, wondering if someone was still in the house. Her father and Peter needed help, but she was afraid to leave them alone.

Maggie went back to Peter, desperation clutching her insides as she held his face in her hands and kissed his cheek. She nestled her head into his neck, wanting to cling to him forever and keep him from slipping away from her. Her heart twisted within her, and tears burned her eyes and blurred her vision as her gaze fell upon her beloved pet and then rose to her father's door. She fiercely wiped the tears away, knowing time was of the essence, and she would fail everyone if she broke down right then. "I love you, Peter," she whispered brokenly.

In the next second the lights went out.

All was silent again. Maggie could feel perspiration break out on her forehead as she struggled to quiet her breathing—the only sound in that small room. An inner quaking spread through her body that she could not still. She peered through the darkness, looking toward the kitchen where she could grab a knife, but she heard a creak in the floorboards—and a shadow suddenly loomed in the kitchen entryway where she had been only moments before. Her eyes darted to the front door and then the back. But the shadow began to move toward her, and she knew she could not reach either exit without rushing past the evil that hunted her.

Maggie bolted for the bathroom, slamming the door and locking it. She nearly jumped out of her skin when something slammed against the door from the outside and the doorknob began rattling loudly.

She stared at the door in horror, waiting for the intruder to break it down. Her gorge rose in her throat, and she realized she'd been holding her breath. Was this how it was all going to end for her?

Silence.

She held her breath. How was it that the silence was so much more frightening than sound? She strained to hear. Where did he go? Her eyes rose to the mirror where she could see the faintest light of morning drifting through the glass window behind her. A pale sheet of ghostly white, it shone weakly into the dark and cramped little bathroom.

She listened intently, but all she could hear was her own breathing. It hummed in her ears like a loud wheezing sound. She held her breath once more, listening, but the deep, steady sound of breathing continued....

She was not alone in the darkness!

Her eyes flew to the mirror once more and this time saw the large dark form that had been standing behind her all along. In that horrifying second, she suddenly recognized the identity of the intruder.

Bret.

Light flashed and caught the edge of the gleaming blade. She released a blood-curdling scream as the death blow rapidly descended toward her head.

"Maggie." Peter's sleepy voice was oddly out of place as it broke into her dream. "Wake up, honey, you're having another nightmare."

Maggie suddenly awoke with a start, finding herself in Peter's arms. Momentarily disoriented, she blinked and glanced wildly around the room. Her mind was struggling to grasp the fact that they were still in the chair and Peter was okay. She clung to him then as if he were life itself, her heart pounding in fright as the events of the dream continued to course through her mind.

"Hey, hey. It's okay, honey. It's just another dream." He gave her a troubled look and wrapped his arms around her, kissing the top of her head. "Wow. That one got ugly, didn't it?"

"I suppose it did," she whispered. "How long have I

been asleep?"

He checked his watch. "I guess we both nodded off. It's early morning."

Since he couldn't convince her to stay at his house, Peter did the next best thing and spent the remainder of the night on her couch. Maggie's father did a double take when he got up later that morning and found him there, but Maggie had been tucked into her own bed by then, and he trusted Peter to his honor.

In English class that day, Maggie kept dozing off, and Peter had to nudge her to keep her awake. He was tired himself.

"You know that we're going to have to talk to the D.A. about last night," Peter whispered.

"Yeah, I know," she replied with sleepy eyes. "Please remind me to never do another trip to Richmond when we have school the next day."

"You don't want to save the lost on a Wednesday?"

"Maybe on a Friday when I can sleep in the next morning. I don't save the lost, anyway. God does."

He grinned at her.

Just as the bell went off, Maggie's phone rang. She answered while the others went piling out of the room. She was surprised when she heard the old man's voice.

"I don't know what kind of trouble you're in, little lady, but you better watch your back. I just received an anonymous call this morning from someone who offered me a significant sum of money to press charges against you for a hit and run."

"What is it?" Peter asked with trepidation.

"Hold on, Peter," Maggie whispered. "I'm truly sorry for the trouble, Mr. Waters."

"You don't sound too surprised."

"I guess I'm not. Was it a male or female who called?"

"It was a male. I couldn't tell the age. Sounded like he might have been disguising his voice."

"Thank you for letting me know. How are you feeling today?"

"As well as can be expected after a crazed teenager tried to take me out in front of my own house," he grouched, but she sensed a note of teasing in his tone.

"Did Dr. Townsend come to see you?" she asked.

"Yeah, and I'll live, so maybe I won't sue you, although I'm not ruling it out as a possibility."

"Thank you...I think. I'm sure I'd appreciate not being sued."

"Goodbye, then. Watch your back, kid."

"Goodbye, Mr. Waters."

"What happened?" Peter asked again. "That was the man you hit, right?"

"Yes. Apparently someone called him and offered

him money to say that I committed a felony hit and run."

Peter shook his head in disbelief. "Apparently you didn't shake the person following you."

"I guess not."

Her cell rang again, and Maggie looked down at the caller ID. This time it was the D.A., Megan Riley. "Hello?"

"Maggie, I need you to come by and see me after school today."

"I don't suppose Tennyson has been talking to you."

"I don't know why you wouldn't suppose he's been talking to me."

Maggie sighed. "All right. We'll come by after our last period class."

The D.A. seemed deep in thought as she sat at her desk when they entered her office. The desk was covered with papers that she'd been going over. She looked up when they came in and shoved her delicate glasses a little higher on her nose.

"Hi, kids. Come on in and have a seat," she said as she tucked a silver-streaked blond lock of hair behind one ear. Always dressed in a business dress and jacket, Megan Riley commanded almost as much respect by her appearance as she did by her reputation.

Maggie and Peter settled into the chairs opposite her desk. "So am I in trouble or something?" Maggie asked straight off.

"You mean for ditching your bodyguard?"

"I didn't do it intentionally."

"Not this time," Megan acknowledged with one brow raised intuitively. "You know, honey, it wouldn't hurt to be just a little more compliant. Tennyson is only working with you as a favor to me, and, in all reality, most agents are not used to chasing down their clients."

"Granted," Maggie conceded.

"So you were followed and neither you nor Tennyson can identify the vehicle?"

"It was dark and his plates weren't lit."

"Tennyson told me as much." She looked from one teen to the other, tapping her pencil on her desk, and it was clear that she was deciding on how to proceed.

"You might as well know the whole truth of what really happened last night," Peter said reluctantly.

Megan removed her glasses and glanced across at him with immediate concern. "Is there something I don't know about?"

Maggie exchanged glances with Peter, and it was clear that both of them were dreading the topic.

"Come on. Lay it on me, kids."

"While she was trying to ditch the car following her, Maggie hit an old man who was crossing the street," Peter informed.

"What? Please tell me you're joking!"

"It was dark. I didn't see him. He was okay, though, and I made sure Dr. Townsend checked on him," Maggie said in her own defense.

"Yeah, but he called her this morning and told her that someone must have seen the accident because he was offered a good sum of money to press charges against her."

"Great…that's all we need right now. Is there any chance he'll take them up on it?" Megan asked anxiously.

"I think it's really unlikely, since he took the time to call me and warn me to watch my back," Maggie answered.

They were silent a moment as this bit of info hung in the air.

"I've heard back from the Organ Procurement Organization," Megan said at last. "They stated that Norfolk Hospital didn't have an AB negative donor during the critical time."

"That's not surprising," Peter said.

"No, it's not. Rosie Dawson, the little girl who received the illegal transplant, was also never accepted onto the list of impending recipients."

"What does that mean?" Maggie asked.

"It means, for whatever reason, that she was not found to be a good candidate to receive a transplant. If the OPO finds the chances of survival to be very low, they will skip over one person and go with a more logical choice. Rosie Dawson beat the odds, though, when she received the operation anyway and survived."

"How's she doing?" Maggie asked.

"She's doing fine. She's a darling child, despite the brood of snakes who designed her. I feel sorry for the poor thing having to be brought up in the middle of this mess."

Maggie gave a shiver at the reference to genetic mapping. The very idea suggested that children who were naturally born were inferior. She wondered how anyone could not consider a child as precious, no matter what their genetic structure was.

"I guess designer clothes aren't good enough. They had to have designer babies as well."

"It didn't start off like that, Maggie. It just turned into that the further the research went on," Peter said. "The more they found that they could manipulate human life, the more they got a God complex."

"Apparently they haven't been able to map out all the desirable genes, or Rosie wouldn't have become sick in the first place...and they wouldn't have desecrated my best friend's body," Maggie responded in bitterness.

"There are infinite characteristics in the human gene pool," Peter continued. "It takes a lot of time and money to isolate the genes and connect them to the characteristics they produce. I doubt they will ever connect every positive or negative characteristic to the gene that generates it."

"You give me shivers, kid," Megan looked at him poignantly. "You should be talking about cars or video games at your age. There's no question that you and those like you have a higher than average aptitude for learning and processing. I'm just glad the adults, as educated as they are, don't quite have that same ability."

"Give it a few years, Ms. Riley. This generation

will soon be the adults running The Inner Society, and then what?"

"Scary thought."

"Thanks," Peter replied.

"No offense, intended," Megan said with a chuckle.

"So have you made any more headway on our case?" Peter asked, unable to wait any longer.

"I've been doing nothing day or night but pouring over information on this case," she informed. "I haven't had a day off since before the first trial. I'm doing everything I can with what I have to work with. I did receive a tip from an anonymous witness who insists James Keller was working for Bret's father, and they weren't on good terms."

"So did you follow up on it? Was it true?" Maggie pressed.

"Of course I followed up on it, but you can imagine what happened when I asked about it."

"Everyone denied knowing anything," Peter finished with disgust.

"Exactly. I have to have proof. I already subpoenaed the records for the law firm where Chambers worked, but if Keller did ever work for him, all evidence has been erased from every file. I can't prove any connection between them.

"Trying to break the links of The Inner Society is like trying to break a steel chain. It's eerie how closely connected their network really is—although I'm sure it's no surprise to you, Peter. They have a network of support that reaches from the city government to the police department, the hospital, even the educational system. Every member manages to obtain an alibi, and every bit of evidence seems to mysteriously disappear. They all serve to protect one another from the repercussion of any illegal activity. It's terrifying how deep this thing goes. The fact that they managed to move the first trial up before I had sufficient time to put together the proof of our accusations is just another example. I've never seen anything like that happen, *not ever*."

"Which means they could move up the next trial, too," Peter said soberly. "We could be rapidly running out of time."

CHAPTER
five

Peter was not in a good mood the next day. Maggie's lack of compliance over the marriage issue and the concern that she was still taking matters into her own hands plagued his mind. He walked across the parking lot, Maggie following directly behind him. She wasn't about to tolerate his mood, and was doing everything within her power to irritate him. As Peter was walking, he felt her shoe make contact with the back of his heel. "You better quit that," he warned. The next time the contact was a little harder. "What are you? Five now?"

She smiled to herself and proceeded to kick him again, this time nearly causing him to trip. Peter turned on her, and she laughed and jumped out of his reach when he tried to grab her. He lunged forward and caught her, though, his hand gripping her jaw just strong enough to keep her from getting away.

"You are about to get it, you little brat!" he promised.

"Don't threaten me with a good time!" she quipped back, fire sparkling in her eyes.

He couldn't help but smile. He loved this girl to distraction. She had become his entire life in such a short time. Pulling her forward, he brought her up against him and tenderly kissed her. But there was heartbreak in that touch, a heartbreak born of the same fear her father was experiencing—the fear that he could still lose her. He couldn't watch her walk away without feeling his heart wrench within him. He wanted to hang onto her every waking moment, but he knew she would never tolerate it.

She loved him—he knew that too; but Maggie was still a free spirit, and she wasn't trusting enough to be bound by anyone. Not even him. He could only be grateful that she had let him get as close as he had.

They walked the rest of the way across the parking lot, hand in hand.

At break time Maggie walked down the hallway at Norfolk High, and suddenly her nerves went on full alert as she spotted the three boys who had surrounded Marci.

Derik Caldwell had her up against a locker. He wasn't touching Marci, but he had an arm up on either side of her to prevent her from moving. Jason and their new friend Conrad flanked Derik's sides. Maggie was at a distance from them, but she could still make out what he was saying.

"What the heck are you doing with a black guy, Marci?"

Obviously terrified, Marci was not meeting Derik's eyes. "We're friends."

"You're more than that. We saw him holding hands with you. You're one of us, whether you like it or not, and there are rules…."

"But he's also one of us," she carefully protested.

"It's not the same thing, and you know it!"

Maggie's steps became more purposeful as her mind suddenly replayed every incident of bullying she had suffered from these boys. The fact that they had now turned their evil intentions upon someone as helpless as Marci only added fuel to the fire.

They didn't even see her coming until she brushed past Jason and Conrad and came at Derik, shoving him backward.

"Oh god," Conrad said under his breath, "this is going to get ugly." There was more anticipation in his tone than worry, though.

He wasn't far from wrong. No sooner had Maggie wedged herself between Derik and Marci than Derik's wrath fell upon Maggie. He towered over her, but Maggie wasn't cowed by him.

"What are you going to do, Derik? Are you going to start messing with Marci now, you jerk?"

His hateful gaze penetrated through her, but before he could respond, his eyes looked past her and saw Peter approaching.

"Derik!" Peter raged. In seconds they were within inches of one another, Peter not intimidated in the least that he was outnumbered. "You guys better not come within ten feet of either of these girls unless you're stupid enough to rack up some more charges against you."

Derik glanced around, realizing they were beginning to attract the attention of others who were passing in the hall. He and Jason were fuming, but they knew their parents would also have a conniption if word got back to them that they were involved in any more conflicts with Maggie Kraus. They didn't have to wait for the trial to suffer repercussions for their actions.

"I didn't go after her," Derik snapped. "She came at me!"

"In defense of Marci. You're amazingly brave when you're bullying someone weaker than you!" Peter was now standing protectively in front of both girls.

"Spoken like a true hypocrite, Peter. The only reason you're going to tolerate this outrage is because Jacob's your best friend."

"It's not going to make a difference to you one way or another when I put you in the hospital!"

They were mere seconds away from coming to blows.

"Whoa! Hold on you guys," Conrad interjected. "We don't need any trouble."

He sounded like the voice of reason, but Peter took in the way he was looking at Maggie and immediately doubted his sincerity. Conrad looked like he *wanted* trouble.

When he became aware that Peter had caught him staring at his girlfriend, Conrad put his hands up in surrender. "Sorry. We're leaving now." He grabbed his friends by the arms and pulled them away.

"Are you girls okay?" Peter asked, still trying to get a grip on his anger. They nodded, but it was obvious that Marci was shaken. "You knew this was coming, didn't you, Marci?" Peter asked, his tone empathetic.

"I…I guess I did," she answered softly.

He turned on Maggie then, his rage renewing in such force that she stepped backward. He pointed a finger at her in warning. "I swear, Maggie, you better not ever initiate a physical confrontation with those guys! I am not kidding! I saw the way you came at Derik. For crying out loud, haven't you learned anything from all this!" He was nearly shouting at her, and Maggie was a little taken back by his wrath, even though she knew she would never be in any danger from him.

Marci watched in amazement as Maggie stood her ground, waiting out Peter's tirade. Maggie caught her expression and knew that Peter's anger had put more fear into Marci than it had into her. This was a side of him that Marci had never seen. Peter had undoubtedly been sensitive and gentle when he'd been with her.

"What was I supposed to do, Peter?" Maggie asked quietly when Peter had finished. "He had her up against a locker."

"You should have come and gotten me!"

"I didn't know where you were."

"You know how to text! You didn't go after Derik simply to protect Marci. You went after him because you were enraged by the injustice of what he was doing. It would only have taken him one second to lose control and shatter your jaw. Apparently you've forgotten what it feels like to get the snot beat out of you!"

"It could have been Marci who got hurt," she reasoned.

"It was unlikely that Marci would have ignited that

much rage in him by herself. You, on the other hand, seem to continually inspire violence in these guys!"

Maggie folded her arms, her eyes narrowing in irritation.

"Don't yell at her, Peter," Marci pleaded gently. "She was only trying to help me."

Jacob joined them then. Maggie could read the dread in his expression when he saw Marci standing quietly by, her face pale. When Marci saw him approach, she ran into his arms, and he held her against him. "What's going on?" he demanded.

All three were silent for a while before Peter finally answered. "They were messing with Marci over your relationship, and Maggie jumped to her defense—*violently*."

Jacob closed his eyes for a moment as the anger took hold. He felt Marci trembling, and his protective instincts surged forth. "I'm going to kill them!" he vowed with lethal intensity.

"No, you're not! You're as bad as she is," Peter said, motioning toward Maggie.

"I seem to remember you threatening bodily injury yourself," she pointedly reminded him.

It was Peter's turn to feel a stab of guilt. "So I did." He took a breath and then looked down at her with a little more self-control. "I'm sorry I yelled at you, sweetheart. But I'm still dead serious about you staying away from Jason and Derik. I'm angry with you because I'm terrified for you. I don't think I could survive it if I lost you."

"I know that," she allowed.

"So you seriously expect me to do nothing?" Jacob asked.

Peter gently pulled Marci away from him. "Give us a moment, Marci, okay?" She nodded in acceptance and Peter took Jacob aside so they could speak in private.

"My god, that chick is hot!" Conrad whistled as he and his friends walked down the hall. "She's got no fear at all, has she?"

Conrad knew who Maggie Kraus was. *Everyone* knew who Maggie Kraus was, but this was the first time Conrad Masterson had met up with her in person. All the teens involved in the recent violence had made headlines in several states now. There was no doubt this situation was going to go national by the time the next trial started.

Jason and Derik exchanged knowing glances.

"She *needs* to have some fear," Derik inserted darkly, adjusting the diamond stud in his ear. "She doesn't know how close she came to dying."

"Oh, I'm sure she knows," Jason disagreed. "That's the thing that's so infuriating. She knows, but she won't let anything back her down."

"I can think of a few times we 'backed her down'," Derik said with meaningful inflection.

"But we didn't keep her broken," Jason replied, "and that may cost us one day."

"There's not a whole lot she can do to us at this point. We'll just have to finish out our community service."

"She can still do damage to our parents," Jason pointed out. "Don't forget we have another trial coming up. Our whole way of life could be on the line."

"She doesn't know enough to do any real damage," Derik countered.

"She doesn't have to. She has the D.A. on her side, and that lady's determined to seek justice. And then there's Peter. He could do some real damage."

Derik gave him a knowing smile. "Peter's too smart to sell out completely, that traitor. He'll try to help her, but he'll be very careful in the way he does it. He knows how powerful The I.S. is, and he knows the legal system can only offer so much protection. He also knows Maggie is too unpredictable to be trusted with too much knowledge. He won't tell her everything."

"Well, I'd like to take that little girl on," Conrad inserted, a mischievous gleam in his blue eyes.

The others again exchanged glances. "No, you wouldn't!"

Peter stopped in front of his locker and turned to Jacob. "You started this relationship with Marci," he said. "We talked about this very scenario. You need to keep watch over her, even if that means walking her to every class and being late to your own. You know I love you like a brother, Jacob, but it's going to break my heart if anything happens to her. I have enough trouble with Maggie."

"I'm sorry, Peter. I had no idea that anyone had seen us holding hands."

"You just had her in your arms a second ago! You have to be careful, man. Marci is a heck of a lot more vulnerable than Maggie."

"I know."

"So don't hold her in public!" Peter hissed. "Hold off until we're out of school."

It wasn't until lunch that Maggie was alone with Peter, and they finally had the chance to talk about what had happened.

"Why did they say that Marci was one of them, and she knew better? I mean, isn't Jacob part of The Inner Society as well?"

"Financially? Yes. His parents were involved in this whole thing when it started, but his mother became pregnant through natural means before they could artificially inseminate her. The Townsends are part of The Inner Society, but Jacob is not the product of genetic mapping."

Maggie pondered that over for a minute before asking her next question. "And since when does Conrad hang out with Derik and Jason? I don't remember seeing him hanging out with them before."

"They've been friends for a while; he just circulated with different people until recently."

"Is he one of you?"

"Can't you tell?"

She contemplated his features, his warm blue eyes, short-cropped golden hair, and the characteristic height and build that was common among those who had been genetically mapped. He looked like an angel of light, but the devilish twinkle in his eyes gave indication to the complete opposite.

"Yeah. I suppose. So they've recruited another demon into their coven."

"Looks like. Stay away from him, too. He might not be involved in all of the crap they've pulled, but you can't trust anyone who hangs out with Jason or Derik. And I don't like the way he looks at you."

"So do you guys all know every name on The I.S. list, then?"

"Yes, anyone local that is. I told you that. This thing has become like a religion, and it's bigger than you think."

"Like white supremacy or something?" The very idea gave her chills.

"No, not quite like that. There are people on the list who are from different races, like the Townsends. The list you saw on Derik's flash drive last year was only one fraction of the total. But, yes, in the sense that they believe we are genetically superior, many of them are supremacists. I don't buy into it, since God obviously doesn't set value on the same things as man, but you ought to know that they are sold out to their belief in our superiority."

"Does that give Marci protection?"

"Again, yes and no. It gives her some protection because she is one of them. We don't generally hurt our own…." He let that hang for a moment, sending her a subtle message that she wasn't getting. "But she is also expected to live by a 'higher standard' because of who she is."

"Does that standard dictate that they only have relationships amongst other members?"

"Not necessarily, but having a relationship with someone outside of her race who is also not genetically perfected isn't going to go over very well. Jacob is accepted because of his wealth and who his parents are. People who started this venture are still considered members of The Inner Society. But that doesn't mean Jacob will have any leeway when it comes to his relationship with Marci."

"Wow. That doesn't smack of bigotry, does it? Apparently all that money that went into genetic restructuring failed to isolate any genes for human decency!"

"Should I be offended?" he mocked.

"You know I don't mean you. You're good, Peter, because you've allowed Christ to put his goodness into you."

A few hours later, Maggie returned to her locker after PE to put her watch away. When she glanced up, she noticed Mark Dawson's ex-girlfriend sitting on a bench that ran between two rows of lockers a little distance away. Her head was in her hands, and she was obviously crying. Maggie hadn't thought about her for a long time. She and Rebecca had never been on good terms, especially after Mark told the court he'd slept with Maggie. It hadn't been true, but Rebecca had believed the lie, and she had broken up with him that same day.

The full impact of Rebecca's predicament hit Maggie at that moment as she contemplated what this girl must be going through. Not only had her boyfriend been shot right after she'd broken up with him, but he had died from complications with AIDS a few days later. It was anyone's guess whether or not Rebecca had been infected as well. It probably didn't help that Mark's complications had resulted from the injury he'd taken while trying to protect Maggie from Chris Fischer's violent tirade.

Maggie remembered seeing her on her first day at Norfolk High. Rebecca had caught her attention when she had sauntered across the parking lot and then sidled up to Mark like a graceful feline. She remembered her glossy blond hair and slim waistline, and how stunningly beautiful she was. Rebecca was still quite lovely, but Maggie noticed her hair was slightly less glossy, and she was looking a little too thin now. It made Maggie wonder if the girl had indeed been infected herself, and her heart twisted in pity.

She paused for a moment of internal conflict. Rebecca had ostracized her just as much as the others; there had certainly been no love lost between them. Yet now Rebecca had become one of the very victims people like her had created. She was the one being ostracized.

Love your enemies, do good to those who hate you, bless those who curse you, pray for those who mistreat you. The Scriptures seemed to speak to Maggie right out of thin air, and she closed her eyes, wanting to mentally block them out. Luke 6:27-28 were probably Maggie's least favorite Scriptures. But then Maggie remembered all the times she had been rude to Marci, and how Marci had never failed to be kind back to her. She knew what she had to do.

Maggie sat down on the bench three feet away from the girl, having no idea of what to say to her. She remembered sitting in this very spot when Mark had taken her there to tell her about the impending drug bust. Of course, she knew now that that had only been a ploy. He had really done it to make Peter jealous.

"What do you want?" Rebecca hissed.

"I don't want to make fun of you, if that's what you think."

"I wouldn't have any heartache if it weren't for you. There's nothing lower than someone who sleeps with someone else's boyfriend."

"I didn't sleep with him, Rebecca. Don't you have any clue of the horrible things Mark did to me? Do you really think I'd sleep with him after that?"

"Why did he say you did, then?"

"I think it's pretty obvious. He wanted to discredit me on the witness stand."

Rebecca thought that over for a minute. "I guess it doesn't matter anyway now. He's dead."

Another moment of silence passed as both girls pondered the terrible permanence of that fact.

"Of course it makes a great deal of difference to you," Rebecca interjected. "If you had slept with him, you would have been infected, too."

"So have you been tested yet?" Maggie asked.

Rebecca looked up at her with resentment, but her expression soon melted in her grief. Tears welled in her eyes, and she hastily wiped them away.

"That sucks," Maggie said. "I'm really sorry, Rebecca—honestly."

"Why would you care...unless you just wanted to gloat?"

"Why would I do such a thing? I'm the one people usually gloat over, remember?"

Rebecca paused, uncertain of how to respond.

"I'm going to die, Maggie. I'm going to die and nobody wants anything to do with me now. My mother cries all the time, my father never speaks anymore, and...I don't know why I'm even telling you this!"

Maggie paused, wondering what she was going to say. But the answer was simple when it came to her. "Because you need someone to talk to right now."

"Do you have any idea what it feels like to know you're going to die?"

Maggie couldn't help but choke on the laughter that erupted from inside her, however horribly inappropriate it was. Then she quickly put up her hands to placate Rebecca. "I'm *so* sorry. I didn't mean to laugh. It's just...you do realize not a day has gone by in the past month when I did *not* think I was going to die?"

Rebecca looked at her as though seeing her for the first time. "Is it true, then, that someone really tried to kill you?"

"More than once."

"You said the guys were involved. Was that also true?"

It was Maggie's turn to feel uncomfortable as she remembered more than one terrifying ordeal at their hands.

"Yes, it's true," she answered quietly.

Rebecca thought that over. "And they got away with it. You must have been devastated."

"I was more devastated by the fact that they got away with killing the only friend I had in the world."

"Yeah, I guess that would bite it," she agreed. "It's funny how I see things so differently now. I don't think I'm the same person I was just a short time ago. Knowing you're going to die changes everything."

"Heartbreak has a way of changing people."

They sat in silence for a moment. Maggie knew that this could be the only opportunity she might ever have to say something that could make a difference in this girl's life. She knew what it was like to be alone and desperate for someone to love her, even despite the mess she was. Peter had shown her that Christ had always loved her unconditionally. Rebecca needed to know this now, but Maggie wasn't too sure how to tell her.

Taking a deep breath, Maggie looked into Rebecca's troubled eyes and said, "You must realize, Rebecca that no one knows the number of their days. Any one of us can go at any time. Jessica thought she was going to become a beautician someday, but she never even made it to graduation. You have already outlived many of the other students of Norfolk High."

"What's your point, Maggie?" Her voice was raw.

What *was* her point? She paused once more, trying to sort out her thoughts before she spoke. "It's not how long we live that counts, but how *well* we live and what we leave behind us when we're gone."

Maggie was coming to new conclusions about her own life even as she spoke, and she had to swallow the sob that caught in her throat as she realized she was talking to herself as much as Rebecca. Jessica had perished without ever knowing the love of God. Maggie wanted to leave something behind her when she died—something that would make a difference in this messed up world.

"You still have valuable time, Rebecca. You're alive now and your time is not over yet. Make the time you have count."

Rebecca remained silent, and Maggie decided she had said enough for now. She left the girl contemplating her future, and Maggie found herself doing the same, grateful once again that she had been given yet another chance to live. Not only had Christ saved her from a life of sin and devastation, but Peter had shown her the love of God and had given her a reason to want to live.

Peter was busy that Saturday picking up a new car for his business inventory, so Maggie stayed home to work on her term paper and spend time with her dad. When she completed the paper, Maggie set about to make some soup.

Her father watched her as she worked, and she was feeling a growing sense of uneasiness as she began to wonder what he was thinking. "What's the matter, Dad?" she asked at length.

He shook his head. "Nothing, honey."

"Quit brooding, then."

He continued to watch her as she stirred the homemade chicken bisque she had cooking on the stove.

The aroma filled the air, and she dipped in a spoon to taste her creation. The creamy flavor washed over her tongue. "Mmmm, this is awesome. Come here, try this, Dad."

He came up to her, and she ladled out another spoonful for him to try. "That's divine, sweetheart. You're just like your mother," he added almost distantly. "She could cook anything out of practically nothing at all."

"Thanks, Dad."

Maggie sliced and buttered a couple of pieces of sourdough bread and heated them in the microwave for a few seconds before serving lunch. The two sat down together in silence, simply enjoying the meal with few words between them.

When they were done, Maggie picked up the bowls and put them in the sink. She eyed her father perceptively. "You're still giving me that look. It's making me uneasy."

"I'm just worried about you, honey."

"I'm fine now that I've got this horrible English paper finished."

"Why do I get the feeling you're planning on going somewhere?"

She smiled ruefully. "Probably because I am."

"I don't suppose your timing has anything to do with the fact that Tennyson had to leave to handle business this morning?"

"I'm nearly eighteen, Dad, and I survived the first part of my life without constant protection. Besides, it would be really awkward if he came with me. I'm just going to go and bring Mr. Waters some of this bisque and sourdough bread. His house is only a couple of miles from here. I'll be right back."

"There's many a slip between a cup and a lip, honey. Any mistake could prove fatal right now. Tennyson told you to stay home and to call him if you had an 'all fire need' to go somewhere." He was worried and rubbing at the stubble on his jaw, something he did when he was agitated. There were worry lines in his forehead.

"I wish Peter hadn't called you the other night and made you worry," Maggie said.

"I'm glad he did. I feel like you live an entirely secret life right under my nose that I don't know anything about."

"That's what teenagers do best!" She went to him and gave him a kiss on the forehead. "Don't worry, Dad. I'll be right back." She poured the steaming bisque into a Tupperware container, popped the lid on, and wrapped up some of the French bread. Holding the bowl and bread in one hand, she grabbed her purse with the other and slung it over her shoulder. "I love you, Dad."

"I love you, too, honey."

Courage followed Maggie to the door. "I love you, too, baby," she said to him. He jumped up on her, and she put her free arm around him and kissed his head. "You be good, boy. I'll be back soon."

Maggie went out the door and gave a violent start as she saw someone rushing toward her.

"Maggie!" the boy said.

Maggie took a moment to get a hold of her hammering

heart as she recognized the Hmong boy from Richmond. He was wearing a remake of the same clothes he'd been wearing last time—only this time he was wearing pale blue faded jeans and a gray flannel shirt.

"Tai? You scared the heck out of me! What on earth are you doing here?"

"My mother said I had to return kindness with a gift. This is very important to Hmong people."

"Really? So what did you do, hop on a bus and travel an hour and a half from Richmond to give me a gift?" she asked incredulously.

"Hey, sarcasm is not appreciated in the Hmong culture," he said, but Maggie could tell he was suppressing a smile. He came up to her and held up a thin, braided red cloth. "It is a neck string, for good luck. Can I put it on you?"

"Just as soon as you tell me how in the world you found me."

"I told you. I am computer genius," he said proudly. She gave him a doubtful look. "I Googled you," he explained at last. "You are only like all over the local news. It wasn't that hard. Okay? I can string you now?"

"String me? It sounds like a hanging!"

He smiled as he approached, and she allowed him to tie the string around her neck.

"You are going somewhere?"

"I'm going to visit a grumpy old man. He's had a head injury and doesn't know what's good for him, so I'm going to bring him some soup."

"Who is this man?"

"His name's Ken Waters."

Maggie sensed the kid doing a double-take at the mention of the name. She was puzzled when he went silent.

"What's the matter?" she asked. "Do you know him?"

"No, why should I?"

He almost sounded genuine, but Maggie was uncertain.

"Oh yes, and here…." He gave her a bamboo plant. "Bamboo is also for good luck for pretty mamas."

"'Pretty mamas'? Really?"

"What? You don't like being called a pretty mama?"

"I don't think so, Tai."

"Hot chick?"

"Definitely not!" she laughed. "I have to go. I've got some soup on the stove. Why don't you go in and have some?" She went back to the front door and shouted to her dad that they had a visitor. Tai smiled eagerly; his appetite had apparently not subsided in the least since the last time she'd seen him. "Oh, yes, and, Tai?"

"Yes, little chicken?"

"*No*, that name isn't going to work either! I just want you to know that if you steal so much as a paperclip, I'm going to kick your butt and then feed you to my very large dog. Is that clear?"

"I won't take nothin'," he promised, almost on a whine. "I only take stuff when I have to."

"And, of course, you have to take computers?"

"It was a career move," he said, standing up straight and mustering what dignity he could manage. One hand rose to check and make sure his gel-spiked hair was still in place. "I'm talented, you know. I could hack into the government's database if I wanted to."

"And you could go to prison for life."

"Juvenile Hall," he corrected with a sly smile.

Maggie was laughing when she got into her Audie. Somehow she had the feeling that she was going to have another puppy following her around.

CHAPTER
SIX

Maggie went up to the doorstep and rang the doorbell.

"Go away!" Mr. Waters shouted.
She shoved the door open and went in anyway.

"It's you again!" the man said, rolling his eyes in exasperation. "Don't you ever go away?"

"Apparently not," Maggie said dryly.

"I don't suppose your mother ever taught you to respect people's privacy?" he snapped.

"My mother is dead," Maggie informed him coolly, knowing that that would shut him up, at least momentarily. "I brought you some soup. You might as well eat it if you want me to leave."

She went into the kitchen and found a bowl in a cabinet. In another minute she had found a spoon and a napkin. She brought them to him, placing them on the coffee table close to where he was lounging on the couch. She set the bread on a napkin beside the bowl.

"You expect me to eat this?"

"If you know what's good for you. Didn't your mother ever teach you manners?"

She sat in the loveseat and leaned back comfortably while he blew on the soup and then took a couple of tastes. He clearly liked it, although Maggie knew he wouldn't admit it.

"What the heck are you wearing around your neck?" he asked with clear aversion.

"Apparently it's a good luck string."

"I know what it is. I just wondered why you were wearing some filthy Hmong relic!"

"So you're not only crotchety, you're prejudiced, too. *Nice touch*."

"So what happened to your mother?" he asked at length.

"We were in an accident. She wasn't wearing her seatbelt. I was."

He was silent as he dipped his bread in the soup and took a bite while thinking that over.

"What about you? Don't you have any family?"

He grumbled under his breath. "My father was tortured to death in Korea. My mother passed on when I was young."

"No wife or kids?"

"You're pushy, aren't you? Yes, I had a wife and a kid. They took a mind to get tired of me. She left me many years ago. I've never heard from them since—not a letter or a birthday card…nothing. Good riddance!"

"So you holed up and shut down. I can see that's working for you."

"I poured my life into the service of my country!" he corrected vehemently. "You know, I'm beginning to see why you have enemies!"

Maggie couldn't help but laugh. "Yeah, I have that effect on people."

He dipped his bread again and took a few mores bites. "So what kind of trouble are you in, anyway?"

"Don't you read the paper?"

He looked at her quizzically with one thick brow raised. He rested his head against the palm of one hand as he thought back. Then his gaze fixed on her as recognition suddenly hit. "Well, I'll be danged! You're that kid!"

Maggie shrugged and got up to leave. She grabbed her purse. "Yeah, unfortunately, that was me."

Mr. Waters released a long low whistle. "You really are in trouble," he mumbled, an uneasy frown crossing his features. He looked at her more keenly. "Be careful, little girl."

She gave him a faint smile and waved. "I've gotta go. Bye, Mr. Waters."

"Bye, kid."

Tai was parked on the couch next to her dad when she got home. Courage was in his lap.

Maggie rolled her eyes in disbelief. "You've gotta be kidding me. Are you still here?"

"Don't pretend you're not thrilled, my little bamboo stick."

Maggie groaned. "Quit with the names already!" she said with genuine irritation, and dropped her purse and sunk into an armchair, noting that the two were watching football. "So," she said to her dad, "the television is still here, and I don't see any appliances missing."

Her father gave her a look of annoyance, but there was humor in his eyes. "Exasperating little cuss, isn't he?"

"You know that in the Hmong culture, it is customary to say bad things about a beautiful child so that the evil spirits will be tricked into not stealing away his soul," Tai said smugly.

"You won't be offended when I call you brat, then!" Maggie quipped.

Tai smiled a toothy grin, his white teeth flashing and his brown eyes twinkling.

"Did you make it to church Sunday?" Maggie interrogated.

"I make my own decisions," he said with as much arrogance as he could muster. "A Hmong man doesn't let others make decisions for him." He again patted his spiky hair to make sure it was still in place.

"A 'Hmong man'? Hmmm. A few minutes ago you were a 'beautiful child.'"

"I am man enough for you, sweetheart!"

"My fiancé is going to kick your butt."

"He will just have to accept the inevitable. You have found a beautiful Hmong man who you are crazy about."

Maggie rolled her eyes. "That was nauseating...."

"You know, you marry a Hmong man and you can have a strong Hmong name."

"Like what? Margaret Sara Lee? I might as well change my name to Wonder Bread!"

A knock at the door interrupted their banter, and Maggie knew it had to be Peter. "Come in," she called. Peter walked in and his expression showed his astonishment when he saw Tai lounging comfortably on the couch as though he owned the place.

"What are *you* doing here?"

"According to him, he came because his mother told him to bring gifts of thanks," Maggie answered dryly, lifting the red string around her neck for him to see.

"That really was true," Tai said with a little more humility. It was pretty evident that he was intimidated by Peter.

"He's hitting on your girlfriend," Mr. Kraus said in jest.

Tai's eyes grew wide as Peter's attention fell upon him. Peter was obviously not threatened in the least by Tai, but he wasn't past having a little fun at the kid's expense, either.

"Really? Is that so?"

Maggie had to bite back a smile as she and her father watched the unfolding scene with amusement.

"No. I just want to compliment her. In our culture—"

"It is very important to hit on the person you are giving thanks to?" Peter finished for him.

Tai looked away a little sheepishly. "Okay, so I think she's a cool chick. Are you going to kill me now?" The question was all the more humorous due to his serious tone.

"Maybe later, when I have nothing better to do," Peter said as he pulled Maggie to her feet and kissed her. He pulled back and looked into her silver eyes. She smiled at him then rested her face against his shoulder, and he wrapped his arms around her.

"How'd you get here, anyway?" Peter asked as he turned back to Tai.

"Our city's finest transportation system."

"You rode an hour and a half on the bus?"

"Well, it took a little longer than that due to all the stops and stuff."

"Did you make it to church on Sunday?"

"I asked him that," Maggie answered. "He said, 'A Hmong man makes his own decisions.'" She smiled smugly, knowing she had just gotten Tai in trouble.

"I…I never actually said I didn't go!" Tai said in his own defense.

"Your mom got the groceries, then?"

"Yeah, thanks, man. She really appreciated it. Things have been…hard."

It was the first time that the boy had revealed anything personal, and Peter thought over his answer.

"It might help if you had a job."

"No one's going to hire me, man. I'm sixteen."

"You can get a work permit. How would you like to do some janitorial work for the church or something on the weekends? I'm sure I could arrange something. I mean, you'd be scrubbing toilets, but you'd also be making some money."

"Really?" Tai's eyes lit up with anticipation. "I'll scrub those toilets until they're shiny clean!" he vowed.

"All right, then. You better catch the bus. You've got a long ride home. I'll call you after I've spoken with Pastor Bradford. It will mean the same long ride down here every weekend, though. Are you sure you're up to it?"

"Yes! I can do this!" Tai assured him.

Tai bolted out the door, eager to catch the bus and get home to tell his mother about his new possible job.

Peter watched him go, then turned to Maggie. "You do realize this kid's going to follow you around like a lost puppy now?"

"Yes, I've no doubt he's going to drive me up the wall, but I'm glad you helped him out, Peter. It was the right thing to do. Underneath that thick layer of annoying arrogance, I think he's a good kid. By the way, can I borrow your laptop so that I can type up my English paper?"

Peter looked at her skeptically.

"What?"

"I…I just think…." He was looking uncomfortable.

"What's the matter, Peter?"

"I don't want you going on Facebook, that's all."

"Why?" But even as she asked she knew the answer. The other teens were slaughtering her. "Oh, I see," she said quietly.

"I'm sorry, honey. I just didn't want to see you hurt."

For a moment Maggie was hit with a feeling of isolation. Since Jessica died, she'd had no girlfriend to confide in. Peter was a tremendous strength to her, but it wasn't the same thing as having someone of the same gender to talk to. Marci was a friend to her, but they were worlds apart in personality.

"Are you okay?" Peter asked, concerned.

"I'm tough, Peter. I can handle this. Life hasn't given me the option of being weak."

He kissed the top of her head, wishing she could learn to let God be strong for her—but some things took time.

For the rest of the afternoon they watched football and ate pretzels with Maggie's dad. From time to time, a commercial popped up concerning the upcoming elections, a reminder that voters should be expecting an intense turnout at the polls.

"What do you think about Pat Jamison?" Maggie's father asked.

"I'm not too sure about that guy, but then I don't generally vote Democrat," Peter said.

"I think Steven Raintree was a strong choice for the Republicans," Mr. Kraus said. "But both of them are going to have to contend with William McFarland."

"I don't know. A third party only serves to draw votes away from the Democrats or Republicans. In this case, I think it will take votes from Raintree. A third party ticket never wins, though."

"Don't be too sure. McFarland has a heavy backing so far," Mr. Kraus replied.

"Well I don't like him," Maggie interjected. She had seen his ads multiple times over the past month, and something in his eyes just made him look untrustworthy. "He gives me the chills."

"Pastor Bradford seems to be supportive of him," Peter commented. "He says he stands for religious freedom and only supports abortion as a last alternative when a mother's life is at stake. I'm not sure what to think of him yet."

The game came back on, and the men tuned back to the TV, but Maggie was left with an unsettling in her spirit. She had always hated politics and avoided the subject in general. But for some reason, she had the feeling that this election was going to be a critical turning point for America.

CHAPTER
seven

Peter and his aunt, Genevieve, met Maggie and her father in church the next morning. They were in for a shock when a stranger stepped out onto the platform to preach.

"What happened to Pastor Bradford?" Peter whispered fiercely to Genevieve. She shrugged, as nonplussed as he was.

A woman leaned forward from the pew behind them. "The board fired him on Thursday!" Her voice had dropped conspiratorially.

The new preacher rested his hands on either side of the podium and introduced himself with a smooth elegance as Pastor Ryan Walcott. The church members, apprehensive at first, were, nevertheless, quickly won over by his suave demeanor and quick wit. Indeed, he was a tall and impressive man, somewhere in his late thirties with wavy black hair and dark arched brows. It had only taken time enough for him to speak his first few words for people to note his impressive eloquence of speech. He was obviously as sophisticated as he was educated.

Peter wasn't so taken in. His eyes narrowed as he carefully absorbed all the details about this new "pastor," and also noted the topic of his message which was reliance on the power every person has within. Though it was implied that that power came from God dwelling inside of a person, Peter was aware that the meaning could too easily be misconstrued to mean reliance on a god-*like* power that was naturally inborn into every person.

Maggie watched Peter's reactions throughout the message, trying to interpret the meaning behind the pastor's words. She had not been a Christian long enough to understand the significance of what was happening, and this was more than disturbing to her new faith. She glanced over at her father, who was quietly listening, and she knew he wasn't any more certain than she was how about the situation.

When the service was over, the organist began playing "Onward Christian Soldiers," and Pastor Walcott went to the entrance to greet the church members as they left.

Jacob and Kevin came up behind Peter and Maggie as they made their way down the aisle. "What do you think of that?" Jacob asked.

"You *know* what I think, Jacob," Peter answered even as his eyes locked on Walcott, who was standing by the door.

A troubled look crossed Maggie's features. "What does this all mean, Peter?" she asked anxiously.

He looked down at her and leaned close so that he could whisper into her ear. "It means Pastor Bradford was becoming too difficult to control. He was no longer letting The I.S. dictate what he was going to preach."

"And this pastor…?"

"Has been hand-picked by some of the pillars of The Inner Society."

A few people brushed passed them, and one cast Maggie a contemptuous glance. Derik's father and mother completely ignored them as they joined the long line of those waiting to speak to the pastor. This coldness was nothing new. Until recently, Sunrise Baptist was the largest church in Norfolk, but like any other church, its members attended for different reasons, and not all of those reasons involved sharing in the love of Christ.

"Maybe we should exit out the side door," Genevieve said.

"No, I want to get the chance to speak to this man face to face. It's important that we get a correct read on him and not judge him just because we are unhappy about losing Pastor Bradford," Peter said.

"I can't believe he didn't call us," Kevin said from behind them.

"I don't know. I get the feeling that this decision, however long in the brewing, was made suddenly," Peter said.

The new pastor stood tall, his dark eyes sparkling as he conversed with each person on their way out. He obviously had a personality which attracted people, and a talent for making each person believe he was delighted to make their acquaintance. He had already received numerous invitations to dinner, and no doubt many had been inspired by the fact that he was most definitely an eligible bachelor.

Maggie could feel her tension rising as they got closer

and closer to the entrance. She was out of her depth in all this and painfully aware of the fact. She realized she was taking in only shallow breaths when she began to feel lightheaded, and she made a conscious effort to breathe normally.

One more step and she was at the front, the others behind her. Pastor Walcott turned and his eyes fixed on Maggie's face as he took her hand in both of his. His dark gaze was so keen and penetrating that she soon felt that she would be overcome by his presence alone. There was something both frightening and alluring about him, something that went beyond his unmistakably handsome features. She could perceive that he was clearly aware of his good looks and intelligence, and was fully capable of using both as the need arose.

Maggie began to feel uncomfortable as she realized she could not break eye contact with him. He had done nothing inappropriate, but there was something about his manner that seemed too...*familiar*. It was as though he could literally touch a person with spiritual intimacy alone, and the very knowledge of it both repelled and attracted her at the same time.

He offered her a cool smile that lacked the radiance he had bestowed upon the others, his gaze still penetrating through her. "A pleasure to meet you, young lady," he said, his voice smooth and steady, almost calculating. He made her feel like a helpless child sitting in the principal's office. "I'm glad you could come." He released her hand.

Maggie was saved from a reply when Peter came forward and shook his hand.

The pastor's gaze transferred from Maggie to Peter, and he smiled, revealing a straight line of sparkling white teeth. "Glad you could make it. Have a nice week," he said.

The youth group met that night at Jacob's house, and this time Genevieve and Marci's mother were in attendance, as was Eric. Even Maggie's father was there. They all sat around the coffee table, settled into the plush sofa, loveseat, and armchairs. A fire burned brightly in the marble fireplace. Jacob's dad sat by the hearth, and Marci helped Mrs. Townsend bring in mugs of hot cocoa for everyone. Kristy sat beside Kevin, who was quietly strumming his guitar as the others spoke.

"Well, I guess we knew this was going to happen eventually," Dr. Townsend broke the silence.

"Did anyone have any indication that Pastor Bradford had been replaced?" Eric asked.

Everyone looked at each other, shaking their heads.

"What are we going to do?" Genevieve asked the crucial question.

"I don't think we should do anything yet," Dr. Townsend answered. "I'd like to get the chance to get hold of Pastor Bradford and hear his side of things first. There could be a lot we don't know. I would also like to get some insight into what kind of impact this could have on the power The Inner Society wields over this city. Leaving one of The Inner Society's churches isn't something its members generally do. They might miss attending, but they don't leave the church. That would certainly have repercussions."

"Like what?" Maggie asked with immediate trepidation.

Peter looked over at her, his expression softening as he realized how frightening all this must seem to her. Church was supposed to be a safe place, but a church where man was in control instead of God could be just the opposite.

"Nothing violent, Maggie. It just means that we could be excluded from meetings and barred from knowledge of their future plans. Then the rest of us won't know what's going on, and we'll lose any power to participate in decision making."

"I wouldn't doubt that is already happening to some degree, since all of this mess with the next trial coming up at the end of the month," Mrs. Townsend said, and the others nodded in agreement. "For the first time, The Inner Society has split camps."

"And the timing couldn't be worse, considering this is an election year," Peter said. "Our people will certainly be strategizing to manipulate the polls in their favor, and we definitely don't want to get blindsided by their political maneuvers. The fact that we have a third party candidate only serves to complicate matters."

"I don't understand," Mr. Kraus said. "Aren't churches supposed to be loving and supportive? And if they're not, why attend?"

The others exchanged glances once more, and then looked at him with knowing smiles.

"That is the ideal, isn't it?" Genevieve said softly. "The whole premise of Christianity is love and acceptance, right? But a church is made up of people, and hypocrites attend church right alongside the righteous. That's why God has to be in your heart, so that you can bring him with you."

"People don't even know they don't have God in their lives until they see his love through someone else,"

Jacob added. "Many of these people are just lost, Mr. Kraus. They have been sucked in by wealth and greed and power, and they have forgotten their purpose in life. Even after the deaths of their children, they still have not found meaning in all of this. If everyone who truly loves God leaves the church, it will leave the others without hope."

"We don't want to abandon them, but we also don't want to *underestimate* them," Dr. Townsend inserted. "They are dangerous, and we will have to protect ourselves."

"I think we should also be careful about judging Walcott too soon," Eric inserted. "It's not Walcott's fault that Bradford was dismissed, and it would be very easy to be biased against him for this."

"I'm sure that's true," Peter said, "but I am uncomfortable with his manner toward Maggie and me this morning. It was as though he had personal knowledge of who we were, and I've never even seen this guy before."

"I caught that," Genevieve said, "especially when he looked at Maggie. It gave me chills. I couldn't help but wonder if the church board has told him something."

"Which would mean that they have taken him into their confidence," Mrs. Townsend surmised.

"He probably *does* have some background knowledge of at least some of the teens in the church," Marci pointed out. "Quite a few of us have been all over the news, you know. No doubt he is terrified of the notorious church members he's just inherited! He probably thinks the teenagers are a bunch of murderous renegades."

Kevin, still quietly strumming the guitar strings, hit a sour note, drawing the attention of the others. "He wouldn't be far from wrong," he retorted with a gleam of humor sparkling in his dark eyes.

It wasn't funny, but the others still laughed, unable to deny that could explain a lot of things.

"I was just thinking...this could be a problem for Tai," Peter pointed out. "I'm not so sure this pastor will be willing to hire a delinquent kid to work for the church, and Tai was counting on the money." He sighed. "I was really hoping that Pastor Bradford could make a change in this church."

"But the board is looking at the numbers," Dr. Townsend said. "There has been a serious decline in attendance and tithing ever since he took the chance and started preaching from his heart. It's all about power with Norfolk, and money is power. You know that. I had hoped that the recent tragic events would bring people around, and I think it has for some, however late. But there are others who only became more embittered as a result. As Jacob pointed out—they haven't learned anything from this."

Maggie listened in silence as the others talked. She was troubled by all this, and since Christianity was fairly new to her, she was ignorant on church politics. These issues were both frightening and tiring, and somehow she knew they went a lot deeper than the surface. She sensed the others had already come to that conclusion way ahead of her. It just seemed like life never slowed down long enough for her to catch up with it. She was exhausted and desperate for a reprieve from all the drama. She needed time to find some peace and rest, but she also knew it wasn't going to come any time soon.

On the way home, Maggie and her father stopped at the gas station. Maggie was still feeling a little off when she went inside to pay the attendant. When she came out, she was taken aback; their truck was no longer parked by the gas pump.

She stopped, peering around the small, dark parking area to see if her dad had moved for some reason. There were no other cars aside from a black Beamer with tinted windows.

Fear crept into her spirit, saturating her with its thick darkness. Something was seriously wrong, but without any knowledge as to what it was, she couldn't possibly know how to fight it. She glanced around anxiously, fighting mental images of all the horrible possibilities that could explain the missing truck. *Oh, God, not my dad. Please—not him!*

Desolation closed in on her like a thick bank of fog. Looking up at the evening sky, she beheld the ominous clouds overhead. Moving rapidly across the pale moon, they soon blocked what little light was to be had, shrouding the city in darkness.

The sound of footsteps came from behind her, startling her, and she quickly turned to see the new pastor approaching her.

"Maggie, right?" he asked, his eyes smiling warmly. "Is everything okay? You look a little…confused." He sounded sincere enough, and somehow Maggie didn't feel he was so threatening when they were standing in a parking lot at a gas station. Maybe it was just that she was desperate to see any familiar face at that moment.

Maggie took in a shaky breath and tried to swallow her hysteria. "Well," she hesitated, not quite knowing what she was going to say. "Our truck was parked by this gas pump five minutes ago. My dad got out to pump the gas, and I went in to pay the attendant. Now my dad and the truck are both gone." As she heard the words leave her lips, the terror of what they might mean sunk into her spirit, and she experienced a sensation of vertigo.

Walcott took her by the arm to steady her. "Hey, hey. Hold on. Let's not get too upset until we have a chance to figure this out." She knew then that he had immediately tuned in to her fear. "Do you have a cell phone on you? Maybe you can try calling your father?"

No sooner had the suggestion gained merit than her heart sank. "No. He never keeps his phone charged. He's still living in the ages before technology."

He smiled gently. "Okay, young lady. How about calling the house phone?" He passed her his cell.

For a moment she stared at it without seeing it, her mind consumed by the knowledge that this was not going to be explained by any small misunderstanding. She felt her body go numb as an icy chill swept over her. Perhaps shock was settling in.

Regaining her attention, Walcott pressed the phone into her shaking hands, and her eyes slowly focused upon it. She dialed her house with stiff fingers. It rang and rang, but there was no answer.

The pastor looked down at her, concerned. A slight frown crossed his features, and his obsidian eyes took on a speculative gleam. "I'm going to take you home to see if he's returned there for some reason. If he's not there, we'll call the police. Okay?"

Maggie looked up into his dark eyes, feeling somehow distant and detached from everything. This couldn't be happening. Her father would never have driven off without her like that—especially when he was afraid of leaving her alone.

Maggie was barely even aware that Walcott was leading her to his car until she was inside and the door was shut.

The sound of that door closing suddenly transported her back to that night when she'd heard the trunk snap shut on her, and a shockwave of panic ripped through her chest. She quickly grabbed for the door handle as the pastor got into the driver's seat, but he caught her arm.

"Hey, take it easy. I'll take you home, and you'll see that all of this is probably some kind of crazy misunderstanding."

She gave a fresh start when the engine started and the door locks snapped into place. She looked up at the pastor in undisguised alarm.

He laughed in soft sympathy. "Calm down, kid. It's a new car; the doors lock automatically."

She looked away, embarrassed by her own instability in that moment. She told him her address and he headed toward her house, the atmosphere in the car both silent and heavy as Maggie struggled frantically to make sense out of everything.

But as they proceeded, Maggie was struck once more

with a sense of ominous foreboding as they drove past her street.

"You missed the turn," she said with barely suppressed apprehension.

He wordlessly looked over at her with those black eyes of his, cool and dispassionate. A cool smile curved his lips, and his gaze cut right into the depths of her spirit. It paralyzed her. He continued driving, his hand steady on the wheel, and Maggie was acutely conscious of every block that took her further and further away from her home, her dread rising into her throat and strangling her.

She suddenly jumped into action, making a desperate grab for the lock on the door, but his hand snaked out, taking her wrist captive in an iron-like grip and holding her in place.

The horror of her situation penetrated her nerve endings like fire as she mentally strove for an escape from her dangerous predicament. They passed two intersections before she saw the lights of an ambulance up ahead.

She was not even aware that she gasped as she snapped to attention, leaning forward to peer out the windshield into the dark night. The flashing red and white lights became brighter as they drew closer—and suddenly Maggie saw her father's truck, a mangled mess of metal.

In sickening horror, she took in the body lying across the hood, and recognized her father.

A scream was torn from her lips as her eyes flew to the pastor's face, and she realized he was watching her reaction quite closely, his lips still curved in dark amusement.

"Stop the car!" she screamed in mindless terror as she made another frantic attempt to unlock her door.

"You're not going anywhere, little girl," he said with dead calm and pushed her back against her seat, keeping a firm grip on her arm so she couldn't jump out of the car.

"Dad!" she screamed, struggling to get free. His grip tightened, and the deep timber of his cruel laughter seeped into her consciousness, absorbing into her system like poison. "Where are you taking me?" she cried.

"To hell, sweetheart!"

Maggie gave a violent start, waking herself with the scream that ripped out of her chest. She immediately began to fight the hands that were restraining her, but soon she found herself caught up in arms of steel, and she was unable to free herself.

"Maggie!"

She belatedly realized the voice was Peter's, and she became still, her mind reeling in its attempt to figure out where she was and what was happening.

"Hey, sweetheart! It's okay." Peter was trying to soothe her, but it was apparent that her violent nightmare had scared him as well. "You dozed off. It was just a dream. Understand?"

She finally looked up at him through tears, and then relaxed slightly in his arms, but he could feel her trembling.

"What the heck was that about?" Kevin asked in alarm, setting his guitar aside.

"She does this," Peter explained. "She's been having some horrific nightmares, and they seem to be getting worse."

"Maybe we shouldn't be talking about this stuff in front of her," Jacob suggested.

Maggie looked around and was nearly sick with relief when she saw her father sitting beside her, looking at her with unmistakable concern. She took his hand for a moment and held onto it as if she would never let him go, but no sooner had she done so than she began noting the attention she'd drawn from the others. Her cheeks burned in hot embarrassment. She dropped her father's hand and pulled herself out of Peter's arms so that she could sit up straight.

"I'm so sorry," she said, her gaze dropping in mortification. "I'm fine...really." She was amazed at how calm and rational she had managed to make her voice sound when she was feeling anything but that. "New Hope said I had a way of bringing a meeting to a screeching halt." She offered them a precocious smile, and everyone relaxed. The others were amazed by her quick turnabout, but there were several chuckles since many were privy to this inside joke.

Peter smiled tolerantly, but as the others began to get ready to leave, he pulled her back against him and whispered in her ear. "Smooth recovery. We can't let anyone think that we have any secret weaknesses can we?"

She flushed and gave him a slight glare, knowing he was chastising her for the charade.

"You're not fooling me, though, Maggie. You need to get some help."

CHAPTER
eight

The next week passed without incident, and Saturday had come around again. Maggie made her usual visit to see Mr. Waters. Tennyson followed her this time.

As they drove down the streets, Maggie noted the signs on the lawns: *Vote for Raintree. Vote for Jamison. Vote for McFarland.* It seemed that Jamison had the majority of support, in Norfolk anyway. She shuddered again at the sense of foreboding that accosted her. She didn't need to be knowledgeable about politics to sense something dark was soon to transpire.

Maggie arrived at Waters's house, and Tennyson parked in front when she went in. She was surprised to find Mr. Waters with his leg in a cast. He was sitting in a wheelchair and looking as hostile as ever.

"My gosh! What happened to you?" Maggie exclaimed.

"The stairs didn't seem to be in the same place I left them last!" he grouched.

"You fell down the stairs?" she asked incredulously. She had her answer when she saw the look of humiliation that briefly flickered across his features before he looked away and mumbled some incoherent reply. "You know, for someone who doesn't want to need anybody, you sure have a knack for putting yourself in a position where you have to be helped."

"I don't need any help!" he rasped. "I made it through Desert Storm and the war in Iraq. I suppose I can make it through my own house!"

"Did you ever suffer a serious injury overseas?" she asked.

"No, not a 'serious injury'."

"Well then, it would appear your house is much more dangerous. You're obviously seriously injured now."

"You little twit. I've shot people for less offense than you're giving me!"

Maggie smiled. He smiled, too. Then they both laughed.

"Would you like me to fix you anything?" she asked. "Is there any food in the fridge?"

"I haven't been able to go shopping, but I think there's some sandwich meat and some bread."

As she headed into the kitchen, she noticed a picture on the kitchen table that she was pretty sure hadn't been there before. It was of a small blond boy on a bicycle with training wheels. A younger Mr. Waters was helping him steady his bike, and the boy's face was beaming.

When she returned with a large sandwich and a glass of milk, she asked, "Is that your son in the picture?"

"You're being nosey again," he complained.

"You're dodging my questions again."

"Yeah," he relented at last. "That was my son on his birthday. It was the last birthday I spent with him." His voice cracked and he cleared his throat.

"And today is his birthday, isn't it?" she asked gently.

He didn't answer. He didn't need to.

"You know, I found it hard to learn to love people again after my mother died, and I...I was jerked around by others. I became angry and withdrawn, too, but someone told me once that depending upon others isn't a weakness; it's a strength. Two people are stronger than one."

He looked at her thoughtfully for a moment. "For an annoying brat, you're all right, kid."

Maggie took out his dish when he was done, and then cleaned the kitchen for him. They sat together watching Jeopardy for the next hour or so in companionable silence.

Maggie was deep in thought as she headed home, Tennyson trailing a block behind her. Perhaps for that reason, she didn't notice right away when the Mercedes pulled to the side of the road.

Her phone rang and she answered.

"Did you not see me pull over, Maggie?" Tennyson

growled.

She looked into her rearview mirror and saw his Mercedes some distance behind her. "I guess I didn't."

"Turn around and come back. I just blew out my tire."

"Do you have a spare?"

"Yes. That's not the point."

Maggie turned around and went back. Parking, she got out of the car. She was surprised to see a board with several nails sticking out of it embedded in Tennyson's front tire. A piece of a paper bag was caught between the tire and the board. "Wow. How did I miss that?" she wondered out loud.

"You didn't see a paper bag in the road? This was inside it."

"No. I was kind of lost in my thoughts."

He went to his trunk and popped it open, fetching a car jack and tire iron.

"Would you mind if I went home?" Maggie said. "It's not far and I have a huge load of math to finish by Monday."

He looked at her skeptically. "I don't think it would hurt you to wait a few minutes."

"You know this will take more than a few minutes," she said with as little irritation as she could muster.

"You know what, little girl, you just go ahead. I can't physically force you to do anything."

"Don't be mad. It's not like I'm late to go partying with my friends. I just need to get my homework done."

He treated her with a look that spoke volumes, but she chose to ignore it as she returned to her car.

Maggie was feeling frustrated as she got into the driver's seat and took off. It had been so long since she'd led a "normal life" that she barely remembered what it felt like. Most teens got frustrated when their parents went into their rooms, and their greatest worry was what they were going to buy at the mall on Saturday. She never had *any* privacy. She had an unfriendly adult following her everywhere she went, and she never had time to think about shopping when she spent most of her time worrying about being followed.

It was thus ironic that, while she was still thinking those thoughts, Maggie glanced into her rearview mirror and saw the Lexus right on her bumper.

"Lord, have mercy!" she breathed. She realized the nails in the board could have been placed in the road intentionally to get Tennyson out of the way. She was once again without protection *and* being followed. This time it was her fault. She should have stayed with Tennyson.

The driver flashed his lights at her—an obvious indication that he wanted her to pull over. *Like that was going to happen!* Maggie upshifted and put pressure on the pedal. The Audi zipped forward and so did the Lexus. It was unlikely she would outrun him, and she knew she couldn't go home. Her dad had been planning on going shopping, and she couldn't chance being caught there alone, not when Courage was in the backyard. If he'd been in the house, she might have chanced making it to the door.

Maggie made a sudden turn down one street and then

another, but the driver kept pace with her. He obviously had no intention of letting her get away. She pulled onto a narrow road that ran parallel to the train track on her left. On her right there was a grove of densely populated trees.

The Lexus was still on her tail. The driver tried to pass her, but she maneuvered the Audi into the center of the road, effectively blocking him. He flashed his lights at her again. She managed to block him once more as he tried to pass, but an oncoming car forced her back into her lane, and, the second the other car passed, the Lexus shot around her before she could straddle the lanes again.

After coming up on her left, the driver swerved his car toward her, and she was forced to swerve in order to keep from being hit. The Audi went off the road, into a secluded area of trees, and the Lexus skidded to a halt in front of her car, blocking her.

Maggie jerked her car into reverse, but not soon enough. The driver was already out and running toward her. She frantically tried to hit the lock button, but he reached her door first, jerking it open before she had the chance. Her heart pounding against her ribcage, she tried to evade him without success as he grabbed her by the arms, hauling her out of the car and slamming her up against it. She gasped as pain exploded into her back.

"Not so tough now, are you, you little harlot!"

Maggie desperately looked around for help, but they were completely alone.

"That's right. You're on your own now. No dog, no boyfriend, and no bodyguard," her uncle rasped. "How dare you pull that crap with me after all I've done for you!"

"After all you've done for me?" she choked. "Are you joking?"

He smacked her so hard she saw stars. Her ears were still ringing from the impact when he started to yell at her again.

"I have provided a home for you and seen to it that you have a good education, and this is how you repay me? By taking off with some inexperienced punk and copping this attitude? You have no business being with that guy, Maggie, and if you don't get rid of him, I'm going to make life a living hell for you!"

"Haven't you already done that?" she cried. "You crushed me when my heart was already devastated by my mother's death. You made me wish *I* was the one who died." She swallowed the lump that had formed in her throat and blinked back the hot tears. Then her rage suddenly took hold. "Now let me go, you monster!"

"You've got quite an attitude. You ought to be grateful you're not in a jail cell right now. I can only imagine how you managed to evade charges and actually befriend the man you hit with your car."

In that instant Maggie knew two things: He had been the person who had followed her the night she had headed home alone and hit Mr. Waters—and he was the one who had turned her in to The Inner Society. Daniel Kraus's wealth was a front; he couldn't have come up with the money on his own to bribe Waters to file charges against her. She also knew he deeply coveted acceptance by the elite members of the city. It was the very reason he had forced her to attend Norfolk High in the first place, even though that had backfired drastically.

"It was you! You told them I hit the old man!" she

choked, unable to believe he'd done it, even though she knew it was true.

"You needed to be taught a lesson," he replied coldly.

Maggie choked on a response, unable to voice the words that were crashing through her mind.

"You needed to be sorry for your disrespect."

Regaining her senses, Maggie's eyes narrowed in anger. "I'm only sorry I didn't let my dog eat you while I had the chance!"

"Enough of this crap!" he barked. "You're coming with me, you little witch!"

Her eyes were still brimming with tears as she cast him a murderous look, her eyes glancing in disdain at the brutal grip he had on her left arm.

But this wasn't over. He suddenly became aware that she had her cell phone in her right hand, and as she held it up in his face, he could see who she'd managed to call the moment before he ran her off the road.

Peter.

Her uncle's eyes narrowed upon her.

"I'll be dead before I ever go with you anywhere, you animal!" she rasped.

"That can be arranged," he said darkly.

At that second, both heard the screech of tires and turned in time to see a blue Camaro skid onto the street some two blocks away.

"You better leave while you can," she solemnly advised. He gave her a terrifying look that promised retribution. She tensed for another blow as he took hold of her and slammed her against the car. But as the Camaro approached, he quickly released her and retreated to his vehicle, unwilling to brook another fateful confrontation with her boyfriend. He stomped on the accelerator, jerking the Lexus back onto the road, and made a hasty retreat before the Camaro reached them.

Emotionally depleted, Maggie slid to the ground, bringing her knees up to her chest and burying her face in her hands. Now that he was gone, she was fighting the tears she didn't want Peter to see.

The Camaro skidded to a halt, a cloud of dust billowing in its wake. She could hear Peter slam it into park and throw the door open, then run to her side.

"Maggie?" he choked. "Are you all right?"

She looked up just long enough to see his incensed gaze follow the rapidly retreating Lexus, and she knew he was aching to chase it down. He dropped to her side and reached for her, but she put up a hand to hold him back.

"Please give me a minute, Peter," she whispered as she desperately tried to collect her churning emotions. She knew what the consequences would be if she completely broke down in front of him. He was just looking for the opportunity to cut off her freedom which he was convinced was putting her in danger.

Peter hesitated but couldn't wait for long. He pulled her into his arms, and she couldn't help sobbing despite all her efforts to do otherwise.

"Are you okay, sweetheart?" he asked again, trying to mask the protective rage that was coursing through him. This was his fault. He shouldn't have allowed her to stop him from pressing charges against Daniel Kraus in the first place.

When she didn't answer, he pulled back, cupping her cheeks and pulling her head up so he could see her face. He brushed her hair away from her face. Then he spotted the redness and slight swelling on the side of her face.

"He hit you! I'll kill him!"

Maggie clung to his jacket. "No, Peter! You can't do anything to him. My dad will find out. It will break his heart. He hasn't been sober long enough to handle something like this. He's barely hanging on as it is. I swear this will send him over the edge!"

He caught her hands and gave her a hard, piercing look. "It ends here, Maggie! I should have taken care of this situation a long time ago."

"But my dad—"

"Your dad is going to be told, and he will just have to deal with it."

"No, Peter! He's not strong enough to handle this yet," she pleaded in desperation.

"Stop it, Maggie. Stop begging me to keep this horrible secret. This has gone far enough." There was a cold finality in his tone that terrified her. "And where the heck was Tennyson during all this?" he raged.

"He blew out a tire, and I went on ahead."

"Against his advice, right?"

She didn't answer. "You can't go to the police with this, Peter. It will end up all over the headlines! Everybody will know what he did to me!" she cried.

"Better that than you making headlines when he ends up putting you in the hospital. I let my love for you break down my reserves before when it should have given me the strength to do the right thing. That won't happen again. I'm going to put that animal away!"

"I won't press charges."

"You're still a minor. I can press charges without your help."

"I'll deny it!" she choked.

"No, you freaking won't!" he said, enunciating each word in wrath. Peter took a hold of her and dragged her to his car, driving her to the police station.

He followed through with his threat, and Maggie was unable to deny the truth since her face still bore evidence of her uncle's latest abuse. When they left the police station, Maggie was devastated and refused to talk to Peter at all. He called to arrange for someone to pick up her Audi after driving back to it and leaving his spare key under the seat.

"I don't want you driving right now," he explained.

"He's going to kill me!" she choked on a sob. "You don't understand."

"He's going to be sitting in a jail cell within the hour," Peter countered.

"But my dad…."

"Maggie, it is a father's duty to protect his child. Do you not get that? You were trying to protect your dad from suffering more grief, and yet you were the one who was being hurt the whole time! Don't you see how warped that is? I'm sorry if he collapses, and if other people find out about what's been going on. I realize you're probably going to blame me—but it's your dad's fault that he let himself sink into alcoholism and neglect you. I'm never going to risk you getting hurt by your uncle, or any man, again. I had a choice: to protect your dad or to protect you. I'm sorry if you can't understand it, but I'm going to choose you every time."

"I'll never forgive you for this." She whispered it brokenly, but with such a conviction that it gripped him with fear.

He swallowed but didn't lose his resolve. "I hope you will."

They pulled into her driveway, and Peter got out.

"Are you coming or not?"

She buried her head in her hands, all the fight gone out of her. "Please don't tell him, Peter. I *beg* you!"

"You know it's too late for this discussion, honey. The report's been made. They're going to investigate. That means they will eventually question your dad. He has to know before it comes down to that."

She shook her head in frustration, refusing to look at him, and he went into the house without her.

Half an hour later, he returned and opened the car door. "You're going to have to talk to him now, Maggie. I'm sorry, but you can't hide from this."

She raised her tear-streaked face up to look at him, and her anguished expression over his betrayal tore at his heart. "How could you do this to me?" she cried. "How could you?"

"You know I didn't have a choice, baby." His own voice was hoarse with emotion as her pain became his. He could hardly bear to see her cry, especially now, knowing he was part of that pain.

Maggie finally headed toward the house, every step bringing her closer to the confrontation she had dreaded for years.

Her father was sitting on the sofa with his head in his hands, much the same as she did when she was trying to cope with something monumental. She knew it took everything within him to find the strength to meet his daughter's eyes, and when he did, she could see that his were red and swollen, a sharp contrast against the pale gray color of his skin.

She was gripped with alarm. She hadn't seen him look this bad since the day....

He staggered to his feet, even though he had not had a drop of alcohol. He stood for a moment, unconsciously wringing his hands together in his consternation. It was clear that he was utterly devastated and didn't have the slightest clue of what he should do or say.

Maggie's eyes clouded with tears of unspeakable shame then. What did her father see now when he looked at her?

But he suddenly came forward, clinging to her and swaying with her in mutual heartbreak.

"How could I have let this happen?" he cried in despair. "How could I not have *known*?"

Unable to speak, Maggie buried her face against his chest.

Peter had remained sitting in his Camaro, praying about what he should do next. His cell phone rang.

It was Jacob. "So what did you decide to do about this guy?"

"I made her report him." Peter's voice was low and full of exhaustion.

"You finally made the decision?"

"I had to."

Jacob was silent for a moment. "You do realize that, without a rape kit, it's going to be his word against hers."

"I know that. But I can testify to the fact that I witnessed him hurting her, and there was evidence of abuse on her face. I didn't see him hit her, but I saw him slam her against the car before he took off. He'll have a record for assault. If nothing else, we'll at least have a report on file against him now. She also has a restraining order. Her father knows now and he owns the house, so that slime has nothing left to blackmail her with. He'll be afraid to go near her from now on."

"How's she taking it?"

"Not well." Peter slid his hand down his face as if he could swipe away all the tension and dread. "She's pretty screwed up over this, Jacob.... I think she's about to break up with me."

"You didn't have a choice, Peter."   "I know."

CHAPTER
nine

Maggie tossed and turned that night, unable to sleep. Peter had texted her several times, but she had not responded, and eventually turned off her phone. She was dreading what people would say about her at school, imagining the barrage of questions she would certainly be subjected to by the media. Reporters were calling all the time as it was. She could only imagine how horrible it was going to be when everyone knew about this tragic, private part of her life.

But most of all, she was terrified that her father would deteriorate back into a life of inebriation, leaving her alone in the world once more.

The worst part of it was that Peter had forced this upon her.

She listened as she lay in the darkness and heard her father's footsteps pacing the floor until the early hours of the morning. She knew he was wrestling against his desire to drink himself to oblivion. She could only imagine the utter shock and devastation he must be experiencing over his own brother's unimaginable betrayal. He had always been so proud of his little brother. There was no doubt in Maggie's mind that it had never occurred to her father what depravity his brother was capable of.

At some point she heard him crying. The sound pierced through her very soul. It was almost more than she could bear—just as the burning conviction that his pain was *her fault*. It wasn't logical, she knew, but it was something she couldn't shake. She was at the center of all this pain. She was always at the center of others' pain.

But just as the thought set in, so did the anger, this time against Peter. He had forced her to reveal her ugly secret. He had refused to listen to her no matter how much she pleaded with him. He had taken the choice away from her.

"Dear God, where are you? Will you allow us to fall apart now, after everything we've been through?" she cried in anguish. "Was all this for nothing? Why can't I feel your presence?"

Courage jumped up on her bed, resting his head against her shoulder. She petted him, and his warmth and loyalty comforted her, refusing to leave her.

The dawn finally came after the long, tortuous hours of the night, and with it came more uncertainty. What was she going to do now? Should she skip church? The minute she walked in, people would know there was something wrong between her and Peter. She really didn't need any more attention right now, but she also knew Peter had been her strength all along and, she had to learn to stand on her own. She needed to find the courage to face the situation.

Courage went into the kitchen and snagged his leash off the hook, carrying it back to her.

"No walks today, baby," Maggie told him. He dropped the leash and lay down in clear disappointment. His whine was almost childlike. She smiled at him in sympathy.

Tai could tell something wasn't right as soon as he walked into Sunrise Baptist that morning. Peter was on one side of the church with his aunt and Jacob, and Maggie was on the other with her father and Marci's family. He made his way over to the girls.

Maggie was surprised when he joined them. "What are you doing here?" she asked.

He studied her face and noted the shadows beneath her eyes. "Things not goin' so good, huh?" he asked. Marci gave him a look that spoke volumes. He held up his hands in a surrendering gesture, and plopped down beside Maggie without another word.

The choir director asked the congregation to stand then, and the choir led the church in the singing of "Blessed Assurance, Jesus is Mine." Unfortunately, Tai couldn't carry a tune in a bucket, and he didn't know a word of the lyrics; so, he just bellowed along with everyone else as best he could. It wasn't far into the song that Maggie and Marci began to pick up on what he was singing. It was something more like, "Blessed insurance, Jesus has wine!" It was all the more hilarious due to the fact that he obviously had no clue he was saying anything off.

Marci surreptitiously leaned forward so that she could see if Maggie had noticed. Maggie met her gaze, and they both tried to keep serious expressions on their faces as they peered around to see if Tai had drawn any attention.

Apparently he had. There were a couple of elderly ladies behind them who were looking utterly scandalized, which was more than either of the girls could stand, and they began to choke on their suppressed laughter, their eyes welling with tears from the effort.

Things only got worse as the song went on. The choir sang, "Oh what a foretaste of glory divine!" in perfect unison, and Tai caterwauled something to the effect of, "Oh what a poor taste in pouring out time!"

By that point, Maggie's stomach was starting to hurt from trying to control her laughter, and she had to sing twice as loud to drown out Tai's voice before she lost it altogether.

The torturous song finally came to an end. Walcott came to the pulpit and told the congregation to be seated. The girls sat down, nearly sick with relief that their ordeal was finally over. Tai looked from one girl to the other with wide-eyed ignorance and solemnly whispered, "I don't get the songs you guys sing. They make you feel closer to God?"

Marci erupted in spontaneous laughter, and she clapped a hand over her mouth in horror as several people indignantly hushed her. Maggie couldn't help but grin.

Walcott went on to preach on the power of positive thinking. It was a well-rehearsed message that was smoothly presented. As he spoke, his eyes roamed the audience, resting briefly upon Peter, and then upon Maggie where she sat some distance away. Maggie shivered as her nightmare returned to haunt her. She knew she would never be able to look at this pastor again without being reminded of it, and she had to remind herself that it was only a dream. Nevertheless, she found herself avoiding eye contact with the man.

When the service came to a close and everyone lined

up to speak with the pastor on their way out, Maggie told her father she would meet him outside and slipped out the side door before anyone could begin interrogating her.

Jacob watched her leave, and then looked to Peter. His eyes dropped when an unwelcome thought came to his mind, but not before Peter caught his expression.

Peter knew Jacob like he knew himself—well enough to know what he was thinking. "I know you're dying to ask if I'll let her keep the car if we break up. I seriously couldn't care less about the car right now, Jacob."

"So will you?"

"I wouldn't doubt she's going to give it back. They showed up in the truck today," he said dismally.

"I'm sorry, man."

Marci came up behind them, a concerned look in her eyes. "Peter, what's going on with you two? Are you two breaking up?"

"I think it's a strong possibility. She's pretty unstable right now," Peter concluded.

Marci bit her lip, a concerned expression crossing her features. "Then now's the time for her to learn to let Christ be her rock and not you."

Jacob put an arm around her, appreciative of her wisdom. "You're right, of course…but there's more to it than that," he concluded intuitively.

Marci looked from Jacob to Peter in question.

"I'm sure you know she still doesn't fully understand

what she's dealing with. She's in danger, and I can't protect her if she won't let me near her," Peter explained.

"I bet she's at least got some idea by now," Jacob commented ominously. "She was pretty badly shaken the night she ended up in my driveway."

The other two met his eyes, the three wordlessly communicating the gravity of Maggie's situation.

"You'd better catch up with her before she leaves," Marci advised.

Maggie was half way across the parking lot when he called her name. She kept walking, but Peter caught up with her before she was able to climb into the truck, and moved in between her and the vehicle so she couldn't open the door. She stopped but kept her eyes averted.

"Please listen to me, Maggie." Peter's voice was hoarse with emotion. "Just give me five minutes."

"What is there to say, Peter?" she whispered, still not meeting his gaze. There was a very clear note of agony in her voice. "Are you sorry? That wouldn't change anything, would it?"

He paused, gathering his courage to face the crisis before him. "I'm not sorry I turned that animal in, Maggie. I'm only sorry I didn't do it sooner. If you had told someone the first time, it never would have happened again."

"So what he did to me was my fault, right? It's my fault because I didn't stop him?" Her silver eyes were sparking fire, but there was pain in her voice.

"No! I would never say that. You know better than that. He was controlling you with fear, Maggie, and that power had to be broken!"

"Maybe dealing with the abuse was a lesser evil than losing my dad," she choked. "He's destroyed over this, Peter, and I'm about to lose him all over again!"

"When will you learn to let God handle your crisis, Maggie? 'All things work together for good for those who love God.' Haven't you learned that by now? Trust him!"

"Don't...please, Peter. Don't say anything else and don't call me. I need some time. This has been hard enough as it is." She fought back tears and forced herself to keep her voice steady.

They both saw Tai heading toward them then. He had obviously been looking for them. He slowed down as he approached, realizing he was intruding.

"It's okay, Tai," Maggie said, her light tone masking the gravity of the mood. Peter knew that she was going to use Tai as a way out of the conversation.

"Is everything all right with you guys?" Tai asked tentatively.

"There's nothing you need to worry about. What did you want to talk about?" Maggie asked.

He hesitated, as though debating on what he should say. "Um...you did say that the church would hire me, right?" Maggie could hear the uncertainty in his tone.

"There have been some unforeseen problems—" Peter began, but Maggie cut him off.

"But I was going to try to see if Mr. Waters would hire you to help him," she said. "He's had a really bad fall, and he can't get around very well."

Tai hesitated. "He's an Army man, right? Maybe he don't like Hmong people?"

"There's no 'maybe' about it. He doesn't like people in general, so don't take it personally. He hated me when we first met. Of course, that wasn't so surprising under the circumstances. I'm just telling you that, even if I can get him to agree to this, it's going to be murder dealing with him. I've never met anyone so stubborn and difficult."

Genevieve appeared at Tai's side, inviting him to lunch. He eagerly agreed and the small gathering split. Peter looked over his shoulder at Maggie as they left, but she would not meet his gaze.

None of them knew it, but Jason, Derik, and a few of their friends stood by, watching the scene with interest.

Derik released a low whistle. "I don't believe it. Looks like she's leaving him!" he said, looking at his reflection in the window of Jason's black and white Trans Am. He threw his head back to clear his dark locks away from his face and removed his sunglasses from where they hung in his shirt, sliding them on.

"Looks like," Jason agreed, raking a hand through his strawberry-blond hair. He was also admiring his reflection in the window before he glanced over his shoulder at Maggie. "Stupid witch. She'll never have it so good again. It'll make things a lot easier for us, though."

"Wonder if he'll let her keep the car," Conrad cut in, his blue eyes twinkling with clear amusement. He leaned casually against the front of the Trans Am, his arms folded loosely across his broad chest. They looked at each other meaningfully. He had voiced the question that had been on everyone's minds.

"Who's that Asian kid hanging out with her anyway?" one of the girls asked.

"I've seen that twerp around town a couple of times lately," Jason answered.

Jacob just happened to come by at that precise moment, overhearing their conversation. "He's a poor kid who sat on a city bus for over an hour and a half to get to church today."

The boys gave a start and turned to look at him.

"There's something to be said for that when you guys have your own cars and can't make the five minute trip to church half the month." Jacob admonished coolly, and walked off to his own car.

They were all speechless for a moment.

"Is he still seeing Marci?" Jason asked then.

"I saw them together last night at the mall," Derik's girlfriend, Shannon, informed. She tied her platinum blond hair into a ponytail, and then slipped an arm around his waist.

"Saw them together *how*?" Derik prompted.

"They were having lunch together at the Pizza Hut, and they were…sitting *very* close together."

"I think it's about time we take care of that little situation," Derik said coldly as he adjusted the backing on his diamond earring. "I don't think Marci got the point of our last conversation."

"You better be careful," Conrad warned. "You're going to be contending with Jacob *and* Peter if you mess with her."

"Not if she's too scared to tell them anything. That's the thing about Marci—*she* can be controlled."

Maggie drove home with her father in silence, but she knew he was aching to say something to her. They walked into the house, and she could feel his eyes upon her. Unable to bear it any longer, she finally turned to him and said, "What, Dad? I know you're dying to say something."

"I'm just worried about you, sweetheart. I can't even contemplate how hard this must be for you, but you can't blame Peter for this."

She had to swallow her anger and the feeling of helplessness that consumed her. "With all due respect, Dad, you don't understand this."

"Make me understand, honey. This boy loves you more than life, and you're not talking to him because he came to your rescue? You're right, I don't understand this. I just understand that he's good for you, and you're about to make the worst decision of your life."

"I can't make you understand this, and I can't talk about it," she said, and left to go to her room.

Maggie listened to her father pace the floor again that night. It became quiet for a short time, and she knew he had finally retreated to the armchair where he would sit by the hour agonizing over everything that had happened. It deeply disturbed her, and she was just waiting to hear him go for the keys so that he could head to a bar. Of course, that wasn't going to happen since she had taken the keys and put them in her dresser drawer. He could decide to walk, though. It didn't help that Maggie was so used to being the only thing that stood between her father and a bar, it never even occurred to her to pray for God's help.

About two o'clock in the morning, Maggie woke from a light sleep and thought she heard her father talking to himself. It terrified her.

What she didn't know was that Peter had driven by. The curtains had been open and he had seen her father pacing the floor. When he quietly knocked on the door, Mr. Kraus had let him in.

"She won't explain this to me," Mr. Kraus whispered, "and I can't see why she's so upset with you. This was my brother's fault, not yours."

"She's mad at me because she thinks I forced her into a decision that will put you at risk," Peter said, his voice heavy.

"She's afraid for me?"

"Of course she is!" Peter was struggling to keep his frustration with Mr. Kraus in check. "She's afraid you're going to turn back to the bottle to escape the horror of what happened. She's been trying to protect you from this all along."

Mr. Kraus's eyes opened wider in understanding and then closed tight as he raked a hand nervously through his dark, gray peppered hair. "I guess I'm the one at fault," he said miserably. "I'm pretty transparent, I guess, and she's right: I have been struggling against the urge to drink. I can hardly stand to live with what my brother did to my little girl, and I can't get those images out of my head. It *haunts* me."

"If you go off the deep end, she'll never forgive me. Do you understand that?" Peter asked pointedly.

He nodded. "I realize that now. But, despite everything, I haven't touched a drop, Peter, I haven't. Doesn't that mean anything?"

"It means you're a lot stronger than you used to be," Peter agreed. "Holding firm when you're feeling your weakest and things are this hard is actually the best sign of strength."

"How long have you known about this?" Mr. Kraus asked at last.

Peter looked at him cautiously, unsure of whether he should answer.

"Please tell me," Mr. Kraus whispered hoarsely.

"For quite a while," Peter admitted at length.

"She confided in you, but she wouldn't confide in me," he rasped mostly to himself.

"She didn't confide in me." Peter countered. "I was the last person she would have told at that time. I just figured it out. I'm not going to tell you anything more than that. It will only hurt you, and it won't fix anything.

"What's done is done, Mr. Kraus," Peter's voice softened as he looked down at the broken father before him.

"We can't change the past, and we can't undo our mistakes. But we can choose to move forward in a better direction. 'In our weakness, he is strong.' I've found that I don't have to be strong when God is my rock. I know everything is in his hands, and he can deal with the things I can't. I just have to remind myself of this every now and then."

Mr. Kraus just nodded, but he was obviously listening intently.

"It comes down to this: you can't get back the years you lived without your wife, and Maggie can't get back her childhood; so you will either decide to live for what you have left, or you will lose the rest of your life over what you've already lost."

Peter finally left, and Mr. Kraus turned out the hall light and went to his room.

He didn't know that Maggie had been lying in her bed listening to the indistinct sound of his voice. Her door had been closed, and so she hadn't recognized the fact that there had been two voices. As far as she knew, her father had been talking to himself. He had done that before…the week when her mother died. It terrified her—and she feared she had lost him forever.

And it was all Peter's fault.

Maggie pulled into the school parking lot and parked next to Peter's Camaro. She grabbed her purse and books and got out of the Audi, locking the doors. Peter had been waiting for her, and he immediately approached her, but neither found words to say, and the silence between them was agony.

Peter looked across the parking lot, noting that others were watching, even though they pretended not to be. His gaze returned to her averted face. He could sense by her spirit where this scenario was leading, and he felt his heart clench within him.

Maggie reached into her purse and took something out, which she held out to him. Her fingers were closed, but he already knew what it was.

"What? You can't look me in the eyes?" he chastised, his voice tight with emotion.

She briefly glanced up and then away again, but she didn't answer.

He took hold of her arm. "Maggie, you can't just walk out on me after everything we've been through!"

His use of restraint only served to tip over the emotions that were already boiling within her, and Maggie jerked herself free from him. "You don't know what you've done, Peter. You've put my most private secrets on public display. The others will crucify me over this, not to mention what this will do to my father."

"Please, listen—"

"You listen! My father was the only family I had left, and you destroyed him. He will never get over this. Why did he even bother to go to rehab and clean up his life, if only to sink back into it again to escape this new hell?"

"You're upset right now." Peter tried again. "Just wait until you've had time to deal with this."

"I'm 'upset right now'? You think?! Upset doesn't even touch what I'm feeling right now."

"Don't do this, Maggie. I beg you."

His intensity seemed to reach through her, and she gave a slight shudder, her own heart twisting within her in, both in rage against her inability to stop his decision and anguish in the pain of their splitting apart. But the haunted expression in her father's eyes came unbidden to her then, hardening her resolve.

"I begged you once."

She placed her diamond engagement ring and the keys to the Audi in his hand and walked away. Even as she did so, she was aware that life as she knew it had just ended.

It wasn't the first time. This was just the way her life was.

The minute she headed for the entrance of the school, Maggie felt the knowing stares and cruel smiles of the others. It was clear that they *knew*. She was sure of it. They not only knew about her breakup with Peter, but also about her uncle. If there were any doubts in her mind, they were dispelled by the brutal comments the other teens made about her as she walked by. How could they be that cruel? Had they no human decency at all, no ability to empathize with how tragic her situation was?

"Apparently she's made her rounds *all over town*," one girl emphasized just loud enough for her to hear.

"What a slut! Her tastes are obviously not even limited to men outside of her own family."

"How disgusting! It's no wonder Peter finally dumped her! I don't know what someone like him saw in her in the first place."

Under normal circumstances Maggie might have been incensed enough to retaliate, but the pain of this hit went so deeply it paralyzed her. Her life seemed to rush before her eyes in a blinding wave of agony, and every unbearable episode replayed in her tortured mind right up until the point she put the ring in Peter's hand.

God help me! Her world had been turned upside down again, and she was left clinging to the only hope she had: that Jesus still loved her, and there had to be hope for her as long as someone was in her corner. This was more than she had ever had before. Before coming to know the Lord, she had had no one for so long.

It wasn't until the others began dispersing that Maggie realized the bell had rung.

CHAPTER
ten

The next day was a staff development day, so there were no classes. Marci was worried about Maggie, so she called to ask her out to the movies.

"I don't think so, Marci," Maggie declined. "I'm really not up to going out." They were friends, but they had very little in common. Marci was sweet and sometimes a little flighty; Maggie was anything but those things.

"Which is why you should, right? Come on. Jacob is taking off with Peter to do guy stuff, and I'm all alone."

Maggie inwardly groaned. She had really counted on a day of not being around anyone, but Marci had a way of being persuasive, and she wasn't going to take no for an answer.

"Come on, Maggie. You're not going to make me go by myself, are you?"

"Take Kristy."

"Kristy's out with Kevin. You know she's never available."

This went on for a while before Maggie finally caved in. "Oh, all right, Marci," she reluctantly agreed. Going to the movies had to be a lesser evil than continuing this conversation.

"Yay! I'm going to wear jeans, boots, and my purple sweater."

"We're going to *coordinate* our outfits now?"

"Well, of course," Marci said as though she was genuinely shocked that Maggie hadn't taken that for granted.

"You owe me, Marci," Maggie grouched.

"Agreed!"

Marci showed up an hour later in her Jaguar to pick Maggie up. Maggie looked her over, noting she looked radiant, but Maggie knew it wasn't because they were going to the movies; it was because Marci was convinced she was helping her. Marci was like that.

Despite Maggie's protests, Tennyson followed behind them and parked by the front of the building, kicking back to wait for them.

They sat in the dark theatre watching a movie with a tacky love story theme—no doubt one Marci picked out to make Maggie start missing Peter. Maggie never ceased to be amazed by this girl. There was a part of Marci that still loved Peter, and yet she wanted Peter and Maggie to be happy so much that she was willing to try to push them back together herself. Maggie couldn't understand such unselfishness, but she was deeply touched by it.

Maggie continued to suffer through the movie, and she was already counting the minutes until it was over.

Sometime later, someone approached unseen and slid into the seat next to Marci. She gave a violent start when the person on her left side leaned toward her. A low voice whispered, "Get up, Marci. We need to have a little talk."

Marci looked up to see Derik standing with his arms folded. Even in the dark, she could see the expression on his face and knew it boded evil. Her heart sank in immediate trepidation, and she looked sideways at Maggie, who had nodded off from boredom.

Derik took Marci by the wrist and pulled her to her feet, leading her down the row. She pulled back and started to protest.

"Shut up!" Derik hissed. "You don't want to get her involved in this." He nodded toward Maggie, and Marci looked back at her in dread as he dragged her toward the back exit.

Maggie awoke with a violent start from yet another nightmare. She glanced to her left and became alarmed when she suddenly realized Marci was gone. She peered into the darkness and her anxiety level spiked when she saw two forms heading for the exit. Her pulse raced as she made to jump up and go after her, but an arm came across her, keeping her seated. Her head jerked in the direction of the person on the other side of her, and she was shocked to realize Conrad was lounging in the seat next to her. She took in his expensive, dark blue Paige Acadia jeans and the Versace leather sneaker that rested on the seat in front of him. *Arrogant jerk!*

Furious, Maggie tried to throw his arm off and rise, but he caught her around the waist and pushed her back into the seat. He got a firm grip on her arm to keep her there.

"You're not going anywhere," he said calmly.

"You better take your hands off me."

"Sit still and I will."

"Like heck!" She struggled harder to get up, wiggling away and jumping to her feet. She managed to make it to the end of the row and broke into a run as she reached the aisle.

Conrad was hot on her heels. "Come back here!" he nearly shouted. Several people in the audience hushed him.

By then Marci and Derik were gone. Maggie had reached the back exit and hit the door with force, throwing it open. Conrad caught up with her just as she stepped outside. Maggie made a frantic visual sweep of the parking lot and quickly spotted the teenagers who had randomly parked their cars next to Marci's Jag. She headed in their direction, but Conrad grabbed her by the arm, halting her.

As she tried to shake him off, Maggie looked toward the others once more. It was then that she recognized Derik's truck—like she could miss the red, mirror-finished 1949 restored classic that had been blueprinted to produce 500hp—or so Derik told everyone. And there was Marci standing beside it with Derik and Jason on either side of her. Maggie's heart lurched in her chest, and she tried again to run to Marci's aid, but Conrad still had a hold of her arm.

She turned toward him, treating him with a murderous glare. "Let go of me, Conrad, or I swear…!"

He smiled at her tolerantly, his eyes twinkling. Despite the fact that he was over six feet tall, he reminded her of a little boy at Christmas, and she deeply resented the fact that he was quite obviously excited by this.

"What are you going to do, Maggie? Go up to them and demand they release her?" He gave a snort of amusement. "You're outnumbered. The others will never let you get near Marci, and, even if you were able to manage it, all you would do is tick them off and make matters worse for her. Stay out of this. They're not going to hurt her. They're only going to talk to her."

Thirty feet away, Marci stood frozen while Derik berated her. "I guess we weren't too clear on this, Marci. You're not going to be involved with Jacob Townsend anymore. You know better than this. I mean, it would be a shame if something happened to him because of you. Wouldn't it? Do you really want to make trouble for him?"

"No!" she choked.

"Well, it's not coming across that way. Shannon saw you together just recently, and now I'm thinking we need to take some measures to ensure that this...*abomination* stops. Shall we start with you or him?"

Maggie could hear Marci sob, and the sound pierced through her. She suddenly turned on Conrad, throwing the full force of her weight against him and knocking him off balance. For just a second, he lost his grip on her, and she ran toward Marci. She made it about five strides, momentarily drawing everyone's attention to her, before Conrad managed to catch hold of her again and jerk her back. Try as she might, she could not break his hold this time.

"Stop it! I told you, they won't hurt her. They might hurt *you*, though. I'm only trying to keep you from getting your butt kicked!"

Maggie looked up at him through narrowed eyes. "They wouldn't dare touch me! It would be all over the news in twenty-four hours if they did, and their parents would kick *their* butts."

Meanwhile, Derik wasn't through with Marci yet. "You're going to be a good girl, Marci, and break up with this idiot. And you're going to make him believe it was your idea. If you don't, you're going to be seriously sorry. I hope you're listening very carefully because I'm not going to have this conversation with you again. Understand?"

Somehow Derik had touched an inner chord within Marci when he insulted Jacob. She looked up at him through tears and was suddenly taken back by her own anger. She took a deep breath and held on to what little courage she had.

"I understand a lot of things, Derik. I understand that Jacob is a brilliant, compassionate, and wonderful person— something you will never be able to fathom. I understand that you are threatened by those qualities which you and your friends will never have. I understand that you hide behind your prejudices because you don't want anyone to know the real reason why you hate him!"

"Really? And why is that?" There was a frightening edge to his tone that dared her to say more.

"Because deep down, despite any genetic perfection you try to claim, you know he's better than you are," she choked. She was trembling, but she had managed to stand up to him.

Derik caught her by the jaw, his eyes boring into her.

"Go ahead and hurt me, Derik," Marci said softly, her voice cracking with emotion. "I can't stop you, but I can't help how I feel about Jacob either."

Jason caught Derik's hand. "Don't touch her, man. You know we can't lay a hand on her."

When Derik released her, Marci looked up at him, her blue eyes bright with tears. "I feel sorry for you, Derik. You and your friends are in bondage to your own hate, and you don't even realize it!"

"Go ahead and go, Marci," Jason said in resignation. He knew they weren't going to get anywhere at that point, and he certainly didn't want to get in trouble for harassing her.

Derik gave Marci a look that terrified her, but he eventually allowed her to go.

Maggie and Conrad had heard the entire conversation. "I told you, Maggie," Conrad said. "No harm done, right?" He released her.

As enraged as she was, Maggie would have walked away…if he had not given her a humiliating pat on the behind. That was all it took. Already furious, Maggie immediately spun and smacked him across the face so hard her handprint left a clear mark on his cheek.

He raised a hand to his burning skin. "Wow. That was impressive!" It was obvious that he meant it.

She glared at him, then turned and went to join Marci.

No one noticed the reporter snapping pictures at the back of the parking lot.

The next morning, Maggie awoke around six. She stretched, unwilling to open her eyes. Her senses belatedly became aware of a sweet scent just as her fingers touched the velvety softness of unfamiliar objects upon the pillow beside her. Puzzled, she opened her eyes and realized someone had placed two dozen long-stemmed red roses beside her. She knew immediately it had been Peter, although she couldn't imagine how he had managed it. She was unwillingly reminded of the first wonderful night she'd spent in the guest bedroom at his house and the pink rose he'd left on the pillow beside her. She blinked back tears, feeling her heart constrict within her.

Maggie went into the kitchen in her long nightshirt and bare feet. She was more than surprised to find her father at the stove making breakfast. She couldn't begin to know what to think. "What are you doing up?" she asked.

"Making breakfast, sweetheart."

"Since when do you get up to make breakfast?"

"Since I need you to know that I love you, and I'm not going to fail you again."

She thought that over, still a little uncertain of what to think. "And the roses?"

He looked a little guilty at that point, and he turned toward the stove so that she wouldn't read his expression with her insightful eyes.

"You let him in my room while I was sleeping? Dad, I can't believe you did that! We're not together anymore. You know that."

"How do you know I didn't bring the flowers in for him?"

"Did you?"

"Well, no...not really. But I made sure you were decent."

"Thanks!" She threw her hands up in exasperation. It didn't help that her room was a mess. He started to speak, but she cut him off with a pained expression. "No, please, Dad. I don't want to talk about him."

"Maybe you don't, but I do. I've thrown away years of my life and years of yours by hiding from my pain instead of dealing with it. I'm not going to sit back now and stay silent while you make the same mistake. The woman I loved is dead, Maggie. She's never coming back, and there's nothing I can do about it. But the boy you love is alive, and you are throwing away your chance at happiness."

Maggie raked her fingers through her hair, releasing a sigh of frustration, but she refrained from answering. The truth was that she was confused and afraid. She was afraid of losing her father to despair. And she was afraid of having to live her life without Peter. She wasn't sure she even knew how. But she had shoved him away, and she wasn't even sure there was a chance for them anymore. She had brought too much heartache into Peter's life...and would continue to do so. He would eventually see that.

A little while later they sat down and had bacon, eggs, and toast for breakfast. The toast was a little burned, but the eggs were perfect, and Maggie felt as if she and her father were actually a family for the first time in a long while. There was a normalcy to it that was strangely unfamiliar.

She realized that she had become so accustomed to living in a dysfunctional home that she had forgotten what life used to be like before the car accident. The thought played in her mind that she would never be more than a product of her own surroundings. It was the very reason she would never be successful in any relationship—she had lost the ability to trust a long time ago. Since coming to God, she was learning to rethink life, but survival instincts still came first, and her dependency upon Peter frightened her, especially when he wielded so much power that he could make such monumental decisions without her consent. He was, after all, a member of The Inner Society, and wielding power came naturally.

The counselor at New Hope had told her that God would become her rock when she learned to trust in him rather than in herself, but it was hard for her to understand that. Even so, there was something inside of her that clung to the one thing she had been able to grasp in Christ: hope that things could one day be different.

Maggie dreaded walking into Language class that morning. It was painful enough dealing with the ridicule of the others, but sharing a class with Peter was more than she felt she could handle under the circumstances. She was grateful to find an empty seat in the back. The others turned to look at her, their interests piqued immediately. They laughed and whispered amongst themselves, and it was sheer agony for Maggie to ignore them. She closed her eyes and swallowed the shame that threatened to encompass her.

It was then that a slender redhead walked in. Maggie had never seen her before, and she surmised that she must be new to Norfolk High. She was dressed in a blue sweater and a long gray skirt—clearly not designer. She was not stunningly beautiful, but there was a vulnerability and innocence in her that made her lovely, and the glossy red hair that reached down her back was breathtaking.

Maggie watched as the girl made her way down the aisle looking for a seat. She heard the others whispering about her, and Maggie knew the girl was pretending not to notice. The scene was all too familiar. The girl got to the front of the room and looked around with uncertainty. She spotted an empty seat and went toward it in relief, but another girl dropped her books onto the seat and, in a snide tone, said, "This seat is taken, honey."

The girl stopped, embarrassed and unsure of what to do. She glanced around her, and then her gaze dropped to her feet.

"There's an empty seat over here."

Maggie recognized the voice as belonging to Peter. It would have to be him. Who else in that class would have had the decency to be kind? Maggie watched as the girl looked up at him and blushed in a way that was very becoming. She then quietly slipped into the seat beside him, and he whispered something to her. Maggie felt her heart twist inside her chest, and she had to swallow a sudden sensation of complete loss. A girl next to her leaned toward her and whispered, "He won't be lonely for long, honey. Peter has never had any problems acquiring companionship." Maggie cast her a look of resentment and turned away.

When class was over, Maggie half-expected Peter to say something to her as everyone got up and made their way to the door, but Peter followed the new girl out. They were talking about something in quiet tones that Maggie couldn't hear.

Maggie was the last to leave the class. She stepped out into the hallway, her heart heavy and the pang of loneliness almost more than she could bear.

Marci came up to her, following Maggie's line of vision. Peter and the redhead were walking away, close beside each other. Marci was silent for a moment as she contemplated what to say.

"You can't be mad at him, Maggie. You left *him*."

Maggie didn't respond and Marci could sense her depression.

"Go after him, Maggie," she urged, "before it's too late."

Maggie gave her a look that made words unnecessary, and Marci shrugged. The tardy bell rang then.

"Hey, you are still going to meet with us tonight at Pastor Bradford's house, right?" Marci was obviously worrying that Maggie would ditch the meeting to avoid Peter.

"Yeah, I'll be there." She wasn't sure she wanted to go, and she wasn't sure why she said she would. It occurred to her that she was probably just afraid of them talking about her if she wasn't there. She'd had about all of that that she could take.

"And please don't say anything about what happened at the theater yesterday. You haven't told anyone, have you?" Marci asked.

Maggie looked at her, studying her. "I'm not making any promises. The way you handled Derik was amazing, Marci. I didn't think you had it in you. I mean, I was really impressed."

"He scared the life out of me, Maggie! And if you tell, it will only cause trouble."

"They're the ones who caused the trouble. We were just watching a movie and minding our own business, remember?"

A security guard turned the corner and was heading in their direction. "Hey, you kids," he said, "get to class. You're late!"

At lunch break, Maggie went into the quad and saw the new girl talking with Marci and the others. She should have known the youth group would take her under their wing. Hadn't they done the same for her? Maggie's heart sank, but she ignored the fact that it did. She knew she had to rise above the situation. This girl hadn't done anything wrong, and there was no way she could have any knowledge of the fact that she had recently broken up with Peter.

Maggie heard Peter say something. She couldn't make out what it was, but apparently it was pretty funny, because the girl burst into laughter, her hazel-green eyes twinkling. Everyone seemed to sober slightly when Maggie showed up, and she wondered if she had just become a "third wheel" of sorts.

"Maggie!" Marci called. "There you are. I want to introduce you to Katie Keller."

Peter gave Katie an encouraging pat on the back, urging her gently forward. She smiled brightly, her dimples deepening as she stepped toward Maggie.

"Hi, Maggie. How are you?"

There was something horribly adorable about this girl, and Maggie couldn't help but detect the charm that seemed to ooze forth naturally out of her. She had been a little backward in class in the threatening environment, but she was clearly comfortable being herself amongst the youth. They had that effect on people in general, but Katie was obviously a people person anyway.

Maggie wondered how much of her notoriety this girl was privy to. "Hi, Katie," she said kindly enough. "Today's your first day at Norfolk High?"

"Yes. My family just transferred back when my dad got a job here."

"Your name sounds familiar somehow," Maggie said.

Marci exchanged glances with Peter, and then she explained, "Katie is Old Man Keller's granddaughter. He's the one who died in the fire."

Maggie's eyes widened in understanding. "Oh, I'm sorry for your loss," she said sincerely.

"Thanks. It was a shock, but the truth is that I didn't know my grandfather very well. When we got the news, we called the neighbors and asked around about what happened to Courage. No one seemed to know, but Peter told me he's with you."

Maggie felt a moment of private alarm realizing she could lose her dog if Katie claimed him. She didn't think she could bear losing him, and she was quiet for a moment, unsure of how to respond.

"I found him at your grandfather's gravesite. I have no clue how he got there. He took the loss hard, and he was pretty sick. I think he was dying."

"Maggie has taken wonderful care of him," Peter said, sensing where Maggie's train of thought was going.

"Oh, thank you so much, Maggie. I'm so glad we don't have to worry about him anymore."

Maggie inwardly breathed a sigh of relief. Losing Courage would have been an unbearable blow.

CHAPTER
eleven

Maggie pulled down the dirt drive of Pastor Bradford's small ranch on Wednesday evening. She parked the old truck under the large oak tree that spread across the drive and formed an umbrella over the small white two-story ranch house with a wraparound porch.

Tennyson had followed her, but he took his leave upon her arrival, reminding her to call him when she left.

Like that was a likely scenario.

She got to the front steps and stopped, suddenly realizing she didn't want to go in. She was feeling depressed, and she definitely didn't want anyone else to know. Despite Marci's insistence that the others were still her friends, Maggie had the persistent feeling that there were whispers among them concerning her, and she wondered if they were turning on her for leaving Peter. Was she going to lose her friends, too? Did Christians do that to people? She knew it went against everything they had preached to her, but the undercurrents were there nonetheless and Christians were still human—they weren't perfect either.

Then there was the other issue: Katie hadn't left Peter's side from the moment she'd set foot on campus, and there was an obvious connection between them. Katie was perfect for him, and Maggie knew her split with Peter was solidifying by the minute. The pain of that knowledge was more than she could bear to dwell on. But then again, she'd always known that Peter would eventually realize he was too good for her.

The pastor's wife met her at the door and welcomed her in, giving her a warm hug that nearly brought Maggie to tears in its sincerity.

Maggie made her way down the hall to the family room where everyone had gathered. Katie was seated in an armchair, and Peter was sitting on the armrest beside her. He got up and moved to the couch when he saw Maggie come in, and everyone in the room seemed to straighten slightly—or was it just her imagination?

Maggie's heart was gripped with pain, but she ignored it. It was too late. Peter had hurt her, she had left him, and her pride would never allow her to crawl back to him. But she also couldn't expect him to be alone forever.

Of course, she had expected it to take him a little longer than this!

The others greeted her warmly enough, and Marci moved over so that Maggie could sit next to her. Jacob was sitting on Marci's other side. The meeting hadn't started yet, and the television was on. Any thoughts that were haunting Maggie were soon dispelled when the local news came on and a scene from her confrontation at the theatre flashed across the screen.

Marci gasped and looked accusingly at Maggie.

"I didn't tell them anything!" M a g g i e q u i c k l y

assured her. The last thing she needed was to get Marci mad at her. "They called my house, but I didn't take the call. I swear it!"

Everyone in the room looked at the two girls in surprise, and Marci inwardly groaned.

"Apparently the infamous teens of Norfolk are still at it," the reporter said. "It was just Saturday when these pictures were taken at a local theatre. The boys involved in Norfolk's recent trial had obviously found a new target to harass."

The picture switched to a picture of Marci standing between Derik and Jason.

"Not surprisingly, Maggie Kraus was present at the confrontation and doing an excellent job of defending herself."

The next picture had captured the precise moment Maggie had smacked Conrad. This immediately evoked several gasps across the room.

The news changed to a different story then, and the room became dead silent as the others looked to the girls, waiting expectantly to be told about the recent events that had been kept from them.

"Oh crap!" Marci whispered, feeling Jacob's hot gaze. The room was crackling with anticipation.

"Where was Tennyson?" Jacob demanded.

"I guess he was in the front of the theatre. We went out the back," Marci answered with obvious reluctance.

"They might as well know everything, Marci. It's out

now," Maggie said. She turned to the group and met their eyes head-on. "We went to the theatre. Derik came in and dragged Marci out into the parking lot where a bunch of their stupid friends were hanging around. Conrad took hold of me so I couldn't try to help her. Derik threatened her and told her to break up with Jacob. He expected to break her down, but he just ticked her off instead. Marci was amazing, Jacob, you should have seen her. She told Derik that, despite all his genetic perfection, he only hated you because you're still better than him."

"My gosh, Marci, did you really say that to him?" Peter choked. He had his answer when Marci would not meet his eyes. "You know better than that! You don't want to piss him off!"

Jacob was standing by then, obviously deeply agitated as he looked from Marci to Maggie.

The pastor and his wife looked to each other, their expressions worried. Mrs. Bradford put a hand to her flushed cheek. "Lord, have mercy!"

Marci was blushing, but she couldn't suppress the smile that accompanied the excitement as she told the rest of the story. "You should have been there when Maggie smacked Conrad. He gave her a pat on the butt when he let her go, and Maggie turned on him and slapped him across the face so hard that it sounded like a clap of thunder! She left a red mark on his face!"

"Yeah. We caught that," Jacob said with rising disapproval.

It was Maggie's turn to feel embarrassed. She averted her eyes from the rapt attention of the others for a moment.

Peter and Jacob exchanged glances; both were not happy. "I don't think we should let them play together anymore," Peter said, only half in jest.

Maggie glanced up at him, ready with a retort, but reconsidered when she realized how angry he was. His eyes were boring into her, and she knew he blamed her for this new side to Marci.

"Did they hurt you?" Jacob said to Marci in a tone that was dark in its intensity. It was the very reaction she wanted to avoid by not telling him.

"No, Jacob, I swear," Marci said, a little more subdued now.

"Well, *I'm* proud of you, Marci," Kristy pitched in with a defiant tilt to her chin. "And I'm glad you smacked Conrad, Mags. I wish I could have a copy of that picture from the news. I'd blow it up and tape it to his locker!"

The others had to suppress laughter, knowing full well that Jacob and Peter did not find the situation amusing in the least.

"You and I are going to have a little talk, Kristy," Jacob promised.

"Oh, I don't doubt it," she said, knowing he was mad at her for encouraging Maggie.

Maggie knew that Peter was dying to question her about the situation, but he was resisting. They weren't together, and he couldn't tell her what she should be doing anymore. The tension between them filled the room.

"Maybe you girls should be a little more careful when you go out," Mrs. Bradford cautioned when she caught

Peter's expression. "At least for a while, stick with larger numbers. Those guys don't have a whole lot of scruples."

Pastor Bradford decided this was the time to change the topic, and started the meeting.

He told the youth about how the church board had "allowed him to resign" due to his "new and disconcerting outlook" on the meaning of Christianity. They all decided that they would hold youth meetings at the farmhouse in the future, which really constituted an in-home church service that their families would be invited to as well. The other members of The Inner Society didn't need to know this, though. Affiliation with a chosen church was an unspoken I.S. requirement. People could skip attendance, but they could not leave the church or attend elsewhere without consequences. The youth certainly didn't want to raise any suspicions that they were starting a mutiny.

They prayed for each other's needs then, each person adding something heartfelt, and it seemed that the tension of the room faded into a peaceful calm. Several even prayed for Maggie, although they were careful to not to say anything too invasive. Maggie was surprised that she was able to relax now, soaking in the gentle spirit that seemed to hover over their meeting. It was the first time since that awful mess with her uncle that the pain faded into something bearable, and she hoped that maybe it meant she really had been wrong about what the others thought of her.

The pastor then gave a message on the true meaning of love and what Christ's love cost him on the cross. He encouraged the teens to love one another in spite of whatever problems arose among them. It was a beautiful message taught from the heart, a blaring contrast to the polished and carefully rehearsed messages that Pastor Walcott preached.

In all fairness, Pastor Bradford had preached those sorts of messages not too long ago himself, when he was in the tenuous position of trying to please the leaders of Sunrise Baptist. But the tragic events that had swept through Norfolk had changed a lot of things—in particular, Pastor Bradford's outlook on his purpose in life. He no longer lived to please people. He was living now to reach out to the lost, and he didn't care what anybody thought about it. This encouraged the others to hold fast to their own faith and convictions.

After the message came to a close, the teens began talking then about current events, and Maggie was surprised when Peter said that Tai and Waters did not get on very well on their first day.

"What does that mean?" she demanded. She was clearly affronted at his interference in what she considered was none of his business.

"I introduced them, Maggie, and worked it out so that Waters would pay him for his help. Both were extremely difficult, and Tai called me at the end of the day, ready to quit. He said that Waters had put him down and assaulted him with racial slurs the whole time. I talked him into having patience with the guy and hanging on a little longer." He was speaking matter-of-factly and ignoring her hot gaze. "At least Tai took a paycheck with him when he left. Handling Waters might teach the kid a little temperance. He makes too many impetuous decisions. Decisions made in the heat of the moment are never wise."

She chose to ignore that last part, knowing it was a thinly disguised attack against her. "But Waters is my friend, Peter. You arranged this without consulting me?"

"It was your idea, Maggie. I just followed through with your suggestion," he replied casually. "Besides, you weren't talking to me, remember?"

The tension between them was sparking again. Maggie wondered if Katie was bright enough to pick up on it. The girl was clearly as sharp as a tack, but she gave no indication that she noticed anything remiss. In fact, she wasn't even paying attention to them. She appeared to be reading something that she had taken out of her purse.

"Well, maybe it's a good thing," Kristy interrupted. "I mean both of them have issues, and sometimes people like that are good for each other...even if they don't like each other."

The conversation finally shifted when the pastor's wife brought in a huge lasagna and a stack of plates and forks. The scent was wonderful, and everyone was starving. They jumped up, eagerly grabbing their plates.

At that moment Katie tripped, and Peter caught her in his arms. It was apparent to everyone that he was a little slow to release her, and Katie looked up into his handsome face, obviously enraptured by the aura that Peter emitted. She blushed in embarrassment, and he let her go. It was a subtle but meaningful exchange.

The others surreptitiously glanced at Maggie to see her reaction, but she was not going to give them any indication that she noticed.

When Katie sat down on the couch, Peter casually sat next to her. He grabbed a fork and passed it to her, and she thanked him. After a while, he said something softly to her and then wiped a smudge of sauce from the corner of her mouth with a napkin.

Peter's chivalry toward Katie continued throughout

dinner, and, after a while, Maggie got up and quietly slipped out. Marci secretly followed her.

She returned a short while later, and everyone stopped and looked up at her expectantly. "She went to the barn. Her Bible is in her lap, and she's repeating Philippians 4:13: 'I can do all things through Christ who strengthens me.' And… she's crying." It was clear that Marci was feeling horrible.

"Well, at least she ran to God, instead of away from him," Kristy said on a sigh.

Katie thumped Peter on the chest. "You brat! You made me hurt her!" she accused. She got up and went back to the armchair with a look of total annoyance.

"She needs to feel some pain over this," Peter said remorselessly. "She's going to try to leave now."

"She won't get far," Jacob said. "I've already disabled her truck."

"She'll never forgive us," Marci said.

"You willingly went along with this, Marci, so don't go weak on me now," Peter said. "There's no doubt she's going to be seriously ticked off when she realizes we set her up, but she'll get over it." He looked at his watch and then got up to go find Maggie.

Kevin watched him go. "Man, this could get ugly!"

"No doubt," Jacob commented dryly.

Pastor Bradford looked to his wife, noting her reaction to this was no different from his own. "You kids better hope this works out in your favor," he said at last. "I wish you had consulted us about this first."

"We were just trying to help, Pastor," Marci said. "Maggie just needed something to make her realize she's not ready to give Peter up."

When Peter came out onto the porch, it was pouring down rain. It was an odd, warm rain, though, not a normal occurrence for late October. The weather patterns had been off that year.

Maggie had already discovered her truck wouldn't start, and she had gotten out, slamming the door. She didn't see him coming as she went around to the front of her truck and popped the hood. The porch light wasn't bright enough for her to see anything, not that she would have been able to fix the truck if she had; nevertheless, she knew a little about cars, and she intended to give it a valiant effort.

When she realized she was getting nowhere, Maggie slammed the hood down in frustration. She was soaking wet and weeping by the time she realized Peter was heading purposefully her way. The fact that he'd caught her in this embarrassing scene only served to add insult to injury. She decided she would rather walk home than talk to him, even if it took her all night, but as she spun on her heels and headed down the drive, he came after her.

"Where do you think you're going?" he shouted.

"Leave me alone, Peter!"

She broke into a run, not caring how ridiculous she was being, and he chased after her. In ten paces he had nearly caught up with her. Unfortunately, at that point, Maggie slipped in a mud puddle. He tried to catch her to keep her from falling, but she tried to throw him off and both lost their balance. Maggie landed on her back in the center of the puddle, and Peter landed on top of her.

A struggle inevitably broke out between the two of them as she tried to get free, and he fought to pin her down. Enraged, she put in a tremendous effort to kick and twist herself away from him, but he subdued her relatively quickly.

"Why don't you go back to your latest girlfriend!" she cried. He laughed, and that only served to make her even madder. She began to fight him again, but to no avail—she couldn't move him. She gave up in defeat on more than one level. "How could you, Peter? How could you act like that in front of me?" She was fighting tears still, but it was raining so hard that it didn't make any difference.

"I did everything for you, Maggie, and you ripped my heart out!" Peter was fighting to keep from screaming at her. "You were the one who called me for help, remember? I protected you, and you turned on me. You didn't think I was going to make this easy for you, did you?"

The rain suddenly dropped off to a drizzle. It hardly mattered since Maggie was still lying in a muddy puddle, and both were completely drenched by then.

When Maggie turned her face away from him, he leaned forward and whispered into her ear, his breath warm against her cold skin. "She's had four years in the theatre, Maggie."

"Well good for you. You're into actresses now!"

He laughed again and she looked up at him in hurt confusion. "You're not getting it—she was *acting*! And you wouldn't be jealous if you didn't love me still."

She blinked as understanding registered, but then the rage renewed when she realized she had been duped. "Jealous? You jerk!" In a fresh fit of anger, she took a swing at him. He was lucky to have caught her wrist, because she would have undoubtedly inflicted pain.

"You must like lying in the mud, because you're going to be here a long time if you don't knock it off!" His tone left her in little doubt that he meant it.

She went still again, and as the tears welled in her eyes once more, he finally pulled her into his arms and kissed her passionately. In that rapturous moment, everything in her gave way to his powerful strength and beautiful soul she had come to love, and she felt herself go limp in his arms. When he finally broke the contact, he tenderly brushed his lips against her cheek.

He pulled back then so he could look at her. It was dark and difficult to see, but he could tell she was soaked and covered in mud. A band of moonlight shone through the clouds, illuminating her face, and he could see the muddy strand of her hair that had stuck to her cheek. He brushed it away with a wry smile. "Do you really have no idea how much I love you? How can you not see it? Do you think my affections are so jacked up that I'm just going to give up on you so easily and go for someone else?"

"I don't know," she admitted. "I know I've never been worthy of you. You're going to realize that eventually. I'm screwed up still."

"No kidding." He shook his head. "You drive me crazy sometimes, but I still love you. Someday you're going to get that into your thick head. God put us together, Maggie. Can't you see that? Our love was ordained from the beginning. None of this was an accident." He buried his face in her neck and held her.

Maggie nestled into him, clinging to him in desperation as though fearing she might still lose him. "I…I'm sorry. I wasn't trying to hurt you. I was afraid of losing my father, and afraid of your power to make decisions for me."

He looked down upon her, studying her. "I know that, honey. But I had to do what I did, and you haven't lost your father." His expression took on a look of concern. "I want to be really clear with you, sweetheart. Just as you said yourself, you are still screwed up, and there has to be at least one stable person in a relationship, right? I'm going to lead in this relationship. Do you understand? That doesn't mean that I won't take your feelings into consideration or listen to you, but it does mean I'll make decisions that you won't always understand or agree with. It also means that you'll never go hungry or unloved or unprotected again. I will love you as long as I live and even beyond life. Can you or can you not you accept those terms?"

She turned her face away for a moment, knowing he was asking for nothing less than complete surrender when she struggled to give in on the slightest point.

He cupped her cheeks and made her face him. He kissed her lightly several times, gently coaxing a response from her. "Can you accept that or not?"

"Yes," she whispered hoarsely. "I'll try."

He smiled warmly, his bright eyes showing his love more than words ever could. He reached into his pocket and took out her engagement ring. "Now, I'm going to put this back on your finger, and you're going to stop acting like a child." He took her hand and slipped the ring back into its place.

She gave him a look of annoyance. "If this isn't romantic, I don't know what is," she commented dryly. "Can I please get up now?"

He laughed and kissed her forehead before getting up and pulling her to her feet. Water was sloshing off of her, and her clothes stuck to her. He didn't look a whole lot better. Peter smiled, suppressing laughter. "I do believe our clothes are ruined."

"Yeah. I figured that out," she said with slight embarrassment. "I'm sure I'm a mess."

"I don't think you've ever looked more beautiful," he said in a husky voice.

He pulled her against him and held her once more. For a moment they simply clung to each other, unwilling to let go.

"Please don't ever break my heart like that again, Maggie."

She clung to him, almost unable to believe that he was still hers.

He finally let go and his gaze swept the length of her, noting again that she was drenched. "We better get back to the others and get you dried off."

"Are you crazy? Look at us! You want us to go back in there like this?" she asked incredulously.

He laughed. "Well, seeing that my keys are in there, yes. And no, I'm not going alone; they'll take one look at me and think I killed you or something!" He caught her by the arm firmly but gently and dragged her along with him up the driveway and up the front porch steps.

Everyone gasped when the two of them walked in. "Lord have mercy!" Marci cried, horrified when she saw them.

Maggie folded her arms, still unsure of whether or not she was ready to forgive them for their part in all this.

"What did you guys do, have a mud wrestling contest?"

"Shut up, Kevin!" Maggie said. The humiliation was already more than she could handle.

Mrs. Bradford ran to grab them a couple of towels before ushering them over to the hearth where they could warm up. "You kids look affright!" she gasped.

Peter sat down on the heart and pulled Maggie down next to him.

"Looks like that unseasonable hurricane they've been talking about just blew in ahead of schedule," Jacob teased.

Maggie looked at him through narrowed eyes. "Are you the one who messed up my truck, Jacob?"

"Yeah, well, sorry about that. But Peter would have done it if I didn't."

"Well then, I will thank you to fix it straight again," she said, and then her eyes met Katie's.

Katie flushed with guilt. "I really am sorry, Maggie. I didn't mean to hurt you."

"Yeah, you did. That was the point, wasn't it?"

Peter leaned closer to Maggie and whispered into her ear. "Take it easy, sweetheart. I talked her into this. It wasn't her idea."

Maggie turned to Marci then. "I can't believe you could be capable of being part of something like this, Marci!"

"I'm sorry, Maggie, but I only did it to help you. You needed to be with Peter, and that seemed obvious to everyone but you," she answered softly.

Maggie was left with mixed emotions. She was embarrassed and angry, but at the same time, she understood that their intentions were good. It was just going to take her a little time to digest all of this.

When everyone left and Maggie got into her truck, Peter got in beside her.

"I'm going to tell you something, Maggie, and I hope you take it the right way."

She looked sideways at him, bracing herself. She knew she wasn't going to like whatever was coming next.

"When you first converted to Christianity, you had been given a dose of humility from Bret and his friends, and that hardness of spirit that has kept you going gave way to dependency upon Christ. But it's very human to start to revert to your natural ways when that newness in your faith starts to wear off. It's also imperative that you don't give in to your anger and pride, sweetheart."

"What? You don't think tonight was humiliating

enough for me?"

"No, I'm talking about the incident with Conrad and Derik at the movie theatre," Peter countered.

Maggie bit her lip and remained quiet.

"I think you better be careful about your temper. It could backfire on you. You have to let the anger go, sweetheart. You have started serious trouble more than once with your temper. You came at Derik in a rage just the other day. Isn't that how this whole thing started from the beginning?"

"I was trying to protect Marci."

"And how did that work for either of you? You pissed him off and made him all the more determined to go after her. I stopped them at school, but they just waited and caught you both alone at the theatre, right? To make matters worse, Marci followed your example and told Derik off. Look what they did to Jessica. Derik is just as dangerous and unpredictable as Bret, and Jason will follow his lead. They could have hurt Marci."

Maggie sighed in confusion. "But Marci is one of you. I thought you said you don't hurt your own."

"We don't...*in theory*. The guys would have suffered the consequences for harming her, but that wouldn't have done Marci a lot of good, would it? You have to watch your temper, Maggie."

"It's easier said than done, Peter."

"I never said it was going to be easy, I just said that you had to do it. If you don't, you'll be imprisoned by your own anger, and you'll wind up right back where you started."

He looked into her eyes then. "I say it because I love you, Maggie. You know that, right?"

CHAPTER
twelve

As fate would have it, Maggie bumped into Conrad's girlfriend, Jennifer Lilbourn, in the hallway on Monday.

"Well, if it ain't the school tramp," the blonde sneered. She faced Maggie head-on and lowered her voice. "I know how you tried to steal Mark away, and now you're trying to get Conrad. You better stay away from him if you have any intelligence."

Maggie looked at her incredulously. She had never even had words with this girl, and yet now she was threatening her? Maggie could feel her anger harden in her chest. "I would rather drop dead than give Conrad the time of day."

"Liar! I saw you on the news. You went to the theatre with him!"

Students were beginning to take notice of them, and Maggie was acutely aware of the negative attention this girl was drawing to them both. Maggie's eyes narrowed upon her in contempt. "This conversation is over," she stated flatly, and turned to walk away.

Enraged, Jennifer grabbed her by the shirt to stop her.

"Let go of me," Maggie threatened with as much self-control as she could manage—which wasn't much.

"And what are you going to do about it?"

She barely got the phrase out before Maggie had turned on her. She nearly hit her, but her arm was seized in a biting grip, and she was jerked backward. She instinctively battled with her captor but without success; he was much stronger than she was.

"Knock it off!" Peter snapped at her, pulling her away and holding her up against a wall. He looked back at Jennifer. "You better walk away, Jennifer, before she beats the snot out of you, and you both get your butts suspended!"

Jennifer cast Peter a look of distain as she turned in a huff and stomped away without another word.

Peter turned back to Maggie. "You weren't listening last week, were you? What are you thinking?"

Her anger slowly dissipating now, Maggie sighed in defeat, her eyes following Jennifer as she retreated with her friends. This self-control thing was going to be harder than she thought.

At break, Maggie received a text message from Peter telling her to meet with him in the Home Economics room. When she walked in, she found Jacob and Peter sitting on the desks and Kevin standing by the door, waiting for her. She knew immediately that she was about to get told off, and she would have walked out if Kevin hadn't shut the door and stood in front of it. Maggie looked up at him in irritation, knowing she wouldn't get far if she tried to move him out of the way.

"What have I done now?" she asked.

"You know what you did," Peter said.

"We're not here to point fingers at you, Maggie," Kevin said. "We all blow it, me most of all, but there are a few things that we want to say to you."

Maggie crossed her arms and waited.

"We're asking you to be careful about your attitude," Jacob said. "You will lose all the joy and peace of your salvation if you can't let go of the anger."

"You've got to remember, Maggie," Kevin spoke up, "that you willingly became one of the youth, and we accepted you when no one else did. Your actions speak not only for you now but for all of us as well."

Maggie knew Kevin struggled to stay in line himself. His passions had gotten him into trouble more than once. "Really, Kevin? I seem to remember your temper getting you into trouble a lot," Maggie reminded him. "How many fights have you gotten into now?"

He nodded in acceptance. "Like I said, I blow it more than anyone. But then I get the same talking to that you're getting. That's why I'm here right now. If we don't all help each other stay in line, then we'll all fall back into our old natures, and everything we've stood for will be for nothing. No one's judging you, Maggie. Any one of us could fall into temptation at any time. It's hard to live by what you believe in a world that hates your values."

"Is this about Jennifer? Or is this about your fear that

I'll put Marci in jeopardy?"

"Both," Peter said.

"Kristy didn't seem to share your views," Maggie said in quiet defense.

"Well, we've talked with Kristy, too, since then, and she's realized our point," Jacob countered. "She doesn't want to see you or Marci hurt any more than we do."

"Now you're talking about that little episode at the theatre. What should I have done?" Maggie asked, her frustration building again. "Neither of us saw them coming. You can't say that I provoked them. And as for Conrad, should I have let him put his hands on me and get away with it?"

"That slap was totally awesome, Maggie." Peter couldn't help but smile. "I'd be lying if I said I wasn't proud of you. But it still wasn't the right response. You walked away from that because he *let* you. He could just as easily have retaliated. You got lucky."

"Marci looks up to you." Jacob tried to reason with her. "You have to be careful how you influence her. If she had hit Derik like you hit Conrad, he could have seriously hurt her, and you know that...."

"Marci looks up to *me*?" Maggie choked in astonishment. She could hardly grasp the concept, considering she had always thought Marci was so much better than her. Then Jacob's meaning belatedly struck home, and pain gripped her heart. "You think I'm going to get her killed... like I did Jessica," she concluded on a hoarse whisper.

"Hey, take it easy. No one said that." Peter slid off the desk and took her in his arms. "But you know these guys are dangerous, and they have some terrifying connections. You have always been like an accelerant to a fire, honey. That has to change. Making these guys angry or getting even with them might feel great at the time, but what are the results? Nothing positive. Quite frankly, you could take a few lessons from Marci on love and humility. She can say things in a way that reaches people."

"We understand that this is new to you, Maggie," Kevin spoke up. "Like I said, none of us are close to perfect, and we all understand your anger—especially me—but we're not going to let you wallow in it."

"What happened today with Jennifer happened out of self-defense," Maggie said.

"Look, we're not defending Jennifer's actions," Jacob inserted, "but you've got to see this thing from a new standpoint. If you're going to act the same way as every lost teen in this school, how are you ever going to be a witness to them? Are you going to knock their teeth out and then tell them Jesus loves them? Look at how many teenagers have ended up dead at Norfolk. We're trying to heal the anger, not fuel it."

Maggie stepped back from Peter, her frustration mounting. "It was self-defense," she said again. "She came at me!"

"It's always self-defense with you, Maggie, right?" Peter said. "Was it self-defense when you tried to hit me Wednesday night? I wasn't hurting you, but you were angry enough to have done some damage if I let you."

"When you react in anger, that anger is eventually going to spread to people you love," Jacob said. "Marci can persuade people to do things by handling them carefully and talking them out of their anger. You need to learn how to do that. If you had learned that from the start, a lot of the violence might have been prevented. 'A soft answer turns away wrath,' you know."

Maggie's heart wrenched inside of her. She could never remember facing any situation as uncomfortable as this one was, not including the events of the last youth meeting, of course. The boys had ganged up on her to make sure she got the point, but she couldn't be angry with them. She knew, deep down, that they were right. *Talk about humiliation....*

"All right, I've listened to you. Can I be dismissed now?" she asked quietly.

"Don't take it like that, Maggie," Kevin said. "None of us are trying to hurt you. All of us had to take it from the others when we joined the group. You're not immune."

"Okay, I think she gets it," Peter said, and the guys left them alone.

Maggie didn't want to face Peter now. She had just been berated by all three of them, and she was deeply upset by it.

Peter gently but firmly pulled her chin up. "Look at me. I warned you about this last week. You have reverted back to the rage that was first eating away at you, and you need to take control of it. I know how tough you are, in some ways, but I also know that your anger is born of fear. You haven't had a day in your life when you weren't afraid, honey. You've been afraid of losing someone you love, afraid of being rejected, afraid of being abused, and afraid you'll never get justice. You try to protect your heart by putting up a wall of anger so that no one can touch you, but it obviously isn't working. That wall also keeps out the Lord and everyone who cares about you. I would bet on it that you're still afraid to let yourself love me because it makes you too vulnerable."

"Well, it does! You broke my heart when I saw you with Katie," she cried.

"It was necessary for you to feel that pain, Maggie. If I didn't let you feel hurt, you wouldn't have come back to me, and you're way too vulnerable on your own right now."

"So you break my heart and then knock me down and pin me in the mud? I don't think I can stand much more humiliation!"

"You know darn well I didn't 'knock you down,'" he corrected, his tone chastising. "I tried to catch you to keep you from falling, and you slipped when you fought me off! That was your own fault."

"You could have let me up."

"I don't think so. I was enjoying that too much. That was one of the most...never mind." He couldn't help the boyish smile that curved his lips.

Her eyes widened and then narrowed again as she choked, "You were enjoying that at my expense?"

"Completely at your expense," he easily admitted. "Consider it payback for leaving me." Her eyes were sparking fire, and Peter pointed a finger at her. "Watch your temper, little girl!"

She would have responded to that immediately, but he caught her up in his arms and kissed her until the fight was out of her. He had a way of being able to manage her. When he finally released her, she was flushed, and she definitely looked vulnerable.

"How…how far would you have gone with her if I hadn't come around?" she whispered, almost afraid to hear his answer. She was staring at her feet.

He studied her carefully for a moment, thinking over how he was going to answer her. "I would have taken it farther if I thought it would get you back," he admitted. "You know my faith wouldn't have allowed me to take it too far, though, and she wouldn't have been willing, anyway. Katie's been a Christian most of her life. I can say one thing for you, Maggie. You were very cordial to her, under the circumstances."

"What did you think I was going to do, attack her?"

"We were debating on the possibility," Peter grinned. "Not that we would have let you near her. She might have surprised you, anyway. Katie's no coward. You've met your match with her. You two would make great friends if you could forgive her." He knew Maggie had ignored Katie since the night at Pastor Bradford's house.

"How well do *you* know her?" she asked intuitively.

"She was part of the youth back when we were in junior high. We've been friends for years."

Maggie shook her head, bringing her fingers to her temples to rub away the tension headache that was forming there. "Is she on the list?"

"No."

She pondered that over, realizing that she already knew as much.

"Now you're going to be good, aren't you?" he said, abruptly bringing the conversation back to its origin.

"Yes," she relented, willing to do almost anything to keep him at that point. How had he managed to turn the tables on her so quickly?

"And you are going to watch your temper?"

"*Yes*, Peter, I'll try. This is hard for me!"

"We all understand that, sweetheart. It's hard for everyone. Did you know that Marci's father emptied their bank account and left her and her mother for his secretary?"

Maggie blinked. "No, no one ever mentioned it."

"Well, believe it or not, she had to deal with anger, too. Her father took nearly everything they had and left them destitute. Why do you think it was so hard for her when I left her, too? And then Kevin...his little brother died of cancer at the age of nine years. He's had a lot of anger and rage to deal with over the past few years, too, believe me. Everyone has pain, sweetheart, and everyone has to face their own demons."

Maggie was annoyed when she realized the others had ditched her for lunch. She soon knew why when Katie joined her at her table in the quad. Maggie was still unsure of how she felt about this girl, and it must have shown on her expression. It didn't help that the others were trying to coerce her into being friends with her. Maggie didn't easily take to being manipulated.

Katie cast her a coy smile. "You're not still mad at me, are you, Maggie?"

"I'm debating on it."

Katie's smile widened. "No harm done, right? You're back together." Her eyebrows rose, her eyes were twinkling again.

Maggie met her gaze with a penetrating one of her own, but Katie wasn't going to be intimidated by her. She held her smile until Maggie couldn't help but smile back.

"You've got a lot of guts, I'll give you that," Maggie said a little begrudgingly.

"I hear the same about you," Katie replied. "Friends?"

"I guess," Maggie finally relented. Katie was a friend of Peter's, after all, so she knew she wouldn't be able to avoid her. Besides, Katie was difficult to say no to.

Katie pulled out her sandwich and took a bite. She was obviously at ease, since she started up a conversation right off the bat. "I see that they cleaned up the lot," she said.

"What lot?"

"Where my grandfather's house used to be."

"Oh, yeah. They cleaned that up after Internal Affairs started poking around. Courtesy of the city council, which said it was a hazard."

"I might as well let you know that I've heard about everything—the trial and everything that's been happening here." Katie shrugged. "The D.A. has been in contact with us, and we've followed the reports on television. You didn't think that fire was an accident, did you?"

"I didn't think it was likely," Maggie admitted.

"And you went through all that crap to keep that lighter away from Bret."

"Did you know him?"

"Not well. I knew of him, though. Why did you go to such great lengths?"

"I hated him, and I knew he was involved. I didn't want him to get away with it."

"But why was the lighter so important?" Katie asked with genuine interest.

"It proved he had been at the house before the fire, or so I thought. It was bent by a beam that had fallen on it during the fire, so it couldn't have been dropped there afterward. There was also soot on it that would have placed it at the scene. It was evidence, but it still wasn't solid proof. Bret must have thought the lighter was significant, though, because he also went to great lengths to get it back. Why would he do that if he wasn't guilty? What did the D.A. have to say to you guys, anyway?"

"She asked my parents if my grandfather knew Mr. Chambers." Her voice had dropped to a conspiratorial whisper, and she glanced around them to make sure no one was close enough to hear them.

"And what did they say?"

"They gave her the impression that my grandfather wasn't involved with him."

"Why do I get the feeling you know that it wasn't true?" Maggie asked, reading her carefully.

"He *was* involved with Chambers," Katie whispered.

"He was working for him."

"Why didn't they say so then?" Maggie asked, leaning forward with increased interest.

"Why do you think? Everyone knows how dangerous people in this city are now. They were afraid. If someone was willing to kill my grandfather, they might be willing to kill any of us, as well."

"And why are you telling *me* this?"

"Because I don't want them to get away with it, either," Katie said. "I wasn't close to him because we lived far away, but he was still my grandfather. He was just an old man, for the love of mercy!"

Maggie was remembering what the D.A. had said. She had come to the same conclusion, but she couldn't prove it because all the records had been destroyed and no one was talking.

A new thought occurred to Maggie then. "What's Bret's dad's first name?" she asked imperatively.

"Brian."

Maggie felt as if the sky had just fallen. The wheels in her head began turning furiously. "B.C.... They have the same initials! Maybe it wasn't Bret's lighter. Maybe it was his dad's and Bret was protecting his father all along! Bret was acquitted of starting the fire, but his father can still be tried!" she whispered fiercely.

Katie was silent for a minute, thinking over the possibility. "Yeah, you're right. Still, there has to be some good hard evidence, and there's nothing left of the house."

"Only the lighter and there's no telling what happened to that. It wouldn't really matter anyway, at this point."

"Why?" Katie asked.

"Because the evidence would have been contaminated by now. I kept it in a plastic bag so I wouldn't smudge any fingerprints, but of course they could have been destroyed a long time ago if the boys wiped it clean."

"There must be some kind of evidence that could connect it, though, a microscopic trace of soot or something," Katie suggested.

"Probably, but I don't know how much it would prove. The men could have met at the house before the fire, and the lighter could have been left behind by accident. It could have been sitting on a table or something when the fire started. We can't prove the lighter started it."

"It still proves that Chambers was there before it happened," Katie pointed out. "It proves they knew each other."

"Well, there is no lighter now, so it doesn't matter one way or another. We need more evidence."

The girls were silent for a moment.

"*I* have more evidence," Katie said.

Maggie looked at her sharply, realizing Katie had been guiding the conversation to this revelation from the very start. "What evidence?" she asked, her heart beginning to beat faster. She was unaware that she was holding her breath.

"Grandpa made a recording of himself on his

camcorder. He made a DVD out of it and mailed it to us in a padded manila envelope before he died."

"Well, what was on it?" Maggie could hardly stand the suspense.

"I haven't seen it," she admitted, "but my parents have. They locked it in a cabinet, though, and they won't talk about it."

"How do you know it wasn't a family video or something? It could have been anything."

She gave Maggie a meaningful look, and one delicate brow rose. "I heard them fighting over it. I couldn't hear everything they were saying, but I know that Grandpa thought he was in danger from Chambers. He apparently caught wind of some pretty damning material that reeked of a definite threat to The Inner Society. When I asked them about it, they told me to stay out of it. He sent a letter with the package, too."

"And what happened to that?"

"I'm not sure. They might have burned it."

Maggie suddenly felt she was being watched, and in that instant both girls realized Rebecca Christensen had just passed by them. Both girls felt a moment of panic. When Rebecca was gone, they looked to one another in question.

"Do you think she heard us?" Katie asked in alarm.

"I'm not sure, but we have to get hold of that DVD, Katie. Everything could depend on it."

Katie shook her head. "I don't know how I could get to it. I don't know where the key to the cabinet is. Besides, my parents will go ballistic if they suspect I've stolen it!"

"What if someone *else* steals it?"

Katie eyed her, humored by her determination. "It would be inadmissible as evidence then, right? Or does that only apply to illegal search and seizure with cops?"

"I think it only applies to cops," Maggie answered thoughtfully. "But it might not matter if the D.A. gets a search warrant. We have to tell her."

"The police will know, and they'll get there first. And...they could come after my family," Katie answered cautiously.

"You're probably right," Maggie agreed. "Just give it a little time. We'll think of something. I really think we should tell the District Attorney, though."

"No, Maggie! She'll go straight back to my parents, and she'll order the search warrant; we'll be right back to where we started. I can't see any way she can get a search warrant without The I.S. knowing." Katie lowered her voice. "They have eyes and ears everywhere."

Maggie looked in the direction Rebecca had gone. "Yeah...no kidding.

CHAPTER
thirteen

After PE Maggie pulled her tan sweater on and sat down on one of the benches in the locker room to pull on her brown suede boots. Rebecca came and sat next to her.

An intense moment of silence passed between them, and Maggie knew the girl had indeed overheard her conversation with Katie. What on earth was she going to do now? If Rebecca told, the consequences would be devastating.

Maggie finally broke the silence. "So…how have you been, Rebecca?" She wished her tone had come across as a little more relaxed than it sounded to her own ears.

"I heard you talking," she informed quietly, knowing right away why Maggie was so tense.

"Oh?" Maggie tried harder to come off relaxed, though she knew she was failing miserably.

"I heard you talking about some seriously taboo topics with a girl you just met. What makes you think you can trust her?"

Maggie didn't bother to maintain the pretenses. "Her

identity should indicate where her loyalty lies."

"That's quite a risk." Rebecca gave her a penetrating look, but Maggie could sense weariness in the girl. She wondered if she was already displaying some symptoms of illness.

"You're not doing very well, are you?" she asked softly.

Rebecca released a light laugh that didn't quite reach her eyes. "I'm no longer just HIV positive. I have AIDS. I've been told I still need to attend school, though, because I need an education for my future just in case they come up with a cure," she said with tainted humor. "The irony is almost too much to bear."

"I'm so sorry," Maggie breathed sincerely.

Rebecca sighed and her eyes dropped to her feet.

"I know where the lighter is."

Maggie's breath caught in her throat, and the atmosphere seemed to suddenly hum with anticipation.

"Mark kept it as a souvenir, if you can believe that. He told Bret that he got rid of it in the bay, but Derik knew the truth. When Mark got shot, Derik went to his house and took the lighter while Mark's parents were at the hospital. He was naturally afraid someone would find it. Now he's the one keeping it as a souvenir. I've heard them brag about the night they took it from you. I can't believe how sick these guys really are. How could I not have seen it sooner? I guess I used to be just as shallow as them."

Maggie closed her eyes. She had to take a moment to get a grip on the rage that suddenly clutched her. That lighter represented many horrible things. She had no doubt that it was a reminder to the boys of their triumph over her and over the legal system as well. It represented power— the power to do anything they pleased and get away with it, even murder. The idea that they were keeping it as a souvenir made her literally ill, and she knew at that moment that she would risk anything to take it away from them.

"So Derik has it?" Maggie couldn't help the urgency that had crept into her voice.

Rebecca's eyes rose to meet hers. "I doubt it will do you any good now since he was tried and found innocent. But, yeah, Derik has it in a small wooden box in his locker. It's been right under your nose."

"Aren't you afraid of telling me this?" Maggie questioned.

"Afraid of what? What are they going to do to me?" Bitterness crept into her voice. "Excommunicate me? They've already done that. Kill me? I'm already going to die."

"I've told you this before, Rebecca: Your life is not over yet. God still loves you, and he still has a purpose for your life as long as you draw breath."

"If he loves me, then why won't he forgive me?" she choked.

Maggie took Rebecca's hand and gave it a squeeze— it was probably the first time in a long while that someone wasn't afraid to touch her. "He forgives everyone who asks. Your illness is not his punishment—it's merely a consequence of your own choices. You weren't ignorant; you knew the risks of having sex. Everyone has consequences for every choice they make. I had to live with the consequences when I crashed the party at Nicole's house and got beat up. I had to live with the consequences when I chose to accept drugs from Mark. It was just that once, but I was hooked the first time. The drugs became my way of coping, and after a while I couldn't do without them.

"God might not take our consequences away, Rebecca, but he will walk with us through them. Do you understand that? Your circumstances can make your life a powerful testimony. If you can hold on to hope and courage in your circumstances, then others might be able to do the same in theirs."

Rebecca stared at her, her eyes brimming with tears. She looked beautiful and lost at the same time, but Maggie thought she read hope in her eyes.

"Do you really believe that, Maggie?"

"Yeah, I do."

Katie and Maggie watched Derik carefully the rest of the day and the next morning, noting his habits. More importantly they were watching his locker. They needed to know how often he opened it and at what time.

At lunch that day, Maggie took her things out of her locker and put them in her car, then slipped her lock into her purse. She met up with Katie at the cafeteria, and the two of them hatched a daring plan.

"This is risky," Katie said. "I'm not sure we can pull it off. If his friends are with him, there'll be others who are watching. I don't mind admitting that I'm terrified of Derik's vengeance, Maggie."

"If his friends are with him, we'll wait for a better time."

"Are you going to tell Peter?" Katie asked critically, her eyes meeting Maggie's gaze head-on.

"He's been…busy with work. I'll tell him when the time is right," Maggie said carefully.

And so they watched until the right opportunity arose. Maggie stood in the shadows between the end of the lockers and a support beam. The bell rang and students began to swarm into the hallways, the perfect pandemonium they needed to pull off their plan.

Sure enough, Derik headed toward his locker as if on cue; his friends weren't with him. He flicked through the combination on his lock and popped it open, allowing the lock to hang on the latch as he checked his reflection in a mirror that hung inside the door. He dragged his fingers through his shiny dark locks and adjusted the black leather jacket he wore over his beige V-neck sweater.

Maggie eyed Katie down the hall, and waited for her move.

Katie watched Derik with narrowed eyes. She was working up her nerve, waiting for the right time. She finally solidified her resolve. Briskly approaching Derik, she pretended to be in a hurry as she brushed passed him. She bumped into him, dropping her books. "Oh, I'm so sorry!" she said with all the believability of a first class actress. "I'm sorry, I didn't see you!"

Derik cast her a look of annoyance, unwilling to take his eyes off his locker for more than a few seconds. Stepping around her books, he got his things from inside and shut the door, making sure to lock it. When he walked off, Maggie joined Katie.

"Jerk. He didn't even bother to help you pick up your books."

"Did you expect him to?" Katie asked.

Maggie shrugged. "Let's see how long it takes him to figure this out."

"He's gone. Are you going to get the lighter now?"

"In front of all these witnesses? Think not! I'll wait till later. In the meantime we have other issues to attend to."

"I told you, Maggie, my parents will kill me."

"Hypothetically, right? What does it really mean when your parents are going to 'kill you'? A hefty grounding perhaps? You were the one who came to me with this and said you wanted justice."

Katie didn't answer. She was debating on how far she was willing to go. She had told Maggie about the DVD so that Maggie would know for sure the fire wasn't an accident; she had never intended to turn the DVD over to her.

Maggie sensed her anxiety. "Okay, Katie, let it go. Let them get away with murder. Can you live with that? Because I'm having a hard time dealing with what members of The I.S. did to my friend. Their evil, spoiled kids killed her, and then their parents took advantage of the fact by stealing her body to save one of their own. If they can do that, they're capable of anything."

Katie gave a shudder at the thought and then fell silent a moment. "I don't even know that the DVD is worth all this, Maggie."

"Your expression says otherwise."

"All right. If we can find the key. I am not busting that cabinet open."

"Fair enough."

Maggie watched from a distance as Derik went to his locker at the end of the day and realized he could not open it. He was obviously furious when he marched off to the office and returned with the janitor, who cut off the lock with bolt cutters. She couldn't contain the malicious smile that curved her lips as he looked through his things and realized they'd been tampered with and the lighter was gone. Baffled as to how such a thing could have happened, he cursed in rage and punched the locker door.

"I'll give you about a lifetime to decipher what happened, you stupid snake," Maggie said under her breath. "You won't be keeping any souvenirs of the pain you've caused as long as I can help it!"

She reached her fingers into her pocket then, feeling the shape of the dented lighter within the plastic bag. A lump rose in her throat as she was engulfed by her memories. She remembered the terror of the day they had overtaken her on the beach, and she remembered them taunting her over the death of her friend. At the mere thought of Jessica, Maggie felt her heart constrict over her loss. She tried to push the pain from her mind, but there were times that she missed her friend so deeply that she could hardly bear it. She blinked back tears, determined to be strong. So much had happened since she had first come into possession of this ominous object. Now things had come full circle, and once more she held it within her grasp.

That evening, Maggie met Katie outside her window after her parents were in bed. A strange warm wind mixed with cooler gusts was blowing Maggie's hair about her face, and she was having trouble controlling it.

"Wow. It's getting weird out there," Katie said, looking out. "The news predicted a tropical storm, or maybe even a hurricane, is going to hit in the next day or two."

"Well, I wouldn't worry about it now. Let me in, would you?"

Katie shoved her window up, and Maggie crawled in.

"Did you hide it?" Katie asked.

"Oh, rest assured. It's safe and sound. It might not be of any value, but it certainly won't be kept as some sick souvenir," Maggie replied.

"I'd pay money to have seen Derik's face when he realized it was gone!" Katie mused.

"What about the key to the cabinet? Did you find it?" Maggie asked.

"No. I looked everywhere. My mom really must have taken great pains to hide it."

"Then we'll take the door off its hinges."

"You've got to be kidding!"

"You know I'm not. Do you have any screwdrivers?"

"There's a junk drawer with a few screwdrivers right underneath the cabinet."

"Let's do it, then."

The girls slipped through the dark house, pulses racing. They moved quietly, stopping from time to time to listen for any movement coming from the other side of the house. Katie grabbed a flashlight, and the girls rummaged through the junk drawer until they found several screwdrivers. They tried each one until they found one that fit the screws on the hinges. One girl held the door while the other loosened and removed the hardware. Then both carefully removed the door, and Katie reached inside, feeling around until she found the padded envelope.

"I seriously hope this is worth the crap I'm going to take when my parents discover this thing missing. Maybe you can copy it to your hard drive and return it?"

"That's doable," Maggie agreed as she took the envelope and removed the DVD. "Here, keep the envelope. They'll never know it's empty. Of course, you could replace this DVD with another one in the meantime. I doubt they're going to watch it, so they'll never know it's not the original."

In a short while the girls had replaced the door, and Maggie slipped out of the house.

Her dad was asleep when she slipped in through her back door a few minutes later, tapping in the code to the new alarm system. Tennyson never knew she'd been gone, since he drove by to check on the house during the night, but didn't spend the night at her house.

She checked her cell and found a couple messages

from Peter. She knew he had been busy that day. He often worked before and after school and always put at least some time in on the weekends, but he never forgot to call.

Maggie closed the curtains and locked the doors before slipping the DVD into the laptop Peter had given her. Somehow she knew that everything she had ever needed to put these people away was suddenly within her possession, and she had never felt more excited.

She felt chills creep up her spine as an old man came on the screen. She had never seen him before, but she knew immediately that it was Old Man Keller. His face was pale, and he looked shaken. She noticed the perspiration that had beaded upon the lines on his forehead.

He cleared his throat and said, "If you are seeing this message, I'm probably dead. I want you to know the truth. I have been secretly working for Brian Chambers for some eight months now to supplement my retirement income. He paid me to deliver envelopes to others within his circle. I do not know what was in them, but I was paid well to do my job without asking any questions. It was during this time that I learned about The Inner Society. As I understand it, they are a dangerous inner circle of the elite who have infiltrated important political positions in Virginia and across the States.

"One day I delivered a package to the chief of police, Thomas Caldwell, in the office at his estate. He left the room to take a call, and I got a glimpse of some troubling files that had been left open on his laptop. These files on the server and on his hard drive contained strange information, such as many long lists of names and businesses across the States.

"Since then I've learned that The Inner Society has a private server, which can be accessed by all of their higher ranking members. That server contains critical information in regards to their future plans. This information seems pretty basic at first glance—but don't be fooled. Their files contain hidden messages only meant for their members to decipher. Certain words, for example, were consistently used in place of other words, which changed the entire meaning of the message conveyed. Errors in spelling, likewise, spelled out certain dates and the names of key people in the Senate and White House. I did some follow-up on the names on one of their lists, and I was shocked when I realized that every name on that list could be attached to an obituary.

"After further research, I have come to the conclusion that The Inner Society has set its sights on the White House, and they are eliminating anyone who gets in their way.

"Caldwell must have become suspicious when he realized he'd left me in the room with his laptop. I know he told Chambers about it, because Chambers questioned me later. I now have reason to believe that my life is in danger, and I am about to reveal to you the very secrets that The I.S. wants to keep hidden...."

Maggie couldn't shake the horrible image of the charred remains of Keller's house. The knowledge that some of those ashes were human was horrifying. She remembered wondering if that fire had been fatal. Now she was looking at the man whose ashes were mingled in with those blackened remains. The thought sent chills into the core of her being.

At that very moment, there was a loud knock on the door that nearly gave Maggie a heart attack. Why would anyone be visiting at this time of night? She felt her heart slamming against her chest as she frantically tried to retrieve the DVD from the laptop. A message came across the computer, though: DEVICE IN USE. CLOSE ALL PROGRAMS BEFORE EJECTING THE DEVICE.

The knocking on the door continued, and Maggie released a low, frustrated cry as she closed out the screen with shaky fingers and tried again to eject the DVD. The tray slowly slid open as her heart raced. She snatched the DVD from the tray, only to realize she hadn't saved it to her hard drive as Katie suggested. With increased anxiety, Maggie ran to the kitchen, dropping the DVD into an empty cookie jar on the counter and replacing the lid.

She gave a fresh start as she heard the knocking once more. Maggie frantically looked around her for some sort of protection. Unable to find the butcher knife, she grabbed a steak knife from the knife rack and went to the back door. Cracking it open, she let Courage in and locked the door behind him. He jumped up on her and licked her.

"Down, Courage! Heel!" she whispered fiercely. Courage immediately dropped to her side in an alert stance. His head snapped in the direction of the door as the knocking persisted, and his ears picked up. He followed her cautiously to the door. Courage was intelligent enough to sense when his owner wanted him to be silent, and he could move like a ghost when it was necessary. It was this unusual characteristic about Courage that had prevented Maggie's uncle from knowing he was there until it was too late.

Maggie reached the door and peered through the peephole. She released a shuddering sigh of relief when she realized it was Tai standing on her front porch. She nervously raked a hand through her hair, taking a moment to get a grip on her nerves, then put the knife down on the hall table and unlatched the door. A gush of wind blew leaves into the house as she opened it.

"What the heck are you doing here at this time of night?" she demanded. "You scared the snot out of me!" She was tapping in the code to the alarm as she spoke.

"I have to help Mr. Waters in the morning and…well, I just got off the bus and walked over here. I was hoping you'd let me crash on your couch."

"Are you crazy? What happened to the iPhone Peter set you up with? Considering you've been texting me daily, it must be in service."

"Yeah, well, I used up most of the minutes for the month, so I'm trying to cut back. Hey, I'm a handsome Hmong man—I have to keep up with the ladies."

"Seriously, Tai? Give me a break! It must be ten o'clock!"

"But I knew you stayed up late, my little honeybee."

"Oh my gosh, quit with the gooshie names, brat!"

"Would 'snob' work better?"

"I suppose that isn't quite as nauseating." Maggie rolled her eyes in disbelief. She could hardly stand the suspense now that she had to wait to find out what was on that DVD. Tai couldn't have pulled this stunt at a worse time. "I can't believe you just showed up here like this, and now you want to sleep on my couch! Really?"

"Oh, come on, snob. Don't pretend you're not happy to see me."

"You're insufferable, you little snot."

"Does that mean you'll let me stay? Waters hates me. He told me to be at his doorstep by 0500 hours or I can forget about working for him."

"5:00 a.m.?" she asked incredulously. "He's being

a real jerk! How'd he even know this hurricane threat has caused the schools to close tomorrow?"

"He watches the news. He said if I wanted to work I should be available, and since school is out, I'm available. He says his fence needs repairs, and the weather won't be any good for working by afternoon. Army men are up before the sun. He thinks I'm a punk kid, and there's no way I'll show. He's just trying to come up with an excuse to get rid of me. I'm not going to let him look down his nose at me, though. I am going to show him. I'll be there early and wake *him* up."

"Wow, I don't think this will be the right kind of weather for this kind of confrontation. I've heard that a lot of people are preparing to leave the area. Are you going to go to a shelter?"

"Probably not. Reporters get viewers to watch by exaggerating the news. I doubt it will get bad enough to do any real damage, but I wouldn't want to be doing any outside work, either."

Maggie's thoughts went back to Waters then, and she looked at Tai dubiously. "Speaking of storms, you two seem to be having your own. You're seriously not doing well, are you? You know, Tai, you need to consider if the money is worth the misery. I mean, you're traveling for hours to get here as it is. If that doesn't show where your heart is, I don't know what will. You've got to understand, Waters is a bitter old man. He is carrying a lot of baggage from his past, and even if he won't admit it, he's lonely. But that doesn't mean you should put up with his abuse."

Tai's expression became more humble. "You don't understand. No one will hire me anywhere. My mom needs the money for her doctor bills and medication. She has no one else to take care of her."

"You never told me what was wrong with her."

His eyes clouded over for a minute before he straightened up and swallowed his emotions. "She's in the final stages of cancer. She has six months to live."

"Oh, Tai...I'm so sorry." Maggie was suddenly overcome with emotion, and it was her turn to get a grip on herself. "I had no idea it was so serious." She was beginning to find a whole new respect for this troublesome kid who had the heart of a lion. She understood what it was like to face being alone in the world, though Tai's situation was worse than hers. Where on earth would he go if his mother died?

Now here he was asking to sleep on her couch so he wouldn't be late to work, and she had nearly tossed him out on his behind. "All right, you can stay." She moved aside, momentarily forgetting the DVD—as well as the possibility that she could be putting him in danger by allowing him to stay there.

She brought out a few blankets and a pillow for him. "Would you mind if I asked you a question?"

He shrugged. "Shoot."

"What happened to your father? Is he living?"

He paused for a moment of inner conflict, and Maggie could tell he was measuring how much he wanted to tell her.

"I never knew him. My mom won't talk about it, but I've heard people talking. A missionary dude who came by her village offered her a job in America as a maid. Her parents encouraged her to take it in order to escape the violence in their own country. They put together all the money they had to buy her plane fare.

"She arrived in Virginia shortly after, and the guy made good on his word. His church set her up as a scullery maid in a restaurant. People say she was taken in by some handsome dude almost right after she arrived. She was scared and alone in a place that was strange to her. I guess it was easy enough for him to tell her whatever she needed to hear to get what he wanted from her. Monster…. By the time she realized she was pregnant, he had already gotten tired of her and split. I don't think she ever knew what happened to him."

"Oh, I see. That must be really hard for her."

"It pretty much sucked. I try to make it easier for her, but she's very lonely. Hmong people are very social. Like I told you before, in places like Laos and Cambodia, people cook meals together around open fires. This is a time where people talk and hang out. When Hmong refugees come to America, they're alone. They don't know the language, and they eat meals isolated in their homes. It's not so easy. It is even worse when a woman is shamed and abandoned; she is treated differently because it is thought that she has bad luck."

"You need to bring her to church, Tai, or maybe we can get people to visit her if she's too ill."

"Thanks," he said. A new thought occurred to him then. "Will Peter be mad at me for staying here?"

She smiled. "Peter isn't the jealous type, but then I don't give him any reason to be jealous." The reality of her situation came back to her then, and she instinctively glanced at the cookie jar on the counter. "You really shouldn't stay here, though, Tai. This has to be a one-time deal. It's not safe. You don't need to end up dead on my account. Anyway, I'm sure Peter will let you crash at his house."

"Who wants to hurt you, Maggie?" he asked gravely. "Is it Derik and his friends or is it your uncle?"

Maggie's heart sank, and she hardened herself against the shame. She hadn't told Tai the details of the boys' anger, or her uncle's treachery, but, like everyone else, he must have seen it on the news. These weren't the kind of things people talked about, but there was no help for it now. What was done was done. She would have to deal with it.

"Maggie," Tai sensed her anxiety, "I would never let anyone hurt you. I would give my life for you!"

Maggie felt a sudden shockwave of fear at the sincerity in his tone. "Don't even talk like that, Tai! I am totally serious. I already have someone dead on my account. I don't need anyone else dying for me, please. And what the heck would your mother do if something happened to you? Have you thought of that?"

"I'm sorry," Tai said, realizing he'd upset her when he mentioned her uncle.

"Don't be. It is what it is."

"Where is the danger coming from now?" he persisted.

"I don't know, Tai. I know I'm being watched. Some anonymous person contacted Waters and offered him money to file charges against me for hit and run. I don't want to get you involved in this. Do you understand?"

Tai was silent a moment. "I have no family aside from my mom. I don't have any friends that aren't in a gang.

You're the best friend I have."

Maggie's heart twisted. She had once had a best friend….

"You're sixteen, Tai. You have your whole life ahead of you."

"And what are you, seventeen?" he shot back.

"You're still a stubborn brat," she laughed.

He grinned. "And you're still a snob."

CHAPTER
fourteen

Maggie watched TV with Tai for an hour or so, debating on what to do with the DVD. She knew by then that there was no way she was going to be able to watch it with Tai sleeping on her couch. Too much was happening too fast. She knew from experience how easily someone could take something from her. She couldn't keep that DVD in her house for long. She had to get it into the right hands before the wrong people figured out she had it. She debated on whether to call Peter or Megan Riley. It was too late for Peter to stop her now that she had both the lighter and the DVD. He would have no choice but to help her. Either way, she had new ammunition against The I.S., and she intended to use it. Justice was getting closer.

By the time their movie was over, Maggie was relatively confident that no one knew she had the DVD and decided it would be safe to wait until morning.

Maggie got up before daybreak, but before she called Peter or the D.A., she had to take care of Tai. She called Waters's house. The phone rang and rang obnoxiously until Waters finally answered.

"Who the heck is this?" he growled.

"I thought soldiers were supposed to be up at the crack of dawn?" Maggie snapped.

"What? Maggie, is that you? I swear I'd give you a good thrashing if you were here!"

"That's what you told Tai—that soldiers are up at the crack of dawn. Shouldn't you be up then, soldier, especially when you have a worker showing up?"

"Dawn hasn't cracked yet!" he raged.

"It has now! There's no excuse for the way you've been treating this poor kid." Waters tried to cut her off, but she wouldn't have it. "I'm not finished yet. This kid has no money, no father, and a mother who has six months to live. After that he's going to be completely alone in this world. Do you get that? The money you're paying him is all he and his mother have to buy medicine and pay doctor bills. So you're going to be nice to him, all right? Oh, and just in case you think he's put me up to this, you're wrong. He doesn't know I'm calling you."

"Are you quite finished?"

"Quite!"

"Then you might consider being less concerned about this kid, and more concerned about the impending hurricane that's coming."

"Seriously? You weren't worried enough to let Tai stay home today. But now that you know he's coming anyway, you want to use this supposed hurricane to keep him away."

"Fine then! Send that kid over here." He hung up on her, and she half-smiled to herself, satisfied. Waters would be furious with her for about two hours; then he would get over it. Their relationship was like that.

Maggie looked out the window and noted Tennyson's car was gone. He clearly didn't expect her to leave the house so early in the morning.

She drove Tai to Waters's house in her Audi, which Peter had, of course, returned to her. An unseasonably warm wind was whipping across Norfolk, and the very air seemed to be charged with electricity. The trees were swaying and leaves were flying everywhere. It was extremely bizarre weather for the first week of November, and Maggie wondered if maybe Waters had been right after all.

When they showed up at Waters's house, they were both a little surprised to find the old man on the porch, waiting for them.

"What took you so long?"

"What took so long is that I'm fifteen minutes early!" Tai snapped.

Maggie stood with her arms folded, glaring at the old man with a look of impending rebellion. Waters mimicked her for a moment but then threw up his hands in exasperation. "Well, then you might as well come in," he said to Tai. Can't have you starting too early—I'd have to pay you more."

Tai went up the steps and into the house, determined not to let Waters get under his skin, and Maggie followed to make sure the two of them behaved.

"Go ahead then. Sit down. Do you drink coffee?" Waters asked Tai. He already knew that Maggie did.

"In the absence of Hmong tea." Tai's reply had an edge to it, and Maggie elbowed him.

"Well, I don't have Hmong tea, or Indian corn, or African reefers, and I don't grow bamboo in my bathtub for good luck, either!"

Maggie couldn't help the laughter that spontaneously erupted from her.

"Coffee it is, then," Tai said with a hint of humor this time.

Waters gave him a double-take, sensing his satire and suppressing the fact that he was amused by it. A few minutes later they were actually sitting across from one another and drinking their coffee in silence as the wind whipped small debris against the windows. After a long while, Tai finally broke that silence.

"So why do you hate Hmong people? Did somebody mess with you in Vietnam, or do you just hate everyone?"

Waters glared at him. "You're an impudent little, cuss, aren't you?"

"So Maggie tells me."

Waters laughed unexpectedly at that. "She doesn't mind speaking her mind, does she?"

"Not too much."

"Hello? I'm right here, folks!" Maggie protested.

"How the heck did you get tangled up with this little hoodlum anyway, Maggie?"

Tai looked away sheepishly.

"I was passing out certificates for free food with the youth group when this little brat took my friend's purse. I tripped him and sent him sprawling on the asphalt. We blackmailed him into attending church in order to avoid pressing charges."

Waters laughed. "What a way to win souls! That sounds like you. She's got a lot of guts, kid," he said to Tai then. "You probably shouldn't mess with her."

After making sure things were okay between Tai and Waters, Maggie was eager to return home. On the way home, she called Peter's cell. She knew he'd be asleep at that hour, especially after working late, but she wanted to leave him a message. She had little doubt that he was mad at her for not returning his texts earlier. They always texted each other before bed, although last night had been an exception. Maggie left him a message apologizing for not replying to his texts and explaining that something had come up. She asked him to call her as soon as possible.

When she arrived home, Tennyson was still not there, and for the first time, Maggie wondered if there could be a connection between the DVD and the fact that Tennyson was absent. The very thought gave her goose bumps, and she couldn't help but think he could have been taken out by someone who was trying to get to her. Past events had taught her that anything was possible.

Maggie glanced around the area cautiously, absently noting all the litter that the wind had tossed into her yard. Her mind raced over all the possible scenarios that could account for why Tennyson was not there. But Tennyson had shown up past five-thirty in the morning more than once, and Maggie decided she was just being paranoid because she was in possession of the DVD.

She went to check on her dad, who at that hour was still sound asleep. She then hurried to the cookie jar and snatched out the DVD. The potential of what it could mean sent a course of adrenaline through her veins, and she shuddered. Keller's testimony could be all they needed to shut The I.S. down. Maggie grabbed the house phone sitting next to the jar, dialing the D.A.'s home phone number. Maggie was sure Megan wouldn't mind her calling so early for something so significant.

"Hello?"

"Ms. Riley?"

"Maggie?" She was on full alert now. "Where the heck have you been, and why haven't you returned my calls?"

"You're going to want to hear this: I've just managed to get hold of the missing lighter...."

"What?"

"I have the lighter, and I also have a DVD that I think will prove Chambers murdered Keller."

"Wait, Maggie, don't say anything more over the phone. Hold on a minute." Maggie could hear her rustling around. "I need to make some arrangements. Does your father know about this?"

"No. You know I never involve him if I don't have to."

"How long have you had this DVD? Wait, don't tell me yet. Go tell Tennyson to come in. I'll call you back on your cell phone in a few minutes. And for crying out loud, pick up your cell when I call!"

"Okay." Maggie looked out the window, but Tennyson was not there. Maggie was about to say so, but the D.A. had already hung up.

Maggie heard her father getting up and heading into the bathroom down the hall. She grabbed her keys and got into the Audi where her father would not hear her. She shoved the DVD into a hidden compartment beneath the driver's seat. A few moments later, her cell phone rang. She recognized the D.A.'s phone number right away.

"Yes?"

"Maggie, come to my house right away. We can talk there. Okay?

"All right. I'll be right over."

Maggie headed for the D.A.'s house but received another call before she got there.

"Hello?"

"Maggie, listen carefully: I have reason to believe your house phone has been tapped. You and your father need to get out of there immediately. Whoever tapped your line knows you have the DVD. Do you understand? If you haven't already left your house, *get out now*. I've got to get off the phone right now, but I'll call you on your cell phone with new instructions right away."

Maggie tried to call home and warn her father, but before she could, her cell rang yet again. She pulled off the road into a grove of trees and snatched up the phone.

"Maggie?" Megan asked.

"Do you still want me to go to your house?"

"No! It's one of the first places they'll check. Meet me at Fleet Park right now."

"But my father—"

"*Right now!*"

As she was heading toward Fleet Park, Maggie received a text telling her to meet at Lakewood Park instead. Maggie was confused. Lakewood Park was clean across town from Fleet Park. Lakewood, in fact, was right down the street from Megan's house. Wasn't that too close to home? Maggie checked the ID on the caller, though, and recognized Megan Riley's number.

Maggie could feel an odd tingling sensation that seemed to be warning her of danger. Instead of going directly to Lakewood, she pulled into a neighborhood that was parallel to it and parked the car. She got out and glanced around her, feeling extremely uncomfortable and vulnerable. She left the DVD in its hiding place and began walking toward Lakewood Park.

Being careful not to be seen, she stopped when she neared Lakewood Avenue, standing in the shadows of a large cypress, as her eyes scanned the area. The park was vacant, of course. It was early, and no one wanted to be out in weather like this. There was a car parked at the far end of the street that she did not recognize. There was no sign of the District Attorney's gold Cadillac anywhere. Suspicious and on alert, she quickly retraced her steps, retreating back to her car.

The wind kicked up, raising goose bumps on her

arms, and she shivered. She zipped up her jacket a little higher. Leaves came showering down from the trees, and Maggie gave a start when a twig smacked her in the head. A plastic bag suddenly slapped her in the face, and she took in a sharp breath. The plastic snapped tight around her mouth, cutting off her air. She ripped the bag away from her face and threw it away from her. The wind kicked it upward, carrying it high into the ominous sky. She took in a deep breath, trying to calm her jangling nerves.

She was feeling panicked as she tried to decide what she was going to do. Did Megan really send her that text message? Should she head to the woman's home that was only a block away, or should she head to Fleetwood Park? Again she glanced around to make sure she was not being followed. All she wanted now was to get rid of that blasted DVD!

Maggie got back in her car and dialed home again, but her father didn't answer. He'd probably gone back to bed. She wondered if he was in danger as she replayed her conversation with the D.A. in her mind. She had said aloud that her father did not know about the DVD. Did that give him some protection? She hoped so.

Maggie thought of going back home to warn him, but she knew that they could be watching and waiting for her to do just that. She could be bringing death home with her.

Megan wasn't here. Maggie was beginning to feel frantic. In a soaring moment of indecision, she decided to go to the D.A's house, even though Megan had said it wasn't safe. She didn't know what else to do at that point. Maggie drove the short distance to Megan's, willing herself to stay calm. She knew, though, that anyone looking for her would be watching out for her Audi, so she pulled into the alley behind the D.A.'s house instead of parking in front.

The clouds had darkened the sky, and Maggie used the cover of that darkness to hop the white picket fence and land in the D.A.'s backyard. Cautiously she made her way across the yard and toward the massive two-story Cape Cod. Anxiously glancing around her, she went around the side of the garage where no one would see her and peered into the window.

Megan's Cadillac was parked inside. She had never even left the house.

Maggie sucked in a breath of air as cold terror began to constrict her airway. There was a loud creaking sound. Her head snapped in its direction, and she saw that the wind was causing the gate between the garage and the house to swing back and forth. It suddenly slammed shut with a loud bang that nearly made her leap out of her skin. After taking another moment to take in a deep breath and still her nerves once more, Maggie looked for a way in, and her attention was drawn to the back door of the house as it stood wide open.

Maggie took several deep breaths and desperately tried to think. She knew this was all wrong, but who could she call? The police? She wouldn't get any help from that quarter! She didn't technically have anything to report anyway. Nothing had happened.

In utter trepidation, Maggie looked both ways, listening intently for any sound as she slipped quietly through the back door. The house was dark, but she had been here a few times before, and knew where she was going when she made her way cautiously through the kitchen and into the living room.

Even in the dark, it didn't take her long to spot the overturned coffee table and the lamp that had been knocked over and broken. Pieces of glass littered the floor.

In that next horrifying moment, Maggie's eyes finally took in the form of Megan Riley, lying on the floor in a gruesomely unnatural position. A large knife protruded from the woman's back, and her white blouse was soaked in blood.

It seemed as if the walls were closing in on her, and Maggie's heart was beating so hard that her blood was pounding in her ears, followed by a high-pitched ringing that clamored through her brain. This was punctuated by a sharp headache. Maggie had seen death before, and she knew instinctively that the woman was dead.

Chest pains suddenly gripped her as the frightening knowledge sunk in, and she began to struggle to suck in air. A panic attack, perhaps? Maggie whispered a desperate prayer, fervently trying to cling to her faith.

Now what was she going to do? She couldn't exactly hang out and make phone calls right then when she couldn't determine whether or not she was actually alone.

But that question was soon answered as a small noise came from the bedroom. Snapping to attention Maggie immediately fled the scene, making her way back to the Audi. She was still struggling against hyperventilation as she slammed the driver's door shut and forced the key into the ignition. Her hands were trembling, and it took her several tries to even get the key into the slot.

"What am I going to do now?"

The question bounced off the walls of her mind as she struggled for an answer that was not coming to her. The car came to life, and she slammed it into drive, pulling away from the curb. She had to ditch the DVD and get hold of Internal Affairs. Without the District Attorney, she didn't know who to trust anymore. She had never realized, until that moment, how dependent on the D.A. she had really become. Megan was one of the only people in the legal system she'd been able to trust. Maggie's heart went out to the poor woman who'd become another victim in this deadly game.

As she made the corner and passed Megan's street, Maggie looked into her rearview mirror and saw a car parked across the street from her house. She wondered if it was the same car she'd seen at the park, but she hadn't seen the car clearly enough to tell. Either way, Maggie just knew she had to get away. She wasn't sure where she was going, but she kept driving. She checked her mirror a half dozen times to see if she was being followed, but no one was behind her. She was terrified for her father and terrified Tai would go back to her house before leaving Norfolk. Whatever she was going to do, she couldn't chance going back to them and leading a killer right into their laps. The I.S. knew about the DVD, and they were serious enough about keeping it secret that they had murdered Ms. Riley within a terrifyingly short time of her finding out about it.

There was no question that their hit man was now enthusiastically searching for Maggie, and that she was going to be at a serious disadvantage since he would know who she was but she wouldn't know him. She had to first put distance between herself and the area and then find a safe place where she could place some calls without being seen.

Maggie made it across town, eastward toward the coast, where she slipped down a dirt road into a grove of trees. She put the car in park and took out her cell, dialing Waters's house.

"Yeah?" Waters's gruff voice came on the line.

"Mr. Waters, its Maggie. I'm…I'm kind of in some trouble."

"What kind of trouble, kid?" His tone did not mask his sudden concern.

"I…never mind that. I need you to make sure Tai does not go back to my house. Please just do that for me."

"Where are you? This weather is turning bad. The news is saying a hurricane will actually hit by four o'clock. Can you get to my house?"

The call suddenly dropped. Maggie gave a violent start as a small branch crashed down on her windshield. No damage was done, but the wind was obviously picking up. She wondered if a storm could give her some ironic reprieve from anyone who happened to be after her, but she doubted it.

The reality of what she had seen at the D.A.'s house began to solidify in her mind, and she could feel her hands starting to shake with adrenaline again. By the time she finally got through with her father, she was beginning to wonder if she wasn't in shock.

"Dad?"

"Maggie! Where the heck are you? Did you know we have a hurricane on the way?" The connection was full of static.

"Listen, Dad. I can't talk over the phone. I'm in trouble and you could be in danger. You need to get out of the house. Go to Peter's. Please, just do as I say. That's all I can tell you right now."

She hung up. She had to. She was afraid that, if her home phone was tapped, someone also might be tracking her cell phone transmissions. She desperately hoped her father would do as she asked, but she knew there was a possibility that he would not leave the house without her.

Her phone went off in her hands, and she jumped. She snapped it open and breathed an inward sigh of relief when she realized it was Peter.

"Peter?"

"Maggie! Where have you been? I've been trying to reach you!"

"Peter, Megan's dead!"

"What are you talking about?"

"I just took the lighter back from Derik, and I got hold of a DVD that's going to do some serious damage to The I.S. I'm sure they'd do anything to get hold of it. Ms. Riley called me and told me they tapped my house phone, so they know I have it! When I went to meet with her, she didn't show. I went to her house and found her dead! Do you hear what I'm saying?" She was screaming in hysteria now. "She was on the floor with a freaking knife in her back!"

"Don't say any more over the phone. Where are you?" Static came on the line again.

"Maggie?"

"I'm losing signal, Peter."

"Come straight to my house, right now!" His voice had risen in urgency. "The governor called for a voluntary evacuation."

"But, my dad…!" There was more static. The line went dead.

CHAPTER
fifteen

Maggie could feel her blood rushing through her veins as her temples began to throb. She was scared out of her mind. She needed to ditch that DVD quickly, but she wasn't ready to leave it just anywhere. She put the car into drive and slammed her foot on the accelerator. Her tires spun and dirt kicked up everywhere before traction took hold, and the car sped onto the road.

It was unusually dark for the hour, and the roads were already deserted. People had either left to shelters or were hunkered down in their homes, ready to wait out the storm. Massive dark clouds were forming overhead, and the rain began to come down in sheets.

Twenty minutes had passed when Maggie became startlingly aware that a pair of headlights had appeared directly behind her car. A sickening sense of déjà vu struck her. This had happened too many times lately. In panic, Maggie pushed the Audi faster and faster, but the other vehicle sped up until it was directly on her bumper. It was so close that she thought it was going to ram her.

Scared out of her mind, Maggie ran a red light; the other car did the same. She then tried to lose him by making a tight right turn. The Audi skidded sideways on two wheels, and she nearly lost control, but she managed to make the turn. The sedan hit the brakes too late to follow. The vehicle skidded past the turn, its tires screaming.

Maggie sped down the wet streets, rain now beating down upon her windshield so hard she could barely see. For one brief moment she looked into her rearview mirror and thought she had lost the guy.

Then without warning, the vehicle suddenly shot out from a side street, directly in front of her.

In abject panic, Maggie swerved to avoid T-boning the car. The Audi skidded sideways on the slippery road, nearly crashing into the other vehicle anyway. At the last second, her tires suddenly gripped the road and shot forward. Maggie nearly lost control and was forced to steer down a dirt side road to keep from crashing into the trees alongside the road. Now the sedan was behind her again, and she was unable to get back onto the main road.

Maggie swerved to miss a large pothole just as an explosion rent the air in two. "Dear God, he's armed!" she cried. There was no longer any question as to the driver's intent. He was going to shoot her down.

"God, I could use your help right now!"

The last thing she needed was to get caught alone in a deserted place. She was keenly aware of how easily she could disappear. It would be only too simple for her to end up as another name on the missing persons list.

Maggie wasn't sure where the dirt road went, but she had the strong feeling that she was heading toward a dead end—in more ways than one. She sped down the slippery road that wound through a forested area, weaving frantically to avoid being hit by a bullet. She was struggling to control her racing senses as she desperately sought any place that was wide enough for her to make a quick turn around and head back out onto the main road. Another shot rang out, and Maggie's back window exploded into a thousand pieces. Cold air rushed into the car.

Rain, leaves, and sticks pelted the windshield, and rain was whipping into the car from the back window. Maggie struggled to see through the glass, and for one frightening second, her vision suddenly focused on a tree that had fallen across the road. She quickly swerved to the right, steering the Audi up a slight incline and around the tree, coming down on the road on the other side. Her heart slammed against her chest as she flashed back to the time she had been driving in similar conditions with her mother and the tragedy that followed....

By the time the driver of the sedan saw the tree, there was no time to evade it and he crashed into it head-on.

"Game over." Maggie hit the gas, speeding down the road in the only direction she could go. In a short time the road looped around, and she was sick with relief when it led back to the main road. She glanced behind her, seeing no sign of the other vehicle. She had miraculously managed to lose the guy. "Thank you, Lord," she breathed in relief.

She continued down the main road, acutely aware that she was still in dire danger. If the driver had survived the crash, he would surely contact his friends. Her cell phone chirped, and she looked sideways at her purse. Leaning across the seat, she fumbled through her purse until she got a grip on the cell phone. Her eyes were straining to see where she was going and at the same time watching for anyone who could be following her.

Her cell phone rang in her hand, this time the tone coming in stronger, and Maggie noticed she had two bars of signal as she flipped it open. "Hello?"

"Maggie? Where the hell are you?" Tennyson cried. "I don't know everything that's been going on, but Megan obviously thinks this is serious. She sent me to find you immediately."

"Megan's dead," Maggie choked.

"What are you talking about? I just talked to her!"

"She's dead. I saw her body!"

Tennyson let loose with another cuss word. "Are you sure?"

"Of course I'm sure!" Maggie nearly screamed. "Do you think I'd say something like that if I wasn't? I'm also being followed. I ditched the guy, but I'm sure he has friends."

"What are they after, Maggie?" he asked.

"A DVD."

"What's on it?"

"I haven't seen the whole thing yet, but I know Old Man Keller named Chambers as his killer."

There was a moment of silence as Tennyson thought that over. "That could change everything, couldn't it? Where's the DVD?"

"I've got it."

"With you?"

"Yes."

"Are there any copies?"

"No. I didn't have time to make any."

"Where are you now?"

She hesitated, realizing she didn't know who she could trust at all right then.

"Now isn't the time for second thoughts, Ms. Kraus. I'm trying to save your butt!"

She glanced down at the phone's screen. "Hold on, I have another call coming through."

"Don't answer that!" Tennyson barked, but she switched the line over anyway.

"Peter?"

"Maggie! Dang it! Where are you?" he yelled, obviously frantic.

"I've just pulled onto Virginia Avenue. Someone is after me, Peter. He shot at me, but I ditched him."

"Dear God, Maggie," Peter choked in panic. "Pull over now, I'm coming to get you."

"No! Don't do that." The last thing she wanted was to get Peter involved in this. The only reprieve she had was the knowledge that he was safe.

"Then can you make it to my house?"

"I think so. Is my dad there yet?"

"What do you mean? No one has showed up here. Was he supposed to come over?"

Crap! Maggie thought. This changed everything.

Peter knew immediately that her silence meant she was planning trouble. "Maggie, don't go back to your house. Do you hear me? You're dad probably went to a shelter."

Without her? Yeah, right! "Look, Peter, I'm driving and these roads are dangerous. Let me off the line now."

"You are coming straight over here, right?"

Without answering she made to switch back to Tennyson, but she lost signal and the call dropped.

Maggie's mind was racing as she zipped down the road. Why hadn't her dad gone to Peter's like she'd asked? She was struck with the sudden fear that the killer had gone to her house. Sick with dread, Maggie took a detour and headed directly home. She knew it was dangerous, but there was no way she wasn't going to go back for her father.

Maggie swerved around the debris in the road but was then blocked off by flooding in the street. She made her way back down the road and found another way around through an alternate street. Driving as fast as she was, it didn't take her long to get to the end of her street, where she cut the lights and parked in the shadow of a large bush. Peering down the street, she strained to see if there were any unfamiliar cars parked anywhere near her house. She saw none. The streets were deserted.

She wondered what the risk was of showing up at her house for even just a few minutes. Her heart was pounding in fear for her father. She had to get him out of there. Maggie checked her cell phone only to see that, once again, she had no reception. She knew there was a good possibility that the storm had knocked out all electricity and cell towers by now.

Eventually she decided it was better to take the risk than to leave her dad in danger. She pulled into her driveway.

Her father met her at the doorstep, and they gripped each other in a desperate hug. "Oh my god, sweetheart, I've been worried sick!"

"Why are you here, Dad? I told you to go to Peter's. You have to leave *now*."

"I knew you were in trouble, and I knew you weren't at Peter's. Two men showed up at our door and asked where you were. I thought they were cops. When I told them I didn't know where you were, they searched the house. I was terrified for you, so I went looking for you myself after they left. I just got back right now."

"Dad, you shouldn't have done that!"

He ignored her worry. "This thing is really bad, isn't it?"

She hadn't told him everything, but she knew he wasn't referring to the storm thundering above their heads. "It's not good. Let's just get Courage and get to Peter's house." Her hair whipped about her as she spoke, and she pulled it away from her mouth.

"He's gone, Mags."

"What do you mean, 'he's gone'?" Maggie cried.

"When I came home from looking for you, Courage was gone. I have no idea what happened to him."

"Was the gate left open?"

"Yes, but I don't remember opening it."

Maggie's mind swirled. She wasn't leaving without Courage. He had been her loyal friend ever since she first came to Norfolk. She steeled her resolve.

"Okay, Dad. We've got to get out of here in case those men come back. Take the truck and head to Peter's. I'm going to grab my stuff, and I'll be right behind you. Okay?"

"Please don't take too long. This storm is getting nasty."

"Okay, Dad. Go now. Please hurry."

Her father reluctantly complied, and she followed him to the truck, giving him a hug before he got in. In a few more seconds, he was heading out onto the road.

It was when she turned back that the front door suddenly blew shut with a bang, and she saw the papers taped to the door with duct tape. She immediately ripped them off, looking over them with apprehension. They were papers from the SPCA with a description of Courage and the schedule for euthanasia. A note was attached, and Maggie's eyes followed the words with trepidation: ***This time it was the dog. Next time it will be you.***

Her heart clenched in anguish, and tears filled her eyes. Maggie swallowed the lump in her throat as every memory she'd ever had with this dog came pouring back into her tortured mind. Courage had given her a reason to live when she'd given up on life. He had been her faithful friend ever since the day she'd taken him in. The thought that he'd been punished because of her was more than she could bear.

Was Courage really at the pound? The pound had to have been closed today, she thought. She looked again at the papers. They looked legitimate. If they were, it meant these people had managed to get someone from the SPCA to participate in this. One of the two men who had been at her house must have brought the paperwork with him. She could only be glad they hadn't put a bullet in Courage's head and tacked the note to his body. But why hadn't they? Why would they resort to threats now when they were trying to kill her earlier? Maybe they wanted to frighten her into silence until they managed to track her down.

She experienced a moment of soaring indecision. What was she going to do now? Time was of the essence, and she had to get out of there for more reasons than one. Even if she was able to avoid the hit men, the hurricane was supposed to strike in full force within hours, and the weather was already wild.

She knew she shouldn't head for the pound. It was a dangerous and stupid thing to do. Someone was out to kill her, and it was obvious that she would be risking her life. Courage might not really even be there, anyway. Besides, if she headed for the pound to see if he was there, no one would ever know where to look for her. On the other hand, if she called Peter or Tennyson and told them she was heading to the pound, she would never make it there at all.

Visions of her beloved dog locked in some cold cell, waiting for her to save him played in her mind. Her anxiety grew. After a final wave of uncertainty, she made up her mind. It didn't matter whether or not he was there. The SPCA was only fifteen minutes from there, given the roads were passable, and she'd never forgive herself if she didn't try to save him. Maggie could feel something in her spirit cringe at the very thought of breaking into the building. She was being stupid, and she was doing wrong, but she was willing to risk anything to save her Courage…even wisdom.

Getting into her car, she headed toward the SPCA, hoping she wouldn't get lost. She'd never been there before, but there was an address on the papers. She'd also seen pictures of the place on commercials and knew it was an old brick building accessed by a long dirt road that led through a park-like property. This meant it was in an isolated location—not a good thing for her. If she had her facts straight, it was also located in a major flood zone.

By then the winds were so strong that she had to fight the wheel to keep the car steady. The streets were filling with water, and it was becoming more and more difficult to navigate. It hadn't developed into a massive storm yet, but it packed a dangerous punch. Maggie peered through the windshield, noting that, not too far away, a car had been abandoned after hitting a power pole. The city was now clothed in blackness, and it appeared that the power was out for the entire area.

To her dismay, when Maggie reached the SPCA, she could see that it was deserted, and a large portion of the gray brick building was under several inches of water. She looked around cautiously, seeing no one. She then parked between a large bush and a dumpster where no one would see it. It was a no-brainer that this could be a trap, and she intended to take precautions. She intended to do what she came to do and get out of there quickly.

At Waters's house, Tai was chomping at the bit. Waters had insisted that Tai remain with him in his basement. The transportation systems were down, anyway, and he couldn't go back to Richmond. So there they sat in a couple of old overstuffed armchairs, bundled up by the propane heater.

The minute Waters fell asleep, Tai snuck up the stairs and out of the house. He had overheard the conversation Waters had with Maggie, and he knew she was in trouble. He was scared out of his mind for her. He had seen the news reports; he could only imagine what these people were capable of. He had to find her, however impractical the odds.

He went outside and quietly lifted the garage door, looking at Waters's new blue Oldsmobile. His thoughts were churning in his head as he glanced up and down the street, feeling incredibly guilty for even thinking what he was thinking. But he shook the feeling away as he popped the hood, removed the dipstick, and shoved it into the slight opening of the driver's side window, working it until he managed to pop the lock and open the car. He grabbed a screwdriver from a workbench and used it to open up the steering and hotwire the vehicle.

He soon made it through the storm to Maggie's house, thankful that it was only about five blocks away. The winds were so strong that the rain was pelting the windshield in sheets, and he was having a hard time steering straight. When he reached her driveway, he found the vehicles gone and the front door unlocked. He went in for a quick perusal and found the SPCA papers on the kitchen table. He scratched his head thoughtfully. She couldn't possibly have gone there, could she? But, then again, Maggie was reckless. That was part of what made her Maggie.

Maggie made her way through the water, which was now a good six inches deep, and peered into one of the windows. She then found a note on the door that read: CLOSED DUE TO WEATHER. There was no one there.

Everyone had sought shelter, leaving the poor animals behind. She had a quick vision of Courage locked up as the water slowly crept through the building. She shivered at the thought and decided she didn't care if she got into trouble; she wasn't going to leave Courage there under any circumstances.

She was scared half to death as she went around the perimeter of the building, checking for a window she could slide open. Unfortunately, the building was old and the windows had to be opened with a crank; there was no chance of getting them to open from the outside. The only hope for getting in was breaking a window. Maggie felt a twinge of guilt over that, but decided God would be more concerned about his animals being abandoned than her breaking in to save them. She hurried back to her car and popped the trunk. She searched for her tire iron without success, forgetting that she had taken it out of the car and left it in her garage after they'd changed a flat on the truck.

Dang it!

Lightning flashed and thunder boomed overhead. A mournful howling sound seemed to rise above the noise of the storm, and Maggie knew it was coming from within the building. Her heart twisted in sympathy for the poor animals, and she was more determined than ever in the conviction that she had to save them.

Maggie wrapped her arms around herself for meager warmth as she braved the miserable weather in her search for a way in. The rain pelted her in the face, and her shoes sunk into the sodden earth with every step, the water sloshing in and soaking her socks. The place was creepy in the dark, with its large oaks branching across the building like long, dark arms with scraggly fingers. It looked more like an insane asylum than an animal shelter.

"You don't listen too well, do you?" A voice came from directly behind her and nearly gave her a heart attack.

"Tennyson? You scared me to death!" Maggie cried. Taking hold of her shattered nerves, she gathered her resolve. "I'm not leaving without my dog!" she vowed, prepared to do battle if he decided to try to drag her out of there. "And how did you know where I was anyway?"

Tennyson fingered his car keys in his hand. "I found out your dad showed up at Peter's, but you didn't. I went back to your house and found the papers. I figured you were stupid enough to actually come out here. I've never met such an obnoxious, rebellious teen."

"Then perhaps you've never met the other teens of Norfolk!" Maggie snapped.

At that moment Tennyson accidentally dropped the keys in his hand, and Maggie snatched them up. She headed for his car before he could stop her. "Hey, stop! What are you doing?"

"I know you have a tire iron in your trunk, and I'm going to bust that window in."

He tried to grab for her, but when he took a step toward her, he stepped into a very deep puddle and lost his balance, landing on his backside, which gave Maggie enough time to reach for his Mercedes.

Maggie briefly fumbled for the right key and quickly popped the hood open before he could catch up with her. She soon realized she couldn't see into the pitch blackness of the trunk. She felt around for the tire iron but found a flashlight instead, and flicked it on.

The light bounced off of a small object. When she

leaned closer to see what it was, the blood in her veins turned to ice.

It was a gold earring, covered in blood. There were more stains in the gray lining of the trunk. She stared unbelievingly at them and then back at the earring. Something in the back of her racing mind told her that it looked familiar. Then she remembered…it was the D.A.'s!

"He killed Ms. Riley!"

A twig cracked behind her, and she spun around, coming face to face with her bodyguard.

"What seems to be the problem, Ms. Kraus?" he asked, his tone foreboding.

Maggie looked up at him through new eyes as he suddenly transformed into a terrifying stranger. He stood there like a shadowy tower, the wind whipping through his dark hair where it was longest at the back by his collar. His focus was so intently upon her that he was oblivious to the rain that pelted down upon his leather jacket. Maggie shivered, unable to suppress the insane notion that the storm itself was generating from within the darkness of his very soul. She was struck by the chilling realization that she was seeing him for the first time.

Feeling icy fingers of terror creep up her spine, she took just one stumbling step backward. Even in the darkness, the fear in her eyes was unmistakable as she secretly slipped the earring into her pocket. She would have run, but like some terrible nightmare, she was somehow frozen in place. He was too close for her to outrun him, anyway.

"I don't understand," she choked.

He cocked his head in mock curiosity. "Understand

what? I get the strong impression that you and I are on the same page now."

"But...Ms. Riley trusted you!"

"We were colleagues, why wouldn't she?"

"But—"

"Where's the DVD, Maggie?"

"Figure it out yourself!"

He caught her by the hair, and her spine snapped rigid when she suddenly felt the cold metal of his pistol against her ribs. He dragged her to the car and began searching, to no avail.

"I'm done playing with you. Where's the DVD?" To Maggie's horror, he took her by the arm and pushed the gun into her elbow. "You have about three seconds. One... two...."

"Under the driver's seat!" she gasped.

He found the hidden drawer, pulled it open, and took hold of the DVD. Her heart sunk as he dropped it to the ground and smashed it with his boot. He still had a hold on her when he picked up the pieces, stuffing them into his pocket.

He surprised her when he tucked his gun into the back of his jeans, but any relief she might have felt was short-lived. In the next terrifying instant, Tennyson suddenly jerked her closer. Positioning her back against his chest, he took a firm grip on her jaw and head with his hands. He leaned close to her ear so that she could hear him above the storm.

"Sorry. I don't want to leave any blood behind if I don't have to. I'll make this quick," he promised, his tone devoid of emotion.

He was going to break her neck. She held her breath, awaiting the crack that would end her life.

But no sooner had he taken hold of her than he suddenly fell forward, collapsing right on top of her, his dead weight taking her down. Maggie gave a cry of pain as she hit the ground and the wind was knocked out of her. She twisted her head sideways and looked up in astonishment. Tai was standing over them, holding the elusive tire iron in a death grip.

"Tai!"

"Maggie, are you okay?"

"Get him off me!"

Tai immediately helped her to roll Tennyson off of her. He went to the agent's side to check his pulse.

"Is he dead?" Maggie asked. Even in the darkness she could see the blood on the side of the man's head.

"I…I think so," Tai said in trepidation as he tried to control the inner quaking that had seized his body.

They were silent a moment as the rain poured down upon them, and both were considering what their next move should be. As they did so, they simultaneously looked around anxiously for any sign of another person, but saw none.

"How did you know where I was, and how did you get here?" she asked at length, unable to stop the trembling that had taken over her nerves.

"I hotwired Waters's car so I could save my gorgeous babe. I went to your house and found the note." He motioned to the Oldsmobile which was parked some distance away. "I told you I would do anything for you, Maggie." He tacked on this last with a more serious note. There was a slight quiver in his voice, the only indication that he was scared out of his wits.

Maggie shook her head in disbelief. "He's going to kill you, Tai."

"How could you say such a thing? The guy loves me!"

"Your sarcasm isn't going to help, either."

They were silent a moment before she spoke again. "You saved my life."

"Don't worry. You were never in any serious danger, my little pumpkin."

"Not in danger? He was going to kill me!"

"Not as long as you're still wearing my good luck neck string," he said motioning toward the red string she still wore around her neck. "See, no harm can come to you."

She couldn't see his expression in the dark, but she could hear the nervous laughter in his tone. "Wow, you have incredible timing for a joke."

"Come on, Maggie. We need to get Courage and get out of here."

CHAPTER
sixteen

Tai went back to the Mercedes and picked up the flashlight Maggie had dropped when Tennyson startled her. She followed him to the large window in the front of the SPCA, where he bashed the glass in with the tire iron.

"Aren't you afraid of setting off any alarms?" she asked.

"Seriously, Maggie, we're having a power outage! I doubt any alarms will be functioning."

"I guess not," she agreed, somewhat embarrassed. Tai stepped through the glass and then helped her to follow. He ran the flashlight through the room, and Maggie noted that they were standing in about three inches of water which had covered the cement floor. It was definitely eerie standing in the water inside a pitch-black brick building. It didn't help matters that it smelled like mold and dog hair.

"If we don't find Courage within five minutes, you have to promise we'll get out of here."

That was fair, after everything the kid had just done—and was doing—for her. "All right," she consented, reluctantly.

Tai went behind a counter where there were several hooks with keys.

"We'll never find the right one!" Maggie cried in dismay.

Tai smiled. "Yeah, we will. It has to be one of these." He grabbed a small towel from off of the counter and used it to retrieve four silver keys that were about the same size and shape off of the hooks.

"What are you doing?" she asked.

Tai looked at her incredulously. "You don't think I'm going to leave my fingerprints behind, do you?"

They proceeded down a long hallway, making a pathway through the water as it filled their shoes and soaked their socks.

"How do you know which keys will work?" Maggie asked.

"I don't exactly. I just have a good idea. I've broken into a few cars and houses. I know keys pretty well," he explained. "Don't touch nothin'."

As they approached the kennels, the dogs began whining and barking. They were obviously wet and miserable. It was cold inside that dark building, and Maggie was feeling a little more than terrified. They made their way past one empty cage after another before the flashlight shone down upon the gray and white face of a skinny Australian shepherd. He whined in misery as he reached a paw through the bars to get their attention. In a few minutes they'd set him free. Maggie gave him a pat, and he bounded off through the water, disappearing through the broken window. They set two other dogs free before making their way through to some more empty cages.

"Maybe they put him down already," Maggie said dismally, but then she heard a familiar whine and her hope renewed. "Tai, that sounds like him!"

They ran to the cage on the end where they found a very wet and miserable Courage. His ears pricked forward when he saw them, and he began jumping around and barking in excitement. Tai unlocked the door, and Courage went flying into Maggie's arms, nearly knocking her over.

"My poor baby!" She clung to him and kissed his head.

"Come on, Maggie; let's get out of here now!" Tai urged, anxious to leave.

Just as they stepped outside, the large SPCA sign came crashing down five feet from them. They gave a violent start and then ran toward the Audi, Courage hot on their heels.

Tai stopped as they neared the vehicle.

"What?" Maggie asked.

"What do you mean, 'what'?" Tai said. "Your entire back window has been blown out!"

"Oh, that. I was shot at." Maggie fumbled with her keys.

"You have to tell me what's going on, Maggie."

"I don't want to involve you, Tai. The less you know the better."

"I just killed a guy for you! Don't you think it's a bit

late for me to not be freaking *involved*?"

Maggie's hair was whipping in her face again. She ducked, too late, as another twig smacked her in the face. "Ouch! Maybe we should have this conversation inside the car, huh?"

They got into the Audi. Wind was still whooshing in through the missing back window, but they were protected on three sides at least. Tai looked at Maggie with eyes of fear. "Please tell me, Maggie."

Maggie sighed but knew it was a bit late for secrets. "I got hold of a DVD that would have incriminated The Inner Society. Tennyson just took it from me and destroyed it. As far as they know, I'm now the only living proof that the DVD existed at all. If I had been able to pass the DVD on to someone on our side, then they wouldn't have needed to shut me up because the DVD itself would have told the story."

"What was on it?"

"I was watching it when *you* showed up and *interrupted* me," she answered with slight irritation. "I didn't get the chance to view it all, but Old Man Keller claimed he worked for Chambers and that Officer Caldwell had some sensitive information on his hard drive and more information on a private database or server or something that The I.S. is linked to. That information made him think they are after the White House and willing to kill anyone who gets in their way."

"So, if you had been able to pass on what Keller said was on Caldwell's laptop, then you'd be off the hook?"

"Well, in theory. They'd have no reason to try to shut me up. Not a hundred percent sure they wouldn't still take me out – just out of sheer malice."

Tai thought that over. He could feel his stress levels rising as he reluctantly came to an inevitable conclusion.

"What are you thinking?" Maggie asked.

He looked over at her, releasing a heavy sigh.

"What?"

"We need to hit Caldwell's house."

She blinked. "Yeah, *right*."

"No. I'm serious. If I can get to Caldwell's laptop, I might be able to recover whatever information Keller found."

"How?"

"I could get access to his computer remotely through a VPN and a private proxy."

"Couldn't they find out it was you?" Maggie asked, acutely aware that, for the first time, Tai was more knowledgeable than she was. That felt weird.

"No. But it won't matter, anyway." Tai was rethinking. "I couldn't get through during this storm, not with the signal being jacked up. The computer would have to be on, anyway."

"What if we could get to that laptop? Could you get past his password and login?"

"If I had time, I could have installed a RAT and got his login. I could then use a Brute-force attack to crack his password, but I'd have to have my Brute-forcing software with me." He looked over at her and caught her expression.

He suddenly broke into a dazzling smile. "I've lost you haven't I?" he asked smugly.

Maggie made a face but otherwise ignored his arrogance. "Well, we don't have time. I'm sure Tennyson is going to have connections, and they'll know something's wrong when he doesn't report in. Can you or can't you get into that laptop if we can find it?"

"I won't know until I see it and mess with it for a while. I mean, I don't know if they're gonna have power, I don't know if the towers are down…. There's a lot of stuff I'm not sure about."

Maggie was silent for a moment. "I don't know. Is it worth the risk? I mean, if we got caught, I don't even want to think what would happen."

Tai watched her steadily, suddenly looking much more sober than usual. "I want this to be over as much as you do, Maggie. I hate feeling afraid for you all the time. If accessing that hard drive or server will give you any kind of protection, then I think it's worth it. Besides, we won't get another shot at an opportunity like this when the alarms are down and people are gone."

Maggie's face broke into a grin. "I love you for this, Tai!"

"Haven't I been telling you all along that it's me you love?" he teased. "Does anyone know where you are?" he asked then.

"No," she admitted with sufficient guilt. She wasn't sure what she would tell Peter, but she was counting on using the fact that Tennyson had tried to kill her as a good excuse for not showing up at Peter's house. *What could be better than that?*

Tai smiled in the satisfaction of knowing Maggie had let him in on something while keeping Peter in the dark. But it also worried him. "What about Peter?"

"He's been waiting for me to show up at his house, worried sick, no doubt. I can't go there now, though. I'm pretty sure Tennyson wasn't the only one looking for me. He couldn't have kidnapped Courage and gotten rid of Ms. Riley's body at the same time without help. Peter and his aunt are unarmed; I can't risk being followed and having these people, whoever they are, chasing me there—we won't have any way of protecting ourselves."

"Waters is armed, and he knows how to use his weapons," Tai suggested.

"That's a thought." Maggie took out her cell. "I need to call Peter and tell him I'm all right."

"Forget it. You won't get any signal."

She tried it anyway, and Tai gave her another profoundly smug look when she found he was right.

"At least now you can say you tried to call," he offered.

"If I think there's any chance that the Caldwells are home—"

"We'll ditch the place. Okay?" Tai conceded. "But think about it. Derik's house is the very last place these people will be looking for you."

She couldn't help but laugh at his obvious logic. She looked back at Courage, who seemed to be following the entire conversation with interest from the backseat. She patted his head and he barked as if in agreement.

"Let's get this over with, then." She turned on the ignition, but then hesitated.

"What?" Tai asked, clearly eager to leave the place.

"What are we going to do about that?" She pointed meaningfully to Waters's car.

"I'm not going to take it with us to break into Derik's house, that's for sure!"

Maggie looked at the Oldsmobile anxiously. "I guess you're right."

She shifted the Audi into drive and started down the dirt driveway. She felt chills go up her spine as her headlights fell upon Tennyson's prone body, and she drove in a wide berth around it. She silently prayed to God that this didn't leave a lasting impact on Tai. After all, he was only a kid, and he just killed somebody.

The rain was still pouring down and the flooding was more extensive by that time. It took a while before Maggie managed to navigate through the maze of passable streets to come to the entrance to the Caldwell's property.

At that moment, Mr. Kraus was at Peter's house, sitting in a chair with his head in his hands, his usual position when things were going very wrong. Peter was pacing the floor frantically when his cell went off.

"Peter?"

"Mr. Waters? Have you heard from Maggie?" Peter asked immediately.

"I talked to her several hours ago."

"What did she say?"

"She said she was in trouble, but she wouldn't tell me what kind of trouble. She was afraid for the kid. She didn't want him going back to her house."

"Is Tai with you, then?"

"He was. We settled down in the cellar, but—" The line went dead.

Peter slammed his fist on the table in frustration. "I'm the last one who talked to her," he said dismally. He tried to call her for the hundredth time, but he was no longer receiving any signal on his cell. The storm was wreaking havoc with transmissions.

Maggie parked the Audi across the street from Derik's house behind a structure that housed a couple of trash cans.

"What are we going to do with the dog?" Tai asked.

Maggie looked from Tai to Courage and bit her lip worriedly. "I'm not sure. We won't be gone too long, right?"

"You won't be. After we scope the place out, you can return to the car. I could be in there all night. It's one thing to steal stuff. It's another to steal information. Of course, if I can't steal the information, I can take the laptop, but then they'll know someone has been here. Those people know you've been out in the storm. They'll suspect you, and they'll have one more reason to off you."

Maggie frowned at the thought. She quickly went to her trunk and grabbed a blanket to make a place for Courage to sleep on the floorboard. "I can't leave him here too long—not in this weather," she fretted and gave Courage a kiss on the nose. He whined and licked her face.

"Like I said, you can return to the car anytime."

They got out, leaving the keys in the ignition before they made their way stealthily down the long driveway that led to the Caldwell mansion. They were cold and once more pelted with debris from the trees as they quickly rounded the house. Since the windows were shuttered, they didn't think anyone was home...until they made it to the back door, where they saw a faint stream of candlelight shining through the cracks of the shutters.

"Oh, crud, Tai. I think someone is home!" Maggie whispered fiercely.

"You're right. Do you still want to do this?"

Maggie hesitated for a moment of indecision. "The power is out, so we won't trip any alarms, right?"

"Right, but the house is dark. Someone could sneak up on us in the shadows, and we'd never know it."

Again she hesitated. She knew this might be their only chance at taking down The Inner Society, permanently. She couldn't chance the power would be out a second time. Still, she didn't like this one bit—she felt like a criminal herself. And the fear of getting caught was significant. If they were caught, they could end up being subjected to all kinds of terrors while in police custody or jail. She thought of the reporters, and her dread mounted. If she made headlines as a common thief, her credibility would be completely shot this time, and the outcome of the trial would be adversely affected.

"We can't do this, Tai. I don't want you to risk the consequences, especially when we know they're home," Maggie finally concluded.

Tai looked at her, reading her for a moment. "So, that jerk back there was your bodyguard?" he asked stupidly, being momentarily distracted by the thought.

"You've seen him before, Tai."

He shook his head in disbelief.

"What?"

"That's real nice—a bodyguard who tries to kill you!"

"Yeah, that would be my luck!"

"Well, anyway," he continued, "the D.A. is dead, your friend is dead, you were very close to being dead, and this wasn't the first time. The police are corrupt, and your protection is gone. If we don't end this thing, it will eventually catch up to you. I'm willing to take the chance, even if it's only a long shot that I can find the laptop and access the information you believe exists. I think this risk is worth it."

Maggie looked into his face, and although she couldn't make out his features in the darkness, for the first time, she didn't see him as a kid. His selflessness brought tears to her eyes.

"So, how are you going to do this?" she asked.

"Just forget about what I'm gonna do and go back to the car, Maggie. There's no reason for you to be here."

"I'm not leaving you alone, Tai. I'm not a coward."

"Don't worry about me, my little bamboo stick. I can defeat assassins, rescue maidens, and bypass the slickest security systems with a single keystroke. I am the mighty Hmong man!" Tai flicked his coat back like a cape, holding his head up high in pride.

"Have you lost your freaking mind? Cut the mighty crap, Tai! I'm staying!"

"All right then, snob. I'll go in through the back, and you can be my lookout."

"Okay then, brat, but if anything goes wrong, for God's sake, don't try to play the hero and come to my rescue! These people have no problems with hurting anyone— *anyone*, Tai. If you can't promise me that, then we're going to turn around right now."

Tai gave her an odd look. He didn't want to lie to her, but he wasn't going to sit back if she got into trouble either, no matter how scared he was. He shook his head. "No dice, snob."

"I'm warning you: don't pull any stupid heroic moves, Tai. There wouldn't be anything you could do against two adults and a six-foot teenager, anyway. So just concentrate on keeping yourself safe. If you can manage to get past three people, I can manage to take care of myself."

"Yeah, you were doing a great job of that earlier!" He checked the backdoor and found it unlocked. He glanced back at Maggie. "At least something's goin' right tonight."

CHAPTER
seventeen

Maggie was standing up against a wall in a breezeway between the garage and the house. She had to consciously get a grip on her anxiety as the silence bore down on her. Oh God, please forgive us if this is a sin, and please protect Tai.

She was exhausted and stiff from the past traumatic hours. She was also soaked, and the wait was torture. It reminded her of last Wednesday when Peter had taught her that horrible lesson, and she had ended up in the mud puddle, cold and wet. She hated all this. She wanted it to be over, wanted desperately to be warm and dry and safe in Peter's arms.

Maggie felt her heart drop into her shoes when a clatter came from upstairs above her head. She moved around the side of the house where she could peer through a crack in the shutters and get a glimpse down a hallway at the fire-lit living room. Her stomach twisted into knots when she heard someone inside say, "What was that?"

Tai was in trouble. Maggie could see movement from the other room and knew someone was heading for the stairway. Maggie didn't have a whole lot of time to think. She kicked over a trash can, and it crashed with a bang on the cement walkway. Having successfully created the diversion, she made a mad dash for the gate that led to the front yard.

But no sooner had she passed through the back gate than a form suddenly appeared directly in front of her. She stumbled to a halt and gasped when she heard the click and felt the cold steel of a pistol pressed against her temple. She froze, her heart pounding erratically. She could feel the color drain from her face.

"I don't believe this!" Derik exclaimed. The wind blew viciously around them, and made eerie howling noises as it tore through the trees. "So now you're breaking and entering? You've got a lot of guts, I'll give you that."

"I didn't break in," Maggie corrected in her own defense.

"How about trespassing? That was also against the law the last time I checked!" He cursed her, the wrath in his tone making her wince. "Start walking," he said, his voice like ice.

"You've graduated to guns now, I see," Maggie commented as he gave her a shove to get her moving.

He laughed unexpectedly, knowing she was alluding to the incident at the hospital where he had held her at knife-point in order to access her laptop. "There are benefits to being a cop's kid. Access to weapons and knowledge of the law are two." He shoved her again when she resisted, pressing the pistol to the side of her head once more. "You can call this a citizen's arrest, if you know what that is, or I can just shoot you!"

"Your dad is just going to let you take his pistol and drag someone into your house?" she asked incredulously.

Derik leaned closer to her. "My parents aren't home," he informed darkly, the words seeping into her consciousness like poison.

The closer they got to the front door, the more the panic set in. She dug her heels in, but he took her by the arm and dragged her along. When they reached the door, he threw her into the house, then slammed the door behind them and locked it. Maggie looked back at the locked door with trepidation.

"Look what the storm blew in!" Derik announced, casting Maggie a look of unadulterated contempt as he removed his leather jacket, shook off the rainwater, and threw it over the back of an antique bench that graced the marble entryway of the mansion.

Conrad and Jason had been sitting on the couch in the adjoining living room, but now they both got to their feet and joined them in the foyer. Maggie's breath caught in her throat as she realized she was now trapped in the house with *all three* of them. She was suddenly reminded of the night she had run for her life from Bret and the boys. Every terrifying minute of her struggle to survive came back in vivid color. They had resolved to kill her as though she were no more than a bug. If Mark had not intervened, she would never have made it out of the situation alive. Now here she was again at their mercy, and Derik was just as volatile as Bret had been. She could hardly believe she'd been stupid enough to put herself in this position.

Derik kicked off his muddy shoes and then turned back to Maggie. "Take off your shoes. We don't want dirt on the white carpets."

She was in such a state of alarm that she didn't register what he was saying at first.

"Take your shoes off!" Derik barked again.

She gave a start and then did as he asked.

"What the heck is she doing here?" Jason asked in disbelief.

"That's what I'd like to know," Derik growled.

"What are you going to do with that gun, Derik?" Conrad asked alarm.

"Cool off, Conrad. I was just making a citizen's arrest. It's perfectly legal, I assure you." Again he turned to face Maggie, taking two strides toward her just as she stumbled backward. "What are you doing here?" he demanded.

"Derik, don't point that gun at her—it could go off!" Conrad insisted, but Derik wasn't listening.

Maggie closed her eyes for a second to get a grip on her terror. It was easier to be brave when she was angry, and it was easier to be angry when she wasn't feeling guilty for being in the wrong. "Why are *you* guys here?" she ventured.

"Derik's parents are out of town," Jason answered.

"And our parents think we're at a shelter," Conrad finished.

"I asked you a question!" Derik shouted.

She cringed slightly, but she stood her ground this time.

"Hey, Derik, take it easy," Conrad cautioned. "She's just a girl. You act like she's actually a threat!"

It was clear that Conrad was taken aback by Derik's

level of hatred. He knew, of course, that Derik and Maggie were enemies, but he wasn't privy to everything that had happened previously between them. For this reason, he wasn't fully aware of just how volatile their relationship really was, and of course the story he'd heard from his friends was very different than the stories given by the news reporters.

"This girl is not as helpless as she seems, man," Derik growled. "She definitely has dark motives for being here, and I want to know what they are." He turned back to Maggie. "What the heck are you up to?" he demanded again. When Maggie refused to answer, his level of anger went up a notch. "My friends are dead because of you, little girl. You better not tick me off!"

That hit home, and Maggie looked up at him with a rage of her own, and in the heat of the moment, she forgot all of Peter and Jacob's warnings about her temper.

"Your friends are dead because of me?" she choked. "I didn't walk into that library with a gun, and I wasn't the one who harassed a messed up boy until he finally cracked. If anything, you're alive because of me, you animal!"

"You better shut up!"

"If you're so concerned about your friends, why don't you tell me what you did when Mark ended up in the hospital? You were such good friends that you abandoned him to die alone! How does it feel to be such a pathetic snake?"

Derik hit her so hard that he knocked her backward against the wall. Pain reverberated through Maggie's face, and she brought a trembling hand up to her split lip.

The instant Derik hit her, Conrad jumped forward to intervene. "Hey! Hold on, man!" He pushed between them, putting his hands on Derik's chest to keep him distanced. "Think about this."

"That's what I mean," Derik said, "look at her. Not a tear—nothing! She didn't even cry out. Tough little girl, aren't you?"

Maggie straightened her back with as much resolve as she could gather. She knew she couldn't cry out without alarming Tai. If he heard and came to her defense, Derik and his friends would undoubtedly hurt him. So she kept in the pain.

"You might get away with a citizen's arrest but not with assaulting her," Conrad warned Derik. "She's half your size, for crying out loud!"

"He's right, Derik," Jason reluctantly agreed. "I don't even want to think of how much trouble we could get into. I don't want to live through the misery of more charges brought against us."

"If it comes down to it, Jason, we're going to be untouchable. We might catch hell from our parents, but we'll never see a day of prison time."

"Let me go," Maggie said quietly. "You know where I live. You can file charges against me later."

The guys looked to Derik to see his reaction.

Just then lightning flashed through the living room window, lighting up the room in brief blinding light. As the boys rushed to the window, a second flash of lightning suddenly struck a nearby tree. Sparks flew and a large branch came crashing down.

"Cool! Did you guys see that?" Jason said with excitement.

Maggie followed them into the room, trying to see her car, even though she knew it was too far away. She felt a chill go up her spine, and fear tore through her as she thought about her dog. She *had* to get out of there.

Derik's attention was still on Maggie, though. "Go ahead, you stupid witch. Go out into that storm. Let's see how long you last!"

Conrad glanced out into the menacing darkness and then anxiously back at Maggie. "He's right, Maggie. You can't leave yet." He looked over her, noting her soaked clothes and the damage that Derik had just done. She was a mess. He cast Derik a look of disbelief. He was beginning to realize just how rapidly the situation was spiraling out of control. His attention returned to Maggie. "Why don't you go sit by the fire and dry off?" he suggested. "Go ahead," he coaxed when he saw her indecision.

She gave one last look at the front door before relenting and going to huddle up by the fire.

Jason turned to Derik and Conrad, glancing back at Maggie to make sure she wasn't listening. "What the heck are we going to do with her?" he whispered fiercely.

"I haven't decided yet," Derik admitted, casting her a look of unmistakable hatred.

"Well, you can't report her for trespassing now without her telling on you for hitting her," Conrad pointed out logically.

Derik let out a frustrated sigh. "I guess you're right."

"Forget her. I'm starving!" Jason announced out of the blue. "What do you have in the fridge, Derik?"

"Go make some sandwiches or something. There's plenty of stuff in there."

"Sounds good to me," Conrad said.

The guys made their way into the large gourmet kitchen that adjoined the living room. From there they could still keep an eye on Maggie.

She watched them surreptitiously, hugging herself for warmth as she listened to them muttering about her. She still could hardly believe she had put herself in this stupid position. It probably served her right, since she had set out to break into the house in the first place. Hadn't Peter warned her about turning her back on God's protection?

The boys made a few monstrous deli sandwiches, loaded with everything, and popped the top off a few bottles of beer. Derik returned to the living room first and came to stand in front of Maggie.

"So how'd you do it?" His voice was low, but deadly.

"Do what, Derik?" she replied with annoyance.

"Get the lighter out of my locker? I know it had to be you."

She looked up at him, still furious over his assault, but then she looked away. She would have liked nothing better than to flaunt that situation in his face, but the painful throbbing in her mouth made her think twice.

"How did you get it?" he repeated with a slight edge of frustration, knowing she had duped him and that he couldn't prove it.

Maggie's eyes narrowed upon him, and she had to suppress the urge to throw back something sarcastic. It had been easy enough: When Katie had bumped into Derik, Maggie had switched his lock with hers. It had been simple for her to return to his locker, unlock it using her own combination, and retrieve the lighter.

"I don't know what you're talking about, Derik," she managed with a tone of relative innocence.

He took a threatening step toward her, and she braced herself.

"Derik…" Conrad's warning interrupted his advance.

Jason came in behind him and plopped onto the couch. "Easy, man. We don't want any trouble, remember?"

Derik cast Maggie a malevolent glare and then moved to sit by Jason.

Jason set his beer on the table and his sandwich in his lap. Maggie's eyes were drawn to the beer and then to the half empty bottle of vodka on the table. She wondered with dread just how drunk they were going to get.

Conrad sat next to Maggie on the hearth, and the others watched him in suspicion as she immediately stiffened. He was close enough that she could smell his cologne. She cast a sideways look at him, noting the light gray sweater that stretched taught over his muscular chest. A silver chain-link necklace hung around his neck. Maggie swallowed, uncomfortable with his closeness, and, once more, she desperately wished more than anything that she was safe in Peter's arms right then.

"Are you hungry?" Conrad asked her.

She shook her head just once, her fingers rising unconsciously to touch her swollen mouth. Conrad followed the gesture, realizing it might be painful for her to bite down.

"What if I cut it up in slices? Would you eat it then?"

"No, thank you. I'm not hungry."

"You're lying."

She flinched when his hand rose toward her face.

"Hey, take it easy, baby," he soothed. He then reached for her again, gently wiping a streak of blood from her bottom lip with his thumb.

Derik and Jason exchanged glances. They already knew where this was going to lead and suspected she did as well.

"You mess with her, Conrad, and we're going to have to get rid of her," Derik warned. "There's no way we can have her telling people that something happened while she was in my house."

Maggie closed her eyes, forcing herself to remain strong. She was going to survive this night. She had to, for her father's sake, if not for Peter's. She then thought of Tai upstairs somewhere and Courage out in the car, and her heart twisted within her.

"I'm not going to hurt her," Conrad said quickly when he felt Maggie's reaction. "Besides, she might not be as unwilling as she thinks she is." One brow rose and he grinned, his blue eyes taking on a mischievous glimmer as he leaned toward her. "Why won't you warm up to me,

Maggie?" he whispered. "I'm good-looking. A lot of girls have thrown themselves at me."

She could hardly stand his arrogance, and she was about to tell him where he could get off, but she remembered the rage she had just incited in Derik and decided to be more careful in what she said.

"Why me, Conrad? If you could have those other girls, why do you have to come after me?"

"You're not like any girl I've ever met," he admitted with a wry smile. "There's nothing wrong with the way I feel about you, Maggie. I just want to get close to you."

"I'm going to clear something up for you, man," Jason informed. "This girl isn't going to be willing, and you're not going to use your overwhelming charm to talk her into anything."

Conrad ignored him, his attention so heavily focused upon Maggie that she began to feel chills crawl up her spine. He smiled, softly amused by her uneasiness. "Come on, honey, relax. I've never done anything to hurt you. Have I?"

She swallowed the lump in her throat and then gathered her nerve, meeting his intense gaze. "No, you only keep friends with cold-blooded murderers! They're not kidding, you know. If you touch me, they're going to kill me."

Conrad's expression was doubtful. He hadn't sorted out who was lying about what yet, and, truth be told, he didn't really care one way or another.

"Look, I know you haven't been treated very well by men in general, Maggie, but just because you hate my friends doesn't mean you have to hate me. I told you before,

I won't hurt you. It's just sex. It's no big deal, right?"

His casual use of the word sent chills up her spine, and for a moment she heard echoes of her uncle's voice. For a moment, Maggie closed her mind against the pain. Then her eyes rose to Conrad's.

"Really? It's just sex? Tell that to Mark and Rebecca. Any one of you could have AIDS right now."

That struck hard. The boys looked to one another for a moment before looking away.

"Right, like you haven't done it, Maggie," Conrad gently chastised. "You were living with Peter."

Embarrassed by the conclusions he had drawn, she turned on him in frustration. "I never slept with him!" Her anger rising, Maggie turned on all three of them. "All you guys think about is getting a quick thrill because you don't have the hearts for anything deeper or more meaningful. You only want your girlfriends to use them, but they don't mean anything to you, so you won't stay around them for long. That's why you always hang out with each other! The truth is you can't give or receive love, and you resent anyone else who can."

"Give it up, Conrad." Derik had heard enough. "Don't waste your time with her. This little girl has an expiration date, and everyone knows it."

"Don't listen to them," Conrad said. He handed her his beer. "Here, drink this. It will take the edge off."

She almost took it out of old habit, but she caught herself. What was she thinking? The last thing she needed right then was for Conrad to get her to compromise her thinking and drop her guard. "I don't drink," she said softly.

"You mean you don't drink *anymore*," Jason corrected. "It hasn't been that long since she got out of rehab," he said to Conrad, "although, her preference usually runs to Phenobarbital, anyway. Doesn't it, Maggie? It really smacks that you think you have the right to preach to us, you little witch."

Maggie felt shame hit her. "I've made a lot of mistakes," she admitted. "I was messed up."

"You're still messed up," Derik said.

"Oh shut up, you guys!" Conrad said. "Lay off of her for a while."

"You're the one who needs to lay off of her," Derik said meaningfully.

Conrad didn't bother to respond. His gaze was still steadily focused on Maggie. It made her extremely uncomfortable. "A couple of beers won't do any damage," he reasoned.

"A couple of beers are what the guy had before he got in his car and killed my mother!" There was an unmistakable raw edge of agony in her tone.

The sympathy in Conrad's eyes seemed sincere enough, but it fell far from eliciting her appreciation.

"My boyfriend is going to kill you, Conrad," Maggie threatened, returning his regard with narrowed eyes.

"Where is your boyfriend, Maggie?" he asked softly, his deep voice like warm velvet. "Does he even know what you're up to?"

"Not a chance," Derik answered for her. "He never

would have let her come over here."

A subtle but distinct thumping noise startled them then, and Maggie's terrified gaze flew to the direction of the stairs. Tai? She couldn't even let herself imagine what would happen if the boys got hold of him.

"What was that?" Jason asked.

"Don't freak out, man. It's probably debris landing on the roof," Derik replied.

Maggie's tension eased. She was acutely aware that the more time Tai had, the better chance he had at completing his mission and getting out of the house.

"So what are you going to tell Peter?" Conrad persisted, undistracted. It was the million dollar question, and all three boys were watching her intently now, waiting for an answer.

"She better not say anything," Jason threatened, "unless she wants to get arrested for trespassing. The reporters would have a field day with that one."

"Someone is going to ask her what happened to her mouth," Conrad pointed out.

"She just came out of a hurricane! Anything could have happened to her," Jason said.

At that precise moment, Maggie's cell phone suddenly gained reception and went off. She snatched it out of her pocket and jumped to her feet, putting distance between Conrad and herself.

"Conrad, take it from her!" Derik yelled.

Conrad lunged for Maggie, but she leaped out of his reach, snapping the phone open and running for the door. "Peter!" she screamed. But she didn't get any farther. Before Conrad could reach her, Derik had climbed over the couch and tackled her.

CHAPTER
eighteen

Derik and Maggie struggled on the floor, wrestling for control of the phone. It snapped shut during the struggle, dropping the call. Derik finally got a hold of Maggie's arm as she tried to keep it out of his reach and snatched it out of her fingers. He shoved it into his back pocket and used his weight to keep her down. "We're not done talking about this, little girl!" he hissed.

She struggled but couldn't move him. "Let's talk about what your parents are going to do when they find out what you've done. I'm not going to lie to Peter about this!" she cried.

"What about what *you've* done? You're the criminal here!"

"Get off of her, Derik," Conrad said. "You're hurting her."

Derik glared at her in warning but finally released her and got up. Maggie immediately scrambled to her feet, her eyes sparking fire. Derik was standing mere inches from her, his stance threatening, but this time she was too angry to be intimidated, and they were at an obvious standoff.

Conrad laughed. "You have to admit, she's got spirit! I think it's *sensual*."

Derik rolled his eyes before giving him a look of total annoyance. "Dude, are you serious?"

"Let her tell Peter," Jason reasoned. "I guarantee it won't go past him. If he tells anyone, it will only ensure she goes to jail. He'll want to keep this quiet as much as we do. Besides, no real harm was done, right? She didn't steal anything, and it's not the first time she's been smacked. She was probably better off than if we had left her out there."

"Speaking of being smacked..." Conrad said, coming forward to stand mere inches from Maggie. "You and I have a little unfinished business, don't we?"

Maggie looked up at him for a moment of uncertainty before his meaning finally struck, and she glanced away nervously, her stomach tightening.

"I think I owe you a little payback, don't you?" He was enjoying her discomfort at that point.

"Dude, that slap was brutal," Jason agreed with a chuckle. "We could hear that from across the parking lot!"

Maggie could feel her cheeks flush. She took a moment to gather her courage, but dread was, nevertheless, settling into her spirit. "You asked for that."

Conrad smiled tolerantly, his brows raised in question. "Really? I deserved that? I gave you a gentle pat, and you tried to knock me unconscious!" Conrad's blue eyes were twinkling as he folded his arms and looked down on her.

"So what are you going to do, Conrad?" she asked quietly. "Hit me back?"

He was silent for a moment. Then, moving even closer, he cupped her cheek in his hand and whispered into her ear, his tone low. "That's not what I had in mind *at all*."

Maggie gave a start, looking up at him with a mixture of reproach and apprehension.

Conrad laughed, his expression softening slightly, and he backed off. "Take it easy, baby; I'm only playing with you."

As they spoke, trash and branches continued to slam against the house. The teens turned to glance out the window. Terra cotta shingles come clattering off of the roof and crashed to the ground. Another streak of lightning lit the sky, followed by an extremely loud boom of thunder. The trees groaned like living beings as they bent under the force of the wind that whipped through their branches. Once more, all four teens had their eyes glued to the plate glass window, their hearts racing and their conversation momentarily forgotten.

"This might get bad after all," Jason said ominously.

"A hurricane this late in the year? Really? How bad could this get?" Derik replied. "It'll never get past a category-1, if it even makes it that far."

"It won't have to if it keeps raining like this," Conrad countered. "We're going to have some serious widespread flooding. Besides, even a category-1 can do significant damage. You could lose your roof tonight."

One of the logs in the fireplace popped loudly, and the boys laughed when Maggie gave a violent start and spun around, her head jerking in its direction. For a moment she was standing with her back to the window, Jason a few feet behind her, his attention still on the raging storm.

Maggie never saw it coming when one of the massive pines in the front yard became too sodden with water to stand and uprooted. There was a loud splintering sound.

Derik and Conrad immediately lunged for cover. In split-second timing, Jason caught Maggie around the waist, pulling her with him as he dove out of the way only a moment before the tree came smashing through the big window. Glass exploded everywhere, and the wind and rain ripped into the living room, instantly showering them with leaves and soaking them. The trunk of the tree had landed on the exact spot where Maggie had been standing.

The teens scrambled out of the way as one final shard of glass crashed over the coffee table, bursting into a thousand fragments. For a moment, they froze, trying to slow their hearts and catch their breath.

Derik recovered first, looking to Jason. "What's the matter with you?" he yelled at him. "You just *freaking saved her life!*"

Maggie's attention went to Jason, her eyes wide with confusion as she realized Derik was right.

"Yeah, well…" Jason couldn't meet her eyes, "she saved my life that day in the library, and now I saved hers. We're even. Next time I'll let her die." He took a step and slipped on a piece of wood, kicking it savagely away. "Come on; let's get out of here before we all end up toast."

"I don't have a basement," Derik said, "but this house is pretty solid, and the storm shutters are closed over the windows in the other rooms."

The boys grabbed some oil lamps, and more beer, and headed down the hall for the family room.

Maggie's heart was still racing. She was worried about Tai. Where the heck was he? And what about Courage? What if a tree came crashing down on her car with him inside? Poor Courage. She knew he must be terrified. This was her fault, too. How could she have even thought of this horrific scheme in the first place? Certainly she hadn't fully thought out all of the possible consequences.

Maggie wanted nothing more than to get out of there, and was willing to risk anything at that point. If only she could be sure that Tai had made it safely out. But how could she know? It did occur to her, though, that she wasn't helping him by her presence there. As stubborn as he was, Tai could easily refuse to leave without her.

The second the boys headed for the other room, Maggie made a run for the open window. She climbed over the branches of the tree and made it as far as the glass-encrusted casement.

Conrad quickly looped back, though, catching hold of her arm before she could climb through, and dragged her back with him.

"Don't be stupid!" he chastised. "There won't be any point to you taking off now. If we were going to hurt you, we would have done it a long time ago, don't you think?"
He became aware she was limping then, and looked down to see a trail of blood coming from her feet. "Oh my god. What did you do?"

She looked down at her feet, realizing that she had

cut herself on the glass. Conrad hadn't been cut himself because his shoes had been clean when he'd arrived, so he'd never taken them off. He shook his head in exasperation as he reached for her.

"Come here."

Maggie knew he was about to pick her up, and she took a couple of steps backward to keep a distance from him. The glass imbedded deeper into her feet with each step, and the pain was excruciating. "I can walk. I'm fine!" she said, more alarmed at the thought of being in his arms.

"Don't be ridiculous, Maggie. Besides, you're getting blood on the carpet. We'll all get in trouble if Derik's parents find out we were here."

He caught her up in his arms, despite her protests, and took her into the other room.

Derik had grabbed a few thick blankets and pillows from a guest bedroom and brought them to the family room. A cold gust of wind was sweeping in from the shattered window, and Jason lit a fire in the fireplace to ward off the chill. Both boys looked up in surprise when they saw Conrad carrying Maggie in.

He set her down on the couch and moved one of the hurricane lamps to the edge of the table closest to her. He pulled her bloody socks off next, examining her feet. She jerked, and he told her to be still as he carefully pulled out several sharp pieces that had become buried in her feet.

"What happened to her?" Jason asked in surprise.

"She tried to run for the window and cut her feet up on the glass. Don't you have a generator, man? I can't see anything in this light."

"If we turn it on, someone might see the lights and tell my parents we're here."

"The windows on this side are shuttered. No one will see the lights from in here. Where is it, anyway?"

"Out back in the shed. There's a switch by the door."

Conrad looked over at Jason. "Go turn it on, dude."

"Why me?"

"Just *do* it."

"Fine," Jason grumbled as he got up and left.

Maggie thought about the generator, realizing that it might be of immense help to Tai. Maybe her cutting her feet up was a good thing.

"Do you have a first aid kit anywhere?" Conrad asked Derik.

"Yeah, upstairs," Derik said. "Second door on the left."

"Well, would you get it already?" Conrad snapped. "She's bleeding everywhere! Do you want her blood all over your house?"

This definitely *wasn't* a good thing. Maggie thought her heart was going to stop as she saw Derik reluctantly head for the stairs. "No!" she nearly screamed, drawing their attention to her immediately. She realized she had just made a mistake, though, and tried to cover up. "I mean, I'm fine. It's not necessary."

"Oh, shut up!" Conrad rebuked.

Maggie watched in anxiety as Derik disappeared up the staircase. *Oh God, please help Tai!*

"What is your problem?" Conrad said, noting her extreme discomfort. "I'm just going to wrap up your feet; I'm not going to give you a flipping tracheotomy!"

Maggie glanced up at him and then away, listening intently for any sounds that could indicate a struggle. She jumped when she heard a door slam, and her heart began beating in a rapid, uneven tempo as she waited for what seemed like ages. What on earth had she gotten Tai into? She was assaulted once more with the conviction that this was her fault. She should have let God handle this instead of taking matters into her own hands. He was certainly powerful enough to deliver these people to justice. Why that concept had been so hard for her to grasp before this was beyond her. Peter had warned her. Jacob and Kevin had warned her, even Pastor Bradford and the other adults. Now all she could do was pray for God to fix her impossible predicament in spite of her reckless interference and lack of faith.

She heard Derik's footsteps on the stairs as he returned with the first aid kit. She took in a deep breath and then released it on a shaky sigh. A second later the light on the end table came on. Jason returned, collapsing in an armchair. He was looking rather wet and put out.

"You're acting seriously weird, Maggie," Conrad said in annoyance. "You're not going to start freaking out now, are you?"

"I don't freak out!" she retorted.

He smiled at her response. "Good, then you won't have a fit when I tell you to lie on your stomach."

She gave him a look of impending rebellion.

Derik and Jason watched the scene with amusement, noting her anxiety, and laughed at her.

"Go ahead and take a freaking infection then! Don't cry about it later, though," Conrad snapped with increasing irritation over her obstinacy.

Maggie folded her arms, her eyes narrowed. She wasn't going to let Conrad tell her what to do...even if she was outnumbered.

Realizing yelling at her wasn't going to work, Conrad tried again. "Would you just do it, please?"

Her pride stinging, Maggie reluctantly rolled over. Conrad was now able to get easier access to the bottom of her feet. He picked out a pair of tweezers from the bag and took hold of her left foot. She tensed as he began to pull out the rest of the sharp slivers of glass. When he was done, he did the same to the other foot. He picked up the beer bottle then, and she gave a violent start as he trickled the alcohol over the cuts.

"Sorry," Conrad apologized, "but you don't need to get an infection. Hold still."

Maggie braced herself against the fiery pain as he took her other foot and did the same. He then wrapped them both up and released her. She sat up, her pride mortally wounded.

"I suppose I should thank you," she allowed.

"I suppose you should," he answered with slight reproof. Conrad laughed then at the look of mortification on her face. "Never mind. You look like you're about to pass out. Go ahead and get some sleep." He handed her a blanket and a pillow. "You should lose the coat first. It's soaked. I'll put it by the fire to dry out. I can only imagine what you've been up to today."

He looked down upon her noting her persisting tension. "No one will touch you, I swear it. Okay?"

"Really?" Maggie looked over at Derik, drawing Conrad's attention to him also. Derik was looking at her with unwavering malevolence.

"Don't be so dramatic. He could have shot you earlier if he'd wanted to," Conrad pointed out.

Maggie glanced from Conrad to Derik and back again, trying to measure Conrad's level of impairment. His words were now slightly slurred, so he must have been starting to feel the effects of the alcohol. Jason didn't look any better. She looked back at Derik once more, and realized he was *stone-cold sober*.

Exhausted, she pulled the blanket over her and curled into the soft cushions of the couch. She was so tired she ached, and she couldn't remember anything feeling more heavenly. For the first time that night, she was finally comfortable. Maggie's eyelids grew heavy and she yawned. She had definitely not intended to fall asleep while Tai was still upstairs, but it wasn't more than a minute before she was out.

Meanwhile, the boys played a game of cards on the coffee table, ignoring Maggie for the time being.

CHAPTER
nineteen

Derik had set Maggie's cell phone to vibrate, so when it went off again, it didn't wake her. Derik pulled the phone out of his pocket and checked the number. "It's the boyfriend," he announced. The boys looked to one another in indecision as the phone continued to vibrate.

"Answer it," Conrad said. "He might as well hear it from us first."

"He's probably right," Jason said.

After another moment of indecision, Derik snapped the cell open and took the call.

"What do you want?"

Peter did a double-take when he heard Derik's voice. "Derik?" he choked. "Why do you have Maggie's phone?"

"Because I have *her*," Derik admitted, bracing himself for an impending fight. He glanced over at Maggie, who was still sound asleep on the couch.

Maggie awoke with a start when she heard Tai's voice scream, "What have you done to her!"

He came racing into the family room with a baseball bat.

"Tai, no!" Maggie screamed back as she saw him lunge for Jason. In that same horrifying second, Courage leaped through the broken living room window and was running toward them. Derik was suddenly standing right in front of her, and Maggie realized, with sickening terror, that he had retrieved the pistol. "No!" Maggie screamed. She tried to run at Derik to stop him, but Conrad caught her by the arm in a biting grip, holding her in place. "Please!" she choked.

But it was too late. Two shots exploded from the gun, shattering the air. Maggie let out a cry as her dog dropped to the floor. Then her eyes flew to Tai. He was just standing there, staring down at the large bloodstain that was rapidly widening in the center of his chest. After a second, he simply collapsed into a heap on the floor.

Maggie cried out in the depths of anguish and writhed in Conrad's arms. "Let go of me! Tai! Let me *go*!"

"Maggie! Hey!" Conrad's tone had suddenly changed.

He gave her a light slap on the cheek, and she gave a violent start, blinking in bewilderment. Her eyes wildly scanned the room, and confusion struck when she realized there was no sign of Tai or Courage.

"Hey there, baby, you were having a nightmare," Conrad said, giving her a gentle shake. Derik and Jason laughed at her, but Conrad was genuinely alarmed by the force of her thrashing.

Meanwhile, all Peter could hear was Maggie screaming.

"Dear God, Derik, don't hurt her!"

"I'm not hurting her!" Derik snapped. "However tempting the notion is. She just had a freaking nightmare, that's all!"

Maggie was still reeling over the possibility that her dream could easily morph into reality. She glanced anxiously up at the dark stairway, wondering where the heck Tai was. Was he still upstairs after all this time? It must have been hours. Maybe he had left already.

"That was a heck of a nightmare," Conrad exclaimed, pushing Maggie's hair out of her face. "Do you have those often?"

"We've given her a few good reasons to have nightmares," Derik said cruelly, holding the phone away, and Jason smiled knowingly.

"What the hell is she doing with you?" Peter demanded, too upset to watch his language.

"Hmm, well, let me see…I caught her trespassing at my house. So if you want to get pissed off, get pissed off at her!"

"She's at your house?"

"That's what I said!"

Peter heard voices in the background. "Who's with you?" he asked, apprehension solidifying in his chest.

"Jason and Conrad. My parents are *out of town*." He delivered this information to Peter with barely concealed pleasure, knowing it would upset him.

By then Maggie figured out Derik was talking to Peter. "Let me talk to him!" she cried.

"Not yet," Conrad said, catching her arm when she tried to get up. "We don't need you making matters any worse." He looked over her doubtfully, noting the obvious swelling and bruising on her mouth. Her silver and gold flecked eyes were accentuated by the mascara which had started to run due to her excursions in the rain. She looked like someone had beat her up and she'd been crying. Conrad turned back to Derik. "Don't let him hang up. If you want to keep this from blowing up, we need to explain the condition she's in before he sees her."

Peter overheard him. "What do you mean 'the condition she's in'? What's happened to her?" he raged. "I swear I'm going to kill you guys!"

Derik put his hand over the receiver. "Shut up, Conrad. He heard you!"

"Pass me the phone."

Derik gave him a look of mistrust.

"Just give it to me!" Conrad insisted. Derik handed it to him.

"Peter, listen carefully," Conrad said, "and I'll tell you everything, but you need to calm down first, okay?"

"Spit it out, Conrad."

"She came over here on her own—I don't know why;

she wouldn't say. Derik caught her while she was trespassing, and she got hit in the process. It was her own fault, man, and he was within his legal right to contain her. You know that."

"How bad is she hurt?"

"It *looks* bad, but she's fine."

"Let me talk to her!"

"Just wait a minute. I want you to really think about what's going to happen if you make trouble for us over this," he reasoned logically. "If you make an issue of this, Derik will press charges against her, and she'll go to jail. Even if it's for a short time, I'm sure you know damage will be done by the press. She'll make a real credible witness on the stand with trespassing charges on her record. You don't want that, do you?"

"Of course, I don't."

"Okay then. We don't want our parents to know that we've been here, and we certainly don't want them to know we've been here with *her*."

Peter thought that over. He knew, despite anything Conrad said, that Maggie must have been through terror at their hands. "I've seen the way you look at her, Conrad. I will still kill you if I even think you've touched her."

Conrad laughed. "Dude, I'd be gay if I didn't notice her, and I'd be lying if I said I wasn't hitting on her. But before you get pissed, you might also take into consideration that I've been protecting her all night."

Derik cast Conrad a look of irritation, but Conrad shrugged, unperturbed.

"She's obviously there against her will, Conrad. Why are you guys holding her?" Peter could tell they'd been drinking, and the knowledge did little to put him at ease.

"Would you have preferred I let her go back out into this hurricane? She tried that, you know. The guys couldn't have cared less what happened to her. You can thank me for keeping her safe. So don't get all desperate and brave this stupid storm to come and rescue her. She's fine."

"You've said what you wanted to say, Conrad. Let me talk to her. Now!" Peter growled.

Conrad put the phone on speaker and then passed it to Maggie. Peter realized he must have been directly next to her in order for her to be able to take the phone so quickly. In fact, Conrad had been sitting on the floor and leaning against the couch where she'd been sleeping.

"Peter?" Maggie said, a note of desperation in her voice.

"Please tell me you're okay."

She hesitated for just a second, and Derik gave her a warning look.

"Don't you dare tell him we've abused you!" Conrad mouthed.

"Yeah, I'm okay, Peter."

"What were you thinking? Where's Tennyson?"

Maggie glanced uncomfortably at the boys, who were listening with rapt attention. She definitely didn't want to have this conversation in front of them.

"Uh, hold on a minute...."

She started to get up, but once again Conrad caught her sweater and jerked her back down. "You're not going anywhere," he ordered. "Finish the call." Maggie clicked off the loud speaker, but Conrad snatched the phone from her and put it back on before giving it back to her. He gave her a look that spoke volumes. She, likewise, treated him with a look of glaring condemnation, but they both knew there was nothing she could do about it.

"Maggie?" Peter's voice came over the line.

"Peter, I—" she tried again, but he cut her off before she could warn him about Tennyson.

"They're listening, aren't they?"

"Yes, but—"

Conrad cast Maggie a look that promised retribution as he abruptly snatched the phone from her. "There, Peter, you've talked to her. She's fine, all right? Now don't forget that you have a good reason not to make a big deal about this. She'll be back with you in the morning when this storm's over."

"Please don't hurt her, Conrad," Peter choked despite his best efforts, his tone suddenly pleading. "She's been hurt by so many people...."

Struck by the rare vulnerability in Peter's voice, Conrad fell silent. He didn't doubt Peter was referring to the new drama that was unfolding concerning the girl's uncle.

"You really love her, don't you?" he said thoughtfully.

"Yes...I do." Peter's voice was raw.

"You'll see her in the morning, Peter. I've no doubt she's in trouble. She's obviously hiding something significant, but nothing is going to happen to her tonight."

When he hung up, Maggie reached for her phone, but he held it out of her reach. "I don't think so. I don't trust you," he said, throwing the phone to Derik, who caught it and put it back in his pocket.

Maggie's dream was still replaying in her head, and the urgency to get out of there was rekindling in force. She had let herself fall asleep, and now she could only wonder if Tai was still upstairs. It was very possible that he'd been waiting for her to escape, unwilling to leave without her.

Then an idea came to her.

"I need to use the restroom."

They looked at her with suspicion, but Derik wasn't about to make an issue out of *that*. "Go ahead. It's that door right around the corner."

"Make it quick," Conrad said. "Clean up your face while you're at it so it doesn't look like you've been crying. And don't get any stupid ideas about slicing up your feet again."

"Why don't you take a flying leap off the back end of a moving truck! You don't own me, Conrad!" Maggie retorted with clear resentment.

He smiled tolerantly. "You know, you're hot when you're angry."

"Maybe another slap in the face will cool you off!"

Maggie was acutely aware of their suspicious gazes

following her as she turned the corner, walking carefully on her damaged feet. Out of sight, she found the bathroom and turned on the light, glad that a fan came on. If they could hear it, they might believe she was in the bathroom. She then shut the door and quietly made her way to the kitchen.

She hadn't missed the fact that Derik didn't have the gun with him when he returned from the kitchen with more beer earlier. That meant it had to be in or near the kitchen somewhere.

She paused briefly, trying to sort out her plans in her head. The fact was that she didn't appear to be in serious danger at the moment, so what would she do if she did get hold of the gun? She knew it wouldn't be long before Conrad came to check on her. She also knew that, even if she got hold of the gun before he reached her, he would feel pretty safe in assuming she wouldn't use it on him. He would easily take it from her, and what would she have accomplished?

As she tried to sort out her dilemma, Maggie hurriedly began easing one drawer open after the next, hoping they wouldn't squeak. She rummaged through them hurriedly, searching for the weapon. It was a big kitchen, though, and there were a lot of drawers.

Peter grabbed his keys and was preparing to leave.

"Where are you going?" Genevieve asked with alarm. She had listened in horror as Peter argued with Derik and Conrad on the phone. Now she was frightened for his safety. "Peter, it's too dangerous to go out there. You'll never make it!"

"She's terrified, Aunt Gen. I have to get her before

something else goes wrong. For crying out loud, what the heck are we going to do? I still haven't gotten through to Internal Affairs! There's a killer out there, and Tennyson's AWOL. We have no protection!"

"If those boys were going to hurt Maggie, they would have done it already," Genevieve said. "They must have had her for hours by now, right?"

Peter felt his stomach lurch at the very thought. "I know Derik has already hurt her, and they were monitoring our call. I know they're holding her against her will, though it made sense when Conrad said it wasn't safe for her to leave." He ran his fingers through his hair, suddenly beside himself. "I don't know what to think!"

"Please don't go, Peter," his aunt begged, fearful for him. "She just found a dead body, for crying out loud. I don't want you to get mixed up in this!"

"Aunt Genevieve, I already *am* mixed up in this!" Peter's voice rose in desperation.

Just then Mr. Kraus came up from where the three of them had been lounging in the large finished basement. "Peter? Is everything all right? I thought maybe you heard some news."

"We're just getting some food, Mr. Kraus. Go ahead back to the basement. We'll be down in a minute," Peter said.

Mr. Kraus looked doubtful, but said nothing and retreated downstairs.

Peter let out a breath. "Don't tell him about any of this," he cautioned his aunt. "It's only going to terrify him."

Just then there was a loud bang at the front door. They ignored it because things had been bashing against the house all afternoon. But the doorbell rang then, and they looked in the direction of the door, surprised. Neither could imagine why or how anyone could have made it to their door in this weather. Genevieve made to head for it, but Peter caught her arm.

"Wait, we have no idea who's out there. Don't open it if you don't recognize the person."

They had not lost their power and the porch light was on, so Genevieve could see who was on the front porch. She opened the door immediately when she recognized Tennyson.

CHAPTER
twenty

Tennyson stepped forward, obviously injured. There was a large gash in the side of his head. He braced himself against the door with one hand. The other hand rested on his hip, next to the gun hidden beneath his jacket.

"Have you seen Maggie?" he asked imperatively, watching her intently for any nuance of reaction.

"You're hurt!" Genevieve gasped. "What happened to you?" She immediately ushered him in and shut the door, checking the injury to his head. His hair was matted with blood, and he had a huge lump. "My gosh, this looks nasty!"

Her reaction set Tennyson at ease, and he relaxed, adjusting his coat to ensure the weapon remained concealed.   Peter stepped up to his side and helped him to the sofa, worry engraved on his face; Tennyson's condition meant something was terribly wrong.

"What happened to you?" Genevieve asked again.

"I got out of my car to move a limb out of the road. The next thing I knew, I woke up on the road with a violent headache, and I was covered in blood."

"Were you attacked?" Peter interrogated.

"I got clocked by a huge board. A piece of the sign from the bike shop, I believe."

Genevieve had already retrieved a clean cloth and was dabbing at his injury. "Looks like you're lucky to be alive," she said.

"Her car's not in the driveway. I'm assuming you haven't heard from her?" Tennyson asked imperatively.

"We just got through to her right before you showed up," Peter informed. He noted the way Tennyson seemed to stiffen, and he wondered if he missed something. "Where have you been all this time? Do you have any idea what's happened?"

"When I got to her house this morning, Maggie was—not surprisingly—gone. I got a call from Megan saying she was in some kind of trouble. I couldn't reach her by phone, and I've been trying to find her ever since. Where did she say she was?" Tennyson pressed. "I have to get to her right away."

"Derik has her at his house," Peter answered, a muscle ticking in his jaw as his anger renewed. "But—"

"Derik has her? You've got to be kidding me!"

"I wish I was." Peter started to pace a bit, glancing out the windows every now and again at the storm. "Conrad and Jason are there with him. Conrad says they caught her breaking and entering, and Derik is going to press charges if I make trouble for them. I know she's been roughed up, and I doubt their excuses for it are truthful. Maggie said they were monitoring our call, and she couldn't talk. But…" he stopped pacing as he realized he'd been sidetracked, "…

there's something I've been trying to tell you." His eyes flashed with renewed anxiety. "The D.A.'s been murdered! Maggie's in serious danger. The fact that she's with the guys now amplifies her danger a hundredfold."

Tennyson's expression became fixed. "How did you...what do you mean the D.A.'s been murdered?" he asked with feigned surprise.

"Maggie said she found her dead in her house." Peter pounded the wall in a sudden passion. "I have to get to her!"

"Absolutely *not*," Tennyson quickly countered. "No offense, Peter. I understand that you've taken on a lot of adult responsibility for a kid, or even for an adult, but this isn't an issue for a teenager to handle. If she's gotten into that kind of trouble, the people who are after her will be extremely dangerous. You don't want to jump in as an overprotective boyfriend and jeopardize both of your lives, right?"

"Take me with you, then."

"Peter, you need to let me do my job. If Megan's really been killed, then we're dealing with something that's more than you can handle. I can't have you getting in the way, and I don't have time to argue about this."

With a sinking heart, Peter realized his logic. "Are you going to go get her, then?"

"If she's really there. We can't know if they were telling the truth about their location. Have you called Internal Affairs?"

"I couldn't get through."

"Don't worry; let me handle it. I'll call until I reach them."

"You're leaving right now?" Peter asked anxiously.

Tennyson clapped a hand on Peter's shoulder encouragingly. "You can count on it."

Since he couldn't get signal from the basement, Peter waited in the kitchen on pins and needles for his phone to ring. But he knew he might not get signal from anywhere in the house at all. Communications had been problematic all night.

Meanwhile Maggie's father was pacing the floor of the basement. He had the terrible notion that there was an entire world going on around him that everyone was keeping from him. It was a frightening possibility that he would never see his daughter again. He could tell by Peter's spirit that whatever was going on was deadly serious.

Peter jumped when his cell eventually did ring forty minutes later. He looked down at the number to see if it was Waters again. Waters had been trying to call and ask about Maggie and Tai all night, and Peter had quit taking his calls to keep the line open.

The number did not belong to Waters this time, though. In fact, he didn't recognize it at all. Peter flipped the cell open with shaky fingers. An incoherent voice came on the other end; someone was shouting in panic. Peter immediately felt the alarms ringing in his head.

"What? I can't understand you." It took him a second to place the voice as Tai's.

"Peter!" Tai was screaming. "They've had her all night!"

Peter thought he would explode when static began taking over the line yet again. "Tai?" he shouted.

"Peter—" More static.

"Tai!"

"He's got...he's...to kill her!"

The line went dead.

Peter let out a cry of rage, picked up the nearest object, and flung it across the kitchen. The expensive vase hit the oven and shattered into a million pieces, cracking the oven's window in the process.

Genevieve raced up the stairs at the noise to find Peter zipping up his coat. She knew he was going to do exactly what he was told not to do. "No, Peter. Don't go!" she cried in terror.

Peter was trembling with anxiety, and his adrenaline was pumping as he kissed her forehead and snatched up his keys. "Tennyson should have reached her by now. I have to find her."

Their eyes locked for a moment, and a wealth of turmoil was communicated between them as they were transported back in time. Every second of 9/11 was racing through their minds, from the moment they'd seen the video on the initial strike, to the tortuous days that followed in which Angela and John Bennett didn't return home.

Peter's expression became set, and Genevieve knew there was nothing she could do to talk him out of going.

"You're all I've got, Peter," she choked and swallowed the sob that was working up in her throat.

"Then pray for me."

She hugged Peter fiercely, wishing she had some way of stopping him and knowing there was nothing she could do. "We'll be interceding for you in prayer every second," she vowed, wrapping her faith around her like a cloak and drawing upon its strength. "I won't let them take you from me."

He squeezed her tight, fear for her, for Maggie, for what he might lose shooting through him for a brief second. His heart was pounding.

"Satan might have won a few battles," Genevieve pulled back and squeezed his arms, "but our God will win this war!"

His eyes shone in anticipation as he looked into her eyes. Then he opened the door, bracing himself against the stiff wind that rushed into the house and took off into the stormy night.

The weather was treacherous, but not as bad as he had thought. His heart was pounding painfully as he veered the Camaro down the wet, abandoned streets, and he had to struggle to ignore the ominous tingling sensation that crept up his neck. "Dear God, please...." he choked, unable to even finish the desperate prayer. The possibilities for a tragic ending to this scenario were limitless. He could find her body somewhere, or she could simply disappear forever, and he'd never know what happened to her.

And what about Tai? He was certainly also in danger. A stab of regret hit Peter; he knew despite how annoying the little punk could be that he was still a good kid. He certainly hadn't deserved getting wrapped up in all this.

It was nearing ten o'clock when Peter came to a skidding halt in front of Derik's house, noting with horror the massive damage done from the fallen pine.

He ran up the front steps, soaked within seconds by the pouring rain. He tried the door and found it unlocked. With his blood racing through his veins, he stealthily opened the door, hanging tight to the handle so the wind wouldn't blow it out of his hands and slam it against the wall. He immediately took in all the devastation in the living room, noting the large tree that loomed inside and the trail of blood that came from the glass. Terror clutched him as he wondered when it had been shed—and whose it was. Was it before or after he had talked to Maggie?

On full alert he rushed down the hall and found Jason and Conrad passed out in the family room. Jason was sleeping, slack-mouthed in an armchair, Conrad crashed on the loveseat.

"Where is she?" Peter's voice was like the boom of thunder, waking both boys with a terrifying start. They quickly staggered to their feet. Both were a little sluggish from sleep as well as the alcohol they'd consumed. Jason, in fact, looked like he was feeling sick.

Conrad glanced at the couch where Maggie had been lying but only the blanket remained. He then looked around the room but saw no sign of Derik either. "Derik!" he yelled.

Peter was seeing through a veil of fear and agony as he noted more bloodstains on the carpet in the family room. "Whose blood is that?" he demanded, his hands balling into fists.

"Whoa! Take it easy, Peter," Jason said with an almost undetectable slur. Peter was helping them to sober up quickly.

"Whose blood is it?" he repeated with all the more rage.

"It's Maggie's," Conrad admitted. He was having a hard time looking Peter in the face. Peter's eyes fell on him, burning holes into him, and Conrad rushed to explain. "She cut herself on the glass in the living room, man, I swear it! I took care of her, though. Look, there's the first aid kit sitting on the table."

Peter's eyes slid from the medical kit back to Conrad. "How much have you guys had to drink?" he demanded, but they didn't answer. They didn't really need to.

Peter never took his eyes off of them. "Maggie!" There was no answer from her either. "Where is she?" he demanded.

Conrad and Jason both looked around, perplexed. "I have no idea!" Conrad said. "She was sleeping right there." He pointed to the couch where the blanket and pillow gave indication that he was telling the truth.

"Jason?" Peter turned on him next, his expression lethal.

"I don't know, man. She was there a minute ago."

"Where is Derik?"

"He was here just a minute ago, too."

If it came down to a fight with the two of them against Peter, there was no doubt they were big enough to inflict some damage, but Peter's very aura was so frightening that neither wanted to take him on.

Forty minutes earlier, Derik had received a call of his own. He didn't recognize the voice, but the man on the other end offered him a grand in cash to take Maggie out of the house, and he was more than willing to be part of the conspiracy. Maggie had awoken to find herself suffocating, Derik's hand cupped firmly over her mouth.

"Wake up and don't make a sound!" he threatened with chilling intensity.

Maggie looked up at him in confusion and rapidly mounting dread, consciously aware that his hair and clothes were damp. Where on earth had he been?

"I don't understand," she choked out when he let his hand drop.

"Shut up!" he whispered forcefully. "You're coming with me."

He snatched up her coat and socks and shoved them into her hand as he took her into the living room. "Put your shoes and socks on," he said, his tone now cold and unemotional—just like Bret's used to be. She wasn't about to give him any more reason to hurt her, so she did as she was told. "Put your coat on." When she was done he took her by the arm and pulled her with him over to a drawer in the kitchen, where he retrieved the gun and tucked it into his pocket.

"Derik—" she cried, but he clamped a hand over her mouth once more.

"Shut up, witch! You wanted to get out of here, and

now you will."

She caught his hand with both of hers, pulling it away from her bruised mouth. "What do you mean?" she rasped.

"You've got dangerous people after you; I can't risk having you in my house." He was dragging her outside as he spoke. "I'm going to let you go out into the storm and meet your fate."

He looked up at the black storm swirling around them. It looked extremely ominous, even if the weather had calmed. He pulled her through the yard and across the street to where her car was parked, or rather, where it *had* been parked.

Maggie's heart jumped in her throat. "Where's my car? What have you done with my dog?"

"You're worried about your dog right now?" He choked on the laughter that caught in his throat. Derik smiled sadistically and pushed her forward. "I parked the car at a gas station while you were sleeping and walked back so everyone would think you left my house in one piece. And don't worry—I didn't leave any fingerprints behind."

On the verge of hysteria, Maggie dug in her heels and tried to wiggle out of his grip. "What did you do to my *dog*?" she cried. She finally managed to jerk out of his grasp, but made no more than one stride before he outdistanced her, caught her, and threw her over his shoulder, carrying her out to the road. It didn't matter that she was screaming now; no one could hear her above the noise of the wind.

The streets were dark since the power was still out, and there was no light from any streetlamps. They were quite a distance from the house when he finally dumped her none too gently on the ground.

"Derik, you monster!" Maggie crawled backward away from him. "Don't you have a conscience at all?"

"Not much," he said with black humor.

"Aren't you even the slightest bit afraid of going to hell?" she choked, her eyes clouding over in bitter tears.

"Not as long as I can stay alive, sweetheart, which is more than you're gonna do. You've got a date with darkness, and he's about to show up any minute."

Derik reached down, took hold of her coat with one hand, and jerked her upward. The muscles and sinews in his arm bulged with the effort as he held her suspended off the ground by several inches. The fact that he was even able to accomplish such a feat made her blood turn to ice water, and she struggled to no avail to make him release her.

Derik suddenly went still. Maggie's blood went cold as his dark eyes seemed to turn even darker. His other hand grasped her by the back of the hair, and Maggie gave a muffled cry of pain when he quite deliberately—and brutally—kissed her damaged lips. She struggled, but she was completely helpless to stop him. *Please God, help me!*

"Let her go!" A voice cracked through the night air.

Derik dropped Maggie to her feet but kept his grip on her.

"Tai!" Maggie screamed.

A surge of desperation hit, and she fought to get leverage so she could strike her captor, but Derik still had a death grip on her coat, and with his long reach, he could easily hold her at arm's length and still keep her powerless to hit him. She did have use of her legs, though, and she managed to deliver a brutal kick to Derik's shin. He briefly doubled in pain and cursed her before he turned back to Tai.

"What the heck is this punk kid doing here?" Derik was only too aware that this unwanted intruder could really screw everything up.

"Let her go." Tai was obviously scared, but he was making up for the fear with determination, and Maggie realized he had picked up a heavy branch that he was wielding like a club. *God have mercy*, Maggie thought. *He's like a Chihuahua attacking a Doberman!*

"Really? You think so, huh?" Derik laughed in contempt as he pulled out the gun. He pointed it right at Tai, who froze in place.

Maggie's mind raced. "What are you going to do, Derik, shoot a kid with a gun that's registered to your *father*? Not even you qualify as that stupid!"

She gasped when he gave her a brutal shake. "The intruder who broke into the house and stole the gun shot him, not me!" he said with cold calculation, taking aim at Tai's head.

Derik was so focused on Tai that he didn't see Maggie reach into her coat pocket. Tai noticed though, and when he saw the bullets in her hand, he lunged at Derik.

He pulled the trigger. The gun only clicked, empty. Derik realized too late that he had no bullets, and Tai clubbed him before he had the chance rethink his strategy.

Derik lost his grip on Maggie's coat, going down hard. Tai made to hit him again, but Derik kicked him in the gut, knocking the wind out of him, which gave Derik the chance to get back to his feet. He lunged at Tai, but Maggie threw herself against him, throwing him off balance. Derik shoved Maggie to the ground, but it was just enough of a break to give Tai another opportunity. He whopped Derik across the head again, harder this time, and Derik hit the ground, his senses swimming.

Tai jumped over him and jerked Maggie to her feet. "Come on!" he yelled. "Let's get out of here!"

CHAPTER
twenty-one

Maggie and Tai fled into the darkness, dodging massive puddles and leaping over wreckage that had been strewn across the streets. The wind was still strong enough that it nearly knocked them over at times. Maggie was struggling against the pain in her feet, and at one point, she stopped to rest under a tree by the main road.

"Are your feet okay?"

"How did you know about that?" she asked with surprise.

"Don't you know by now? I'm your guardian angel, babe! I was watching. I saw what happened."

"It appears my guardian angel has tire irons and clubs instead of wings," she said dryly.

"Yeah, well, that's what you get when you pick up an angel from Richmond!" he replied. "But don't hate the Richmond angels. You're one of them, remember?" He smiled and she laughed.

"I don't think he followed us, but I think we better keep moving, just in case. Can you keep going? I don't think

I can carry you," Tai said.

"We don't have much of a choice," Maggie agreed. "Derik was waiting for someone, and I don't want to meet up with whoever he was." They began moving as fast as Maggie could manage.

There was a beeping noise from Tai's pocket. "Great. My cell battery is going dead!" he complained. "Do you have your cell phone, Maggie?"

"No," she said with sudden remembrance and a sinking heart. "Derik has it!" The implications of both of them being without any means of calling for help were more than distressing.

The wind was whipping around them, strong enough to make it hard to run. Their faces stung from the small pieces of debris that kept pelting them. A groaning sound above them drew their attention to a limb hanging over their heads as they ran beneath the trees. There was a loud crack as it suddenly broke off. The teens barely had time to leap apart as it landed directly between them. They looked to one another in a moment of shock.

"We have to make it to a safe place," Tai said.

"We have to make it to the nearest gas station," she corrected. "Derik said he drove my car to a gas station so everyone would think I left. I've got to find it."

"Even if he was telling the truth, how the heck would we know which gas station?"

"Well, it would have to be close enough for him to walk back to the house," Maggie surmised.

"We don't have time to wonder around lost."

"But Courage was in my car!" she cried.

Tai shook his head. "The dog is a lost cause, Maggie."

Knowing he was right, she fell silent. She had to struggle to keep her mind from imagining all the horrible things Derik could have done to him.

Back at the Caldwell house, Peter was having a heated argument with Conrad.

"I swear I don't know where they went." Conrad insisted when Peter grabbed him by the shirt. "I'm into her, man. I don't have any reason to hurt her."

"That televised slap in the face would be a good reason!" Peter yelled.

For just a second, Conrad's expression changed. "You've got that wrong. I wasn't mad at her for that. I was *turned on* by it."

Peter punched him, rocking him backwards. Conrad wiped a smudge of blood from his nose. "I suppose I deserved that," he admitted. "But I meant it, Peter. Derik never gave us any reason to believe he was going to do anything to her. Did he, Jason?"

"No, man. We were just playing cards. She was sleeping. We had a few beers and fell asleep ourselves."

"This is your fault, Conrad!" Peter accused. "You said you were going to protect her! If you weren't drunk off your butt, she wouldn't be missing right now!"

"I only had a few beers." His words were only slightly

more slurred than Jason's.

"You had enough to knock you out and leave Derik alone with her. Your drinking could have cost her her life!"

"What reason would he have to kill her, Peter?"

Conrad's naiveté infuriated him. "Are you seriously that clueless? What reason did they have to put her in the hospital? What reason did he have to waste her friend?"

Conrad eyed him with some annoyance. It was clear he wasn't convinced that all the stories were true and more than convinced that Maggie could have been lying as easily as his friends. "You know they were acquitted of the murder charges."

"That doesn't mean they didn't do it!" Peter yelled. "And you know darn well they weren't acquitted of the freaking assault charges! When are you going to get it through your head that your friends are punk criminals?"

Conrad fell silent. He'd been feeling guilty since Peter arrived, knowing he had allowed his guard to drop. Peter was right: there had to be foul play involved in her disappearance, and Derik had shown an inclination to hurt her.

He joined Peter in making a complete sweep of the house and property then, returning to the house a few moments later, where they found Jason passed out again on the sofa.

Peter's mind was reeling over the possibilities of what could have gone wrong, and he felt a stab of unease as he wondered again what had happened to Tennyson.

Tai's iPhone beeped again, but this time it sounded more like a malfunctioning chirp. He halted and answered eagerly. "Hello?"

"Tai," Peter said, "where are you? Tennyson said he was going to show up at Derik's to get Maggie, but we haven't heard from him since. I showed up here, but—"

The iPhone chirped a third time, and the connection was dropped.

"Maggie, we didn't kill him!" Tai cried.

"Kill who?" she asked in trepidation.

"Your bodyguard! Peter said Tennyson was looking for you. They don't know about him."

"Why didn't you tell them?" she accused.

"My freaking call was dropped!" he yelled back. Their frustrations were coming to a boiling point. "My gosh, Maggie, you must have the *worst* bodyguard ever. Whoever heard of a bodyguard who tries to kill you? That's jacked up."

"I think you already brought that up once."

"Well, it's worth repeating."

Maggie pondered over this new and disturbing information. She put her hand to her chest as she felt it constrict painfully. "He must have been the guy that Derik was waiting for," Maggie breathed in dread. "We should have taken his gun while we had the chance. We have to get out of here." She was exhausted by then, but her adrenaline was rushing through her. Visions of the dead D.A. were swimming in her mind, followed by the blood in the trunk.

They made their way down the main road, doing their best to hide in the shadows. Just as they went down an alley, a black Mercedes passed by, its headlights briefly illuminating them. They quickly hunched down.

"Do you think that was him?" Tai asked.

"Well, it wasn't anyone out for a joyride in a hurricane," Maggie replied.

No sooner had she spoken than the vehicle backed up.

"He saw us. Run!" Tai yelled.

They fled down the alley, making it to the other side before the vehicle turned in their direction and picked up speed.

"Isn't that your bodyguard's car?" Tai asked, breathless from their exertion.

"Yeah, it is."

They came to a large dumpster. Next to it was a case of empty beer bottles.

"Here, help me," Maggie urged and began grabbing the bottles. She smashed them against the dumpster and began kicking the pieces into the alley. Tai quickly followed suit, smashing the rest of the bottles and scattering the glass. The entire process only took up a few seconds, but it was long enough for the vehicle to have come within twenty yards of them.

"Come on, Maggie. Let's get out of here!" Tai warned in panic.

He grabbed her coat, pulling her after him. Snapping to, she followed, the two of them tearing around the corner before the Mercedes could reach the end of the alley. The rain poured down on them as they fled in terror. The vehicle came skidding around the corner and was barreling toward them, but the tires ripped across the glass, exploding.

"Run faster, Maggie!" Tai cried. "Even if we've destroyed his tires, he'll still be able to outrun you with your feet all cut up."

"I know. I'm *trying*."

They reached the end of the next block, and both of them skidded in the muddy street as they tried to make the next corner. Maggie went down on one knee, but scampered back to her feet immediately.

The car was heading directly for them, sparks flying from its rims. "He's riding on his rims now," Tai noted.

"He's still going to run us over!" Maggie cried. The two glanced back in panic as they ran. Tai grabbed one end of a large limb that had broken off of an oak tree. Maggie grabbed the other end, and they dragged it into the middle of the street. They began dumping trash cans and anything they could to throw into the street and then continued to run. The Mercedes had lost all four tires by then and couldn't bypass the mess. It also couldn't properly brake, and it plowed into the trash, shoving it several feet forward before grinding to a halt.

Even above the sound of the storm, they could hear a door slam, and a loud explosion suddenly ripped through the air as a bullet went whizzing past Maggie's head. Maggie let out a scream as it hit the base of a street lamp, mere inches from her.

Tai led the way down another street, where they made their way around bushes and jumped a picket fence, ending up at the back door of a large colonial home. They banged on the door screaming for help, but no one answered. They ran to the next house, but it was also abandoned.

"Time for a new tactic," Maggie said. To Tai's surprise, she snatched up a rock and broke the glass in the door. Reaching in, she unlocked the deadbolt and threw the door open.

Instead of going inside, though, she grabbed Tai and dove into the nearby bushes. There they hid, with their blood rushing through their veins and their chests heaving from sheer terror.

Not a second later, a dark form appeared out of the darkness and crept stealthily to the open door. He took note of the glass, and cautiously looked around before quietly creeping inside.

"That ought to buy us some time," Maggie whispered, pulling Tai up. "It'll take him forever to search such a big house. I guarantee he's going to get back-up, though." They dashed back onto the street and made their way down the road.

After searching the Caldwell's place to no avail, Peter got into his Camaro and slammed the door in frustration. He was pulling the car out of the driveway when he saw Derik through the windshield, walking down the driveway toward the house. He was drenched and his clothes were a mess. Peter slammed on the brakes, the Camaro sliding on the wet pavement before coming to a halt, and shoved it into park.

Jason and Conrad, who were watching him from the broken living room window, came running out just as Peter leaped out of the car and headed toward Derik, with all the fury of the hurricane swirling around them.

Derik halted when he saw Peter coming. In fact he took a few steps backward.

"Derik, you freaking animal! What did you do with her?"

Just before Peter reached Derik, Jason and Conrad caught up with him. They were about to grab his arms and hold him back, but Peter quickly pivoted and treated them with such a look of hostility that they reconsidered. "Don't even *think* about it," he threatened, enunciating each syllable in wrath.

They backed up, and Peter went straight for Derik, clutching his sweater in his fist and slamming him against the Camaro. "What have you done to her?"

"Wait, Peter, I can explain!" Derik tried.

"Where is she?"

"I don't know! I woke up and she was gone. I went out to get her, but I couldn't find her."

Peter looked at him so keenly that Derik felt he was seeing straight into his soul. "Where is her car?" he asked with deceptive softness.

"How should I know? It was gone. I assumed she

drove home."

Everything he had said made sense, but there was something about his tone that convinced Peter he was lying.

"I hope you really get this, Derik, because your life depends upon it. If she's dead because of you, I will find out, and if I don't kill you myself, I will spend every waking moment for as long as it takes to see to it that you get the death penalty. You're going to get strapped into an ugly chair and feel a massive, continuous jolt of electricity go through your body. Then you won't feel anything at all but hell's fire!"

"You've got no proof we did anything to hurt her!" Conrad protested.

"Are we going to have this conversation again?" Peter spat in disgust. "Derik has motive, and she is *missing!*"

Derik said nothing, but the passive look on his face convinced Peter that he had a hand in all this.

"The truth's not always so clear cut, man," Conrad reasoned, trying to reign in the hysteria that was crackling through the atmosphere.

"And you can't prove anything," Jason rasped.

"You better shut your mouth, Jason!" Peter threatened darkly.

Jason unfortunately had a point, though. Peter glanced down at Derik beneath him and noted the lack of remorse in his eyes. But there was nothing he could do, not without proof.

Peter finally let Derik go. He opened the driver side door but hesitated as he turned to Conrad one last time.

"You need to choose your friends more wisely. They're going to get you into more trouble than you can handle!"

With that he jumped into the Camaro and slammed his foot on the accelerator. The tires spun, throwing muddy water in all directions that pelted the boys. The tires finally took hold, and Peter sped down the driveway.

All three boys watched Peter leave in silence, Derik and Jason still trying to shake the mental picture of the electric chair.

"I swear, Derik, if you did something to her, I better not get dragged into it!" Conrad rasped.

"I didn't do anything to her!" Derik said, but he caught Jason's expression and knew Jason wasn't going to buy that for a second. Derik's mind was churning frantically over what was going to happen if Maggie got away. He had screwed up royally. There were two witnesses now, and everything depended upon Tennyson getting rid of them before they could talk to anybody.

CHAPTER

twenty-two

Peter scoured the streets looking for Maggie. His heart skipped a beat when he finally spotted the Audi at a closed gas station.

Parking next to it, he got out and found that the car was unlocked and the keys left in the ignition. He leaned inside to give the car an apprehensive inspection. He saw the blanket and noted the dog hair which had not been there the day before. He realized Courage had been with Maggie at some point and wondered darkly what had happened to him.

Just then something slammed into his back, knocking the wind out of him and forcing him face down onto the seat.

On the defense, Peter instantly attempted to twist onto his back, but no sooner had he done so than he was hit again. The second his senses cleared, he suddenly detected the familiar scent of…wet dog.

"Courage!" Peter cried, wrestling himself out from underneath the canine. "You scared the heck out of me, boy! You and your way of sneaking up on people—" He didn't get much further before he got licked in the teeth and was effectively silenced. But the dog was the most welcomed sight Peter had seen all night. He hugged him, soaked fur and all, his heart still heavy with fear for Maggie and Tai. He hoped, though, that if Courage was okay, they would be too.

Peter's mind again went back to the day of the terrorist attack, when he had seen the Twin Towers collapse on national television. He had been young, but old enough to understand that his parents had been there. He and Genevieve had then suffered through the brutal torture of wondering if they could possibly be alive and suffering somewhere beneath the immense debris.

This felt sickeningly similar. He knew a killer was on the loose. He knew the killer was after Maggie and Tai. He didn't know if they were alive or dead or alive and suffering out there in the darkness somewhere.

Despite everything he had been through, Peter thought he had never felt as alone in his life as he did standing in the dark at that empty gas station. For a moment Peter closed his eyes tightly, rubbing his throbbing temples with his fingers. He took in a deep, shaky breath and slowly released it. Courage nudged him worriedly, and Peter hugged him again, tears prickling his eyes.

"I will not walk by fear!" he vowed. "I will not hinder God's hand by my lack of faith. Lord God, I trust you have a reason for everything, and I trust you will bring them back safely...." He closed his eyes, choking on the next words. "But, even if you don't...I will still serve you all the days of my life!"

Sensing his distress, Courage whined and rubbed his head against Peter's.

Peter took out his phone and sent up a quick prayer of thanks when he saw it was finally getting signal. He returned to the Camaro and opened the door so Courage could jump in. Then he got in and closed the door.

Peter gave a violent start as an old shutter came flying out of nowhere and crashed against his windshield, cracking it. His heart pounding, he took a steadying breath, thankful that it hadn't bashed through the glass. He glanced over at Courage, who let out another nervous whine, shifting his weight from foot to foot anxiously.

When he called Internal Affairs again, Peter finally got through this time. He could barely force himself to speak slowly enough for them to understand what he was saying as he went through every incredible detail.

"You would tell me, wouldn't you," he asked then, "if her bodyguard took her into hiding?"

"No, we probably wouldn't," the man on the other line admitted, "but since that isn't the case, I can tell you that's not what happened."

Agents were going to be dispatched immediately, despite the storm, their first destination being Megan Riley's house. The last thing Peter was told was to go home and stay out of this. It was too big for him to handle, and he needed to let the professionals deal with it. They would meet him at his house as soon as possible.

When Peter hung up, he took in another deep breath. He was tremendously relieved that he was going to get some help but deeply concerned that it was coming too late. He put in a quick call to his aunt to apprise her and Maggie's father of what was happening. Afterward he sat in the driver's seat in silence for a moment as he considered what to do.

At that moment, a lamppost came down, glass shattering on the pavement. Trash and leaves were being whipped across the small parking lot of the gas station. Peter looked around, again noting that the storm had wreaked a lot of havoc. Telephone and power lines were down, there was flooding everywhere, and many buildings were sporting broken windows.

The darkness and desolation around him were a shallow echo of the devastation within him. Worse was the conviction that this was somehow his fault because he had failed to protect Maggie.

Peter dropped his head back onto the headrest and, in a sudden fit of rage, slammed his fist into the steering wheel, crying out in bitter anguish.

Courage barked and pawed at Peter's leg to get his attention, undoubtedly trying to communicate his distress. "Take it easy, boy," Peter soothed, rubbing him behind his ears. Courage put his head in Peter's lap then like he did with Maggie when he sensed she was upset, and Peter knew that, like him, the dog was worrying about her.

Maggie and Tai made their way to a small church off of the main road. They circled the perimeter, looking for a way in.

"Do you think anyone could be inside?" Tai asked.

"No. There aren't any cars anywhere. I doubt anyone walked here—unless someone else is out here hiding from an assassin!"

Tai released a small laugh in acknowledgment of her humor.

They pulled the board off of a small bathroom window then and managed to pry it open. Tai climbed in and helped Maggie to follow. Once both were inside, they closed the window.

The building was cold and dark, although one of the shutters had come off one of the windows. A very faint light poured in through the stained glass window, casting a haunting glow of red, blue, and green over the whitewashed pews. They looked around them, listening intently for any sign that they had been followed. For a moment they just stood, afraid to move and unsure of what to do.

"I don't think we've been followed," Tai whispered. He was obviously terrified but was doing everything within his power to keep the fact from Maggie.

Maggie sunk to the carpeted floor, so exhausted she thought she'd never be able to get up again. He collapsed next to her, also wiped out. Maggie lay on her back, staring at the dark beams above her and wondering what they were going to do next.

"There'll be a phone here somewhere," Tai said, his voice raspy from fatigue.

"Yeah, and maybe in another twelve hours or so, they'll have the lines functioning again."

They rested for a while in silence. Then Maggie turned to face Tai. "So what the heck happened at Derik's? I never saw any sign of you—aside from the loud crash that forced me to make a diversion that got me caught," she added with annoyance.

"So that was my fault?"

"Yeah, I believe so," she said without remorse.

He glowered at her for a moment before getting over his irritation. "It took me forever to find the dang laptop," he complained. "I've hit houses in the dark, of course, but there's usually some kind of light coming in from the moon or a streetlamp or something. With the shutters closed, it was pitch black up there for most of the time. All I had was the light from my phone. I also generally have some kind of information on the person I'm going to hit beforehand."

"So could you get past the passwords?" Maggie asked.

"It was actually pretty easy. He had a touch screen with a picture password."

"A what?"

"You know—a password where you touch a picture at the right points in the correct order."

"How'd you know where to touch the picture?"

"I blew on the screen, and my breath made the fingerprints show up. There were four touch points on the screen, and I just tried them in different orders until I figured it out and got in." He smiled, full of self-importance. The old Tai was back. "I can't imagine these people having such an easy form of password with so much at stake. For educated boobs they're the stupidest intellectuals I've ever seen! That's like, uh, an oxymiron or something, right?

"Oxymoron," Maggie informed dryly.

"Did you just call me a moron?"

"No, moron! 'Oxymoron' is the word you meant."

"Oh. Okay then…. Hey, wait a minute. You just

called me a moron again!"

Maggie grinned despite herself. "Okay, get over it. Are you sure the laptop you found belonged to the police chief?"

"Oh yeah, I'm sure."

"Well, did you get into the database?" she asked anxiously. "Did you find any of the stuff Keller was talking about?"

"He had FileZilla. It's a program that enables you to go to Quick Connect for recent connects and use the last login. Just like that: bang, I was on their server. It was sheer luck that the broadband towers were still up and running, at least for most of the time. They went out after a while. Didn't the fed guys go through any of The I.S. computers?"

"I assume they did."

"Well, they either missed some whopping files, or they were deleted off of the computers before those guys in charge—"

"You mean Internal Affairs?"

"Yeah, those guys. It's possible that The I.S. sabotaged their own computers with a Nuke so that none of their data was traceable on any computer on their server. They could have reinstalled their files after the big guys finished checking them. I don't know. I wasn't really sure what I was looking for—but some things seemed a little off."

"What do you mean?"

"Like all kinds of stuff. They have a huge network. They have people from all over the country on their list. It's no wonder you've had such a hard time getting justice. And they have some whopping plans for the future."

"What kind of plans?" Maggie asked with uneasiness.

"Like big stuff. They've been getting some jerk ready to be president. I didn't understand all of it, but it seems to me that they also pretty much own the third guy that's running."

"Are you talking about Pat Jamison and William McFarland?" she asked incredulously.

"I think that was them. I don't remember the names."

"They're going to get McFarland to split the right wing votes so that Jamison will take the election," she breathed. She remembered Peter and her father having a conversation on this very topic. "I can't even imagine how scary it would be to have these people running the country." She gave a shiver at the very thought. "I don't think that's illegal, but I bet people would like to know that "Independent" McFarland is hiding his identity as a Democrat. That won't get him the Republican votes."

"Well, there were also lists of names of like people and companies, and they had large amounts of money in the columns next to them. Whatever that means. It didn't look legit."

"This was on the server?"

"No, that was on Caldwell's hard drive."

"I wonder if they're buying votes or accepting illegal contributions. Are you sure about them owning McFarland?"

"No, I'm not sure about anything. I don't understand

most of this crap. I haven't spent a whole lot of time following the elections while I was out on the streets! But there was something that seemed pretty clear. They have this, like, big plan to change everything."

"What does 'change everything' mean?" Maggie asked, annoyed at his ambiguity.

"Like religion and stuff. They want to promote their jacked up ideas on...what did they call it? Oh yeah, 'genetic perfection.' These people are something else. How is it that no one knows about them?"

"Everyone around here knows about them, but no one will talk about them because either they're working for them or terrified for their lives."

"Wonder why?" he said with heavy sarcasm.

"Were you able to print out any of this stuff?"

"Yeah, like I'm going to turn on a noisy printer with the boob gang downstairs."

Maggie rolled her eyes in frustration and thumped her palm on her forehead. "You mean all this was for nothing? It's good to know this, but without proof—"

"Just hold on. I didn't have internet connection long enough to get everything, but I was able to save a chunk of those files to my iPhone before it died completely. Otherwise, that couldn't have happened. I don't mind telling you that Derik scared the freaking life out of me when he came upstairs."

"No kidding. I about had a heart attack when I saw him head upstairs. So, what else did you get?"

"I told you. I was able to save a chunk of those files, but I wasn't really sure which files were important and which weren't. All this stuff takes time, Maggie, and it's hard to concentrate when you're scared out of your wits. Oh yeah, and what Derik said about that hit-list...."

"You heard that?"

Tai nodded, wide-eyed. "He wasn't joking. Keller was right. Caldwell has a blacklist with tons of people on it in one of the files on his hard drive. Your name is on that list. I ran a check on a bunch of those names before the internet went down. Like Keller said, I was able to match an obituary to nearly every name. The ones I couldn't match, I found on the Missing Persons list in Caldwell's files from the office. Oh, and guess what?"

"What?"

"I found *Keller's* name on that list."

Maggie gave Tai a penetrating look. "Tai...no matter what happens, you can't ever let anyone know you found out about this stuff. Your name will end up on that list in a heartbeat if you do. I should never have agreed to letting you do this. If I'd had more faith, I would have trusted God to take care of this in his own timing." She fell silent for a moment. "I don't think I'll ever forgive myself for getting you involved."

"I whacked Tennyson on my own. I whacked Derik on my own. So, you didn't get me involved; I involved myself. Anyway, they know I'm in this thing with you, so it's too late to pretend ignorance now. Besides, haven't I told you that I'd do anything for you?" he added with quiet sincerity.

She smiled at him through the darkness of the sanctuary. "I hope you know how much I appreciate you, brat."

He grinned back at her. "So, are you ready to become Wonder Bread yet?"

"Don't hold your breath!"

They sat in silence for another long moment.

"If you're so good at doing things like this, how come you and your mom aren't living it up?" Maggie asked at length.

He was silent for a moment before turning to face her. "I don't want to do those things, Maggie. I only do them when I have to. The risk is too great. If I get caught, I'll go to jail, and my mother will die even earlier than the doctors said she would. Her medications are very expensive. She can't survive without them now, but she would also probably rather die than find out about the things I've done."

Maggie's brow raised in disbelief. "And you're really going to tell me you don't *enjoy* hacking into computers, when your room is full of computer hacking junk?"

"Okay, so I admit I used to think the challenge was a total rush, but I don't like…you know, hurting people. I do it when I need to, and like I said, internet fraud is safer than stealing a car or taking valuables. The authorities don't even look into most identity theft cases if the theft is less than $5K."

Peter had told her as much. "But, Tai, you have to know how much damage that can do. People default on loans in situations like that. They could even miss a mortgage payment and lose their homes. Some of them might have loved ones who are also sick and in need of medication. Have you ever thought of that?"

He remained silent.

"You realize you're never going to be right with God until you set things straight with those people," Maggie quietly chastised. When he said nothing, she nudged his arm to make him look at her. "We *both* have things to set right."

"Yeah, I know."

Maggie finally dragged herself to a sitting position and carefully pulled off her shoes. Even in the darkness, Tai could see the blood seeping through her socks. He cursed and Maggie told him to watch his mouth.

"For crying out loud, that really looks bad, Maggie!" he whispered.

She pulled her socks off to survey the damage. The bandages that Conrad had wrapped her feet with were soaked in blood.

Tai was frustrated, not knowing how to help her. He got up and disappeared into the darkness of the back rooms. A while later he returned with a box that had some limited medical supplies. "There isn't much here, but there are some fresh bandages. That might help a little, although it doesn't help that your shoes are wet and your feet have been soaked for so long."

He helped her change the bandages.

"Quit hovering, brat," Maggie said at last. "I'm not helpless."

"Well, you play the part pretty well, snob!"

She smiled in spite of herself.

"Hey, there's a kitchen back there. Do you think they'll have any food in the fridge? I mean that would be okay, right? It's not like stealing from a church or anything?"

"You hit houses and break into people's bank accounts, and you're seriously worried about eating the church's food?"

It was his turn to smile.

He got up, and Maggie moved to do the same. "Sit down," Tai said. "I'll go check the fridge when I put this stuff back. There's no point in you walking on those feet."

She gave him a look of annoyance and got up anyway.

"Stubborn," he mumbled under his breath.

"Thief," she said under hers.

When they opened the fridge, they found very little besides some juice for communion. Maggie found a bag of communion crackers in a cupboard.

"Won't we get struck by lightning or something for touching sacred food?" Tai asked again, genuinely concerned.

Maggie laughed. "I seriously doubt it. Jesus ate grain on the Sabbath, and when David and his men got hungry, they went into the temple and ate the holy bread that was consecrated by the priests. I'm not making any promises, though, brat. If you go up in smoke, it's on you!"

He glanced at her in irritation.

They found some matches and lit the gas burners. It

gave them some light and heat, and the two of them climbed up and sat on the counters, drinking the juice and eating the crackers.

"I don't think I've ever been so hungry," Maggie said. "I'm still struggling to pretend that this tastes good, though."

"Have you had anything to eat at all tonight?" Tai asked.

"Well, Conrad offered me something, but I was too proud to take it from him. I'm regretting that now. What about you?"

"Mr. Waters made some sandwiches around four."

"How's that situation going?" she asked.

"He was a little better to deal with today, but he still looks down his nose at me, and I still hate him. It won't help that I stole his car."

"He might understand under the circumstances."

Tai shook his head in denial. "He thinks I'm just a dumb Hmong kid. It shows in everything he does, even when he doesn't come out and say it." Tai's voice became more and more bitter the more he talked. "I work hard for him, Mags. I've always been on time. But nothin' I do matters. When he pays me, he acts like I'm a charity case, not like he's paying someone who's worked for the money. If it wasn't for my mom, I'd tell him to take a flying leap!"

Maggie sensed his shame and tried to encourage him. "The fact that you would put up with him so that you can make money honestly when you could have made more money dishonestly speaks for your character. You know, Tai, you shouldn't try to measure your value by what other people think, anyway. Christ is the only one you need to please, and he loves you, even with your faults."

"It's easier said than done," he said with a raw edge of frustration.

She thought about it, knowing how many times she'd been talked about and put down by others. "I realize that. I'm the target for gossip for the entire school, remember? But when you find yourself in Christ, you see yourself through his eyes and everything changes. It doesn't feel good when people trash you, but it also doesn't matter so much anymore because you know you still have value in the eyes of the one who created you."

They sat in silence then as they finished the rest of the crackers.

"Tai?"

"Yeah?"

"We need to split up before we end up with a swarm of these guys after us."

"Why should we leave?" he objected. "We're safe here. We need to wait out the storm. When it gets to be daylight, people will be around. The lines will be fixed."

"They know who I am, but they don't know anything about you," Maggie insisted. "You have to get out of Norfolk and do something to change your look."

"It's a bit late for that! I'm sure Tennyson has seen me with you before."

"He never saw you come up behind him. He doesn't

know you're with me," Maggie objected.

"Derik does. He'll tell them we were together."

"I doubt Derik knows you're from Richmond. Did you ever fill out a church visitor information card?"

"I don't think so. It doesn't matter; I'm not leaving you!"

Just then they saw a flash of light coming from the sanctuary. Tai ran to the nearest window and looked out just as two vehicles came to a stop in front of the church.

CHAPTER

twenty-three

Maggie and Tai froze before Maggie jumped into action and flicked off the burners. They crept back into the main room, where the headlights were casting a sheet of ghostly light through the missing shutter. The stream of light reached across the sanctuary all the way to the pulpit. Maggie quickly snatched up her socks and shoes and slipped them back on.

"Could these people be on our side?" Tai asked.

"Extremely doubt it!" Maggie whispered fiercely. "Do you want to find out?"

"I'll pass on that! I'm sure Tennyson sicced them on us. How the heck did they find us, anyway?"

"They probably saw the missing boards on the bathroom window and are wondering if we broke in," Maggie surmised. "They know we have to take shelter somewhere. They'll probably search every building within walking distance from where we were last seen."

"If that's the case, they might not know we're here. They could just be randomly searching this place, right?" Tai suggested.

"They'll know we were here when they feel the heat coming in from the kitchen. There's no way they won't figure out that the burners are hot!"

They watched in trepidation as the shadows from several people crossed in front of the headlights on their way to make a sweep of the perimeter of the church.

"Come on!" Maggie choked in mounting trepidation. "We have to get out of here!"

They rushed toward the back rooms of the church, slipping on the wood floor as they rounded a corner and nearly tripping over each other in their haste. Running down a hall, they found a stairway that led to the basement.

"Let's go," Maggie whispered fiercely, motioning to the stairway.

"I ain't gonna get trapped in a basement!" Tai hissed.

"Would you rather be shot right here?"

Tai swallowed his panic, unable to argue with her logic, and they quickly made their way down into the darkness, treading carefully in case the boards creaked.l

Meanwhile, two men in dark clothes knocked the remaining board aside and climbed through the bathroom window. With the aid of a tiny flashlight, they made their way stealthily through the silent church. They eventually came to the kitchen, both immediately noting the heat that hovered there just as Maggie had predicted. At one point one motioned to the other and shined his flashlight on the floor. A bloody footprint had been left behind.

"Looks like one's wounded," he whispered ominously.

"Bullet wound?"

"Hard to tell."

"Lord God, help us," Maggie prayed under her breath.

She and Tai stood silently, holding their breath and listening with their hearts pounding loudly in their ears. As careful as their predators had been, the teens had heard them enter the building.

"What are we going to do?" Tai hissed. "We obviously can't go out the way we came in. We'll never get past them!" Hysteria was beginning to surface.

"When we came in, I saw a stairwell outside that led to this basement. It's on the north side," Maggie said, thinking aloud. "The headlights are shining on the east side. We might be able to slip out in the cover of darkness if we can find the door and get it open."

They both tensed as they heard a slight creak coming from the top of the stairs. A small, narrow beam from a flashlight shone into the darkness, and they both ducked for cover as it went right past their heads.

"Make sure you don't run into anything. We can't afford to make any noise!" Maggie whispered into his ear.

"Do you think I don't know that?" he whispered back.

Both in panic mode now, they quickly made their way past chairs, boxes, and furniture to the north wall, where they felt their way along until they found the door.

"Someone could be right outside, watching the door!" Tai warned. They hesitated in indecision. There was another creaking noise just then, and both of their heads snapped in the direction of the stairs.

"Well, someone is definitely in here with us!" Maggie whispered.

They quietly pushed on the crash bar of the door, experiencing another moment of terror when the door didn't budge. Their panic increased. They knew they couldn't push harder without making noise. They also knew they were dead if they gave away their location and still couldn't get the door open.

There was another creak on the stairs that inspired them to immediately throw caution to the wind, this time pushing with all their strength. The bar popped and the door opened. They hurriedly scrambled through the opening, and were hit with a gust of wind that nearly blew them backward. Both caught their balance, glancing back at the door. There was no question that whoever was coming down the stairs had to have heard the noise.

As they tore up the cement steps to ground level, they could hear a loud clattering coming from the basement. "The idiot must have found the boxes!" Tai whispered as they reached the top of the stairwell and looked frantically around them.

There were several shouts just then, and they knew their time was running out. A dark form emerged from around the corner of the church, but not before both teens had taken cover behind a storage shed. From there they made it across the street to an empty two-story commercial building. There was a large oak tree that grew directly next to it.

"Come on!" Tai said as he climbed up into the tree, scrambling up the branches to the top and then climbing onto the roof.

Maggie followed, struggling to ignore the burning pain in her feet. They both flattened against the roof where they could take cover behind a chimney stack but still watch what was going on across the street.

"We're sitting ducks on the ground," Tai said, "but they'll never think to look for us up here."

"Yeah, and as long as the wind doesn't pick back up, we might not die!" Maggie replied. Even as she spoke, they were getting pelted with sticks and leaves, and it was a struggle to move on the wet roof without slipping.

"I guess there is that."

They watched anxiously as three men raced around the church, meeting in the front by their cars. They couldn't hear what the men were saying, but they could tell they were frustrated by the way they were gesturing.

The men quickly spread out and made a wider sweep of the area just outside the church property. One headed across the street in their direction.

"Crap!" Maggie said.

"Just stay low. He'll never see us," Tai assured her.

"It's extremely dangerous up here, Tai."

"It's dangerous? *Really*?" Tai replied sarcastically.

It was then that Maggie looked to the east and spotted a light in the distance. "Look, Tai! The power is on in that section of the city," she whispered. "Maybe the phones are working, too."

It was raining again by then, and a streak of lightning snaked its way across the angry sky. A rolling boom of thunder followed.

Tai looked to the distant lights. "You're right, but that's a long ways off."

They watched as the men returned to their cars. Their engines had been left running, and in no time they had split up in three different directions, driving around the area. From their vantage point, the two could see the vehicles stop from time to time, the men getting out to ring a doorbell and question the occupants or check the perimeter for break-ins if the occupants were not home.

"Wow. They're pretty thorough," Tai said with a shudder. "We need to get help."

"From who? How do we know who to trust? These guys are hitting all these houses. They've probably told the residents we're dangerous criminals or something."

Tai thought that over. "They might recognize you and suspect those men are lying."

"Yeah, and they might flat turn us over to save their own butts! I doubt anybody could protect us against these men, anyway. We could end up getting an entire family killed! I mean, think about it, it's not like they could call for help with the phone lines being down."

Tai shut his eyes against the image, knowing she could easily be right.

They watched as the vehicles finally disappeared from view. They waited another fifteen minutes, afraid to move, then scampered back down the tree. Tai made a break for the garage of a home that was about a hundred yards down the road.

Maggie was hot on his heels. "What are you doing?" she cried.

Ignoring her, Tai wrapped the end of his sweater around his hand and tried the garage door. It was unlocked.

"These people are home, Tai!"

"Which is why they will have a car parked in the garage," he said meaningfully.

As the door opened, they got a look at the vehicle parked within.

"What the heck is that?" Maggie asked with sarcasm.

"Haven't you ever seen a smart car, Maggie?" Tai laughed.

"It looks like a pencil box with wheels!"

"Well, it basically is. Get in."

"I don't think so. This is grand theft auto!"

"Which is what I committed when I took Waters's car to find you at the SPCA. Would you rather take a bullet in the head?" he whispered fiercely.

"*I* am *not* doing this. Breaking and entering was bad

enough."

They heard the crunch of gravel on pavement then and turned just in time to see a vehicle creeping down the street with its lights off.

Tai shut the garage door, and they waited until the vehicle had passed.

"Oh great, they have their headlights off now; we won't see them coming!" Maggie said, her anxiety increasing once more. "We won't hear them, either, as long as this storm keeps up."

"Get in the car, Maggie!" Tai said again, his voice betraying his terror.

"No, Tai, this isn't the way. Besides, if we're in a vehicle, we'll be confined to the streets and they'll spot us for sure. On foot we can roam anywhere."

Tai was going to argue further, but he finally relented, and they went back out into the night on foot.

It was early morning when they reached a gas station in the portion of Norfolk that still had its power. By then the storm had abated. They peered into the glass windows and spotted a phone on a desk some ten feet from the door.

"Now what?" Tai asked.

"Well, I guess we're back to breaking and entering if we want to get to a phone," Maggie confessed, cognizant of the fact that they were facing breaking the law yet again. "But I'm sure the law will understand under the circumstances." The minute she said it, she realized how ridiculous that was, and she laughed spontaneously.

"Oh, and your famous Norfolk Police Department is going to let that pass, despite the fact that you were just trying to get away from their murderous buddies who they probably hired to shoot us in the first place."

She couldn't help but laugh again. "They'll probably say we've gone on a huge crime spree, taking advantage of the storm to break into the homes of unsuspecting victims. That most likely carries a hefty sentence."

"No kidding!" Tai exclaimed, but he wasn't smiling. "We know the alarm systems are going to be functioning now, but we don't know if the telephones are."

"Well, can't you cut the lines to the system or something?"

"That doesn't always work. Cutting the lines could set off the alarms, and I guarantee whoever has been following us will be here in a heartbeat."

Maggie thought that over. "We're still too far away to make it to Waters's, and even if I could reach him...you stole his car, which is still at the pound, so he can't come get us."

"So what, then?"

"We need to contact Internal Affairs."

Tai raised an eyebrow. "Can we trust them?"

"As a whole? Yes. That doesn't mean they don't have any members who've converted to the other side. I mean, dang, my own bodyguard ditched me for these mobsters!"

"How far away are their offices?"

"Pretty far," Maggie admitted. "About seven or eight miles, I'd guess. But I don't know if they're even open. I mean, if I call the cell number I was given, I could be getting an agent at his home or anywhere."

"Do you think they'll get here before our buddies do if we do set off the alarms?"

"Probably not, but we might not set of the alarms, right?" Maggie said optimistically.

"We could also set off the stupid alarms and then find that the phones don't work anyway!"

Maggie was wracking her mind for a solution when her gaze drifted down the street and she saw the local news station. "Tai, who's the first to be at a crime scene?"

"The cops, of course. But in this case, if they are working with these guys who are after us, they will probably be late on arrival on purpose."

"Sure. But who's right after them?"

He followed the direction of her gaze, his eyes suddenly widening. "The news reporters!" he shouted.

"Bingo. They are always ready to go after a story when things get crazy, right? They'll certainly be looking for a story about this storm. What would you bet that they'd rather get our story? I bet those reporters are so used to being ready on a dime that they'll show before Tennyson and his buddies do. I'm sure they won't mind risking this weather to get that interview they've been hounding me for. They'll be witnesses, Tai. The assassins wouldn't be stupid enough to try to take down a whole crew of reporters, and they certainly won't want to get caught on camera. The reporters can give us safety, at least for now."

Tai's eyes glinted in anticipation. "Do you have any numbers to call?"

"They call all the time. I've got a couple of them memorized by now."

"All right then."

Tai made an attempt at disabling the gas station's alarms, but just as he predicted, he set them off instead. They immediately ran for the door, busting in the glass with a rock and unlocking it before running in, making a quick search, and finding the phone. Maggie snatched it up and nearly passed out with relief when she got a dial tone.

"Hurry!" Tai cried.

"I am!" She punched in the numbers for one of the reporters who had been leaving her messages for weeks on end. She knew the number by heart.

A sleepy voice came on the other end. "Hello?"

"Daniela Parker?"

"Yeah, speaking?"

"Listen, I've only got a minute. This is Maggie Kraus."

"Maggie Kraus?" she asked, waking out of her sleepy state immediately.

"Please listen. I've been on the run for my life all night. My bodyguard tried to kill me, and now he has hit men who've been hunting me and my friend. We're at the gas station by the Denny's restaurant, and we've set off the alarms. They're going to be here any minute—we need help!"

"Hold on, kid! I'll assemble my crew and be there in five minutes. Can you hang on that long?"

"I don't know. They're armed!"

"Okay, I'll meet you there!" She hung up.

Maggie called I.A. next. A man came on the line, and she identified herself.

"Ms. Kraus! We've been looking for you all night!"

Tai cautiously peered out the window and into the darkness. From a distance of several blocks away, tiny headlights suddenly appeared. "Oh god, Maggie, here they come!"

She was out of time, and Maggie gave their location and rushed to tell the man as much as possible. She finished with, "Tennyson has switched sides. He's armed and he's got friends. They're coming to kill us *right now*!"

No sooner had Tai spotted the first vehicle than a second car came skidding from a side street and pulled in front of the first car.

"There's two cars now!" Maggie screamed into the phone.

"Okay, hold on, Ms. Kraus! Find a place to hide immediately. We'll be right there."

Maggie slammed the phone on the hook as she and Tai dove behind a tire display.

Just then the two sedans came to a skidding halt, one by the front door, the other by the back door.

Before the drivers could get out, though, two vans pulled in and parked twenty feet from them. Six reporters piled out of the vans with flood lights and camera equipment in hand. When the drivers of the sedans spotted them, they suddenly backed up and spun out of the parking lot.

"They left, Tai!" Maggie cried, weak with relief. "Stay here. Don't let them photograph you or get your name. Got that? I have to talk to the reporters before the cops show up and put their own spin on this."

Ms. Parker cautiously entered the building, looking around and spotting Maggie right away. "Are you kids okay?" She glanced around the room, looking for the other teen as she approached.

"Yes," Maggie said. "Did you see those vehicles?"

"They left when they saw us. We couldn't get their plates. Now talk to us before the police arrive. Where's your friend, Maggie?" Ms. Parker asked.

"If I talk to you, it has to be under the condition that you don't take his picture or give out his name. Can I trust you on that? If you tell, these people will come after him. If you don't, I will make sure you have any exclusive we give the press."

"All right, agreed, but you've got to know the police could still give out that information."

"I guess you're right. If the hit men are working for the cops, they already know there are two of us, and they'll keep searching until they find him." Maggie sighed in frustration. "Tai, you might as well come out," she called.

Tai approached from the back.

"This is my friend who saved my life," Maggie said, unable to help the pride that was in her voice.

"Nice to meet you." Ms. Parker held out her hand, and Tai shook it. She then guided him and Maggie outside, where the cameramen were already stationed. "We're running out of time, honey. Talk to me."

"I can't tell you everything, but I will tell you that Agent Tennyson, who was supposed to be my bodyguard, tried to kill me last night."

"Why would he do such a thing?" she asked, confused.

"He wanted to get rid of me because he knew I had some incriminating evidence against The Inner Society. He had to get hold of it and make sure I didn't tell anybody. My friend showed up, though, and messed up his plans."

"How's that?"

"He cracked him over the head. We thought he was dead, but he came after us later and shot at us. I...." She thought twice about what she was going to say next. "I didn't have my cell phone, and all the phone lines were down, so we couldn't call for help."

Sirens could be heard in the distance.

"What evidence did you have, and did he get it from you?" she interrogated quickly.

"I can't tell you what it was, but, yes, he took it from me and destroyed it."

"So you have no proof that it ever existed?"

"No. I mean, yes!" Maggie was becoming rattled as she glanced anxiously at the oncoming cars. Her time was out, and she rushed to finish. "But you need to know that William McFarland is only running as an Independent to take votes from Raintree. He's really working with The Inner Society to make sure Jamison is voted into office. He's lied to the public about his intentions all along. Do you understand? Jamison and McFarland are both working for The Inner Society! People need to know this. Election Day is right on top of us!"

"Can you prove this?"

"In another hour, Internal Affairs will be able to confirm it."

All at once three police cars pulled into the lot. The policemen jumped out. "You need to leave the premises now!" Caldwell's chief deputy told the reporters.

"Don't leave us!" Maggie cried to Ms. Parker. "You know they're corrupt. They're probably working with the assassins!"

Ms. Parker turned to the deputy. "The free right of the press is a Constitutional right," she protested.

"You are interfering with a crime scene, and that is not your right. You will vacate, or we'll arrest you too!" The deputy raged and took hold of Maggie's arm in a biting grasp.

Another officer took hold of Tai. Both he and Maggie found themselves slapped in handcuffs.

"My crew and I are not leaving these kids," Ms.

Parker insisted.

The deputy looked at her with exacerbation before turning back to Maggie and Tai. "You are being arrested for vandalism, and breaking and entering with the intent to commit theft. You have the right to remain silent—although I find that hard to imagine. You have the right to an attorney. If you cannot afford one, one will be appointed for you. Do you understand your rights?"

The officers took the teens and hauled them toward their vehicles. The reporters followed, getting everything on tape.

"I'm going to confiscate your cameras!" the deputy threatened.

Maggie's eyes darted around, looking for any solution at all to get out of this mess. She could only hope and pray that Internal Affairs got there in time.

Just then a new gold Impala and a blue Chrysler came screeching into the lot and pulled alongside the police cars.

"What is this, Grand Central Station?" the officer bellowed.

The drivers got out of their cars and flashed their badges. "You know who we are, Deputy, and you know we have jurisdiction," Agent Ralph Brawley said sternly. "Let these kids go immediately."

The deputy looked resentfully at the agents, knowing he had no choice. He jerked Maggie around and undid her handcuffs. "Let the kid go," he told the other officer who had Tai.

"You and your men can leave now." Agent Brawley

dismissed the police, and they reluctantly returned to their cars. Maggie let out a breath of relief and a prayer of thanks. Maybe this horrible night would finally be over.

Agent Brawley turned to Maggie and Tai after the police left. "I hope you haven't said too much to those reporters," he whispered. "Now get in the car, you two."

CHAPTER
twenty-four

Not long after, they arrived at a three-story red brick building on Brooke Avenue, and went up to the top floor. By then the storm had finally passed, the black clouds parting to reveal patches of midnight blue sky. The moonlight shone through the patches, shedding a pale light on all of the destruction that had occurred during the tumultuous hours of the night. Although no serious damage had been done, many of the streets were under several inches of water, and there was trash and debris everywhere. Quite a few trees had become uprooted, but there was no damage worse than that done to Derik's house. Power and communications were still down in several areas, and two people had reported suffering concussions from being hit by things strewn by the wind, but news reports said they weren't expecting any reports of fatal injuries.

Now Maggie, Tai, and three agents sat in gray-cushioned chairs around a massive glass table in a luxurious conference room. Both teens were soaked and suffering from exhaustion. Their muscles were sore from their excursions, and they looked like they were about to drop. An agent brought them each a cup of hot cocoa, and the others gave the kids their jackets since they had no blankets to offer them.

Maggie and Tai were half-starved and sipped gratefully at the cocoa, feeling it warm their cold, stiff bodies.

Brawley turned on a tape recorder. He was a man in his fifties, with dark bushy brows and brown hair peppered with gray. He was growing bald on top and had put on a little weight, but his keen gray eyes missed little, and Maggie discerned that he was the one in charge.

The agents began grilling them with questions. They asked about the District Attorney, and Maggie told them how she found her dead in her home. They then asked several questions about Tennyson. They wanted to know where the two kids had been between the time they knocked Tennyson out and the time he came after them on the road. The agents didn't miss the fact that Maggie and Tai quickly exchanged glances.

"You better not keep anything from us," Agent Dennison, a tall, skinny man in his late thirties, threatened. "Your lives depend on it."

"I am so tired," Maggie said, so exhausted that she could barely keep up. "We've been running all night. Can't we finish this later?"

"She's hurt," Tai informed. "Look at her feet."

"We know you two were at the Caldwell residence. Is that where you got hurt?" Brawley asked, genuinely concerned.

"A tree crashed through the window, and I cut my feet on the glass."

Before she could go into any detail, the door burst open, and Peter, Mr. Kraus, and Genevieve came in. Maggie jumped up and ran into Peter's arms. He clung to her so tightly she could barely breathe.

"Oh, baby, I never thought I'd see you again!" There were tears in his eyes, and his voice cracked with emotion. He pulled back from her so that he could assess her for injuries. He took her by the jaw and gently turned her head to the side as he absorbed the damage done to her mouth. He closed his eyes for a moment and swallowed the rage that clutched his heart. "Derik did that to you?" he asked through clenched teeth.

Maggie only nodded. In the scope of things, her bruised mouth hardly ranked as important.

"Did it happen while you were caught trespassing or later on?"

"I made him mad at me," she confessed softly.

"Where did the blood come from, Maggie? Conrad said you cut your feet."

"That's basically what happened. I just told the agents about it."

He pulled her close, encouraging her to just relax now. "You all right, Tai?" Peter looked to him, relieved to see he appeared to be unhurt.

"Yeah, I'm fine, man. You know, same old stuff I get every day in Richmond: people trying to run me over, shoot me, or knock me down in the street." He looked over at Maggie when he added on that last part, and she gave him a knowing smile.

Maggie's father came forward and hugged her, too. "Honey, I've been so worried! I didn't think I'd survive not knowing what happened to you! Are you okay?"

"I'm fine, Dad. I mean I've been better, but I'm upright and breathing."

"Let's have a look at those feet, honey," the female agent who'd given them the cocoa said. Maggie sat in a chair, and Agent White knelt on the floor beside her and pulled off Maggie's shoes and socks, examining the damage.

Peter's heart constricted when he saw the bloody socks, and he came to her side and put his arm around her. She leaned into him and sighed, drawing comfort and strength from his presence.

"Yeah, this looks pretty bad," the agent said. "You've been walking on your feet in this condition all night?"

"Well, for a few hours, anyway. I don't think the fact that we were walking through dirty water most of the time helped."

"No, it hasn't. We'll have to get you tended to."

"In the meantime," Brawley continued, "we still have a few more questions. I'd like to know about the DVD."

"Old Man Keller made a video that outlined some dark secrets The Inner Society has kept on a private server."

"All of the higher ranking members of The I.S. members have access to it," Tai said.

"We've accessed their server already," Brawley informed.

"But Keller said there was information in the files on their server that was carefully encoded so someone reading it wouldn't really know what they were reading," Maggie corrected, with a nod from Tai that she had her technical facts right. "If you didn't know it was there, you wouldn't have thought to look for it."

"I think some of that information could have been deleted from the server before you got access to it anyway," Tai said.

"What's on it?" Agent White asked.

Maggie's attention was drawn back to the female agent. "I never saw the whole DVD," she admitted, "but Keller said he found lists of names, a kind of hit list, and some of the files had political plans that were a threat to the United States. He thought his life was in danger because Chambers suspected that he'd gotten access to information that had been left open on Caldwell's laptop."

"So where is that DVD?" Brawley asked imperatively.

Maggie sighed. "Like I said, I called Megan Riley and tried to pass it to her, but she never showed at our meeting place. Instead I found her with a knife in her back at her house!"

"We'll discuss Ms. Riley later, Maggie," Brawley said. "We need to know where the DVD is."

"Tennyson took it from me and destroyed it."

It seemed like most of the people in the room released the breath they'd been holding up until that point. Brawley groaned and rested his head in his hands for a moment as he pondered this unwelcome information. "That leaves us with nothing, then."

"All right, you can now explain why, on God's green earth, you decided to break into your enemy's house during a flipping hurricane!" Agent Dennison interrogated. "Mr.

Bennett," he nodded to Peter, "has informed us about your nocturnal activities, Ms. Kraus. You want us to trust you, but then you recklessly break the law and take matters into your own hands instead of letting us do our jobs!"

Maggie and Tai looked to one another again, and the agents became restless.

"I really don't like this undercurrent that I'm getting between the two of you," Brawley said. He wasn't any happier than the others at being up at that brutal hour. "We'll separate you and question each of you alone if I think you're comparing notes."

"It's not that," Tai said. "We just don't want to get in trouble."

"I've got news for you, kid: you're way past that mark!"

"I was scared," Maggie confessed. "Ms. Riley said my phone was tapped and someone had overheard our conversation. They knew I had that DVD. When I found her dead, I tried to call you guys, but I couldn't get through. I didn't know what to do. I thought Tennyson was going to help me, but then I lost the DVD to him, and I knew without any other evidence, it was once again just my testimony against all the other witnesses. I would be the only one who could verify what was on that DVD. I knew The I.S. was going to get rid of me for real this time."

She stopped, the reality of her long, terrifying night sinking in. She could feel her body trembling, but a squeeze from Peter's hand on her shoulder encouraged her to finish. She took a deep breath.

"I felt I had to find some concrete information to pass

on to you. If I could manage that, then maybe they'd call off the hit on me because I would have already given you everything you needed to prosecute them."

Brawley sighed, understanding her fear, but still frustrated with her recklessness. "So, what 'concrete information' did you think you could obtain that the entire Internal Affairs Department couldn't have obtained on our own?"

"I thought I could access their server," Tai spoke up. "I was scared for Maggie, and I thought this was the only way to stop these people."

"So *you* talked her into breaking into Derik's house? Are you crazy?" Peter choked.

"We couldn't see any other way out of this mess," Maggie jumped to his defense. "Ms. Riley was murdered because of that DVD. We didn't have her to turn to, and you know we couldn't have gone to the police. Tennyson turned out to be a murderous freak, and we couldn't get hold of you. We were scared to death, Peter!"

"Why didn't you come to my house like I asked you, Maggie?" Peter said, summoning what patience he could. Everyone was exhausted by that hour, and he wasn't immune to the effects of a sleepless night, any more than anyone else.

"She was afraid of putting all you guys in danger," Tai said in her defense.

"I would have brought death to your door," Maggie said, "and you guys would have had no way of defending yourselves at your house."

Genevieve, standing on Maggie's other side with Mr. Kraus, said nothing but rubbed Maggie's shoulders in a motherly way.

"So the two of you went into the house and the boys caught you," Brawley surmised.

"They caught me. They never caught Tai. He was free to go through their laptop all night."

"And don't you kids think I.A. could have done that, and done it without such extreme risk?" Agent Dennison rebuked.

"Well, did you?" Genevieve asked then, reproach in her voice.

"Like we said, we already accessed their server," Brawley informed carefully. "The Inner Society has the Constitutional right to congregate and perpetuate their own beliefs. Nothing on that database was illegal."

"Well, I don't think you accessed Caldwell's hard drive—at least not the one at his house," Tai said. "If you had, you would have seen the hit list that has her name on it!" He motioned toward Maggie. "I found the obituaries of a whole bunch of people on that list, too!" Tai was smart, but he was also way out of his depth with these people. It was terrifying to stand up to them, but he knew what he knew. He was also not ready to accept that everything they'd been through that night had been for nothing.

"So enlighten us, then," Brawley said. "How the heck did a kid get access to a private server?"

Tai hesitated. "If I tell you, will you offer me protection against my crimes?"

"It definitely won't go in your favor if you don't."

"If you saw his room, you would understand," Peter answered for him. "He's fixated with computers. He must have over a hundred books on computer hacking alone."

Maggie glared up at him. *You're not helping*, her eyes said.

"You do realize that computer hacking is a serious offense, right, kid?" Dennison put in.

"I came clean with you, though. And I won't do it again!"

"You just did it!"

"I wasn't stealing or anything, though. Doesn't it matter that I was trying to help?"

Maggie's heart twisted. Peter too felt a pang of regret; Tai was a good kid—even if he was mad at him for helping Maggie with this hare-brained scheme.

The agents looked to one another with raised brows but remained silent.

Tai grew pale. "I'm going to jail, aren't I?"

"You might," Brawley said.

"But this time it was my fault!" Maggie jumped to his defense again. "I'll take the responsibility."

"There will definitely be some consequences which could easily carry over to both of you," Brawley said, giving them both a stern look of disapproval.

"So what else was in that database, and were you or were you not able to print it out or save it to a disk?" Agent White interrupted.

"I didn't have a disk, and the power was out, so I couldn't print it out either. But I found another solution," Tai said smugly, momentarily forgetting about his possible fate. Even with dark rings under his sleep deprived eyes, he hadn't lost his arrogance.

"Well?" all the agents asked at once.

"I sent some of the files that looked important to my iPhone. I didn't have time to send them all, though. The internet was down most of the night."

The agents looked to one another with sudden interest.

"Okay. Hand it over, kid." Dennison put his hand out toward Tai expectantly.

"Am I gonna get my phone back?"

"Not until we get the information off of it and delete it from your files."

Tai reluctantly handed it over, obviously not too happy about the situation.

"Are you going to let us in on this information?" Genevieve asked Agent Brawley.

"Not until we've had the chance to go through it thoroughly."

"And probably not even then, right?" Mr. Kraus said. It was the first time he had spoken, being as absorbed as he had been over everything that was being said. His daughter's activities never ceased to shock him into silence. "I think the rest of my black hair has turned gray."

Brawley's attention went from Mr. Kraus and back to Maggie once more. "I will tell you this. We went over to Megan Riley's residence."

"And?" Maggie asked anxiously.

"And there was no sign of any disturbance."

"What?" Maggie and Peter both gasped.

"Doesn't a *dead body* count as a disturbance?" Peter asked incredulously.

"There was no body—no signs of any disturbance at all. The doors were locked, and her car was gone."

"But I saw her car in the garage!" Maggie cried. "And that was right before I discovered her body. She certainly didn't get up with a knife in her back and drive away!"

Brawley nodded. "We'll look into it soon, considering no one in this room has had any sleep tonight."

"Are we going to jail?" Tai asked hesitantly.

"You should for all the stunts you kids pulled tonight!" Dennison snapped.

Brawley put a hand out to quiet him. "We can discuss that later as well. We'll see if the Caldwells press charges."

"Can we go home then?" Maggie asked.

"The others can. You certainly can't. If you still don't understand the danger you're in by now, then I don't know what to tell you."

"Then where will she go?" Peter asked, worried.

"We'll set her up somewhere where she can rest for now. She obviously needs some medical attention, but then she'll have to get her things together and get out of Norfolk. We'll find a place for her until the trial is over."

"You let her stay at Jacob Townsend's house once before. Would you consider that again? I mean his dad is a doctor, and they have security like a prison."

"Sure, we'll consider that, but we don't want to put the Townsends at risk, either."

By then Maggie would have been happy to sleep in a motel bed so long as she could have a shower first. She was stiff and aching all over, and she wondered if Tai wasn't feeling just as bad. "What about Tai?" she asked.

"Did anyone ever get a good look at him?" Brawley asked.

"The police did. So did Derik, and I'm sure Derik remembers seeing him at church. That means they could find him, right?"

"Do you live around here, Tai?"

"I live in Richmond with my mom."

"There are nearly eight million people living in Virginia. It is highly doubtful they'll locate Tai without a name or address within the next two weeks," Brawley concluded. "Would the church have his information?"

"I don't remember if I turned in a visitor's card or not," Tai admitted.

"They can trace him through the transportation system," Peter said.

"You take a bus to get into Norfolk?" Brawley asked.

"Yes."

"Well that screws things up." Brawley was looking exhausted himself. "Okay, fine. Let's see if the Townsends will agree to letting you crash their house again. In the meantime we're going to turn over this case to the FBI."

It was four o'clock in the morning by the time Maggie finally shed her dirty clothes and got into the hot shower in one of the guest bedrooms at the Townsend mansion. She'd been under so much pressure for so long that she finally burst into tears.

A long while later, she got out, towel-dried her hair, and dressed in a soft pink robe that zipped up the front and clung gracefully to her curves. Mrs. Townsend had been kind enough to let her borrow it, although it was a little long for her.

Peter got up from where he was sitting on the edge of the bed when she came out. His attention was unwillingly drawn to the zipper on her robe that was just a little too low. Maggie smiled covertly at the attention she'd drawn. Peter grasped the zipper, hesitating for just a second of indecision, before zipping it up to her throat.

"You better quit messing with my emotions, little girl," he said, his voice husky. "Things are already difficult enough."

She blushed and looked away.

"Come on now, beautiful," he said, scooping her up in his arms, "your feet have an appointment with a doctor."

"Peter?" she said, her mood becoming somber.

"Yeah, baby?"

"Derik ditched my car somewhere, and...and he did something horrible to Courage!"

He looked at her, surprised that she'd been thinking that all along and hadn't said anything before. "No, he didn't, honey! I found Courage by the Audi at a gas station. He's back at my house. I'll have one of my guys go pick up the Audi later today."

Her eyes clouded over in tears. "He's okay?"

"I'm *so* sorry I didn't think to tell you earlier. Get it out of your head right now, okay?" He kissed her forehead. "You've had a traumatizing night, and we need to get you calmed down. Maybe this will make you feel better." His voice grew lighter. "I got a text from Marci this morning."

"And?"

"And Pastor Bradford made the trip out to visit Chris in prison a few days ago. Chris finally broke down and wept over what he'd done. I think it won't be long before he comes around. It always amazes me how much we can mess things up, but even then, God loves us enough to take the pieces and start putting them back together when we let him."

Maggie's expression softened, and she smiled. "I'm so glad for Chris. I only wish someone had reached out to him in love before it was too late."

"It could have prevented a lot of heartache," Peter agreed.

He carried her downstairs where Dr. Townsend was

waiting with bandages and ointment. "Put her on the couch," he said, and Peter did as he asked. Dr. Townsend examined the cuts and lacerations on her feet. "Wow. You have some hefty cuts, young lady." He applied some hydrogen peroxide to clean out any infection, and she tensed when it burned. "Sorry, honey," he apologized.

"I can't thank you enough, Dr. Townsend—" Peter started to speak, but didn't get to finish.

"Don't even mention it, Peter. You know you're like a second son to me." He gave Peter a hug, and then finished bandaging Maggie's feet.

"Can I sleep now?" Maggie asked groggily.

"Of course you can," Dr. Townsend answered, his eyes softening in compassion. "You can take her back up, Peter."

Peter carried her back upstairs and put her down on the bed, pulling the soft down comforter over her. She was asleep before her head touched the pillow. He sat on the edge of the bed next to her, gently brushing a strand of hair from her face. Then he put his head in his hands and wept for the first time in many years.

Maggie awoke four hours later to find herself wrapped in Peter's arms. He awoke when he felt her stir.

"How are you feeling, sweetheart?" His voice was sleepy. He shifted his weight so that he could pull her more closely against him, his hand rising to brush his knuckles against her cheek.

"I'm still so tired," she said. "Do Jacob's parents

know you're in here with me?"

"I'm not sure, but I didn't hide the fact. I left the door open."

"Are you going to hover over my every move because of what happened last night?"

"You know I will."

She sighed in resignation, and he kissed her ear. His breath tickled her, and she giggled.

"You need to marry me now, Maggie. I'll never have a complete night's rest if you're not next to me. There isn't a time that I wake up during the night and don't have to fight the urge to call you and make sure you're okay."

"Peter...I really can't think about this right now. You know how complicated this is." She changed topics. "Genevieve told me last week you got accepted into Harvard. When were you going to tell me?"

"When the time was right."

"And when was that going to be? Harvard is nearly eleven hours from here."

"By car. It's close enough by plane."

"And you didn't tell me because you were afraid I wouldn't go so far away from my father."

"I knew you wouldn't. But Harvard has the best research program of any college, and its law school is unrivaled. My parents went there. Most of The Inner Society members go there. Marci and Jacob have already been accepted."

"And what am I supposed to do?" Maggie was suddenly frustrated. "You know it's too late for me to get accepted into a college like that, even if I was willing to go so far away."

"No, you won't. You spent too much of your high school years messed up. You don't have a whole lot of options now, and I'm glad you don't."

"What's that supposed to mean?"

"It means that if you got accepted to a college four states away from Harvard, we would be having a problem!" Peter sat up, looking at her full on. "You're going to marry me and go with me, Maggie. I am not waiting another four years for you. You can enroll in a junior college for a couple of years. After you pull off a decent GPA, you can transfer to a four-year college. Your dad will be fine without you for a while, and I'll send him a plane ticket when he wants to visit."

Maggie listened quietly, her mind working over the implications of what he was telling her.

"Of course, we'll have to take it a bit easy," he continued. "I've taken a few financial hits lately—you know, wrecking hundred thousand dollar cars, giving away Audis, and such." He smiled mischievously, and she couldn't help smiling with him. "But seriously, Harvard is going to be extremely expensive, and I also will not be able to keep up with the business while I'm in Boston. I won't have time."

"So what are you going to do?" Maggie asked, a slight worried frown crossing her features.

"I knew this time would come. Aunt Genevieve already plans to retake control over the majority of Bennett

Motors until I graduate with my master's in Research and Technology. After that I'll find work, and Bennett Motors will either become a side job, or I'll continue to let Genevieve run it. I could also relocate the business and teach you to run it. Either way, I don't intend to live in Virginia with all this drama going on. The Inner Society will give me trouble over that, though. They will expect me to join their local team of scientists, and I'm sure they'll want to keep tabs on me."

Maggie stared at the ceiling, her mind churning over all the things he was telling her. "So The I.S. generally sends their offspring to Harvard, and, of course, they usually get in, right?"

"Of course."

"Does that mean Derik and his friends will be there?"

Peter hesitated for a moment. "You know they have powerful connections, though the negative publicity could easily eliminate their chances. They would also have to be able to indicate they've been involved in charity work. The youth group's missionary work in Africa and in the local communities is a perfect example."

"Of course, they would never falsify records or make a hefty donation to sweeten the deal," Maggie said with barely concealed sarcasm.

Peter lay back down next to her. "We've been taught from birth how to get what we want, Maggie," he whispered, his lips brushing her jawline and sending shivers through her belly.

"You're not talking about college anymore," she said, a smile playing on her lips.

"No…I don't suppose I am."

CHAPTER
twenty-five

Dr. and Mrs. Townsend took off work that day, and Mrs. Townsend made a large late breakfast of bacon, breakfast burritos, and sliced oranges. Peter and Maggie headed for the dining room when she called them.

On the way they looked in on Tai. He was sprawled across the bed in the downstairs guestroom, snoring up a storm, and they decided to let him sleep in.

Jacob and his parents joined them at the breakfast table, and the five of them were wrapped in conversation over the events of the previous night when the doorbell rang. Mrs. Townsend met FBI Agent Barnes at the door and let him in. He joined the others in the dining room but declined breakfast when Mrs. Townsend offered him a plate.

"I've got some information for you kids. We went to Ms. Riley's office, and her secretary said that she was taking a leave of absence due to her mother's sudden illness."

"It's a lie!" Maggie cried immediately. "Don't you think that's an incredible coincidence?"

"Yes, we did, in fact. That's why we called the

forwarding number and *spoke* with her!"

Maggie blinked, shocked. "They…they weren't talking to her, Peter. I swear I saw her dead! She had a huge knife coming out of her back!"

"Either way," Barnes continued, "this is going to set the trial back until they get another District Attorney to take her place. We are going to continue this investigation, but we wanted you to know where things stand right now. We're also planning on moving you and Tai out of the city tonight, Maggie. Oh, yes, and one more thing. You never told us why you believed Tennyson killed Megan in the first place. Did he confess, or did you just come to that conclusion?"

Maggie's eyes suddenly widened as something occurred to her. "Oh my gosh!"

"What?" Peter asked.

"My jeans. Where are my jeans?"

"I took them into the laundry room," Mrs. Townsend said.

"You want to get dressed all of a sudden?" Jacob asked in confusion.

"No. You don't understand! Did you wash my jeans, Mrs. Townsend?"

"Well, no, not yet. Why?"

"What's this about, Maggie?" Barnes asked, tiring of the suspense.

"I found a bloody earring in Tennyson's trunk! I completely forgot about it. It was hers, Agent Barnes; it was

Ms. Riley's earring. I saw her wearing one just like it! I put it in the pocket of my jeans."

"Hold on!" Mrs. Townsend left the room, returning moments later with the jeans and handing them to Maggie.

Maggie jammed a hand into the front pocket and took out the earring. "There, are you satisfied now? He was the one who killed her. He had to be the same person who cleaned up the crime scene after I left, which is why her earring and her blood was in his trunk—he had to dump her body!"

"Which could explain why no one could find him yesterday morning," Peter said.

Mrs. Townsend retrieved a plastic sandwich bag from the kitchen and handed it to Barnes. He carefully took the earring out of Maggie's hand with a clean napkin and dropped it into the bag. Then he held it up to the light, examining it. All eyes in the room were glued to the small object, and more than one of them gave a shudder at the thought of what it represented.

"He had to have put her in his trunk," Peter confirmed Maggie's theory. "How else could that earring have gotten in there? Can't you run tests for blood in his trunk or something?"

"Sure we could...if we could locate him, or at least his car. Tennyson's vanished without a trace. We could go back to the 'crime scene,' though, and run some tests to see if we can detect any traces of blood left over from a cleanup. Not that we won't use Maggie's testimony; we just know the opposition will try to discredit her again. Hard proof is crucial."

When Barnes took his leave, Jacob and Peter followed him out.

"You're not taking her away from me," Peter said at once.

"You need to leave this in the hands of the authorities, Peter. Maggie and Tai will be in good hands."

"I've heard that before." Peter's tone was laced with hostility despite his efforts to conceal his emotions. "If she goes anywhere, I'm going with her."

"Now listen, kid...."

"I might be eighteen, but I own my own company and gross a heck of a lot more than you do. I'm not some stupid kid off the street, and I'll be dead before I see another of your guys walk off with her!"

"Whoa, hold on, Peter," Jacob cautioned, alarmed by his growing hostility. He turned to the agent then. "He didn't mean anything by that, Agent Barnes, but he does have a point. We don't know who to trust anymore. Can't we work something out? I don't see why Maggie can't just stay here."

"We told you this was going to be temporary. It's too dangerous for your family, Jacob. You of all people ought to know what we're up against here."

"They won't touch my family. The I.S. does not harm their own."

"Thus far they seem to adhere to that, but that's no guarantee for their future intentions. From what I've seen, that little girl in there is the most danger-prone witness I've ever come across. She doesn't understand boundaries, and she doesn't know when to be afraid!" Agent Barnes replied.

"We viewed those files Tai saved this morning. Keller was right. There were hidden messages and encoded words in those files that Internal Affairs missed. It made the hairs rise on the back of my neck. She's really pissed off some scary people. After seeing that there's no way we would even consider leaving her or Tai at an obvious location. They've got to get out of here."

"Then I'm going with her," Peter insisted again, his voice like steel.

Barnes stared hard at him for a long moment. Jacob looked between them anxiously.

"All right, Peter." The agent reluctantly gave in with a look of irritation. "You three will need to be ready by eight o'clock tonight. We'll send a car to pick you up."

"Where are you going to take us?"

"You know I'm not going to tell you that. Just as you're not going to tell anyone you don't have to tell. You won't be taking your cell phones, either. There won't be any contact with anyone you know. In the meantime, that little girl does not leave the house for one flat second, and neither does Tai. Understood?"

"Understood," Peter agreed. Jacob nodded his agreement.

Barnes walked to his car then, shaking his head. "Eight o'clock," he repeated.

Jacob and Peter returned to the living room, where the others were gathered around watching the election coverage. By then, the story Maggie had given the reporter was all over the news.

"So Tennyson just disappears, and no one can find him," Maggie said. "He's going to get away with everything he's done!"

The others exchanged meaningful glances before looking back to Maggie. Tai sat back, waiting to hear how the others would respond. He'd been thinking the same thing as Maggie.

"He's not going to get away with anything," Jacob said quietly.

The room fell silent for a long while, and it seemed his words hung in the air.

Dr. Townsend was the first to break the silence. "He was paid to take you out, Maggie," he explained grimly. "He not only failed, he involved Derik, one of The Inner Society's teenagers, in the crime. Do you understand what I'm saying?"

Maggie looked to Peter for clarification. Peter took her hand, and for a moment everyone fell silent once more. "He's missing because he's dead, Maggie," Peter said.

It was three o'clock that afternoon when Peter received a call from Barnes. He put the call on speaker so that Maggie could hear it, too.

"We used a black light to detect blood stains on Ms. Riley's living room carpet, but not enough to prove it constituted a loss of life. We also matched them to the blood on the earring, so we can assume it was Ms. Riley's. However, there was a medical kit left out on the bathroom sink and a few band aid wrappers in the wastebasket, suggesting someone had a little accident and patched up the damage."

"A little accident?" Maggie choked. "Are they *freaking kidding?!* Does no one believe me?"

Peter covered the receiver for a moment and patted her leg in comfort. "I believe you, sweetheart." He then summed up his patience and spoke to Barnes. "Haven't you even considered the possibility of those things being planted to draw you to the very conclusion you just came to? You can't prove the woman you spoke with on the phone was Ms. Riley until someone stands face to face with her and identifies her."

"Easier said than done, Peter."

"And why is that?"

"She's visiting her mother in California. She left early this morning. That's a long flight. We can't just meet her for coffee in the next hour."

"And there were actually flights that took off this morning?" he asked in amazement.

"Apparently. And, yes, we checked to see if someone by that name boarded, and she did. Look, Peter, there were a lot of things going on last night. She was scared out of her mind. I'm not saying you're lying, Maggie; I'm just saying you could have been confused by what you thought you saw. It's possible Megan was hurt, but not dead. Maybe she thought her life was in danger and fled. Either way, without a body and without evidence of enough blood, we can't prove the woman is dead."

"It's possible she was *hurt*? I think a butcher knife in the back would hurt a little! And it's not even a little suspicious that her bloody earring was in Tennyson's trunk?"

Maggie asked in disbelief.

"With all due respect, Agent Barnes," Peter intervened, "my girlfriend doesn't crumble under pressure. If she says the woman was dead, then she was *dead*."

Barnes was silent for a moment, and his voice was grim when he spoke next. "Just keep in mind…she saw the blood on Tennyson and thought he was dead, too."

CHAPTER

twenty-six

FBI Agent Stevenson was posted outside the Townsend house when Peter left to quickly collect his things from his house.

After he got his things together, he turned to say goodbye to his aunt, and she hugged him fiercely.

"I love you, Peter. You are the son I never had. Please be careful."

"I will and I love you, too," he said.

He headed out to Maggie's house to get her things for her. As he pulled into the driveway, his phone rang. He flipped it open but didn't even get to say hello.

"Listen carefully, Peter...." The voice on the other end was low and even.

His blood froze. "Who is this?" he demanded.

"You know who we are. Shut up and listen. The FBI will never get that girl out of Norfolk alive; we can promise you this. You have betrayed your own, and there is a price to pay for that. You might be untouchable, but there are others you love who aren't. What's going to happen in the next hour is a warning. We're not merciless, you know. There is forgiveness, but you better get that girl away from those agents and disappear until after the trial. Then you better put a bridle on her if you don't want to be looking over your shoulder for the rest of your life."

The line went dead.

Peter felt immediate panic overwhelm his senses as he rapidly dialed Jacob with numb fingers and warned him to keep Maggie close. He dialed his aunt next.

He had just left her minutes before, but there was no answer. His heart sank. He knew only too well that Genevieve was not a member of The I.S., and she had no protection from any backlash. He'd been so worried about Maggie all this time that he hadn't even considered they might try to hurt others close to him to make their point.

Fearful of calling the agents and having the call traced, he took a second to scramble through how he was going to handle this. Since he was already at the Kraus home, he ran into the house without knocking. When he did not find Maggie's father, he went into the garage and found the truck missing. He was out.

Peter ran back to the Camaro and jumped in, jerking the car into drive and skidding out of the driveway in his haste. Five minutes later, he slid to a halt in front of his house. His heart skipped a beat when he saw the front door wide open.

"Aunt Genevieve!" He bolted up the porch steps and tore into the house, his heart racing. He went from one room to the next calling her name, but she didn't answer.

Then he heard Courage bark and ran to the service porch. Genevieve was sitting on the floor with Courage hovering protectively over her.

"Aunt Genevieve!" he cried when he saw her. She had a bruise on the side of her face.

"I'm okay, Peter," she said, but she was holding her head.

"What happened?"

"A man broke in and attacked me," she said on a slight rasp. "He was only able to hit me once before Courage tore into him and bit the snot out of him. He sent him running for his life!"

She didn't appear to be seriously injured, but Peter's hands were shaking as he helped her to her feet and checked her over. He was alarmed by all the implications of this attack. Until now, The Inner Society only went after people they considered as a direct threat. Jessica Carter's death had been a mistake—she had been driving Maggie's car. But now The Inner Society had taken a new step: they had deliberately attacked an innocent person in order to silence someone else.

"Courage saved me," Genevieve said.

"Good boy, Courage," Peter said, giving the dog an enthusiastic hug. Courage yipped and wagged his tail proudly in response. He already knew he had done a good job.

Peter called the Townsends. "Dr. Townsend, Aunt Genevieve's been attacked!"

"Is she okay?"

"I think so. She's banged up, though." Peter swallowed hard, unable to look at the bruise on his aunt's face. He couldn't help but feel this was his fault.

"Get her over here right away."

"I will. I'm worried about Mr. Kraus, though. He could easily be next."

"Not likely. He just showed up to see his daughter. Get over here, Peter, now!"

Genevieve grabbed her things and followed Peter and Courage to the car. It wasn't long before they reached the security gate at the Townsends'. Peter popped in the combination, and the gate opened. Dr. Townsend and Agent Stevenson met them at the front door, where they were ushered into the house.

Dr. Townsend looked over Genevieve critically. Genevieve winced when he touched her face, but she was no quivering coward and was handling things amazingly well under the circumstances.

"That was quite a hit," he said, mulling over the gravity of the situation. Like Peter, he was alarmed by what this new turn of events could mean.

"It would have been a lot worse if Courage hadn't been there," Genevieve said. "I think that guy intended to put me in the hospital. As things stand, he's the one needing medical attention. He'll need at least ten stitches."

"Well, if he shows up at a local hospital, the FBI will track him," Dr. Townsend said.

They looked up and saw Maggie standing in the doorway with her father. Her eyes were wide with shock as she saw the bruise on Genevieve's face.

"This is my fault!" she choked.

Peter came up to her and pulled her aside. "Don't start that, Maggie. You need to go back inside."

"No, Peter, this is my fault. This wouldn't have happened if it weren't for me! I hurt everyone who comes near me!" She was quickly becoming distraught, and Peter gave her a shake.

"Stop it! Now isn't the time."

She quieted, but Peter knew she was deeply disturbed in her spirit as she was drawing new conclusions.

"If they'll go after Genevieve, then they'll go after my father, too!" Maggie said.

"Don't worry about me, sweetheart," Mr. Kraus interjected. "You have enough on your plate right now."

Peter looked at her, but he couldn't deny the possibility when he'd already come to the same conclusion himself. "Pull yourself together, Maggie," he said, putting his arms around her. "We can't let ourselves go to pieces now. You didn't send that guy over to my house."

Agent Stevenson interrupted them to ask for Peter's phone. "I want her cell phone as well," he said, pointing to Maggie.

"Derik took it from her," Tai reminded him as he entered the family room. He looked rested and relaxed, the only one out of all of them.

"Well, I guess we're going to have a full house," Mrs.

Townsend said as cheerfully as possible to lighten the mood.

"No dilation," Dr. Townsend said after checking Genevieve's pupils. "She's going to be all right."

"There's no way I am going to impose on you," Genevieve said.

"Come on, Genevieve, we've been friends for years. Besides, our two biggest troublemakers are about to fly the coupe," Mrs. Townsend said, motioning to Peter and Maggie. "That only leaves you and Mr. Kraus."

"What do you mean me?" Mr. Kraus said. "I only came to see my daughter!"

"She's right," Agent Stevenson conceded. "You're not safe either. These people are obviously desperate and willing to use any means to keep Maggie and Peter out of this. If the Townsends are willing to put themselves out to this extent until this trial is over, you should take them up on it."

"I realize that this is going to feel awkward to you, Mr. Kraus," Dr. Townsend agreed, "but I'm sure you don't want to put yourself in a position where people can use you as leverage against your daughter."

"Our home is large enough to house an army without its soldiers ever running across each other," Mrs. Townsend said with a comforting smile. "Everything we own belongs to the Lord, anyway. We are open to using anything at our disposal to be of service to others. So please, get settled. We'll set up rooms for you."

Peter took Stevenson aside to speak with him in private.

"The caller said I better get Maggie away from you, because if you guys try to take her out of the city, they're going to dust her!"

"All the more reason we have to get her and Tai out, Peter," Stevenson reasoned. "We know how to do this. It will be extremely difficult for anyone to track us when we head out. There will be several cars with tinted windows heading off in several directions."

"And their people could split up and follow, right?" Peter wasn't convinced.

"It's possible, but it's unlikely they will be able to track us. The alternative is to stay where you are and jeopardize everyone in the house. They will hit the house if she stays."

Peter gave a sigh of frustration. "Are you sure the roads are passable?"

"We've got people checking on it. Don't worry—this is routine."

Peter gave him a look that spoke volumes. "Nothing is routine in Norfolk."

A few hours later, their time was up and Maggie was becoming agitated. "I don't want to leave," she protested, her fear showing through her thin veneer of bravery. "Anything could happen on our way out of here."

"At least you have some clothes," Tai grouched. He was wearing the only clothes he had—those he had on the night before. Mrs. Townsend had washed them for him.

"Genevieve's clothes!" Maggie countered. "Peter wasn't able to get mine, remember? Besides, you would only try to grab another flannel shirt and pair of faded jeans, anyway. I've never seen you wear anything else."

"Hey, don't hate on the threads, little chicken! I happen to *like* my flannel shirts."

"We'll figure something out later," Peter said.

"What's going to happen to my mom?" Tai asked, his tone tinged with worry.

"Don't worry about her, Tai," Peter said. "I made a call to a local church in Richmond. The pastor promised to come by every day to check on her until you can return."

Tai thought that over and nodded, satisfied.

"I'm sorry I got you into this, Tai," Maggie said for the hundredth time.

"Quit with the apologies, snob. You didn't drag me into this. It's not like you can bat your little eyelashes and no man is immune to the power of your persuasion." He gave her a smile, and she realized that he was glad to get to go with her. Even if he was scared, the entire thing was probably more excitement than he'd ever had in his life.

Within the hour, there were three Mercedes Bens enclosed in the Townsends' massive garage. All three were identical: black with tinted windows.

The group gathered together for a final heartfelt prayer. Dr. Townsend asked for the Lord's protection over the teens and that God would give them all a spirit of peace and not fear. But Maggie could feel her tension rising as she stood by her father and Peter. Even Peter's hand in hers didn't help alleviate the nausea in her gut. Something just didn't feel right about what they were about to do.

Not long after, the three teens were told to get into the middle vehicle, but Maggie hesitated. "I don't like this!" she protested and looked back at her father's stricken face. She was clearly not the only one who was uneasy.

"A little late for that now," Stevenson said. "Get in. We have to do this on schedule."

Her sixth sense was still bothering her. "I have a bad feeling about this...."

"Get in!" Stevenson and the driver shouted at the same time.

Maggie bit her lip and shut her eyes, still debating on whether or not to comply when Peter got into the car and pulled her in with him. Tai got in after them. Stevenson waved them off, and the three Mercedes pulled onto the street and headed out.

"Be ready to do exactly as you're told," the driver told his passengers, "and do it without talking. Is that clear?"

They agreed.

They followed the first car down several roads. Maggie was watching carefully. She looked back several times at the car behind them.

"Settle down, Maggie," Peter whispered, but her agitation was transferring to him. He had learned to trust her instincts, and he was becoming nervous.

The first vehicle swerved into a parking garage, and the other two followed. Maggie watched as a fourth car blocked off the entrance. Within minutes they had all parked on the second floor. The kids were ordered out of the vehicles and shoved into a blue sedan. "Duck down!" two new agents in the front ordered.

The three easily recognizable vehicles had turned into five everyday vehicles, which made their way out of the garage intermittently and headed off in different directions. The blue sedan pulled behind a couple of other cars that happened to be exiting at the same time. The three Mercedes left soon after.

"Where are we going?" Maggie whispered.

"Apparently north on Interstate 64. They're going to expect us to go east toward the airport," Peter surmised.

"Are we being followed, then?" Tai asked nervously.

"I'm not sure."

The sedan headed north, pulling up alongside a large big rig just before it went over the overpass on Bayview Boulevard. Just as they reached the center of the overpass, the big rig suddenly swerved into them.

The agent in the front passenger's side cried out a warning, but it came too late. Maggie screamed and Peter covered her head as the semi smashed the sedan against the guardrail, attempting to push the vehicle over the edge. There was a horrific sound of crunching metal, and sparks flew everywhere as the side of the car ground against the guardrail. The truck veered off, and the sedan slid for several yards before coming to a stop. The guardrail had held firm, but the side of the car was completely crushed.

"Are you okay?" Peter asked hoarsely as he looked Maggie over for injuries. She nodded, shaken. "Tai?"

"I'm okay," Tai said. They looked to the front seat and realized the agent in the passenger's seat was dead. The driver was injured. There was blood and smashed glass everywhere.

"Lord Jesus, help us!" Maggie choked, the horror of the situation making her flashback once more to similar scenes from her past.

Peter glanced at her in a moment of panic as he realized this could completely unhinge her, but the driver cut him off before he could speak.

"Get out of the car!" the driver yelled, his hands clamped on his leg. "My leg's broken; you have to go now before their assassins show up to finish the job!" He pulled out his gun and called for backup on his cell phone.

Peter didn't argue and jerked Maggie and Tai out of the crushed vehicle. They fled northward along the overpass until they reached the other side and were able to hop the guardrail and make their way under the overpass onto Bayview.

"Waters's place is only three blocks from here!" Maggie cried as they ran. "He's armed. He might be able to protect us."

No sooner had she spoken than they heard shots exchanged.

"They're already here!" Tai exclaimed.

"They must have shot him!" Maggie cried between breaths. "They shot the driver!"

"Shut up and keep moving!" Peter demanded.

They made it down the boulevard and managed to hook left onto Culfor Crescent Drive. Peter glanced back over his shoulder to see if they were being pursued, and in the next horrifying second, he heard the screeching of tires coming up from behind them.

As the vehicle came hurtling toward them, they realized there was no time to get out of the way.

Tai was the first to see the red laser beam on Maggie's chest. He threw himself in front of her, and a scream tore from Peter's throat as the gun went off.

Maggie and Tai crashed to the ground.

"Maggie!" Peter screamed.

He instinctively ducked as another shot was fired right after, but this one took out the driver who had fired at them. His head dropped onto the steering wheel, his car crashing into a nearby tree.

Confused and terrified, Peter glanced up to see Mr. Waters standing on his porch with a rifle in his hands.

Peter made it to the others and dropped to his knees, panic coursing through him. "Maggie? Tai?"

Tai coughed, the sound rattling in his chest. The next time he coughed up blood.

"Tai!" Maggie choked. She tried to reach for him, but she was struck with a strange numbness and found that she couldn't manage it. It wasn't until then that she realized she'd been shot, too.

Peter's face went white as he saw her sweater rapidly turning crimson. "Oh God, please, no!" He dragged her into

Melinda Louise Bohannon

his arms, desperate to stop this from happening. "Don't leave me, Maggie! Please! Just hold on!" He buried his face in her neck and wept.

He looked down into her lovely eyes, feeling he would die with her. Her eyes held his, softening in the love she felt for him. It was then that he saw something in them he had never seen before: absolute peace.

She choked, battling the sensation that everything was slipping away, even as some opposing force called to her to give in to it.

"I'm sorry, Peter."

"Maggie…?" Panic seized him.

In a moment more, she closed her eyes and went limp in his arms.

"No! Dear God, no!" Peter screamed.

He was barely aware that Waters had reached them. He was on his knees and had ripped open Tai's shirt, revealing a bullet hole that had pierced his right lung. He removed his coat and used it to plug the wound. "Peter!" he shouted. "Peter!" He shook the boy's shoulder to get his attention. "Look at her! She's still breathing. You have to stop the bleeding!"

His words suddenly registered in Peter's tortured mind, and Peter put her down. He put his ear against her chest and was able to register a heartbeat. He instantly tore off his own coat, pressing it against her wound. It quickly soaked with blood. "What should I do? I can't stop the bleeding!" he cried.

"Keep pressure on it!"

383

A gold Toyota Avalon came zooming around the corner then, coming to a stop just in front of them. The driver jumped out and ran to them, phone in hand. Peter absently heard him yell, "I need an ambulance on Culfor Crescent Drive, right now!" It seemed only a few more seconds before two more vehicles arrived on the scene, and Peter was suddenly fighting off the hands that were trying to drag him away from Maggie.

"Let her go, Peter," someone urged.

"Maggie! Maggie!" Peter was shouting, fighting to stay with her, but there were too many of them, and they dragged him away.

CHAPTER

twenty-seven

People filed into Sunrise Baptist Church on that somber November day. Funerals had become common place in Norfolk by then, and the people who attended them seemed to do so in sorrowful numbness. It was almost routine. There was a surprisingly large attendance. Among others, the members of the youth group had entered with their families and slipped quietly into the pews. Several reporters had also shown up, but were asked to remain in the back out of deference to those who were mourning.

At the front of the church was a large, ornately carved wooden table, and in the center, a beautiful gilded urn. It was surrounded by pictures of Maggie Kraus, taken throughout her life. One picture had captured her working in the garden with her mother as a child, before tragedy had swept through her life. Large vases of red roses lined the entire front of the sanctuary like a red velvet blanket. Their glorious scent perfumed the air, a royal tribute to a girl who'd once been a neglected outcast of society.

Under the circumstances, many of the key members of The Inner Society, including the Caldwells and members employed by the council, were absent. Their involvement in the shooting was an unspoken fact understood by both factions of The Inner Society, and no one wanted to ignite an already explosive situation.

Although Walcott was pastor now, Pastor Bradford had been asked to preside over the gathering. Walcott was still in attendance, though, having quietly slipped in the back. He was dressed in a black turtleneck shirt and slacks with a polished belt and patent leather shoes, which was rounded off with a black sports jacket. The outfit was appropriate enough for a funeral, but it smacked of Inner Society.

As Jacob entered with his parents, he took note of Walcott's presence with a guarded expression. He knew too much not to question whether or not he'd been sent to keep an eye on the situation and report back to his superiors. He exchanged glances with his father and knew he was thinking the same thing.

"Time will tell where this pastor stands," Dr. Townsend whispered. "But, one way or another, he's been put in a place of power. We can only hope he uses that power for good and not evil."

They slipped into the front row beside Peter, who sat silently next to Maggie's father. Peter sat with his head hung low and his hands curled in his lap. Genevieve was on Mr. Kraus's right, and Kevin and Kristy sat together in the row behind them. Kevin looked to Kristy, thinking of how short life was. He couldn't contemplate life without her, and he could only imagine how Peter was feeling right then.

Peter's mind was a million miles away as he listened to the pastor talk about the tragic life of a young girl who had awoken the conscience of an entire city.

As he drew to a close, Pastor Bradford looked over

the congregation for a moment before concluding. "We are suffering the death of yet another one of our children. Our city has been rocked by the vain struggle for power that rightfully belongs to God. God save us all from our reckless intentions."

Marci got up from her seat then, and Peter's attention followed her as she went to stand at the front of the church. Tears filled her eyes as she sang "Amazing Grace" in her sweet angelic voice. His eyes clouded with tears as well, and he thought she had never seemed more beautiful.

Peter's eyes roamed the pews as Marci sang, and to his left, he noticed Rebecca Christensen. She briefly met his gaze before her eyes dropped to her hands in her lap.

After the song came to an end, Marci quietly placed the microphone down on the podium and made her way over to Peter, hugging him. He clung to her for a minute in mutual comfort and then released her so that she could return to her place beside her mother.

When the pastor motioned to him, Peter made his way to the front. He had thought about what he was going to say, but it took him a few minutes to sort it out. He cleared his throat, and looked up at the expectant audience. His voice was soft, but surprisingly strong, when he spoke at last.

"You know, people often live their lives with no purpose. They live day to day thinking there is nothing but time. But the people of Norfolk know only too well that life is fragile. It is a blessing not to be taken for granted." He paused and cleared his throat again. "It wasn't long ago that a messed up teenager stepped into Norfolk and challenged the thinking of our entire city. Maggie, by her own admission, was far from perfect, but she taught us that a person's worth is not in their money or in their clothes, but in who they are.

She lived her life by her convictions and in total gratitude that God could love someone like her when few others could."

Peter paused and steadied himself from the swell of emotions rising in his chest. "When Maggie came to Norfolk, people hated her because she made them face their own shallowness. She brought to light unspoken issues that many would rather have buried than faced. Maybe all of us should find a reason to live that is more meaningful than the pursuit of our own selfish ambitions. Maybe we should step outside of ourselves long enough to reach out to others through the love of Christ. I look back at the lives that have been lost in this city, I look at all the pain, and I can't help but wonder, *What for? Was it worth it? What have we learned? And where will we go from here?* It took a joint effort to create the society we live in, and it will take a joint effort to stop the violence and hatred that have come from it."

The service concluded with these last words, just as this journey in his life had come to an end. It was true, after all: There were no guarantees in life, and it was not possible to hold a person to this world by strength of love alone. In the end, everything was in God's hands, not man's.

Katie met Peter outside and gave his hand a comforting squeeze, and both inwardly winced when a reporter snapped a picture.

"Don't blame yourself for any of this, Katie," Peter spoke first. "You might have gotten caught up in this, but you didn't involve Maggie. She became involved in this mess long before you met her."

Tears sprang to Katie's eyes, but she nodded. "So what are you going to do now, Peter?"

"I don't know. I have a few things to attend to, and then I have to get out of here for a while. I just have to clear my head before I go crazy."

"Where will you go?"

"I don't know. I haven't decided yet."

Rebecca Christensen glanced up at Peter and then away as she made her way around them, but he caught the sleeve of her sweater to stop her.

She looked up at him through haunted eyes. "I'm... I'm sorry for your loss, Peter," she whispered uneasily.

He looked down at her thoughtfully. "Are you still going to speak at the next assembly?" he asked.

"I know Maggie wanted me to; I'm not sure I have the courage to get up there and talk about it, though. People already treat me like I'm contaminated."

"You need to do this, Rebecca. It's important. Norfolk High needs to hear about the dangers of contracting AIDS, and they're not going to listen to some adult who gets paid to make a speech. If you save the life of one person by making them more aware of the possible consequences of their behavior, then it's surely worth what you have to go through to make the speech, don't you think?"

She looked away for a moment of turmoil before coming to terms with her fears. "Okay, Peter. I'll do it."

He caught her hand and gave it an encouraging squeeze. "I'll pray for you, Rebecca. In the meantime I think you should join the youth group. We're not perfect, but none of us will ostracize you. You don't have to walk through this alone."

She looked up at him, tears sparkling in her blue eyes. Then she nodded and walked away.

Peter said a few more goodbyes then made his way to his car. He had something else he had to do.

Peter drove to the hospital where Tai had been placed in critical condition. A guard had been stationed outside the door and another inside the room. Since he had called ahead of time, Peter knew that Waters was there.

The guard allowed Peter to pass, and he went in to find Waters sitting in a chair beside Tai's bed, his crutches resting against the chair. He looked up, his eyes tired. Though he wasn't going to let himself show emotion, Waters was showing his age.

Tai was lying in the bed unconscious with wires and tubes hanging out of him. There was a monitor next to him that ticked off his steady heartbeat, but his skin was gray, and he looked like he was barely clinging to life.

"You know, I told that kid he would never amount to anything." There was a rough edge to Waters's tone as he tried to swallow his own guilt. "And yet he might have just given his life in his attempt to save Maggie. Who would have thought it?"

Peter sighed, but he wasn't going to just let Waters off the hook. "You know, Mr. Waters, we don't always get a second chance in life to get things right. But you had yours, and you never knew it."

"What do you mean?"

"I mean you let your family walk out of your life, and you've spent the rest of your years being lonely and bitter. Then you met a kid who was just as lonely as you, but you could never see him as anything more than a Hmong kid."

"This is the last thing I need to hear from you," Waters rounded.

"Then maybe you should see this." Peter pulled out a folded piece of paper out of his pocket. "They found it in Tai's jeans pocket when he was brought in here. He had it with him when he went to work for you on the night of the hurricane. I'm sure he meant to confront you with it, but so much was going on, he didn't get the chance." He passed the paper to Waters.

Waters hesitated, looking at it with trepidation before taking it and unfolding it. He examined it with confusion, but then it became clear by his expression that understanding had begun to strike home. "This is his birth certificate."

Peter watched him for a moment, measuring his reaction. "It names you as his father."

Waters was too stunned to react at first. Then he swallowed, and his eyes slowly lowered to the paper once more. He said nothing, but Peter noticed his hands beginning to shake.

"He must have known all along," Peter said. "That's why he tried so hard to win your respect."

"It's a forgery!" Waters burst out adamantly. "There's no way this could be true. Maggie introduced us. We met by chance."

"Really? Tai is sixteen. Are you going to tell me you *didn't* get involved with a pretty young Hmong girl sixteen years ago and then dump her when you got tired of her?"

Waters was frozen as the truth in Peter's words slowly seeped in and took hold. "Dear God!"

"God had nothing to do with it!" Peter snapped, his caution now gone. "That's your son lying in that bed, Mr. Waters, while his mother lies dying of cancer alone at home with no way to come and see her only child."

Waters's eyes were shiny now, and he gazed at the stricken young boy beside him as if seeing him for the first time and began to note resemblances he'd never recognized before. Tai looked Hmong without question, but his jawline and the shape of his ears and chin bore witness of his paternal genes.

"It was no accident that Tai became entwined in our lives, and it was no accident that Maggie hit you with her car that day," Peter continued, though gentler now. "God orchestrated that in order to put you together with your son. It's way too much of a coincidence for me to believe anything else. Now, you can live the rest of your life as a bitter and lonely old man, Mr. Waters, or you can get on your knees before God and beg him for the life of your son. It's time to set things straight before it's too late."

Later that afternoon, Waters put in a call to Peter from his car. "All right, which apartment is it, Peter?"

"You're going to try to attempt those stairs in crutches?" Peter asked incredulously.

"Forget about that. I'll manage. Just give me directions."

"I don't know the number, so keep me on the phone. Do you have your Bluetooth in? "

"Yes."

"Are you at the front of the building on the south side?"

"Yeah."

"There are five entrances on that side of the building. Go in the second to your right. There will be a hallway and a flight of stairs. Go up one flight."

Peter waited. He could hear Waters struggling to make it up the steps and wondered if there wasn't a better way to handle this. But Peter knew as well as Waters that Mai Lee would probably not have met Waters downstairs if he'd tried to call her and arrange it.

A laborious ten minutes later, Waters came back on the line. "All right," he said, panting. "Which apartment?"

"Turn right at the stairs. Her door is four doors down on the left."

"She'll slam the door when she sees me."

"Maybe God allowed you to break your leg to gain sympathy," Peter suggested with suppressed humor. This situation really *wasn't* funny.

"Thanks for the encouragement," Waters groused. "I think I have it from here. I'll talk to you later."

"I'll pray this goes well, Mr. Waters."

"Thanks, kid." Waters had taken a sudden dose of humility that day, and his usual gruff tone had dissipated.

They hung up the phone, but not a second later, Peter got another call. He answered, soon realizing Waters's had butt-dialed him when he shoved his phone in his pocket.

Peter wasn't about to hang up. He listened as Waters knocked on the door for quite a while before there was a sound of a bolt sliding. The door opened and then there was silence. Peter envisioned Tai's mother, beautiful but frail, and wondered if she would recognize Waters. Then he heard Waters's voice.

"You don't recognize me, Mai?"

Her gasp answered Peter's question. There was the sound of the door creaking, and Peter surmised she was trying to close it.

"Wait! Please give me the chance to speak to you. I'm not leaving until I speak with you, so you might as well let me in, Mai."

Peter listened intently as the silence soared.

"I'm not here to hurt you, honey. I just need to talk to you. Look at me, Mai: I'm not Hmong—it's not disrespectful to look me in the face. I want to make this right. Please let me do that. I know about the cancer," he explained.

"Please. Please go. I beg you." Peter heard her whisper brokenly in what little English she knew. His heart twisted in sympathy at the heartbreak in her voice.

"Did Tai tell you he's been working for me?" Waters asked then.

"Tai?" she whispered.

"He's been trying to come up with the courage to

tell me I was his father, and I made it so hard for him that he never did. I didn't find out he was my son until today.

"There's a kid…I believe you know him—his name is Peter Bennett? He told me God brought me together with my son, and I shouldn't blow my chance to set things straight. I'm trying to do that in my clumsy way…."

Peter hung up after that. God had given him a sense of peace over the situation, and he knew this would somehow work out. The odds of any of these things happening were nothing less than miraculous, and it was obvious that God had had his hand in it from the start.

CHAPTER
twenty-eight

Three days later, Peter was sitting alone in a lounge chair, overlooking the small, private beach in Georgia. He was shirtless and wearing his black silk pajama bottoms with his Bible open in his lap. The gentle, rhythmic crashing of the waves soothed his spirit, and he rested his head back for a moment, his eyes wandering across the waters where an otter was floating on her back and cracking a shell with a rock. It was quiet and peaceful, both things he never could have experienced in Norfolk.

Dr. Townsend came out the back door of the white beach house behind him and came to sit down on the sand next to his chair. The doctor smiled. "I told you I would come to visit, son. I just wanted to check on things and make sure you were okay."

"Thank you, Dr. Townsend. I appreciate it, but you know I'm fine. How is Tai doing?"

"That's a whole other story. Whatever you said to Waters must have hit home."

"Why?"

"He took Tai's mother from her apartment and moved her into his guest house so he could take care of her, and she could be near her son."

Peter grinned, amazed. "Wow. I never would have expected him to take it that far. But you never answered me; how's Tai?"

"He's going to be fine, Peter. God has a way of bringing things together. The bullet pierced his right lung. It was touch and go for a long time, but the doctors did a good job on him, and that kid is a real fighter. I am just amazed how this worked out."

The two men gazed out over the sea in silence for a few moments, relishing the peace.

The silence was broken when Dr. Townsend stood up, brushed the sand off his pants, and took his leave. "I have to go now. I just wanted to say something before I left, though. You've spent a large portion of your life mourning, Peter." He paused and looked down on the young man he had come to view as his second son. "Don't mourn *too* long."

Peter looked up at him, and their eyes met. Then Peter smiled in understanding. "I won't," he promised. Dr. Townsend gave him an affectionate hug before taking his leave.

Peter looked out over the beautiful landscape once more as he put his Bible on the edge of the chaise lounge and rose to his feet. He turned and made his way back to the house. He went up the steps of the back deck and in through the French doors, padding across the wood floors with bare feet.

Entering his bedroom, his eyes immediately fell upon the form of his lovely new wife as she lay in his bed, wearing the top half of his pajamas. A delicate silver heart hung from a chain around her neck that he'd given her for her birthday two days before. There was a fresh bandage that had been recently applied to the bullet wound that had pierced her five inches below her right clavicle.

Maggie stretched languidly as she watched him enter, a soft, sensual smile curving her red lips. Peter's smiled in response, knowing she was teasing him again, but, this time, she wouldn't be getting away with it.

He slid into bed beside her, pulling her gently against him. "You can tease me all you want, baby, because the doctor just informed me that you're doing just fine, and I don't need to 'mourn' any longer."

She looked up at him in question, and her cheeks flushed when understanding struck.

He took her hand and kissed the golden rings on her finger, his love and adoration for her shining in his eyes. "I'm sorry we had to do things out of order, honey. I promise you, though, that we'll have a beautiful wedding and an awesome honeymoon when this is over."

"It's okay, Peter. I understand."

"Have I told you I loved you yet today?" he asked in a husky voice.

She couldn't help but smile. "Twice this morning."

His lips molded over hers then, and she relaxed in his arms, the memories of her past melting away beneath his loving touch.

AFTERWORD

Any hopes that the death of the District Attorney would delay the trial were in vain. Once again, The Inner Society managed the nearly impossible feat of moving the trial up to cut the time the new DA and the opposition had to prepare their case. It was also not surprising that, since they had failed to get the last trial moved out of state, despite obvious bias, this new phase of the trial would, likewise, be tried within the boundaries of Virginia.

All of the accused were able to post bail, however substantial the cost, and not one had to wait in jail for the trial date.

Some had wondered why Maggie Kraus's name had not been stricken from the docket, and there were many gasps in the courtroom when the new D.A. called her forward to testify as their key witness. It was too late for the defense to do anything about it.

The trial was brutal, dragging on past Christmas, as multiple charges were brought forward against key members of The Inner Society, Brian Chambers and Thomas and Derik Caldwell among them. It was one of the most complicated court cases that had ever been tried, but this time the evidence was substantial.

Even though the lighter had been handled and the evidence had been marred, its mere existence proved Maggie had been telling the truth about the boys in the first trial. The lab was able to find a minute trace of soot left on the silver lighter, which was traced back to a sample taken from the crime scene by Internal Affairs before the lot was cleaned up. A partial fingerprint was also matched to Brian Chambers. This didn't prove he burned down Keller's house, but it did prove he had been in possession of the lighter that had been at the scene of the crime. It was more proof that the initials on the lighter were his and definitely pointed toward proving Chambers had some kind of dealings with Keller.

The DVD had been destroyed, but Maggie testified that Keller had found private information on Caldwell's laptop, and he was in fear for his life from Chambers because of it. The fact that Keller's name was on a list of people who were dead convinced the jury that Chambers and Caldwell were both involved.

The defense was very careful in taking responsibility for certain issues while expertly dodging others. In Jessica Carter's case, they couldn't exactly deny wrongdoing, so the attorneys played on the sympathy of the jury by claiming The I.S. had done wrong but had done so to save the life of a child. They brought in little Rosie Dawson as evidence, asking if anyone could convict parents of taking desperate measures to save their child's life. This didn't prove their actions were less criminal, but it undeniably softened the jury. It also cast some doubt in the minds of the audience about whether or not the motives of The Inner Society were really as dark as they were reported to be.

In the end, multiple members of The Inner Society were still given hefty sentences, Brian Chambers among them. Enough evidence had been put together to nail him for murdering Keller, and several other names had been implicated along with his.

All efforts to locate Megan Riley in person had

proven to be futile. And, although Megan Riley's body was never found, foul play was obviously involved, and Tennyson now had a warrant out for his arrest. The problem was that Tennyson was also nowhere to be found, and without him, the D.A. couldn't establish his connection to The Inner Society.

Officer Thomas Caldwell was charged with destruction of evidence in the death of Jessica Carter. Derik was tried as an adult and sentenced to a year in jail for reckless endangerment for his part in trying to forcibly deliver Maggie to Tennyson.

The Federal Bureau of Investigations had worked in conjunction with the new D.A. to search out every name on the "hit list" that Tai had discovered. They had been alarmed to learn that every name on that list could, indeed, be matched to an obituary—every name except those who had become "missing persons." All of the people who had obituaries, though, had reportedly died from either freak accidents or "natural causes," and even though the evidence presented by the FBI managed to raise suspicion, they were unable to prove foul play. Having the list of names was certainly suspicious, but it wasn't illegal, and The Inner Society's attorneys simply stated that their clients kept a list of those affiliated with them who died and kept track of their causes of death.

The heads of Norfolk General Hospital also had serious charges brought against them; the Association of Organ Procurement Organizations saw to that for what happened to Jessica's body. They were slapped with fines that ran into the millions, and control of the hospital was turned over to others who had been elected to clean up the corruption.

The most alarming information Tai had accessed

from the database of The Inner Society, however, were the implied intentions for an intricate takeover of the presidential seat. The documents Tai discovered had also suggested plans for revamping the powers of church and state in a way that could slowly put an end to democracy as the US knew it. Either way, their intentions were very clear: The Inner Society wanted total power, and they weren't going to be satisfied with anything less.

After several long weeks in court, the youth group and their parents congregated at Pastor Bradford's house to listen to the results of the trial broadcasted on national television.

Maggie curled up in Peter's lap on one of the couches and put her head on his shoulder. "So what does all this mean in the end?" she asked at last.

Everyone in the room looked to one another before looking at her. Most of them knew exactly what the outcomes would mean.

"Well, you and Tai did a good job screwing up The I.S.'s political plans for this last election. The media saw to that," Peter said. "If hiding the fact that McFarland was working with the Democrats while implying he had Republican sympathies was only unethical, buying votes was definitely a crime. They would have gotten away with it, too, if Tai hadn't gotten access to their files."

"They thought they had the election in the bag. No one thought Raintree would beat Jamison to the White House, especially with McFarland drawing votes from the Republicans," Mrs. Townsend said.

"But you have to understand that it's only going to be a temporary setback," Dr. Townsend added. "The government can fine The Inner Society all they want to, but they can't legally dissolve us."

"But they planned to take over the country!" Maggie gasped.

"They can plan to do anything they want," Jacob answered, sitting next to Marci on the opposite couch. "As long as they haven't done it, there's no proof that they ever intended to follow through with it."

"Then what is going to happen now?"

"A lot of The I.S. members have taken a huge financial setback, though not enough to cripple us permanently," Peter informed quietly. "The I.S. will only relocate, and go forward with new plans for the future."

"The Bible has warned us of these kinds of things happening in the end times, Maggie," Dr. Townsend spoke up, "but we aren't going to live our lives in fear. We do need to ask for God's protection, though, because this is just a taste of what's to come."

Everyone fell uncomfortably quiet as the weight of their new reality settled down upon them.

It was Pastor Bradford who broke the silence. "Just remember," he said, "'We battle not against flesh and blood, but against the rulers, against the powers, against the world forces of this darkness, against the spiritual forces of wickedness in the heavenly places.' We might be fighting a battle, but the Lord will win the war. In the meantime, we need to stand strong…because I have a feeling things will get a lot worse before this war is over."

Read the Complete Trilogy!

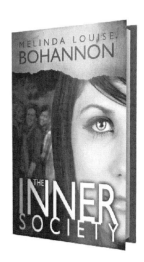